9/12

Queen of Wands

Queen of Wands

John Ringo

QUEEN OF WANDS

Copyright © 2012 by John Ringo

A Baen Books Original

Baen Publishing Enterprises
P.O. Box 1403
Riverdale, NY 10471
www.baen.com

ISBN: 978-1-4516-3789-2

Cover art by Dave Seeley

First printing, August 2012

Distributed by Simon & Schuster
1230 Avenue of the Americas
New York, NY 10020

Library of Congress Cataloging-in-Publication Data

Ringo, John, 1963–
  Queen of wands / John Ringo.
      p. cm.
  ISBN 978-1-4516-3789-2 (hc)
  1. Demonology—Fiction. I. Title.
  PS3568.I577Q44 2012
  813'.54—dc23

                                                    2012016682

10   9   8   7   6   5   4   3   2   1

Pages by Joy Freeman (www.pagesbyjoy.com)
Printed in the United States of America

To Miriam. Just because.

And as always
For Captain Tamara Long, USAF
Born: 12 May 1979
Died: 23 March 2003, Afghanistan
You fly with the angels now.

Acknowledgements

I'd like to thank Wendy, Scott, Bryan, Joe, Tony and Carol for assistance in building bits of this story and providing research assistance when the spiritual journey of Janea (quite suddenly) came together.

I'd like to thank George Spence for help in details of the development of the Chattanooga Art District. And for ignoring my complete violation of reality in that regard. ALL THE WAY!

As always I'd like to thank Miriam for her help, understanding and support. Not to mention a memorable lecture on pageant drama.

As usual the members of RingTAB especially Supervisory Special Agent Jon Holloway for lending credibility to both the FBI side of things and unarmed combat.

Again I'd like to thank Rogue and Cruxshadows for giving me a foundation on which to build a story.

This book has been in the works for a long time. From well before *Warehouse 13* came on TV. The *Warehouse 13* reference at the end of one of the stories was a very late but I think humorous add. I'd like to thank the writers and producers for not only making a really good television show (words that are very hard for me to type as they're *so* uncommon) but for featuring my novels in one of the backgrounds. ☺

Last, I'd like to thank the entire staff of Dragon*Con. I'd have placed odds on major body count and they *somehow* managed not only to keep it to zero but to hold one of the best Dragon*Cons in memory. Great job, guys and gals. By the way, the Dragon*Con that is pictured in this book is from 2007 with some modifications. It's changed in layout since then. And gotten bigger. And bigger and bigger and Bigger! When LSU fans that have been "goin' ta Mardi Gras since I could hold a can a be'r!" get freaked out ... GEEKS RULE!

☺

And on that note:

> *If we shadows have offended,*
> *Think but this,—and all is mended,—*
> *That you have but slumber'd here*
> *While these visions did appear.*
> *And this weak and idle theme,*
> *No more yielding but a dream.*

The Queen of Wands

A Card in the Aleister Crowley Thoth Tarot deck

The Queen of Wands is the joining of water and fire, representing fire's flickering movement, and is a card of restlessness and relentlessness. The Queen of Wands represents an individual who is well-grounded but prone to recklessness when challenged, who is self-initiating and goal-oriented, a firm friend and a formidable foe. The Card represents the Seer and is the symbol of Vengeance.

Book One

The Shadow of Death

The Mother's Tale

Chapter One

*Y*ou okay?" Mark Everette asked as he came out of the bathroom. The executive was already dressed and had a suit coat over his shoulder on a hanger. "You don't look so good."

"Thank you for your phrasing," Barbara Everette replied. Mark's thirty-four-year-old—one year his junior—wife was sitting on the edge of the bed with her head in her hands. She'd been in much the same position when he started his morning ablutions. Normally she'd have been dressed and getting breakfast ready by now. "I'm fine," Barb continued, looking up and wincing at the light from the bathroom. "Just a headache."

"Okay," Mark said, frowning. "You've been getting a lot of those lately. Maybe you should see Dr. Barnett."

"I doubt that the good doctor could do much for me," Barbara replied. "You're going to be late. Allison can fix breakfast."

"I don't have time to take the kids to school," Mark pointed out.

"I've got it," Barb said. "Just...go. And let Lazarus in when you leave."

Barbara sighed in relief as Mark left the bedroom, then felt a pang of regret. She really should be drawing strength from her husband, not feeling drained. But Mark had never been much of a nurturer. He expected to be supported and comforted, not the other way around. And explaining her current problem as anything other than "a headache" would have the men in the white coats at the house faster than you could say "Mommy had to go away." Because Barb was hearing voices.

A year ago this never would have happened. Just a year before, she'd been a nice, normal homemaker with, on the outside, the perfect life. Nice house in a nice neighborhood, steady husband with a good job who neither cheated on her nor abused her, three great kids and the respect of her friends and fellow homemakers. Need a hand with the bake sale? Call Barb. Charity auction? Barb's your gal.

Oh, Barbara Everette had her oddities, anyone would admit. Most of her fellow homemakers did not pack a pistol in their purse. And when the rest of the gals were down at Curves going through a gentle workout guaranteed to raise no more than a glisten, Barb was practicing and teaching a variety of Oriental martial arts and tossing around men twice her size. Both of those oddities were legacies of an Air Force dad who'd dragged his family around to a multitude of Far East postings, as were the occasional loan-words she'd slowly filtered out of her vocabulary. The church ladies of Algomo, Mississippi were unfamiliar with such pejoratives as *kwei-lo* and *gaijin*.

But a year ago she'd made either the greatest or the worst mistake of her life. Tired of the endless domestic routine, she had insisted on "just one weekend" alone. She just wanted two days to do whatever she wished, mainly find a nice hotel and sit around reading.

A series of chance happenings, or more likely God-driven choices, had left her marooned in a backwater Cajun town. One that had been taken over by a demon.

That was when Barbara Everette discovered that there was more inside her than she'd ever dreamed. She had been a committed Believer since she was quite young, it was just part of her makeup. She'd inherited the full measure of an Irish temper along with the slightly curly strawberry-blonde tresses. Faith kept that in check.

But in Thibideau she'd discovered there were times for that full-blown rage to manifest in the *service* of the Lord. Such as when a cult was killing women to feed their demon master. And she discovered that true devotion, faith and service paid off when the Lord gave her the power to not only challenge the demon but blow its lousy ass straight back to Hell.

She'd survived. Police had become involved. Then psychiatrists had become involved when she refused to admit to "reality." There were, of course, no such things as demons. Yes, a group had been committing serial crimes, but *demons* weren't involved, Mrs. Everette. Take the nice pills.

Fortunately, there were people to deal with the police. Barbara was recruited by a group that dealt with "Special Circumstances." That was the euphemism the FBI had coined, very quietly, for those rare cases where things got "beyond normal activities." When werewolves stalked the night, vampires drifted through open windows, when demons and their worshippers gathered their powers. When the supernatural intruded on their normal and customary doings.

To fight the supernatural required very special skills, ones that the majority of the populace, much less the police, did not develop. It required not only Belief but a firm commitment and connection to a god.

"A" god was the part that at first surprised Barbara. She was the *only* member of the Foundation for Love and Universal Faith who was a Protestant Christian. The rest were pagans of various flavors, Hindu, Wiccan, Asatru worshippers of the Norse Gods. The group was in contact with and occasionally drew on support from the Catholic Church, and in some cases, specific rabbis became involved when a Hebrew rite was of use. But she was the only Protestant for sure.

But she had, by then, become able to sense the power of others, its source and level. And the people she now associated with were, unquestionably, on the side of Light. Otherwise, she could not have fed power to her closest friend when a demon drained her soul. Given that Janea was a high-class call girl, stripper and a High Priestess of Freya, the Norse goddess of fertility, joining FLUF had required some reevaluation of the details of her Belief. "Suffer not a witch to live" simply did not compute.

The current problem was just a new development. She knew that, intellectually, and generally she could wrap her emotions around it. But it was a royal pain in the ass. It wasn't ESP; she couldn't read minds. She just heard voices. If she couldn't feel the similarity to her God channel, she'd simply go to the shrinks and get the nice pills to make the voices go away.

The voices were generally simply unintelligible whispers, but sometimes they got comprehensible. And generally when she could hear them clearly, they were negative. "You're no good." "You're not a good mother." "Everyone hates you." Sometimes there were positive messages, but those were rare. She could ignore it, mostly. She knew she wasn't a bad mother, that she wasn't a bad person. But it was just so *constant*.

And then yesterday she'd seen something. She wasn't sure what it was, but it looked like a black snake wrapped around a young woman's neck. The head, which was more humanoid looking, had its fangs sunk into the woman's shoulder.

Barb had almost asked the woman about it before she realized that nobody else was noticing the snake. And she'd received a serious "death stare" from the woman, more like a girl, for no reason she could determine. As she passed the woman, the thing had hissed at her quite clearly. Again, nobody in the grocery store noticed. The woman herself didn't even appear to notice.

But things were getting seriously weird in Barb-world these days.

Mark left the door to the bedroom open, his back set in disapproval, and a black cat oozed into the room and up onto her lap.

As soon as Lazarus curled into her lap, the voices didn't stop, but they were muted. She scratched the cat on the back of the head and pulled him in close.

"What's happening, Laz?" she whispered. "What in the *hell* is happening?"

"Mark, I'm going to have to go out of town," Barb said as she pulled the half-and-half out of the refrigerator. It had taken her nearly thirty minutes to put on a bit of makeup and a jogging suit. Something had to be done.

"Again?" her husband asked, surprised.

"It's been nearly two months since I went to a Foundation meeting," Barb said, trying to keep a combination of annoyance from the voices, annoyance at Mark and low blood sugar from causing a blowup. "It's beyond time."

The problem was, okay, in honesty, she'd coddled Mark. She had, throughout their marriage, managed the household. It could, arguably, be other than coddling. Mark was a disaster in the kitchen when they were first married, to the point that she'd thrown him out. And, frankly, it was just easier to pick up after him than get him to do it. So she cleaned the house, she did the cooking and the dishes. Over the years, Mark had gotten to the point where he barely knew where the pots and pans were. So going away before Allison stepped into the breach was a serious problem; the entire household generally fell apart.

The *other* problem was, no one knew what Barbara did on the side. Mark was not someone she could sit down with and calmly explain that she was now fighting demons. Demons didn't exist in the world of peanut processing. Besides, the Foundation was as secret as the best mystics in the world could make it. So she had to lie. Lying wasn't one of those things good Christian wives were supposed to do with their husbands, but there really wasn't another choice.

"Allison will manage the house," Barb said, looking over at her fifteen-year-old daughter. A year ago she'd have said that with the greatest of trepidation, but since the night Barb had "adopted" Lazarus, Allison had been an absolute model child. In fact, Barb was fairly sure that Allison knew damned well that Mommy's trips didn't have much to do with prayer meetings. Oh, there was quite a bit of praying, but it was generally along the lines of *"Lord, please keep the demon from eating my soul."*

"I've got it, Dad," Allison said, looking up from the book she was reading. Normally, there was no reading at the table. Breakfast was generally an exception. "Jason and Brooke will help."

"Oh, yeah?" Jason asked grumpily. The male twin had his father's dark looks, as did Brooke. Allison seemed to draw almost entirely from her mother. "Who's gonna make me?"

"*I* will," Allison said, staring him down. "Or do you *really* want to take me on, little brother?"

"No," Jason admitted, bending his head back down to his plate. "Allison's got it. We'll help."

"Fine," Mark sighed, picking up his suit. He'd finished breakfast and was on his way out the door. "Whatever. Write when you get work."

"I love you, too," Barbara snapped as the door closed. "Lord, forgive me for that."

"He will," Allison said, handing a bit of bacon to Lazarus. The cat licked it for a moment, then got it into his mouth and disappeared under the table, purring.

"It was uncalled for," Barbara replied, pouring a cup of coffee. Her hand shook so badly that she slopped some of it on the counter, and when she tried to pick up a spoon to stir the cream and sugar, she dropped it back into the drawer.

"Mom, are you okay?" Allison asked.

"Everyone keeps asking that!" Barbara snapped, then sighed. "I'm sorry, Allison. No, I'm not okay. But I will be. I just need to go . . . see some people."

"It's not cancer, is it?" Brooke asked worriedly. One of her friends had died of juvenile leukemia when she was still in preschool, and it had left a scar. "You're not dying, are you, Mommy?"

"No, it's not cancer," Barbara said, getting the mess cleaned up and her coffee stirred. She could perform a full Swan Drifts Over Mountain Above Clouds maneuver, something that no more than ten people in the world could equal. She could damned well stir her coffee. "I'll be fine. I just need to go see some friends and get some advice."

"It's the Change, isn't it?" Jason said, not looking up from his plate. "Bobby Townsend's mom is doing the Change. That's what he calls it, anyway."

"It's not menopause, Jason," Barbara said, trying not to laugh. "I'm only thirty-four. That won't happen until I'm in my fifties. You'll be out of the house."

"Good," Jason said. "Because Bobby says his momma's going crazy."

Lazarus had finished his bacon and now oozed back out from under the table and rubbed against her leg. Whenever the familiar touched her, the voices became less. But she couldn't pet him and use both hands. She looked down at him then picked him up and set him on her shoulder. "You. Stay."

"That looks . . . really weird, Mom," Allison said as Barb pulled out the makings of breakfast. The cat had all four feet planted on her left shoulder and was swaying to keep in place. But he wasn't moving.

"Yeah," Barb admitted, preparing some instant oatmeal. It was about all her stomach was going to take this morning. "But it works." She glanced at the clock and shook her head. "Time for you guys to be done. Out the door in ten."

"Brooke, eat it or throw it away," Allison said. "Moving it around your plate doesn't count. Jason, three bites then head for the room."

"Yes, Mother," Jason said, sarcastically. She really had sounded like Barbara, who had gotten *her* parenting skills from a military spouse and her officer husband.

"Mom, what's really wrong?" Allison asked as soon as the younger kids were gone.

"Not something I can explain, honey," Barb said, sitting down at the table.

"Mom, I *know*, okay?" Allison said, gesturing with her chin at the cat still perched on Barbara's shoulder.

"No, you don't 'know,' Allison," Barbara replied, tartly. "You suspect some things and you think you know others. If the time ever comes, I'll explain as much as I can. But you do not 'know' anything."

"I know where that cat came from," Allison pointed out.

About six months ago, Allison had fallen into bad company. The bad company in this case being a softball coach with almost "magical" abilities. Barb had at first feared that there was hanky-panky going on when the coach started taking the girls off for "team-building exercises." Then, after using her connections in the Foundation to get background information, her more paranoid side had starting ringing alarm bells. The coach had previously been associated with both Satanic and Santeria sects. And the change in the team had been...demonic. Metaphorically.

Barb had charged in in full demon-slayer mode: battle gear, bell, book and cross, ready to take on demons or acolytes with mundane or magical weaponry.

In fact, the coach had been a poseur. He used the trappings of Satanic rites to convince the girls they had magical backing. When Barb burst out of the darkness he'd literally wet himself.

What had Barb charging in was a "magic rite" involving the sacrifice of a young cat. She'd gotten there just a bit too late to save the black cat's life, but not too late to save the souls of some young girls. They got the immediate impression that playing Satanist was not in their best interest.

And then God had given her a greater gift than she had ever imagined; the ability to raise that cat from the grave. Lazarus came back not as some sort of zombie but as a fully functional cat, albeit one that could not be far from Barbara. Will she, nil she, Barb now had a familiar. Another thing the Bible was unquestionably dead set against. It got confusing.

And Allison had proof positive, every single day, that Mommy was something special. Barb had been in full-fig down to the balaclava, but there was no way that a daughter wasn't going to recognize her mother's voice. And when Mom had turned up at home, there was that same cat. Seeing God's power manifest tended to change a person, and it had changed Allison immensely.

"I mean, 'Lazarus' is a little *obvious*, isn't it, Mom?" Allison continued.

"It seemed appropriate," Barb said, realizing that she was for the first time admitting she had been the battle-armored figure in the night. "What on earth got you to bring that up *now*, of all times?"

"I think it took me this long to work up the courage," Allison said.

"What I do on these trips is not open for discussion," Barbara said and then held up a hand to forestall a reply. "It's simply not. Among other things, there are aspects that are really and truly legally classified. And there are things I just don't want you to know. There are things *I* don't want to know. But the current problem is...complicated. I'm not going to discuss it with you, but I am going to get help. Okay?"

"Okay," Allison said, biting her lip. "You *are* going to be okay, right?"

Barb stopped considering blouses and decided to get it over with. Digging into the back of the closet, she finally found the Black Bag.

The bag had at first resided in the back of the Honda. But as she came to accept that her place was in Algomo, not slaying demons, it had crept slowly through the house and eventually been covered by shoes in the back of the closet. Pulling it out was a wrench, the final statement that it was time to go be Other Barb.

She didn't like that side of her. It was more than the fear of pride, one of the deadliest sins. It was that that side of her awoke an anger she fought every day. She had tagged that side of her Bad Barb and, at first, she had mentally translated Bad as Evil.

Over time she had come to realize that the words were right, but the meaning wrong.

"Though I walk through the valley of the shadow of death, I will fear no evil," Barb said, pulling the bag out and setting it by the bed.

"Because He comforts you?" Alison asked, tearing up. "Because that's not a comfort to *me*, Mom."

Barb reached down and slid open the zipper of the bag, throwing back the cover.

Only the top layer of the materials in the bag were revealed but that was enough. One side of the bag held a katana, a long, curved, Japanese sword that had already slain one demon. The other side held an AR-10 carbine that had helped slay another. Between the two were a cluster of stakes, knives, bottles of holy water and a King James Bible.

"No, sweety," Barbara said, kissing her on the head. "Because I am the baddest bitch in the valley."

"Sharice," Barbara said, hugging the woman.

Coming to the Foundation had been a good choice. Apparently the mystical barriers that protected the fortress of the Foundation were proof even against the voices. They'd stopped the moment she drove through the gates.

The Center for the Foundation was located in the western North Carolina hills, not far from Asheville. A collection of buildings from several different architectural styles, it rambled through a fifteen-acre wooded park.

The main parking area was by the administrative building, which was a Chinese pagoda. It was flanked by the Asatru House, a mostly traditional Norse longhouse. There were Swiss chalets, Japanese teahouses, a small Gothic chapel and still more buildings on the rambling walkways.

Sharice Rickels was a plump, bright-eyed, silver-haired woman in her late sixties. She was dressed for work in a paisley patterned dress and wearing her normal collection of gobs of silver jewelry; the woman lugged around at least ten pounds of metal. One of the most notable Wiccan High Priestesses in the United States, she had been a field agent for FLUF for over thirty years before going into semi-retirement. Given that the normal lifespan of a field agent was less then ten years, she was both a survivor and a powerful and fey mystical fighter. She hugged Barbara back, then looked her in the eye.

"You are a *mass* of energy, girl," the witch said, frowning. "Your aura is out of control. What have you done to yourself?"

"I didn't do anything!" Barb said, almost crying. The relief at finally having the voices stop, and being able to talk about it with someone who wouldn't think she was crazy, was almost overwhelming.

"You need tea," Sharice said, nodding firmly. "Everything else will wait."

"You're not crazy," Sharice said after Barbara's, to her own ears, unintelligible report of the recent events. "You're just getting new Gifts."

"Gifts," Barbara said with a snort, sipping the herbal tea. "Gifts."

"Gifts," Sharice replied, nodding. "Gifts aren't easy, girl. That's why the All doesn't give them to everyone. You already had Channeling and Projection, which is so rare it's almost unheard of. I had to look it up in some really obscure tomes."

"Projection?" Barbara said.

"When you shot The Dark One in Louisiana," Sharice said, refusing to use the demon's name. "You Projected your White God's power into the bullets. Very rare."

"And the sword in Roanoke," Barbara said, nodding. "But this is..."

"Oh, these are normal Gifts, dear," Sharice said, chuckling. "I think you might have gotten more than your fair measure, as usual, but they're quite normal. Sight and The Ear."

"Sight?" Barbara said. "I don't see..." She paused and realized that she could see a glimmer around Sharice. She shook her head and it went away. "At least I don't *think* I see auras."

"You're able to suppress that one, I see," Sharice said, dryly. "But, yes, you've got the Sight. I've heard its common for the White God's acolytes to see the lesser infestations. That's what you're seeing."

"The...things on people?" Barb said. She'd seen even more in the trip to North Carolina. In one restaurant they seemed to be on every shoulder.

"Lesser demons," Sharice said. "Ever heard the term 'I've been wrestling with my demons'?"

"But that's..."

"Not always a metaphor, dear," Sharice continued. "In far too many cases it's quite real. They are drakni, the lesser demons that possess people all the time. They come in a variety of flavors and can be a real nuisance. They can even be deadly if they work through humans. Ted Bundy was covered with the things, what your people refer to as a Legion. And more had sunk into him. Most serial killers are their playthings. But drakni have to have something to latch onto in the first place. There must be the psychological and mystical equivalent of a shoulder. Most people have them, but for drakni, it needs to be...broad. They can't work with nothing."

"And they can't be *stopped*?" Barb said, aghast. "I saw dozens of them just in this one trip! Are you saying..."

"Thousands, millions of people who are possessed?" Sharice said, sadly. "Yes. I am. And, no, there is nothing we have found to wipe them out short of killing them one by one. And that requires something that's very hard to get; full Belief and agreement on the part of the possessed. Try going up to one of those people you saw and saying, 'You have a demon on your shoulder and it's getting into your soul. I can get rid of it, but only if you give your soul to the Good Lord Jesus...'"

"Ouch," Barb said. She was not a proselytizer. She believed in the doctrine of Witnessing, being the best Christian you could be every single day and converting by example.

"I'd suspect that more than one of your Christian screamers truly has the Sight," Sharice said, sighing. "They are quite serious in their intentions if they do. The problem is separating them from the ones that simply use it as a metaphor. But that is your one new Gift."

"That I can see demons and not be able to do anything about them?" Barb said. "How is that a *Gift*?"

"Well, you *can* see demons, even if they're not manifest," Sharice pointed out. "Remolus would have left a visual clue to someone with Sight. You would have been able to detect him in Krake the first time you saw him."

One of her previous investigations had involved a serial killer who was stalking science fiction conventions. She had had to deduce who it was at one convention by a process of elimination. When the killer decided that she was closing in, the elimination had been of lives.

"You say it's fairly common," Barb said. "Why not send someone with Sight on the investigation?"

"Sight is a tricky power," Sharice said. "All of them are. People, even very good mystics, tend to suppress them. To repeat: Gifts are not easy. Most of the operatives we have with Sight can see auras well enough but have a hard time with demons. Admittedly, as deeply as Remolus was possessing Krake, it should have shown up in his aura. But we didn't know that at the time. But you're backwards, as is usually the case with Christians. You can't suppress the sight of demons yet, but you can suppress auras. You'd have spotted him almost automatically. And when you do get to reading auras? Fully possessed individuals, their auras will be almost black."

"Nice to know," Barbara said. "Not. The Ear?"

"The only drakni you're going to see are those that have attached," Sharice said, carefully. "There are far more that are not."

"I'm hearing demons?" Barbara asked.

"Demons, ghosts, which are often associated with demons, psychic echoes," Sharice said, shrugging. "You're hearing mystic voices. The good news is that if you learn to tune it, The Ear can do many things for you. You can find out what a demon's True Name is. There is an undercurrent to the voices, like data in a router packet that tells the system what the origin of the packet is. It repeats the True Name of the demons. It's also sometimes an audible channel to your God and his servants. You might just be able to hear angels, although they rarely have anything more complicated to say than 'Wheeeee! Look what I can do!' We're going to have to do some serious work on you, girl. I'll be fascinated to see the limits of your Gifts. If you have them."

Chapter Two

*I*see a light purple," Barbara said, looking at the monk who was bent over a scroll. "Tinges of orange, but that might be from his robe."

It had taken two days of very careful practice for Barb to learn to open up her ability to see auras. It wasn't a matter of concentration, quite the opposite. It was more a matter of opening up a part of her mind. She had to obtain a nearly Zen state to see one consistently. They had also practiced closing off her Sight with small, inoffensive neutral entities that Sharice conjured. Today was the day of practicing on the real thing.

They'd gone to the Foundation's extensive library to find some subjects for aura reading.

"And I'm seeing a coral color," Sharice said, sighing. "Very pure. And there we go with the fun of aura reading. Different people see different auras . . . differently."

"What's purple mean?" Barb asked, flipping through the tome on her lap. "Vanity? That doesn't seem right. Chun Chao is one of the least vain people I know."

"Which is the problem with reading auras," Sharice said. "Most people see them one way, but others see a completely different spectrum, if you will. Demons are the same way. I might see a spider. You see a snake. Chun Chao might see a snarling traditional Tibetan demon. Nobody sees these things the same."

"Why?" Barb asked.

"Isn't it *your* Holy Book that says the mind of God is ineffable?" Sharice asked back. "Ask Him. The guesses are all over the map. My favorite theory is that it has to do with the mind of the viewer. What your Sight is Seeing gets translated by your brain into something that you can recognize, the same way that a hallucination converts images into something your brain can recognize."

"So if the book's useless," Barb said, tossing it lightly onto the side table, "how do I figure out what auras mean?"

"By watching them," Sharice said. "You just watch auras and deduce from what you know about people and their actions what the auras truly represent. What do you know about Chun Chao?"

"Studious," Barbara said. "Meticulous. Intelligent. A serious researcher..."

"Cowardly," Sharice added. "Afraid of his own shadow. Unwilling to leave guarded premises unless he's in the company of someone like, well, you. He came here with a group of more powerful monks and hasn't left the grounds to so much as take a walk."

"So...purple..." Barb said carefully. "That's probably related to his studiousness and intelligence. And the flashes of orange... are nervousness?"

"Very well hidden, mind you," Sharice said. "And that's just for you. Me, I see mostly coral. You don't, by the way, See with your actual eyeballs. Once you become accustomed to it, you can See with your eyes closed. It's one of the really advanced techniques in martial arts, when the Master puts on a blindfold and *still* wipes the floor with all the rookies."

"Seen that," Barb said, nodding. "I figured he was just hearing them."

"Nah," Sharice replied, grinning. "It's cheating, really. He can still see their auras. And when you get good enough, auras can tell you what a person's actions are going to be much better than body language. So not only can he See them right through the blindfold, he can tell what they're going to do before *they* know."

"*That* would be a useful skill," Barb said, nodding thoughtfully.

"And you develop it the same way you get to Carnegie Hall," Sharice said. "Practice, practice, practice."

"See this box?" Sharice asked, pulling an elaborately carved wooden box out of a niche.

They'd moved from the library to a building Barb had previously never even seen. If she'd been asked, she would have said that the path to the building looped back to the main path to the rear of the grounds. But there was a small side branch that led to the heavy stone building. Thinking about its position, she realized it was very close to the center of the compound and flanked by the prayer houses of four major gods. The doors of the building were heavy wood and steel with mystic symbols inscribed all over them and a massive lock.

The interior was simply one large room lined with niches. Boxes filled most of them, and above each niche were more mystic symbols. There were four tables set at the cardinal points of the compass, and in the center of the room was a large pentacle, the sort of symbol that always made Barb very uncomfortable.

"Okay, I don't *need* to look in it," Barb said, backing up. "I can *feel* the evil radiating off of it. Don't let the EPA know about this place."

"We have a permit," Sharice said, setting the box on a table. "The feeling of evil comes from buildup more than anything This is, in fact, a very unpleasant but minor drakni. It's a gluttony demon, a demon that is, alas, common in the United States. They're damned hard to catch, by the way. You have to have someone who is willing to be exorcised, and pull the thing out in this plane, then capture it. Much, much easier to dispel them back to their own. Now, I'm going to open the box. Even with the lid open, the drakni cannot escape. It's in a different sort of box. However, you'll be able to See it. A person without Sight would just see an empty box. Ready?"

"Ready," Barb said, raising her hands into a panther position. She wasn't particularly worried about the demon attacking her. Gluttony had never been one of her weaknesses. But if it got out, she wasn't planning on it just going back in the box, tough to collect or not.

What was in the box... wasn't really a snake. She hadn't spent much time staring at the demons before, she simply tried to avoid looking at them. But this time she could examine the thing.

It was about four feet in length including the coiled tail. Scaly like a snake but with a humanoid body, stubby arms and long fingers. The abdomen was vastly swollen, taking up most of the interior of the box, but the head was the strangest. There were no horns, but it had enormous, whorling red-and-black eyes with pupils nearly the size of her fist. The mouth that the thing opened to hiss at her was lined with back-curved teeth like an anaconda's and had four long fangs.

"Once that thing bites down..." Barb said.

"It's very hard to remove, yes," Sharice replied. "I'm seeing something like a small dog with very nasty teeth. You?"

"More snaky," Barb said. That was about as simple as you could put it. "Or an Indian naga."

"One of the traditions of the myth, I'm sure," Sharice said as the thing hissed and tried to rear up out of the box. "Back, you," the witch added, flicking her finger at it. Barb saw a very brief flash through the air, like a flicker of static electricity, and the thing sank back down. Lazarus had flared up into full Halloween cat mode and hissed back, but as the thing settled down, so did the familiar.

"Now, here's the trick," Sharice said, setting the box on a table. "Make it disappear."

"You mean dispel it?" Barb asked, raising her hands. "Didn't you say they were hard to catch?"

"Just complicated," Sharice corrected. "But, no, I mean turn off your Sight. You've Seen it. Now don't See it. Suppress, as you did with your aura reading."

Try as Barbara might, she could not get the drakni to disappear. She tried concentrating on it going away, which worked with auras. Nothing. Then she tried the Zen state which was required to read auras. Still the thing obstinately remained. And it appeared to find the whole thing very amusing, making occasional whistles of derision. It was getting annoying.

"Okay," Sharice said, patiently. "Try this. This guy really is a total nothing. If he got loose there'd be one more seriously obese person in the US, which is already awash. He's a total loser. Demons are like very stupid artificial intelligences. They have a simple program they follow. Dispel one of these guys and it's like stamping on an ant. He's nothing. Not worth your notice..."

"That worked," Barb said as the demon slowly faded from view. She could feel the change in her brain. Concentrating on the demon again, he faded into view. Ignoring him caused him to disappear. "That works. But what if I'm in ignore mode and there's something really deadly around?"

"Ever get one of those feelings where you just don't like being somewhere?" Sharice asked. "The vibe is wrong?"

"Yes."

"If you'd had Sight and opened it up, you'd have probably seen demons," Sharice explained. "Probably a lot and probably more powerful than this fellow. But you could still sense them vaguely. If you get that feeling again, open up and check out your surroundings. I'll give you a hint and we'll practice it later. If you open up your Sight but keep suppressing your aura, which we worked on the last time, you can stay under their radar. Don't look directly at them, don't open up your power or use anything but Sight, and you can pick them out without them realizing it. If you want to challenge, just look straight at one and open up your power. But be warned, if there is more than one, they're all going to get onto you. They can't hurt you, but they're annoying as hell."

"Yeah, dealt with that already," Barb admitted. "And if I attack one?"

"You?" Sharice said with a chuckle. "You'll blow it apart. But once they're attached, they sink a mystical barb into their target. If you blow one off of the person, they'll just grow back. The only way to get rid of them is to have the person be willing to be exorcised. They've got to believe they're there and they have to want to get rid of them. Note, *really* want and *really* believe. Otherwise it's pointless."

"That doesn't seem right," Barb said, frowning. "That's not the world of my God. You don't mind if I experiment a bit, do you?"

"Feel free," Sharice said. "Who knows. You might be able to blast one out of a person's soul, with all the power *you* draw. Not sure what it would do to the person, mind you. And unless they had a change of heart, they'd be a ripe target for the next drakni of the same type they run across."

"Where do they come from?" Barb asked. "I mean, from hell, obviously..."

"Hell might not be a *there*, but we'll go with it," Sharice said, smiling. "Besides, your own Holy Book clearly states that the earth was given over to Satan. But here on this plane, they get generated by lesser Mothers, minor versions of Tiamat, in other words. There aren't a lot of those, comparatively, but getting rid of *them* is even harder than getting rid of drakni. They generally attach to a family, being handed down generation by generation. Each produces specific drakni.

"There is actually something of a sovereign remedy for drakni Mothers, drakia, in certain Christian beliefs," Sharice said, frowning. "Let me see . . . Saints, saints."

In the antechamber to the prison was a small bookcase. Sharice pulled a book down and flipped through the pages, looking for something.

"Alas, I don't think it would help you, though," she said, flipping back and forth. "Most of the saints whose patronage is possession aren't recognized by the Episcopalian church."

"We don't do saints quite the same way Catholicism does it," Barbara said. "But any port in a storm. Well, any reasonably Christian port in a storm."

"Your best bet, if it works for your theology, is Saint Dymphna. She's a Catholic saint for the possessed and anyone suffering from mental illness. Strange story. Her mother died, and her dad looked high and low for a woman who was as beautiful as his wife. Finding none, he noticed that his daughter *was* as beautiful."

"Ick," Barb said.

"Ick indeed. Story goes on, including fleeing to a far land and being tracked down by the father. Martyred herself to escape his attentions. The interesting aspect to it is that it was believed her father was possessed by a demon of lust."

"And with what you've just told me, that's distinctly possible," Barbara said. "But he'd have had to be a pretty sick puppy to begin with."

"So Dymphna, despite being an otherwise quite inoffensive creature, is reputed to have a real case of the butt with demons, especially drakni and drakni Mothers. I'd suspect the deep story is that it was a drakia who possessed him, and it may have been generational."

"So I'm supposed to pray to St. Dymphna if I'm dealing with drakni?" Barbara asked. "That's not really how Episcopalians handle things. More of a Catholic approach."

"Not . . . exactly," Sharice said, biting her lip. "I'm afraid to tread on your theology if I go further. My simple answer is that should be unintrusive. Christian theology is a bit opaque to me sometimes."

"Try me understanding Wicca," Barb said.

"Point. Here's the thing. And it's simply the real and skinny. Your White God allegedly gave over the world to Satan, which means Satan's troops, within limits, have free reign."

"Because we have free will," Barb said. "We can choose to resist."

"Accepted," Sharice said. "However, there are indicators that just as demons can possess, so can higher spirits. Angels *and* saints. There is historical basis for the latter."

"If you're saying you want me to call on St. Dymphna, who, if I get this right, was a teenage girl, to possess *me*, to help me fight drakni..."

"It's more likely that she would possess someone similar to her," Sharice said. "And it's *very* hard to arrange. *Extraordinarily* rare. It would require someone who is pure of soul, about the right age, preferably has the right look, and who is in mortal danger from a demon. Preferably a similar one to the one that possessed Dymphna's father. And it would probably require some type of...free pass? I'm trying to put this in Christian terminology. In pagan terms, it would require that the door be opened from both sides of the planes, that another entity opened the door for her to pass through. Not to mention a nod from the White God and acceptance of His Gift upon the part of the possessee. And you don't have to have help to fight drakni. Or even drakni Mothers. But Dymphna would probably be able to wipe out a whole *Legion* of drakni Mothers. Or at least dispel them. Cast them back into the infernal realms. Of course some idiot would probably just summon them again, but it's a point on our side. If a person became possessed of Dymphna and we found out about it, trust me, we'll recruit *her* in a heartbeat."

"I'll keep it in mind," Barb said. "Especially if I can stop seeing these things all over the place."

"Now, this is just a gluttony demon. That's not too bad. But there are others. All the usual sins, of course. Then there are anger demons, hate demons, lust, as in Dymphna's father, and the worst, murder drakni."

"Serial killers?" Barb asked.

"As far as I know, universally," Sharice said. "Even the ones the FBI considers 'common.' Ted Bundy, a Legion, at least sixteen separate types including several flavors of murder drakni; Charles Manson, Son of Sam. I don't actually know of one that wasn't infested. But the point to remember is that *they had to have an opening.* The demons might have pushed them over the edge, but they had the desires and the interest. As you said, there is free will. The person has to be willing to take the demon into their soul. Whether they realize that willingness or not. And they have to choose to carry out the agenda of the demon."

"So we don't chase these?" Barb asked, incredulously. "They cause mayhem and death and they're just off our *radar screen*?"

"Not always," Sharice said. "But mostly. We just don't have the *time*, Barb. You've been taking family time over the last few months. I'm not meaning to guilt you, but the rest of us have been stretched. We could have used a Level Three at least five times while you've been playing Suzy Homemaker down in Mississippi. A Level *One* can dispel a drakni if the possessee is willing. A priest that's not even particularly holy can get rid of one. Drakni are training demons, mostly for sight and hearing as we're doing here. Now, a drakni *Mother* might require a Level Three. And if when we find those, we get rid of them if we can. But, again..."

"The possessee has to believe and be willing," Barb said with a sigh.

"Right," Sharice said. "So, you ready for the next step?"

"Which is?" Barb asked suspiciously.

"To dispel one without using massive amounts of power, you have to have its True Name," Sharice said, grinning. "As I said, you can get that with The Ear. But he's going to have to be out of the box."

Barb glanced at the pentacle, then looked at Sharice.

"You have *got* to be joking."

"Ready?" Sharice asked, opening the box.

"I hope," Barb said, getting into panther position again.

"Confidence is pretty important with any demon," Sharice said, touching one of the symbols on the box and muttering. "There's a reason I chose this one."

"Which is?" Barb asked as the demon popped its head up over the top of the box. She heard it almost immediately, the whispering in her mind. It was more of a craving for...Cheetos? Okay, so she liked Cheetos. It wasn't like she was...Man, she really wanted some...

"You've never shown much interest in food," Sharice replied.

"Now, me, I've got all my defenses up. But I've worked with him before. But I figured there wouldn't be much of a hook with you, not with your figure."

"Thank you," Barb said.

"Don't make me get out the vanity demon, skinny," Sharice said.

"I can handle it," Barb replied.

"Or the pride one."

"Okay," Barb admitted. "Point. But it doesn't really matter. It found a hook."

"Not much of one," Sharice said, gazing at the demon. "It hasn't leapt. What's the hook?"

"So I like Cheetos...And fried chicken. Is that a sin?"

"Not if you don't overindulge," Sharice replied. "But ignore the Cheetos and cheesecake..."

"I hate cheesecake..."

"Never mind. Ignore it. But open up your Ear. Don't focus. Just stay calm..."

"Zen..." Barb said. "Ignore the dressing with gravy..."

"It's there," Sharice said, hypnotically. "Can you hear it? It sings its name along with the food. Very faint, an undercurrent, almost unnoticeable..."

"Zagnatag," Barb said. "Is that what you mean?"

At the sound of its name, the demon dove into the box.

"How long have you...?" Sharice asked, hands on her hips.

"Pretty much from the beginning," Barb said, straightening out of her defensive crouch. "It was louder than the Cheetos. I just figured it was white noise or something."

"There are times I really dislike you, Barbara Everette," Sharice said, half bitterly. "I've got years of training, and having someone as Gifted as you come along is just...I had to sit with this thing for a *week* to catch its True Name!"

"Yeah?" Barb said. "Well, do you go around with whispers and shouts filling your head all the time? Huh?"

"Good point," Sharice admitted. "One which we're going to have to work on. But since you know its True Name, control it."

"How?" Barb asked, crouching again.

"Oh, quit that," Sharice said. "Fix the name in your mind and call it out. Tell it to move around. If your will is stronger, it will have to obey. You don't even have to open your mouth."

Barbara raised her hand to do just that, then paused.

"I'm not sure I should," Barb said.

"It's not hard," Sharice pointed out.

"No, I mean I *should* not, not I *cannot*," Barb corrected. "My religion does not control demons or consort with them. We destroy them."

"Jesus sent the Legion into a herd of pigs," Sharice said. "Think of it that way."

"And it wasn't a popular thing to do," Barb said. "Can I do it? Probably. Should I do it? That might take some soul searching. It feels wrong."

"Well, you can find out a True Name faster than anyone I've ever seen," Sharice said with a shrug. "And once you have that, and your level of power, he's basically putty in your hands. If you really feel the need to dispel him, feel free. We'll have to find another one eventually..."

"No," Barb said, shaking her head. "The Foundation does God's work. But each..."

"Must find their own God," Sharice said, nodding. "Okay, you seem pretty solid on this stuff. Pulling out the rest of the boxes would be fairly pointless. Well, the ones I'd normally pull out for beginners; and I don't have a couple more trained adepts to pull out the advanced. So... Time for field work."

"Fun, fun, fun," Barbara said. "Where?"

"Rubs."

The bar and grill was part of a small chain in the Asheville area. Copying the success of a much more notable national chain, the waitresses were invariably chosen for their looks, and dressed appropriately.

"Oh, my God," Barb said as they walked into the bar. It was just the beginning of the evening shift, and while there were still few customers, the full crop of waitresses was on the floor.

"Don't stare, don't Reveal," Sharice said, walking over to a table with a view of most of the bar.

"They're... everywhere," Barb hissed, setting Lazarus's carrier on the table. The cat slid open the bi-directional zipper she'd installed and poked his head out, hissed and ducked back in. Probably because every second woman in the grill, not *just* the waitresses, had a small demon on her shoulder.

"I'm sorry, ma'am," a man said, hurrying over to their table. "There are no pets allowed..."

"I have a doctor's excuse," Barb said, pulling out a sheet of paper. "Under the Americans with Disabilities Act, you have to allow companion animals. My cat is registered as a psychological companion animal. I'm aware that that makes me crazy, but I'm covered under Federal law."

The response was automatic and rote. Living with a familiar was a pain, but Barb blessed the otherwise incredibly stupid court orders that had expanded the ADA far beyond its original intent. Designed to force companies to make their places wheelchair accessible, the Ninth Circuit, using its usual logic, had decreed that "companion animals" including yappy dogs that were "psychologically necessary" to crazy ladies, were covered by the statute.

Barb was willing to be considered crazy if it meant she didn't have to put up with the headaches she got when Lazarus was more than a few dozen meters from her.

"Yes, ma'am," the manager said through gritted teeth.

"I promise he won't go peeing on the furniture," Barb said. "Laz. Stay. See?"

"Yes, ma'am," the manager repeated, walking away.

"Familiars," Sharice said. "Can't live with them..."

"We've been spotted," Barb said, craning her neck around. She wasn't staring at any of the small demons, but she definitely felt eyes on her. Of course, it might have been some of the patrons. Despite her age, she could easily have *been* one of the waitresses.

"I feel it, too," Sharice said. "Not sure..."

"Now what is that?" Barb asked, blinking. *Now* she was staring, even though there wasn't a demon on the girl's shoulder.

The waitress was bending over, talking to a customer. Pretty. *Very* pretty. She looked much like Barb had when she was in her early twenties. Long legs, blond hair, tight derriere and solid double-D chest. On closer examination, though, Barb was fairly sure that was in part fake. But the sense of being watched, even though the girl wasn't looking at them, was coming from her.

"Aura," Sharice said, quietly. "Read her aura."

The girl's aura wasn't black but it was darned close. It was a red so deep as to be almost indistinguishable.

"So...I repeat. What is *that*?"

"*That* is a drakni Mother, a drakia," Sharice said. "That girl is the reason that there are all these drakni here. They're all vanity demons, by the way. Well, almost all. Now, look around. Do you see some of the girls who should have drakni but don't seem to?"

"Yes," Barb said. "And their auras are dark, too. Not *as* dark…"

"Their drakni have settled all the way in," Sharice said, then paused as their waitress approached the table. "There are a few who don't have them. Call them girls who don't have that particular hook. Stronger-willed, not self-critical and vain at the same time. But they're rare in a place like this."

"Welcome to Rubs," the girl said perkily. "Our Happy Hour specials are…"

"I'd like a Coca-Cola and a plate of hot wings," Sharice said when the girl was finished with the recitation.

Barb had been trying and failing to not notice the drakni on the girl's shoulder. It was tiny, no bigger than a small rabbit, and seemed barely attached. But she found herself studying it, and then it noticed. It hissed at her, and she had the hardest time in the world not hissing back. Lazarus had no such reservations, letting out a soft warning yowl from the cat-bag.

"Uhm, ma'am, your cat…" the girl said.

"It's okay," Barb said, mentally sighing. She focused on the demon and then Displayed, releasing the mental hold on her own aura and showing just a portion of her true power.

The drakni nearly hopped out of its skin and cowered down, blinking its huge eyes in a way that was vaguely appealing, like a puppy that had been shouted at.

"Down, Laz," Barb added as the cat released a meow that sounded vaguely like a snicker. "I'll take the grouper burger, hold the bread."

"They're not ganging up on me," Barb said quietly as the waitress left.

"They saw enough to know not to," Sharice said, sighing. "But they'll follow. And they *are* ganging up on you. You've just managed to learn to suppress your Ear."

"Not really," Barb said. "I Hear what you mean, now. But there's so much other white noise…" Now that she paid attention, she could hear the demons cat-calling at her. They were commenting meticulously on her looks and promising that they could make her look better if she'd just take one of them…

"Concentrate on one," Sharice said, quietly.

"Kavam," Barb said. "The one on our waitress's shoulder. I can name off the rest."

"The Mother?" Sharice asked.

"Uhm..." Barb said, looking over at the waitress. "She's not talking."

"Concentrate," Sharice said. "It's going to be there anyway."

"Long..." Barb said after a moment. "I can hear it in my head, but I'm not sure I could pronounce it."

"And thus we get to the whole unpronounceable name thing," Sharice said. "But it's not necessary. Concentrate on the name and then call it over."

"It's in someone," Barb said.

"Just do it and watch."

Barb concentrated on the waitress, who was delivering a tray of beers to a table, and fixed on the name of the demon, calling it to her. The waitress finished delivering the beers, then instead of heading to one of her tables or the waitress station, came over to Barb's table.

"Welcome to Rubs," the girl said, smiling. "Haven't I seen you in here before?" she added, looking at Sharice.

"I love the atmosphere," Sharice replied. "You've been here a while?"

"Since I turned eighteen," the girl said. "But I'm getting tired of it. I'm thinking about changing jobs. Don't tell anybody."

"Of course not," Sharice replied, smiling. "Our secret."

"Uhm..." the waitress said, uncomfortably.

Barb realized that on concentrating on the demon, she'd been staring at the girl's breasts.

"Sorry," she coughed. "I was thinking about something. Penelope, that's a nice name."

"Thank you," Penelope replied. "Well, I hope you gals stop by more often."

"She thinks we're lesbians," Sharice said with a chuckle.

"I wonder where she's going to move to," Barb replied.

"Nowhere," Sharice said. "This place is too fertile a ground for her Mother. New girls all the time, most of them fixated on the importance of looks. She'll end up being a manager when she's lost the looks to be a waitress. And with that demon riding her, that's going to be quicker than normal. Vanity demons are like that. They promise beauty and make you ugly faster than smoking."

"There's nothing wrong with looking good," Barb said, frowning.

"I agree," Sharice said. "But there's looking good for looking good's sake, and looking good because it's all you consider yourself to be. When *you* dress well and do your makeup, it's almost a sacrifice to your God. It is one form of worship, whether you recognize it or not. In Janea's case, for example, it truly *is* a form of worship. I've never brought her here. I'm frankly afraid of the effects."

"Where *is* Janea?" Barb asked.

The Asatru High Priestess had been Barb's partner on her first true case. While Barb was immensely more powerful, Janea, despite giving the air of being a bubblehead, was much more educated in the occult. They'd made a most effective team.

"In Chattanooga," Sharice said, frowning. "There's a really strange case up there. Not one case, actually. The problem is, there have been several people who have changed from quite normal to psychotic literally in moments. The FBI's trying to figure out if it has Special Circumstances. Most of the killers haven't fit the normal profile. Janea's up there checking it out. In her own inimitable way, I'm sure."

While Barb tended to dress well and becomingly, Janea went straight from "becoming" to "scandalous" without any of the normal intervening steps. When she got teamed with FBI agents, it was . . . humorous.

"Any reports?" Barb asked.

"Not that have come across my desk," Sharice said as her phone started to play Ozzie Osborne's "Over the Mountain." "I'll be right back. That's Augustus."

Barb had just picked up a chicken wing and bitten into it when Sharice came in looking for their waitress.

"We have to go," the witch said, her face tight. "Right now."

"Why?" Barb asked, setting down the wing and wiping her fingers.

"Funny you should have asked about Janea at that moment," Sharice said. "Where *is* that waitress?!"

Barb closed her eyes and Called.

"I hope that's not a sin," she said, quietly. "Lord, I'm only using this demon, and the person that it rides, in Your works. If I have done wrong, I request some sort of sign."

"Well, it worked," Sharice said. "Here she comes."

"Now what about Janea?" Barb asked.

"She's in the hospital," the witch replied. "I need the check. Now. A friend's been hurt."

"Yes, ma'am," the girl said. The demon on her shoulder was shuddering as if in pain.

"What did you do to that thing?" Sharice asked.

"I concentrated," Barb said. "Hard. Janea."

"It seems she might have found what is causing the problem," Sharice said. "Unfortunately, they don't know if she's going to live. Augustus has arranged a plane."

Chapter Three

"We're not sure *what* is wrong with Miss Grisham," Dr. Stewart Downing said.

The neurologist was tall and slender with a saturnine air. Barb, in fact, found him somewhat creepy.

The trip had been . . . odd. It was the first time Barb, who had traveled extensively and in most forms of transportation, had ever flown in a Gulfstream. Now she knew how the other half lived. She'd already been packed; Sharice and Germaine apparently kept a traveling bag readily available, so the real question was, given that the plane had been prepped for takeoff when they arrived, did FLUF maintain a private jet? As it turned out, no. The *FBI* maintained a private jet *for* FLUF.

By the time the team had reached Chattanooga, Janea had been moved from ICU to a semi-residential "long-term care" facility located near Memorial Hospital. Her condition had been determined to be non-life-threatening for the time being.

The move was fortuitous since it meant nobody commented on Barb bringing a cat into the room.

"Do you know where she was found?" Augustus Germaine asked.

Augustus Germaine was the head of Special Circumstances for the US and Europe. In the US, the SC organization was called the Foundation for Love and Universal Faith: FLUF, pronounced

"Fluff." The inoffensive acronym was intentional; FLUF was the antithesis of a public operation. And in many cases it was even on point. Many, most even, of the Special Circumstances investigators were highly non-violent Wiccans and Buddhists.

He was not an adherent of any religion. Nor was he agnostic or atheist. He knew gods existed, but for him, that was like saying air existed. You can't see it, it's there anyway, so what? Being strictly neutral was also the only way that he could settle the more-than-occasional disputes between his various agents. He didn't care what kind of air it might be, as long as you could breathe it and not die.

"Coolidge Park," the neurologist replied. "Initially police thought she was under the influence of drugs. She was, at that time, conscious but incoherent, and attacked the officers. They started to place her under arrest and her heart arrested, so she was transported here. She was thought to be suffering from drug toxicity, until her tox screen came back negative. Then the FBI identified her as a consultant and, well..."

"I understand," Germaine said. "From your medical point of view, what is her condition?"

"There were some small surface contusions," Dr. Downing continued, pursing his lips in thought. "Possible indication of a struggle. That might actually have come from the altercation with the officers. No indication of sexual assault, and even the contusions are problematic. But nothing that would cause a coma. And it's not a coma. She's just *very* asleep. She has had a full CAT scan, EEG, and radiological MRI. There is no gross trauma to the brain but she remains in REM sleep. Only REM, not deep sleep. Heartbeat is up, blood pressure is high. Indications are of a more-or-less continuous nightmare. Which, sorry, isn't good. The body can only stand so much stress. When I got all the tests done we administered a sleep antagonist, which is when it got truly unusual."

"She coded," Sharice said.

"Yes," the neurologist said, frowning. "How did you know?"

"I've seen the condition before," the witch said. "I take it you administered an antagonist?"

"And she went right back to this condition," Dr. Downing said, nodding. "Do you know of a cure? I haven't been able to find anything in the medical texts on this condition."

"It's not common," Sharice said. "And no, I don't know of anything you can do to cure it."

"That's a rather broad statement," the neurologist said with a sniff.

"It's a rather accurate statement," Germaine replied. "I know two neurologists in the world who are familiar with the condition. I'll have one of them e-mail you."

Barb laid her hand on her friend's shoulder and prayed to God for guidance. In return she received a very slight feel of life, of struggle.

"Sharice..." she said a moment later in a strained voice.

Sharice laid her hand on the patient's other shoulder and then nodded.

"She's so far..."

"I think that the good doctor has other things to do," Germaine said. "We can stay with our friend, can we not?"

"Absolutely," the neurologist said. "If you need anything else..."

"Not at all, Doctor," the head of FLUF said. "But I appreciate your briefing in this matter."

"Her *ka* has been ripped from her body," Sharice said after the door was closed. "This wasn't an intentional projection. It was *pulled* out. The silver cord is barely holding."

"She's fighting," Barb said. "I get a feeling like dozens of... things ripping at her."

"Harpies," Sharice said. "Probably the origin of the myth. That's what most call them, anyway. One of the things to avoid on the Moon Path. She's held, trapped. And being tortured astrally."

"How do we get her back?" Barb asked.

"That's a tough one," Sharice said. "Augustus, I'm going to need help."

"Who?"

"Drakon and...Hjalmar," Sharice said. "I'm going to have to go onto the Paths and battle. If we keep her here, I'm going to need physical security on her as well. She should be moved to a more secure location. We'll need a nurse that can keep her mouth shut, support equipment and an on-call MD. Then Drakon to watch my astral back. Hjalmar, because if Freya doesn't get involved pretty damned soon, we're going to lose her."

"What can I do?" Barb asked.

"Right now, what you're doing," Sharice said. "Send her power. It's helping her, I can tell. We may need to bring in a coven to raise the support we'll need. But you've got other things to do."

"What?" Barb asked.

"Someone or something did this to her," Sharice said, looking over at Augustus. "Am I right?"

"Presumably," the senior agent said. "There has been an upgrade in the case. It is now officially Special Circumstances."

Chapter Four

*S*ee the Boss."

Kurt snorted at the post-it on his computer monitor and then crumpled it up and tossed it in the trash. Special Agent Kurt Spornberger had been an FBI agent for barely two years, but he wasn't exactly a newb.

He'd been a street officer with Chicago PD for three years before moving to investigations and had worked his way up to Homicide before being *recruited* by the Bureau. The Bureau was, at the time, going through one of its periodic reevaluations, and some bright consultant had noticed that many investigations that the Bureau had been credited with solving could better be credited to local LEOs. It just made sense in many ways. Bureau agents rarely spent enough time in any one area to really develop relations with the local informants. They didn't spend their early careers working the streets of a city. They often didn't really get the zeitgeist of the local culture. Local law enforcement officers—at least the good ones—did.

The suggestion of the overpaid consultant was taken to heart by at least one member of senior management in DC, and the order had come down from on high: *Recruit some local guys.* Kurt had good relations with the local office. After he turned up a critical lead in a local serial-murder case, an eyewitness to an abduction who just happened to be a street whore who would

34

have *never* talked with a Fibbie, the local Supervisory Special Agent had recommended him. He had the requisite four-year degree, albeit in anthropology, not pre-law or criminal justice, and he had a good rep. He was a little less "STRAC" than the Bureau normally hired, another way of saying he didn't look like he had a ten-foot spike jammed up his ass, but the idea was to look at different cultures and everyone agreed Kurt Spornberger was "different culture."

But he had an interesting time at the FBI academy. Some of the classes were taught by agents who had "been there, done that." You could tell by the look. These were guys who had spent decades looking at bare scraps of evidence, trying to find that one word buried in billions that would pop the perps, turn up the terrorists, break the bank-robbery team.

Those instructors looked him in the eye, looked at his record, listened to his answers and then nodded. He might be a greenie to the Bureau, but he wasn't green. They'd brought him in on some techniques he hadn't known and let him slide through the stuff that was rookie material without being assholes. He got along with the Old Guys.

Then there had been the classes taught by the Belts.

Suits were the upper echelon. Some of them were old agents who had been there and done that. Too many, though, were overgrown Belts. A Belt was like a Chairborne Commando in the Army. They were the agents who had somehow managed to *never* work outside the Beltway. Oh, they might have gone as far as Quantico, but that was about it. They had no field experience other than an initial tour.

But *my God*, did they know how to run an investigation. They were investigating supermen, one and all. They had every answer, just ask them. And ask the Suits, all of whom they knew by name. You clearly got the impression that the FBI Director did not shit without their fully prepared Action Report on Shitting Method-ology. And make sure that form 493-628-QX is filled out fully.

Kurt had barely managed to survive the classes given by the Belts. He'd dealt with Belts before. Every department had them. You just had to learn to live with them because killing them forced you to fill out even *more* paperwork. And there were so many, you'd never get any real work done.

On the other hand, the shooting instructors were pretty good.

They believed in the FBI Way of shooting. But when Kurt proved that the Kurt Spornberger Way of the Gun was going to get him through the qualifications, they'd left him alone. The hand-to-hand stuff, well...

It had taken him quite some time to convince them that he Did Not Want to move to Quantico to be a HTH instructor. Seriously. He had a house in Chicago, he liked Chicago, he did *not* like Virginia and he didn't want to live in Virginia. He understood that the FBI meant he'd move at some point. But the idea had been to get *local guys* working *local areas.* Not get local guys to come teach HTH. I'm sorry about the arm.

He'd graduated from Quantico with fair marks, really high on shooting, investigation techniques and hand-to-hand—pretty high from the Been There Done That instructors, pretty marginal from the Belts. Any BTDT Supervisory Special Agent who looked at the results was going to be able to parse it. Good field agent, not a natural diplomat.

The last week of Academy, the postings came out. He was unsurprised to find that at least two of the natural Belts in the class were going to DC. Most of the rest weren't untoward, either, except that they were actually posting the one Native American they had to a reservation. Of course, the guy was a Cherokee and they were sending him to a Hopi reservation in Arizona, but at least they were *trying.*

Then he got to "Spornberger, Kurt M."

Chattanooga, TN.

The whole effing idea had been to recruit guys for their local knowledge, and where did they send the guy from Chicago?

Chattanooga. What, it started with a "Ch" so it had to be the same place? Belt thinking in a nutshell.

Fucking Chattanooga. Goodbye, Lake Michigan, hello...Tennessee River? He could hear the echo of banjoes just saying it. Goodbye kielbasa, hello...What the fuck did they *eat* in Tennessee, anyway? Grits...God almighty, he'd be forced to eat grits. And...chitlins...Oh...God...

Over the last couple of years he'd come to terms with living in the wilderness. Chattanooga wasn't awful. Some of the local cops, with whom he'd quickly established a close relationship since his own BTDT came across fast, even insisted that they'd never live anywhere else. He'd tried to explain the inherent superiority of the only truly civilized city on Earth, but they just couldn't comprehend it. It was probably something in the water.

But he survived. Someday, he was assured, he could get transferred back to the center of the universe, the city with broad shoulders. They just wanted him to get accustomed to working with other areas. "Think of it as broadening," his Supervisor had explained.

"Morning, Kurt," Supervisory Special Agent Garson said as the agent entered the office. "How's case nine-forty-eight?"

"I don't think these guys have got a record," Kurt said, sitting down and spreading his legs out. "We picked up one pretty clear print, but it wasn't on file. And the way they move, I'd say military background. Wouldn't be the first time. I've put in a request for access to the military database of fingerprints, but you know how sticky they can be. They're going to want to know which guy, and we don't have that yet."

"Well, I may have to transfer it," Garson said, sighing. "We have a change of status on another case. A series of cases. The Madness cases."

"Oh?" Kurt said, neutrally. Everybody in the office, everyone in the *area*, knew about the Madness cases. Technically a series of unrelated cases, they'd gotten tossed together because while the MOs and perps were different, the patterns were remarkably similar. In seven separate cases, otherwise more-or-less normal people had suddenly gone bat-shit nuts. Violently psychotic. They'd gone crazy, started attacking people around them, in one case partially cannibalizing a victim, and had never gotten their act back together. All seven were in long-term psychiatric holding, and the doctors couldn't do more than dope them to the gills with antipsychotics.

"A consultant attached to the overall investigation has been injured," Garson said carefully. "I was asked to find someone to assist the replacement. In your files there is reference to an unusual murder investigation you were involved in in Chicago. The South Side Cult Murders."

"Yes, sir," Kurt said, trying not to wince. The reality was, he had to get out of Chicago PD *because* of his final report on those murders. He'd been the guy who cracked the case, but putting in your report that you'd seen "a shadow" leave the body of the perp after he was shot and killed in the raid... Well, if Kurt had played it off and put it down to "combat fatigue," it would have been one thing. But sticking by his statement and what he was sure he'd seen with his own damned eyes...

"What I'm about to explain to you his highly classified," the Supervisory Special Agent said, interlacing his fingers and leaning forward. "Codeword Sierra Charlie. Sierra Charlie stands for Special Circumstances."

Barb was used to the stares. It wasn't that pretty women didn't work for the FBI. It was that she was *unusually* pretty, and that attracted attention. Once upon a time, that had been a big thing for her. These days she found it to be a pain. And it was only getting worse.

The bag over her shoulder with the black cat head poking out of it, said cat looking around with interest, didn't help.

She really didn't care at the moment. "Focused" didn't begin to cover it. Laser beams were lazy compared to Barb.

"Barbara Everette, Foundation for Love and Universal Faith, to see Supervisory Special Agent Garson," she said in one sharp rush.

The rent-a-cop manning the security station couldn't seem to get past the various views. He shifted from her face to the chest to the cat then back to the face, and his mouth opened.

"Do I have to repeat myself?" Barb asked.

"Uh...ma'am, you're on the list," the guard said, finally looking at his computer screen. "But cats aren't allowed..."

"Fine," Barb said, switching to command tone and whipping a copy of her affidavit out of the bag. "I'm crazy. Under the Americans with Disabilities Act, the cat comes with me. I need him or I get all upset. This isn't upset. This is firm. You don't want to see upset. Just call SSA Garson and tell him I'm here. Is that *simple* enough for you?"

"Yes, ma'am," the guard said, picking up the phone.

"Hubba, hubba, hubba," Special Agent Spornberger said at the sight of the woman. He was watching her through the glass of the supervisor's office, and it was apparent she hadn't seen him yet.

"Let me remind you of the department's policy on sexual harassment, Kurt," SSA Garson said, sighing.

"Understood, sir," Kurt said, wonderingly. "But she's stacked like a brick shi—"

"I get the point, Agent Spornberger," Garson snapped. "Now *can* it."

"SSA Garson," Barb said professionally as she strode into the room. "I'm *Mrs.* Barbara Everette."

"Mrs. Everette," Garson said, standing up and shaking her hand. "This is Special Agent Spornberger. He will be assisting you on this investigation. He has...previous experience outside the Bureau and has been briefed in on SC investigations."

"Hello," Barbara said, extending her hand.

"Nice cat," Kurt replied, shaking it. He slowed in his shaking and then shifted his grip.

"If you want me to put you on your knees, Special Agent, continue," Barbara snapped, shifting her own.

"Tao-ki?" Kurt asked, withdrawing his hand.

"Yes," Barbara replied, wrinkling her brow.

"Bù dào huáng hé xīn bù sǐ."

"Bù dào huáng hé xīn bù sǐ."

"Tiānshēng wǒ cái bì yǒuyòng," Barbara said, smiling thinly.

"I think I'm in love?" Kurt said, his eyes wide.

"Note the 'Mrs.,' Agent Spornberger," Barbara said, tartly. "And I am a servant of the Lord Jesus Christ, who, forgiveness or not, looks poorly upon extramarital affairs. So put your dick back in your pants and your tongue back in your head or I'll rip both off and feed them to you."

"I'm sort of new to the bureau," Kurt said, puzzled. "Was that sexual harassment?"

"No, that was her promising to kick your ass, Agent Spornberger," Garson said, trying not to grin. "But the question I have to ask, Mrs. Everette, is, can you work with him? Because this is, alas, Kurt. We've been trying to potty train him for the last couple of years and so far it's had no effect."

"The problem is not 'can I work with him,' but 'can he survive,'" Barbara said, sighing. She sat down and laid Lazarus's bag on her lap, letting the cat out to sniff around the room. "In these investigations, legally or not, the truth is that the Bureau agent is the innocent bystander. The civilian, in other words. We have to work with the Bureau and local law enforcement agencies, but we'd rather not. Because while the casualty rate of our agents is high, the casualty rate of the agents we're assigned is higher. Agent Spornberger, you clearly have some martial-arts skills, and you're old enough you may have some street skills. But this is a different kind of street and you are no more powerful than a baby on it. Can you face the fact that there may come a time when I tell you to run away as fast as you can, and if you don't, you're going to die? And probably have your soul ripped out and taken straight to hell?"

"Well, ma'am," Kurt said, grinning uneasily. "You clearly have some martial-arts skills, but..."

"That's the problem," Barb said, looking at Garson. "The 'but...' That, right there, is almost sure to get him killed no matter what I do. Because there is no 'but.' Special Agent, are you a Believer in any religion? What religion *are* you?"

"Catholic, ma'am," Kurt said. "I mean, I'm sort of Catholic. I haven't been to confession in..."

"Then you are *totally* unprotected," Barb said. "It's like going on a drug raid without a vest. Or a gun. Or backup. Even if whatever we're dealing with can be deflected by a cross, for example, you have to *believe* in the cross and be in touch with your God. And your God has got to believe in *you*. Otherwise, you're totally and completely *scr*...unprotected, Agent Spornberger. With what we may be up against, it may be necessary for me to *kill* you, Agent Spornberger. If you cannot, when the time is right, follow my instructions to the letter. And I don't think that you can."

"Mrs. Everette, if you wish, I'll replace him," Garson said, crossing his arms and leaning back in his chair.

"Do you have any other agents with experience in the paranormal?" Barb asked, looking Spornberger up and down.

"None," Garson said. "Including me. I've been briefed on SC, I'm aware of some of the reports, the stories. But I can't say that I'm totally convinced."

"And the same would be the case with any green agent," Barb said, sighing. "They just can't *believe*. Okay, tough guy, you're the one that's seen a ghost. I'll leave it up to you."

"It wasn't a ghost," Kurt said. "It was a shadow. I'm not sure what it was, but I...I got this feeling it wasn't a ghost."

"Demon, then," Barb said. "Tell me about it later. I need to get briefed in. Who's doing it?"

"Spornberger," Garson said. "He's got all the reports. Note that we only have the attack on your agent to indicate that there is anything to the SC designation. That and the fact that the case is just so damned weird."

"Well, I know the area's not a total dry hole," Barb said. "I can feel the...currents? Whatever. But it's possible the attack on Janea wasn't related to the investigation. We have enemies of our own. However, we'll just try to follow up on her leads and see where it takes us."

"What's the paranormal read on this?" Kurt asked as he sat down in the secure conference room.

"I'm not a paranormal expert," Barb said. "But I've got some people to do the research. And the short answer is there isn't one. Have you ever heard of Kali?"

"I've been studying oriental martial arts since I was in high school," Kurt said dryly. "And by extension the Orient. Yes, I've heard of Kali. Hindu death goddess, right?"

"More complicated than that," Barb said, biting her lip. "Also a goddess of fertility and childbirth. And murder. Life and death, alpha and omega. The point being that there are references to worshippers being used as avatars of Kali, taken by her and turned into killing machines. But even the...deep references, if you will, the studies that assume the existence of the goddess, indicate most of those killers were using drugs to simulate the effect. And Kali, being what Christians recognize as a demon, is tightly bound by the Fall. Even though God gave the world to Satan, the greater demons and demonesses, ancient gods in most cases, are tightly bound. Freeing them, even drawing upon their essence, requires powerful rites which have not been used in this case. So it's not a possession by Kali or another greater demon. And according to the initial report Janea turned in, none of them show current signs of possession. They have been...sensitized to the supernatural. But they may have been sensitives to begin with."

"In short, you have no clue what is going on," Kurt said.

"No," Barb admitted. "But that's why I'm here. But we've got one piece of evidence we didn't have before. *Someone* attacked Janea mystically. That makes it personal."

Chapter Five

"Oh, thank *God* we're here!" Kurt gasped as Barbara came to a screeching halt at the guarded entrance. The drive had been short but traffic had been heavy. Normally, it would have been quicker to walk with the jammed cars on US 27.

But any belief that Kurt retained that he'd been landed with Suzy Soccer Mom was disabused by the drive. Much of it had been in the oncoming lanes, or turn lanes, or in one case, slightly on the sidewalk. The *opposite* sidewalk.

It wasn't that Barbara drove *badly*. It was that she drove like a cop. One in a hurry and with enormous ability behind the wheel.

"What's wrong?" Barb asked, hitting the window switch and smiling at the frowning corrections guard manning the gate. "We got here in one piece."

"You are insane, Madame," Kurt replied. "Kurt Spornberger, FBI," he continued, holding out his ID. "This is Barbara Everette, a contractor with us."

"Yes, sir," the guard said, hitting the control to open the gate. "Try to keep it down on the campus, ma'am."

"Will do," Barb said.

"Next time, I drive," Kurt said as Barb hunted for an open visitor's parking space.

"Like I'd let anybody else drive me," Barb said.

Moccasin Bend Mental Health Facility was a sprawling set of brick buildings originally founded in 1961, located across the river from the downtown area. It served twenty-eight counties in the area as a regional inpatient care facility.

Barb ... didn't like Moccasin Bend. She wasn't "open" to Sight at the moment, but she didn't have to be to feel the malevolence of the area. The entire place was just ... weird. The buildings were straight out of a horror movie and the layout was decidedly odd. She looked at the map again and realized that the buildings were laid out in a sign she'd only seen once in her "catch-up" research. Specifically, in a grimoire that was kept under lock and key at the Foundation.

"This place is unhealthy as ... hell," Barb said, looking around the parking lot. "Nearly literally. I mean really, really bad."

"You're serious?" Kurt said, grinning nervously.

"*Bad* bad," Barb said. "Bad on toast. Like, my first instinct is to burn it down and kill everyone near it."

"Don't," Kurt said. "I know you're covered for stuff, but that would be pretty hard to cover up."

"Seriously bad," Barb said, taking a deep breath. "Makes me want to scream ..."

"The patient exhibits many classic signs of psychosis with, however, some idiosyncratic additions," Dr. Downing said.

Oddly enough, it was the same doctor who had been treating Janea. Now that Barb knew he was associated with this mental facility, she intended to get him unassociated as fast as possible.

The patient was restrained. Tightly. Barb was familiar with restraints, having spent some time under them herself after her first encounter with a demon and before Augustus pulled some strings to get her out of psychiatric care. But the ones they'd used on her were light compared to what they had on the young man in the bed.

"How idiosyncratic?" Barb asked, disturbed by the sight of the otherwise healthy young man's condition.

"Most patients in this type of condition tend to bite," Dr. Downing said, pulling out a probe. "Most of those, however, do not tend to swallow whatever they bite off. These patients do. And, observe," he continued, pressing the probe into the base of Darren's foot.

"I didn't see anything," Kurt said. "Except him continuing to ..."

"Writhe," Barb finished.

"You should have," the psychiatrist said. "That should have elicited a pain response, even in a patient suffering from psychosis. A yell, a howl, some type of response. And," he continued, pulling out a small rubber mallet. "Observe."

He tapped the subject just below his knee and raised an eyebrow.

"I'm pretty sure his leg didn't twitch," Barb said, frowning. "He should have had an involuntary movement, a reflex response. Right?"

"Correct," the doctor said, smiling as if at a marginally bright student. "No reflex responses, no pain responses, but their autonomic nervous systems continue to function, they breathe, their hearts beat and they have control over their voluntary muscles. But, if I were to remove the restraints and let him walk, you would observe that his motions are powerful but uncoordinated in the extreme."

"I . . . need to check something," Barb said, then frowned. "I take it that anything that goes on in here is confidential?"

"Yes," Dr. Downing said, frowning in turn. "What sort of examination?"

"One that's going to make you shake your head and wonder if the Bureau is going nuts," Kurt said. "And one that you're not going to comment on under any circumstances. Under the Uniform Federal Code Section Eighteen. In a real and legally binding sense."

"Oh," Dr. Downing said. "O . . . kay?"

"It won't take a moment," Barb said. She hated to Open in this place, but it was going to be necessary. Because there was something screaming at her about the patient. He looked healthy enough at first glance, but something was . . . screaming.

She laid her hand on his brow, careful to avoid the gnashing teeth, then Opened up her Sight.

The first thing she noticed was, in fact, the neurologist. His aura was as black as the ace of spades. She saw him tense and looked over with a thin, fierce grin.

"Okay, I suppose this isn't quite as unusual as I'd have thought for you," Barb said.

"What . . . are you?" Downing asked, carefully.

"As it turns out, your worst nightmare," Barb replied. She reached for the soul of the afflicted and paused. "Jesus Christ," she said, softly.

"I wouldn't have expected you to curse," Kurt said.

"That wasn't a curse, Special Agent," Barb said. "That was a prayer. This person is dead."

"Dead?" Dr. Downing said, snorting. "I can assure you, as a physician—"

"With what's riding you, there's no way that you heal," Barb said. "So calling yourself a physician, Doctor, is a stretch. Research. Poke. Prod. Possibly advance science. But that . . . thing in you isn't going to allow you to ever heal. And when I said this person was dead, I was very specific. This . . . thing has no soul. None. No *ka*. No *ba*. It is a walking dead thing."

"Zombie?" Kurt said. "Please, not zombies."

"Not the movie zombie," Barb said. "I'm not sure what it is or how it was created. But this person has no more soul than a rock. How it's continuing to exist is a real question. There is power coming from somewhere that is continuing to give it the semblance of life." She stepped back and started to close down. Then, just as an exercise, she fully Opened her Power.

Dr. Downing immediately took an involuntary step backwards and grunted. In the distance, one of the patients started howling, setting off others.

"What just happened?" Kurt asked, looking around.

"*That* is what I am, Doctor," Barb said. "Is that clear enough for you?"

What was clear was that it wasn't simply the neurologist that inflicted the place. It stank with evil, and shadows filled every corner.

"Yes," the doctor said in a strained voice.

"God has given me the grace to be His sword upon this land, Doctor," Barb said, softly. "Your Master cannot prevail against me, for I wear the armor of righteousness, and the power of the Lord is held in both right hand and left. So fill us in and quit playing power games. I have neither the time nor the patience, and this place quite frankly wants me here slightly less than I want to stay."

"I have a short video I'd like to show you."

The video started with Darren apparently asleep in the traditional rubber room. He was slumped in one corner, his mouth open and flaccid but his limbs twitching.

"I thought these things were a myth," Kurt said, looking at the view.

"They are not a preferred environment," Dr. Downing said. He'd managed to calm down a bit on the walk to the meeting room and was still trying for suave and debonair. However, he was keeping the special agent between himself and Barbara.

"But there are conditions in which they are useful. Such as this one. I wanted to observe his actions under a variety of stimuli, and given the reports of his admission, I was unwilling to do so outside of a controlled environment. He was heavily sedated when placed in the room, and the first part is rather boring. I'll fast forward."

The digital file skipped forward until, in fast motion, Darren lurched to his feet and started walking.

"There," the doctor said. "Note the nature of the motion."

"He *looks* like a zombie," Kurt said, his brow furrowing. "Christ, why'd it have to be zombies?"

"Yes," Dr. Downing said, smiling faintly. "He does, doesn't he? Arms extended, although more to the side than the traditional zombie look. And that would be why?"

"His balance," Barb said, nodding. "He's got real balance problems."

"Due to the lack of reflex," Dr. Downing said. "It gives him the equivalent of an inner-ear infection, and he uses his arms to maintain his balance."

Barbara leaned into the video and nodded.

"His lips are moving," she said. "Is there audio?"

"There is," the doctor said, turning it on.

The syllables were harsh and guttural, mixed with moans and occasional shrieks.

"It appears to be random babble," the psychiatrist said. "Not entirely idiosyncratic, but uncommon. Normally the patient would be speaking recognizable words but disconnected in syntax. Along with occasional disconnected threats or pleas."

"I'm not sure that's babble," Barb said, listening for a moment longer. "Get me a copy of the audio file. Actually, copies of the audio and video."

"Of course," Dr. Downing said, fast forwarding again. "However, after this had gone on for some time, I sent in guards to restrain him again. And... watch."

The two guards entered fast when Darren's back was turned.

They were wearing some sort of full-coverage white body armor including helmets and gloves. They looked like they were suited up to work with an attack dog. They also carried clear plastic shields, and one of them was carrying an air injector presumably filled with a tranquilizer.

A third guard shut the door when they were barely in the room, but before they could even approach the subject, Darren turned, showing more coordination than had previously been evident, and charged, screaming a ululating cry of what sounded like rage and pain. He hit the shield of the guard with the syringe so hard the man was thrown off his feet, and the patient fell on top of him, screaming and scrabbling to get past the shield.

The guard flipped the syringe out from under the pile and the second guard picked it up quickly, then fell onto the patient, pinning him between the two guards and injecting him in the back of the neck.

"And that's about it," Dr. Downing said, turning off the video. "The patient is fast and strong beyond the norm, but very clumsy. In part, I believe, because of the lack of reflex response. The patient's balance is particularly bad probably because, at some level, he has to think about standing up. It's notable that when the patient has had to be . . . restrained, he falls down quickly and tends to fight on the ground. The precise symptoms have never been recorded in literature. I'm considering doing a paper on them. It's possible it may be an entirely new psychiatric condition. If so, I'll have to name it."

"Chattanooga Zombieitis?" Kurt asked.

"Thank you for your input," Dr. Downing said dryly. "But . . . no. Among other things, 'itis' is the suffix for irritation and swelling."

"Neurological indications?" Barb asked. "For laymen?"

"Due to the nature of the problem, we were, fortunately, able to fund a full neurological workup," Dr. Downing said. "Various tests I won't detail. Certain neurotransmitters appear to be out of sync as well as various hormones. Testosterone and adrenaline levels are abnormally high, for example. Dopamine levels as well. Which may explain the lack of reflex response. Glutamate appears to be inhibited and certain portions of the brain are acting in uncharacteristic ways. Mid- and rear-brain activity is overexcited, while forebrain activity is virtually quiescent. The medulla in some of the older patients appears to actually be swelled. We're monitoring that because we're afraid that if the condition progresses it will lead to death."

"Forebrain is conscious thought," Barb said musingly. "Midbrain is sort of higher animal, the puppy brain, and rear brain is the old animal, the lizard hindbrain."

"In layman's terms, more or less," Dr. Downing said.

"So...they're thinking like animals?" Kurt asked.

"I would hate to put it that way in any sort of report," the neurologist said. "But...yes. Very angry and vicious ones."

"What about treatment?" Kurt asked.

"So far there doesn't seem to be one," the neurologist said. He seemed indifferent to the possibility.

"Trust me, Kurt," Barb said. "These things are beyond treatment. Not. Alive. Take my word for it."

"Wait," Kurt said, his brow furrowing. "PCP is a glutamate inhibitor. Right?"

"An NMDA uptake inhibitor," the doctor corrected. "But it has the practical effect."

"So it's like they're on PCP?" Kurt asked. "Sort of PCP zombies. Ouch."

"Again, I did not say it," the psychiatrist said. "But the effects have some similarity to PCP overdose. That was the initial finding of the admitting doctors. But it's not PCP. What it is, we're unsure. As I said, psychotic break, homicidal, cause unknown."

"Double ouch," Kurt said. "Cannibalistic PCP zombies."

"And I don't think that will be in any reports, either," Barb said, nodding. "Good summation. That's enough." She looked at Downing and snorted.

"I don't know exactly why you let that thing ride you, but you did. And apparently with some understanding of what you were doing. It wasn't a good choice. It wasn't even an intelligent choice. But it was a choice. And for that, Doctor, you are damned." She chuckled and shook her head. "Literally, not figuratively. How you could have been that stupid, I don't know. I'll just mention, in passing, that Jesus is pretty forgiving. If you can get your head around getting that...thing out of you, you *might* just be forgiven. On the other hand, if you keep on your current path, you're choosing one life of whatever it gives you in exchange for eternal torment. Again, your choice. But I'd suggest that you start thinking about alternatives."

"I'll keep that in mind," Downing said, frowning slightly.

"Me, I'd damn you and be done with it," Barb said. "But I tend to be rather Old Testament. Jesus is the forgiving one."

"So," Barb said as they headed back to the office. "Tell me about PCP. You said you were a street cop once, right? Ever deal with it?"

"Rarely," Kurt said, holding onto the door handle as Barb weaved through traffic. "It's not as big as it was in the eighties. When something gets a bad street rep you know it's bad. But, yeah, I had to handle a couple of guys on it."

"How bad?" Barb asked, slipping into a narrow gap between a semi in the left lane and the truck ahead of her in the right. "I hate semis that go slow in the left lane and just barely pass other trucks."

"Pretty bad," Kurt squeaked. "They don't feel any pain so when you hit them with a K-11 it's like you might as well not even bother. They'll dislocate their own bones if you put them in a lock. You pin them to the ground and they end up doing one-handed cop push-ups. They get ahold of you, and you'd better have some good escape techniques. They bite like nobody's business. Lost a chunk of flesh on my forearm to one. You start to recognize the signs after a while and call for backup if you've got time. The best bet is to do a Rodney King on their ass, but departments frown on that. And, hell, hitting a guy on PCP with truncheons just pisses him off. You get enough Tasers on one, you can knock him out. That's about your best bet, five or six Tasers more or less simultaneously. And hope he's got a good heart."

"Don't have to worry about killing these things," Barb said. "They're not human anymore."

"You think you're going to find anything in here?" Kurt said, setting down another stack of folders.

"I have no clue," Barb replied. "I hope so."

"Because one thing you've probably noticed is that these attacks have been getting closer and closer together," Kurt said. "The first one that we've pinpointed as being similar in nature was two years ago. Then a year after that. Then three months. Then four in the last six. The last three in the last two months. That's when we got called in."

"I've noticed the pattern," Barb said. "I'm looking for any indication of what may be causing it."

"That's what over a dozen agents have been doing for the last two months," Kurt pointed out.

"They weren't looking for what I'm looking for," Barb said. "Most of this seems to be looking for an environmental cause. A drug that's not detected by the usual tox screen. Some environmental toxin they've been exposed to. You're not going to find a mystic cause by taking a surface swab. The good news is, it's not movie zombieitis."

"That would be bad," Kurt said. "You're sure they're zombies?"

"That or something damned close," Barb said. "Did they go nuts then lose their souls? I suspect it's the other way around."

"So what are you looking for?" Kurt asked.

"I'm not sure," Barb admitted. "Patterns that normal investigators would dismiss. Unfortunately, so far I'm going over tilled ground. All males in their twenties."

"Tilled," Kurt said.

"So I've noticed," Barb replied dryly. "Mostly students at the University of Tennessee, Chattanooga branch. All residents of the Chattanooga area. But none of them from the same area of Chattanooga."

"UTC is a commuter college," Kurt said. "Most of the students don't live on campus. They're making more dorms but it's still mostly commuters. That's just FYI."

"Thanks," Barb said. "Some of the information I need about them isn't even in these files. The investigators talked to people who knew them, but they weren't asking the right questions. I need to . . . talk to some of the same people."

"Most of them lived with their parents," Kurt said.

"And most of them went to school in the area," Barb said. "I think it might be better ground to talk to people who knew them for a while but are less . . . disinterested than parents. I need to know who these guys really are, not what their parents want people to think they are. Were. Religious or atheist, subculture . . ."

"Teachers?" Kurt asked. "Fellow students?"

"Guidance counselors."

Karen Gill was medium height with long, dark hair, a lined, tan face and bright black eyes. The guidance counselor's office was small and cluttered, with the most notable feature being a large inspirational poster on the wall of a man standing on a mountaintop. The title was "Success," and the inspirational quote was "Success means knowing who you are."

Barb was not much given to cynicism, but she wondered if the counselor considered her life a success.

"Darren was not a natural student," the guidance counselor said, sitting in her chair after ensuring her guests did not want drinks. "He struggled through his courses. I give him credit for his efforts in that regard."

"Ms. Gill," Barb said carefully. "Darren is currently in long-term psychiatric care for attempting to eat another person. He is but one of seven recent cases of similar problems. We are trying to prevent a reoccurrence and, if possible, find what happened to him so that doctors may be able to give him a normal life. I'm afraid we really do need something besides 'He was a nice boy and not a natural student.'"

"I am an accredited psychological counselor," Ms. Gill said, making a face. "Communications with my clients are privileged."

"Can you tell us anything that is not from a counseling session?" Barb asked. "Was he counseled frequently?"

"As an alternative, we could come back with a court order," Kurt said. "I'm not making a threat; I'm just saying if that would help . . ."

"No," the counselor said, sighing. "The thing is . . . I'm trying to balance my professional distance with my . . . personal distaste."

"Oh?" Barb said, raising her eyebrows. "For Darren?"

"Yes," Ms. Gill admitted. "I did counsel Darren on a number of occasions but never with much success. I won't delve into those discussions absent a court order, and I don't think I need to. The truth is, I counseled his . . . victims far more often than he."

"Victims?" Kurt said, pulling out a notebook.

"Not physical," Ms. Gill said, then shrugged. "Well, in two cases physical. Darren . . . Darren was a bully. From what I've gleaned from talking to his earlier counselors, he had been since he was a child. He was always picking on other children and intimidating them. We try to keep physical violence to the minimum in school, but kids learn early that if you stand up to a bully they don't always back down. In two cases, when he was a freshman here, he got into fights. He was suspended for both. The second one, he was very nearly charged with assault. I call them fights but what they were were massacres. In the second case he beat a sophomore boy to the point I felt he should be sent to the hospital to be checked. The principal . . . overruled me on that, so he was treated by the school nurse. Jacob's parents didn't press charges when Darren was suspended.

"He was somewhat larger than the majority of the freshmen, or even seniors, and very . . . well, he was just nasty. Mean as they come. Being more professional, Darren had anger management issues. But from the description of his actions on the news, his actions go so far beyond that, it is hard to believe."

"But he wasn't just some nice boy?" Barb asked. "That is certainly the indication I've had from his records. I've even looked at clips about him on the TV. That was sort of the theme. 'He was a nice, normal kid.'"

"No," Ms. Gill said, taking a sip of herbal tea. "He was not a nice boy. He was on the basketball team in freshman year and got benched for the last half of the season since he almost invariably fouled out. He was a decent football player, but only on defense. And even then he received frequent fouls for 'unsportsmanlike conduct.' He was popular only to the extent he was feared. In two cases I suspect him of date rape but was unable to get the girls involved to come forward to testify or even make charges. He was a brutal, nasty, brutish bully. All that being said, killing someone and then attempting to eat them is far beyond his normal unpleasantness. Is there any indication of what caused it?"

"Not so far," Barb said, stroking her hair in thought. "But this has been helpful. Thank you."

"So he got into fights," Kurt said as they drove back towards downtown. "I got into fights in school. Big deal."

"It's more than that," Barb said thoughtfully. For a wonder, she was driving sedately, but that was clearly because her mind was elsewhere. "He was filled with rage. Anger, rage, except in certain specific circumstances, is a sin against God."

"I've got a short temper," Kurt said. "Does that mean I'm going to go off the deep end?"

"You have a short temper and don't handle frustration well," Barb said. "That is a whole other thing than going around filled with rage all the time. There are various reasons that might have caused that. Physiologically, he might have had a testosterone imbalance or even over-production of adrenaline. Environmentally, he might have been in an abusive family. Mystically, he might have already have been possessed of a demon or even carried one that was attached to the family. I have seen one report that families that have a genetic flaw for adrenaline overproduction caused by an otherwise benign tumor on the adrenaline gland *also* tend to carry generational rage demons. The McCoys in the Hatfield and McCoy feud have the gene. Whether the demons cause the tumor or the affinity for rage makes it a good home for a demon is a chicken or egg question. The point is that this wasn't just some nice kid who snapped. He already had the predisposition to hurt and kill."

"Which means... what?"

"When I figure that out, I'll let you know," Barb said. "Do we have Janea's notes?"

"Not that I'm aware of," Kurt said. "She's staying at the Fairfield Inn on Shallowford Village Drive. As far as I know, she hasn't been checked out yet. If she stays in her current condition for another few days, the Bureau will probably clear out her room."

"Can we get in her room?" Barb asked.

"Probably," Kurt said. "Depends on how cooperative the hotel staff is when I flash my FBI credentials."

"What is she wanted for?" the desk manager asked, wide-eyed. "I remember her. What is she, a bank robber or something?"

"No, actually," Barb said. "She's a consultant to the FBI. She was injured during an investigation and we need to see if there are any clues to how she was hurt."

"I can open the room," the desk clerk said, swiping a card. "But I'll have to accompany you."

"This is probably going to take some time," Barb noted.

"I'll get someone to cover for me."

"I think somebody tossed this place," Kurt said, going on guard. There were suitcases covering half the bed, all the other horizontal surfaces, and a good bit of the floor. Clothing was scattered everywhere up to and including hanging on the bedframe, the TV, chairs and even a light fixture.

"No, this is just Janea's idea of housekeeping," Barb replied. "It always looks this way. She throws random stuff into random suitcases, lots of them, and can never find what she wants, so she throws the stuff in every direction looking for her other shoe. And then complains when she can't find what she's thrown around. Sharing a room with her is beyond a pain."

"Finding anything in here is going to be beyond a pain," Kurt said. "But I suppose we have to look. How does she keep records?"

"You're joking, right?"

"Here's something interesting," Barb said.

They'd been picking through the detritus of Janea's life on the road for three hours. A notebook with some notes on the investigation had been found under a pile of dirty laundry. Unfortunately, it only had a few brief entries dated to the first two days Janea had been in town. There were good notes for the first few minutes of her in-brief, after which they were mainly on the subject of the personality and dress failures of the briefers. One of the entries was about a cute guy she'd seen at a coffee shop. Another was on the quality of shopping at the local mall. There was nothing to indicate that she'd actually been investigating anything, but the mall was one of the noted overlap points.

"What?" Kurt asked, tossing another pair of underwear into a growing pile. He'd decided the only way to make sense of anything was to sort the room and had been hard at it, occasionally gulping when he ran across something extremely personal, for the last hour.

"It's a card from a paranormal society," Barb said. "Tennessee Area Ghost Hunters. Hugh Yeaton, Senior Investigator."

"Any number of reasons she'd have that," Kurt said, wincing and placing a very odd-looking device in his "very odd-looking devices" pile. "She might have called them to find out if they had any leads."

"We try really hard not to get involved with any of these guys," Barb said, placing the card on the notebook. "Most of them are kooks and wannabes. And a goodly number of the ones that can actually sense stuff get their powers from the wrong side of the street, if you take my meaning."

"Hey, aren't those the guys who have got a TV show?" Kurt asked, lifting up a piece of clothing and considering it. "I have no clue which pile this should go in. It gets a pile of its own."

"I dunno," Barb said. "I don't watch much TV."

"It's on A&U," Kurt said, distantly. "I'm not sure I *want* to know what this is for..."

"Well, it's the only thing we've got from this mess," Barb replied. "But we'll check it out later. We're missing something."

"You always are," Kurt said, sighing. "It's why the Monday morning quarterbacking you get from stuff like Congressional investigations is so stupid. Sure, all the data is there, and in hindsight it all makes sense. But when you're looking at it, it's just mush."

"What do we know?" Barb said, leaning back on the dresser and closing her eyes. "Janea was found in Coolidge Park."

"Over on North Shore," Kurt said, nodding. "But that's a dry hole. No actual connections to that immediate area. And her car was on the other side of the river. Which means she probably took the walking bridge over the river. But we interviewed everyone we could find in the area and nobody saw her crossing. Either way."

"But that's where she *was*," Barb said. "On the North Shore. She was conscious, then. But already incoherent. Probably already on the Paths but sort of functional to move in the mundane world. So it couldn't have happened far from where she was picked up. We need to pay a visit to Mr. Yeaton."

"Good afternoon, ma'am," Kurt said, holding out his ID. "We're looking for Hugh Yeaton."

The address listed on the business card had led them to a suburban two-story house in a working-class neighborhood in East Ridge and, presumably, the lady of the house. The thin, dark-haired woman looked at the ID suspiciously, then sighed.

"I'm sure whatever it is, officer..." she said.

"We just need to ask him some questions about a case we're working on," Kurt said, smiling. "He's not in any trouble. Honest."

"He's at work," the woman said. "Bennington Subdivision, Lot Fourteen."

"Oh," Kurt said, nodding. "Thank you for your help."

"He's not in any trouble, right?"

The woman seemed ambiguous about the question, as if she half hoped that he might be.

"None that I know of," Kurt said, shrugging.

"Well, this is odd," Barb said as she pulled up to the indicated lot. Bennington Subdivision, Lot Fourteen, was a partially constructed residence. Currently, it was just being framed.

"It's got to be the right guy," Kurt said, looking at the card again.

"We'll see," Barb said.

"Hugh Yeaton?" Kurt shouted.

The shout was necessary because the man they'd been directed to was operating a power saw, cutting a long rip in a strand of plywood.

"What?" the man shouted, holding one hand to his ear. The carpenter was burly and had a sour expression on his face. He also clearly was enjoying messing with the "suits" by continuing to operate the saw.

"FBI," Kurt shouted, holding out his badge. "Want to shut that off?"

"Sorry," the man said, turning off the saw. "What do you need?"

"Are you Hugh Yeaton?" Kurt asked.

"Yes," the man said, somewhat nervously.

"Then we *have* what we need."

"Yeah, I remember her," Yeaton said, taking a drink of Gatorade. "Hot redhead, right?"

"That would be Janea," Barb said. "Where'd you meet her?"

"When we went out for the Art District investigation," Hugh said. "She was walking around when we showed up. It was after most of the stuff had closed, so that was a little strange. You know, young woman, by herself, dark streets..."

"I doubt Janea was much worried," Barb said dryly.

"Kinda got that impression," Hugh said. "One of the team, Pete Crockett, kind of latched onto her. Since Pete's about as straight as a hula hoop, it wasn't 'cause he was hitting on her or anything. We'd been looking for a new researcher, and when I was talking to her, it was apparent she knew her occult lore. I said if she was interested to give me a call."

"Art District?" Barb asked.

"It's a collection of museums and shops downtown by the river," Kurt said. "Old houses. It's supposed to be haunted. Nice place. Great restaurants, and Rembrandt's is to die for."

"Yeah," Yeaton said, frowning. "You've clearly never been there after everything shut down. I hate to *ever* admit anything's haunted. It's what makes us different from most of the paranormal groups out there. But if there's any place I've ever visited that has ... some sort of not-normal activity, it's the Art District."

"Where is it?"

"Across the river from Coolidge Park, come to think of it," Kurt said, nodding. "Near where her car was parked. What day was this?"

"Sixteenth of March," Yeaton said. "She left when Rembrandt's closed."

"That's ten days before she was attacked," Barb said.

"She got attacked?" Yeaton said. "One of these damned Madness things?"

"Not ... directly," Barb said. "She ... I take it you're somewhat familiar with the supernatural, Mr. Yeaton."

"Depends," he said, looking at her suspiciously. "I've seen a couple of things over the years that are hard to explain."

"She's currently in something like a coma," Barb said. "But not a coma. She just won't wake up. Are you familiar with the term *ka*?"

"Sure," Yeaton said. "And I don't believe in it. If I can't measure it, it's myth, not science."

"Well, be that as it may," Barb said, smiling, "her *ka* was stripped and is lost on the Paths. I'm trying to find out who or what did that to her."

"Well, if that search leads you to the Art District after closing time, you'd better be a pretty steady person," Yeaton said. "Because that place scared the crap out of me. And I don't scare easy. I've got work to do. Is there anything else?"

"No," Kurt said, handing Yeaton his card. "If you think of anything else or hear anything you think we should know, please call me. This does have to do with the Madness investigations."

"Hmmm ..." Yeaton said, looking at the card. "You might want to come by my place. I'm pretty busy with work and the investigations but ... Say, Friday afternoon? I've got some stuff you might want to look over."

"Okay," Kurt said. "Around seven?"

"Works."

∼

"Where to now?" Kurt asked.

"I'm drawing a blank," Barb said, looking at the papers on her lap. "I think we need to interview the cops that found Janea."

"I'll get ahold of them," Kurt said.

"What's the FBI doing out after dark?" the police officer asked as Kurt slid into the booth.

The City Café, Chattanooga, was part of a small chain in the area. The cafés delivered and had one of the largest menus in the world. Everything from pizza to omelets, passing through Greek, Italian and various American dishes, was available. Twenty-four hours a day. Which meant it was the pit stop of choice for Chattanooga PD.

"Hi, Teach," Kurt said as Barbara slid in next to him. "This is Mrs. Everette. She's consulting on the Madness cases. She's the replacement for the lady you found in Coolidge Park."

"Oh, *that*," the policeman said. "That was one fricking weird incident."

"Walk me through it," Barb said, sliding Lazarus out of his bag and setting him next to her. She'd already had her standard encounter on the way in.

"We were contacted direct," Tom said. "That is, we got the call from the station, not from nine-one-one."

"That seems strange," Barb said. "Anonymous caller?"

"No," the policeman said, wincing. "It's not all that strange in this area."

"Chattanooga nine-one-one is notorious," Kurt said, chuckling. "They've got the worst call-through in the nation. Only about thirty percent of the calls to nine-one-one get through to the people that need them. People have gotten used to calling the local fire station if they've got a fire, the police if they need a cop..."

"Caller's name was Jeremy Carons," Tom continued, looking at a notepad. "Twenty-four. Was walking in the park with his girlfriend. They saw this lady staggering around, shouting, stuff like that. They sort of wondered if she was a homeless person or something, but her clothing was nice. So they called us and kept an eye on her. She was moving erratically, with which I agree. I arrived, and when I observed her I called for backup."

"Why?" Barb asked.

"She was nonresponsive when I asked her to calm down," the cop said. "Like she didn't hear me. Tell you the truth, I was afraid she was one of these Madness things."

"Do you recall what she was saying?" Barb asked.

"Something about freeing and shields and light," the cop replied. "It wasn't really coherent. Some of it sounded German."

"Norse," Barb said. "And was it 'freeing' or 'Freya'?"

"That...sort of sounds right," Teach said. "What was that word?"

"Freya is her goddess," Barb said. "She's Asatru. She was praying."

"Oh..." the cop said, frowning. "Really?"

"Really," Barb said. "It was the equivalent of a Christian minister calling upon Jesus. 'Jesus aid me.' or something. What happened then?"

"Officer Lawrence Atchison responded to my request for backup and we called for a medical response," the officer said. "I'd determined that we were dealing with a 10-103m..."

"Cop-speak?" Barb asked.

"Nutjob," Kurt said. "Wacko."

"Got it. Go on."

"We approached the subject and requested that she desist in her actions," the officer said. "She continued to ignore us. By that point the ambulance had arrived. Officer Atchison and I attempted to physically restrain her at which point she resisted...well."

"Even stuck on the Paths, Janea's a handful," Barb said, smiling. "I hope you were okay."

"We hadn't realized she was as...fit as she was," the cop said, grimacing. "I was glad I was wearing body armor. And a cup. We managed to physically restrain her, and with the help of the paramedics, we got her strapped to the gurney. The paramedics had gotten authorization to tranquilize the subject, but when they did, she arrested. She came back when they gave her some juice. They then transported her to Memorial. I wrote up my report and continued with the night. We found out the next day she was working with the Fibs...Sorry."

"Heard it before," Kurt said, grinning. "Used it, for that matter."

"Anyway, we found out the next day she was a special consultant. I've sort of been scratching my head about it. Any idea what happened to her? I figure she's not normally like that. Did somebody drug her?"

"Something like that," Barb said. "Anything else? Anything unusual?"

"She was wet," Tom said.

"What?" Barb asked, sharply.

"She was wet," the officer repeated. "From head to toe. Since she was wearing a white shirt, it was pretty noticeable, but when we grabbed her it was *really* noticeable. I got soaked, so did Larry. Looked like she'd been swimming."

"That's one hell of a swim," Kurt said, looking through the binoculars.

The Chattanooga Art District was a cluster of buildings perched on a bluff overlooking the Tennessee River. Consisting of a bed and breakfast, two high-end restaurants, a coffee shop, an art gallery and a museum, it was a pleasant place on a warm morning in spring. The close-set stone buildings created shaded paths, and vegetation crawled over trellises, creating cozy nooks perfect for book reading or just contemplating life.

From the bluff, North Shore and Coolidge Park were clearly evident across the river. Adjacent to the stone buildings was the Hunter Museum complex consisting of three buildings, an Edwardian mansion, a 1970s "modern" building and a modern art annex completed in 2005. Just down the hill, accessed by a daring transparent bridge, was the Tennessee Aquarium. Connecting the collection to North Shore was a walking bridge that soared nearly a hundred feet over the river.

"Hell of a climb, too," Barb said. There was no way to get to the edge of the bluff; stone walls ensured that, but it was clear getting down wouldn't be easy. "And no way she jumped off the bridge. The fall would kill her."

"So, assuming she was swimming, where'd she swim *from*?" Kurt asked, lowering the binoculars. "Dive off the bluff? Looks pretty suicidal to me."

"That is a very good question," Barb said. "For which I need coffee."

Rembrandt's was built into a portion of the first floor of one of the stone buildings. The front counter created a narrow area that, at the moment, was packed with patrons waiting to access the single cash register. At the far end of the counter were some tables, which continued into a back room.

"Oh . . . my," Barb said, looking at the collection of pastries on display. "I think I'm gaining weight just looking at them. I can see more than one reason Janea would come here."

"Anything . . . else?" Kurt asked, quietly.

"Not right now," Barb said, just as quietly. "I'm Shielding. It works both ways. I'd rather be sitting down to do a full survey."

The patron in front of her, a society matron very similar to the ones Barb dealt with every day at home, looked over her shoulder and frowned.

"Private conversation," Barb said, smiling thinly.

The woman sniffed and turned back to the wait.

"And the other reason I'd rather not get into anything in line," Barb said, trying not to chuckle.

Eventually they got up to the cash register and the harried brunette working it.

"Croissant and a mocha," Barb said, smiling. "No whip cream."

"I'll take an espresso and an éclair," Kurt said.

"Those will make you fat," Barb noted.

"And mochas won't?" Kurt asked.

"Everyone has their weaknesses," Barb said as she paid for the food. "Mine is chocolate. I'd love an éclair. But I will not be tempted into gluttony."

They chose to sit outside and picked one of the iron tables at the back of the large, stone-flagged courtyard near a dry fountain. The area was shielded by large, mature trees and had a pleasant air. Barb had a hard time imagining it as a seat for malignant powers.

"Okay, let me be clear," Barb said, taking a sip of her mocha. "When I open up, it's possible that whatever attacked Janea will attack me. Unlikely, but possible."

"What do I do if that happens?" Kurt asked.

"I'll try to keep the uproar down," Barb said. "But I may get strange. *Things* may get strange. Operate as if there is a bomb threat and I'm the bomb squad. Figure out a way to evacuate the civilians, cordon the area and leave me to the battle. I'm . . . somewhat more powerful than Janea."

"You're not going to start chanting or anything, are you?" Kurt asked.

"Not unless things get bad strange," Barb replied. "And it's very much like a bomb tech. If I start running... try to keep up."

Barb still wasn't totally up on the psychic thing. The Lord granted her powers to fight evil manifest in the world, but He didn't always tell her where it was. And this time the best she could get was a slight feeling that things were not quite as pleasant as they seemed. She was trying to get a better feel for it when she sensed a presence near the table and opened her eyes.

"Are you well?" the woman standing by Kurt's shoulder asked.

"I'm fine," Barb said. "Slight headache."

Which was made worse by the woman. Like the neurologist, she had a demon that had so fully consumed her, her aura was black.

"I am Vartouhi," the woman said, smiling at her. "I welcome you to Rembrandt's. I always like to say hello to our new customers."

Vartouhi was tall and slender with an olive complexion and looked faintly Italian or at least Mediterranean. Pretty, edging to beautiful, she was elegantly dressed in a rose pantsuit with orange-yellow highlights. Her one touch of accent was a strange brooch. It was similar to some Celtic designs Barb had seen but much simpler, just three curves forming three lobes. And, simple as it was, it was sounding alarm bells in Barb's soul.

"I'm Kurt," Kurt said. "And this is Barbara. She's just visiting."

"Yes, Kurt, I've seen you here before," Vartouhi said, smiling again. Perfect teeth, Barb noted. Something about the woman, possibly her too-perfect attitude, just made her skin crawl. "Barbara, we hope that you enjoy your visit and come back often."

"It's a lovely place," Barb gushed. "When was it built?"

"At various times," Vartouhi said. "The buildings used to be apartments and were built mostly during the sixties. They were rather run down when the current owners bought them and fixed them up."

"Well, it's one of the nicest coffee shops I've ever visited," Barb said. "And you seem to do a brisk business."

"It suffices," Vartouhi said. "I'll leave you to your coffee. Take care."

"Nice lady," Kurt said. "She's always circulating."

"Uh-huh," Barb said.

"What? Did you, you know, sense anything?"

"Well, 'something is fishy in Denmark' is about the best I can do," Barb said, watching the hostess. "Except about the hostess, who is anything but a 'nice lady.' There's something here but I can't put my finger on it. And I'd bet dollars to donuts that our hostess could. I wonder what's *under* these buildings…"

"Rock," Kurt said, looking at the set of blueprints he'd requested. "The sewer runs down towards the Aquarium then across the river via the Market Street bridge. They've got a couple of basements…"

"There was *something* there," Barb said. "I'd say not far above river level. But it's hard to tell distance with this kind of thing."

"Well, if it's there it's not on the blueprints," Kurt said, rolling them up. "We're going to have to find a way to search for it. I can ask the management, but if they get sticky we've got nothing for a search warrant."

"It's possible that the management is totally unaware," Barb said. "Equally possible that they're some sort of source. Who owns it?"

"A corporation," Kurt said. "I'll check into ownership of the corporation."

"And see what you can find on that hostess," Barb said. "Vartouhi."

"What are you going to do?"

"Check on Janea."

Barb had to show ID to get into the house where Janea was being kept. At one level she was relieved—whoever had attacked Janea might try again—but on the other hand she wasn't sure that a rent-a-cop, okay, a high-quality one from the look, was going to do much good.

On the other hand, as soon as she stepped through the door she realized there was far more than mundane security on the house. It was "clean." Not just physically clean—in fact, it was rather cluttered—it was mystically clean. She hadn't examined it mystically the last time she was there, but this time it was clear that there were no malevolent entities or "vibes" to the place. Mystically it was more like a really good church. In fact, instead of dark shadows, there were flashes of light in the corners of her eyes. She wasn't sure what that represented, but it wasn't bad, whatever it was.

However, the house was *physically* crowded. There were six people in robes holding hands in a circle in the center of the main room and a young woman in a blouse and peasant skirt sitting on a chair watching them. Barb quickly realized that it was, in fact, a "circle." A Wiccan prayer group that was "calling power." She suddenly realized that although she worked every day with pagans, she had some deep-seated prejudices about being around a Wiccan gathering. She knew they weren't evil per se. She wouldn't be able to do what she did to support them if they were working with the devil. But watching them essentially worshipping "false gods" triggered childhood responses.

The young woman stood up and tiptoed over, putting her finger to her lips.

Janea? Barb mouthed.

The young lady motioned for Barb to follow her upstairs. Barb let Lazarus out of his bag and followed her.

The cat checked out the circle for a moment, sniffed, then followed.

"I'm sorry," the young lady whispered as they reached the top of the stairs. "I was afraid you'd disturb the circle. We would have put it somewhere besides the front room, but the energies were best there. Are you Mrs. Everette?"

"Yes," Barb said, shaking the young witch's hand. "Call me Barb."

"Janea's in the back bedroom," the young woman said, leading the way.

It wasn't just Janea in the room. Cots had been moved in, and Sharice, Drakon and Wulfgar were stretched out on them, apparently asleep. All three of them were clearly in REM sleep; their eyes were twitching like mad, and Janea was slowly writhing as if struggling against invisible bonds.

"Wish *I* could take a nap," Barb said.

"Astral projection requires a trance at the least," the witch said. "They're actually deep in the Moon Paths. Can't you feel it?"

"I'm ... just starting to figure some of this out," Barb admitted. "I only recently got the, hah-hah, 'Gift' of Sight. And given some of the stuff I've seen today, I'm just as glad that Sharice taught me how to *not* use it."

"You have many other Gifts. Use your Sight. There are no dark spirits here."

"I noticed," Barb said, opening up to the mystic.

The first thing she Saw had nothing to do with the foursome. There were clouds of...*sparkles* hanging in the air. She wasn't even sure what they were. But there were *a lot* of them. The room was *packed*. It looked like a bad special effect.

"What are...*those*?" she asked, pointing.

"We call them light spirits," the young witch said. "You would call them angels."

"Angels?" Barb asked. "Like, angels of the *Lord*? Messengers of *God*?"

The angels suddenly swarmed around Barb in a dancing light show that was hard to ignore.

"Uhmmm...Yes. And...no," the young witch said, chuckling. "More like guardian angels. These are what Christians term cherubim. Not the little babies with bows, but..."

"Cherubim are fairly high angels," Barb said, wonderingly. "Higher than seraphim, according to most texts. Where did they come from?"

"They apparently come with the house. The house belongs to Memorial Hospital."

"Catholics," Barb said, nodding. "Okay, starts to make sense."

"They sometimes carry messages," the young witch said. "But mostly they just sort of swirl around and squeal 'Look what *I* can do!' They're not warrior light spirits, they haven't been tested greatly. Cherubim are mostly concerned with the element of air. When they get out of hand they tend to cause storms. And they're always glad when someone notices them. These are... *young* isn't the right word. Innocent. Early. Lacking in mass or sophistication. But they serve as effective mystic guards for the house. Not because they would battle well, but because demons avoid *all* angels, and if one was powerful enough to try them, they could call for fiercer guardians. Seraphim, although lesser in power, tend to be *way* more serious. At the worst, they could call upon the true warrior spirits. Let us hope it never comes to that. It's worth remembering that all demons were once light spirits. It is why we simply call them dark spirits. And the warrior light spirits are different from greater demons only in which side they take. They're really rather unpleasant, from what I've been told."

"You hold to the doctrine of the Fall?" Barb asked.

"Not...exactly," the young witch said. "But we have some similar understandings."

"I'm getting a lecture on angels from a Wiccan," Barb said, shaking her head. "What, exactly, happened to my life? So...Janea?"

"They were able to extract her from the place of torment. Other than that, no change."

"Any idea what is happening in there?" Barb asked.

"Not so far."

Lazarus jumped up on Janea's bed and sat down in a perfect Egyptian cat pose, looking around the room. Barb realized that he was tracking on the Cherubim.

"He can see them," Barb said. "Is that some effect from him being bonded to me?"

"You're serious?" the young witch asked. "*All* cats can see spirits. So can babies. At least light spirits. The only place I've ever seen more packed than this place with light spirits is a neonatal ward."

"Nice to know."

Lazarus licked his shoulder, swatted at an angel that got too close, then climbed up on Janea and lay down with his head between her breasts.

"That cat is *definitely* a tom," the witch said with a chuckle.

"Oh, yeah," Barb said, putting her hand on Janea's forehead. The Asatru was so still, Barb worried that she'd feel the same complete lack of soul that she'd felt in the victims of the Madness. But Janea was still alive.

"Lord, bless and keep this warrior," Barb prayed. "Though she walks a different path, she walks a path of righteousness. I beg of You, give unto her Your aid in this battle. In Jesus' name we pray."

"Amen," the young witch said. "Hope that doesn't bother you."

"Nope," Barb said. "Every little bit helps."

She wasn't sure it had helped at all, but Janea seemed to be resting more comfortably.

"I guess it's time to get back to work," Barb said, holding out the bag. "Come on, Laz."

The cat just looked at her. He looked comfortable where he was.

"I need to go," Barb said, gesturing to the bag.

"Cats have minds of their own," the young witch said.

"Well, this one has to keep with me," Barb replied.

"I'm familiar with your..." She paused and frowned, "companion."

"Come on, Laz," Barb said, reaching for him.

Laz didn't even get up, just swatted at her hand, claws retracted. Then he held up one of them with the claws extended. The meaning was clear.

"I can't get far from you, dummy," Barb said.

Laz plunked his head down between Janea's breasts and looked at Barb out of one eye, balefully.

"Seriously," Barb said. "You're staying?"

"I think he's staying," the witch said, frowning. "Generally the familiar bond is not something to be stretched. But yours is... unusual. And at least you can be assured he will be safe in this house."

"Hmmm..." Barb muttered. "Okay, I'll try it. If it doesn't work, though, you are definitely coming with me."

Laz got up, turned around, kneaded Janea's breasts for a moment, then plunked back down and closed his eyes.

"I have never been sure that cats can walk the Moon Paths," the witch said. "But it looks as if that is his intent."

"A year ago I was a housewife," Barb said. "I had, still have, a husband that couldn't cook. I was president of the PTO. Chairman of the bake sale. Now I see angels and demons and have got a familiar wandering around the astral plane."

"It *does* take some getting used to."

"I've got some interesting information," Kurt said, looking up then frowning. "Where's the cat?"

"He seems to prefer Janea's company to mine," Barb said, shrugging. "I was warned that I shouldn't get too far from him and always make sure he was safe. But it seems I'm going to extend the distance. We'll see how far I can go. What's the info?"

"You're going to love it," Kurt said, gesturing to one of the seats in the empty waiting room. "I ran a search in the 'mundane' files on that symbol of Vartouhi's you didn't like."

Barb clicked on the link and blanched. The link led to the website of a corporation that used the same symbol. And, again, it gave her what her daughter would call "major creep factor."

"Trilobular," Barb said, flipping through the pages. "Pretty widely invested... Defense contracts. Biotech. Coca-Cola bottling stock?" She paused and blinked rapidly.

"You hit the part on 'psychological research,' didn't you," Kurt said, grinning. "Skip the rest of the brochure and take a look at their grant list."

"Dr. Stewart Downing," Barb said, musingly. "First we infect them, then we cure them. How interesting."

"Still doesn't tell us what's going on," Kurt said. "But I think I'm starting to get an interesting smell. You think this is some sort of bio research gone wrong?"

"No," Barb said. "Or not in any normal way. This is paranormal. Those patients are D-E-D dead. It's possible they're combining scientific neurological research with paranormal, but you'd be surprised how hard that is to do. The various powers that be seem to have an aversion to mixing the two. And since they have all sorts of earthly controls, they can make sure that paranormal activities *don't* conform to clinical results. That seems to be the case for both sides of the street. God prefers Believers, thank you. Trying to derive some philosophical rationale for God? All well and good. Trying to prove His existence empirically? He is going to make sure you cannot. The Adversary seems to agree on that subject if nothing else. If they are combining paranormal with standard biological research . . . it's going to require a power supporting them that is at odds with both the Lord and the Great Adversary."

"Which are?" Kurt asked.

"Don't know," Barb said. "As much reading as I've been doing since I started this job, I'm still playing catch-up. But there are experts I can call and ask. That's still only a possible, anyway. There is a Power here, and a group of supporters, and five gets you ten it's connected to Trilobular or the Art District. Somehow. What did you get on Vartouhi?"

"High school graduate," Kurt said. "A local private school called Girls' Preparatory Academy. Scholarship; she's not from money by any stretch. Community college. Address is listed in a house near the Art District. High-end housing for a high school grad but no indications why. About all I can get without a court order."

"So what now?" Kurt asked.

"It's late," Barb said. "Let's go find out what the Art District is like after everyone's gone."

At night, with everyone gone, the Art District was definitely spookier. The pleasant paths reflected the surrounding lights oddly, as if they were going through thick glass. The wind from the river whistled between the buildings with the moan of a dying man.

Barb ignored that, walking along the sidewalk with her thermals on. Some demons had been reported to produce an image of heat higher than the ambient. If there was something stalking the grounds, she wanted to see if it would turn up on thermal imagery.

"Anything?" Kurt asked.

"The feel from underneath is stronger," Barb said. "But I don't see anything under thermals."

She took the goggles off and looked around. There didn't seem to be anything abnormal—then she caught a flicker in one of the upper windows. It wasn't hot, it didn't even have the feel of a demon. But something was up there.

"There's something there, but not the target," she said. "I wonder how long the demons, if they're here, have been on this hill? They don't have the feel of American Indian spirits."

"Your side of the investigation," Kurt said. "I'm not seeing anything. But here's an interesting fact."

"What?" Barb asked, looking around. There was no one and, as far as she could tell, nothing in sight except the buildings.

"Chattanooga has its fair share of street people," Kurt said, looking around. "Lots of sheltered nooks and crannies in this area. As far as I know, the cops don't specifically roust people around here. So where are they?"

"Not here," Barb said.

"As if they know better?" Kurt asked.

"Possible," Barb said, nodding. "It would probably be a question for one of your cop friends. We're supposed to meet with Hugh tomorrow evening, right? Let's pack it in."

"There, I told you," the woman said, peering through night-vision binoculars. "They've sent another."

"Not a powerful one, though," the man with her said. "Not from what I can see."

"She's strong. She tries to Cloak it, but she does so poorly. On the other hand..."

"They're looking in the wrong place."

Chapter Six

George Grosskopf, Assistant Deputy Director, Special Investigations Unit, thought that he might as well buy stock in Pepcid AC and Ambien. There were things man ought not wot of. And he, for his sins, was the guy in the federal government in charge of all of them.

During his slow climb up the FBI ladder George had tried, like any sane agent, to stay off the Special Circumstances call list. Unfortunately, not only did he get more than his fair share of SC investigations, he managed to survive them all, not a common characteristic of the positions. If you weren't killed by your third, you were generally driven insane. Statistically, five was about the maximum any field agent could handle. He'd had a total of eight.

So since he'd managed to get up to Section Chief when the previous head of SIU had dropped dead of an almost assuredly natural heart attack, he'd been tapped to replace him. Since that day he'd never gotten a night's sleep without a triple dose of the strongest sleeping pills known to man. And don't even get started on the acid reflux.

As an ADD, even of the smallest and most secret section in the Bureau, he reported directly to the Deputy Director. And while other ADDs might have to wait on hold or call back later, he never did. Of course, he rarely hit the red button on his STU-III.

But when the DD got a call from SC-SIU, he dropped *everything*. Because it meant the shit was about to hit the fan.

Nobody visited SIU. Damned few people had any idea what it was other than a box on the manning chart. It was deliberately buried deep in the belly of the Hoover Building. If he didn't occasionally have to run to the DD's office like a bat out of hell, he'd rather it be in the satellite office in West Virginia. SIU didn't exist, and he liked it that way.

So he'd been sort of surprised to be asked to meet with a guy from DARPA. The Defense Advanced Research Projects Agency often interacted with the Bureau on aspects of national security and counterintelligence. But how the guy had picked SIU for his visit was anyone's guess.

"Doctor Roland," George said as the scientist entered his office.

Roland was a "suit" scientist. Nice suit, no less. Armani. Probably an egghead as well, but he'd gotten far enough up the feeding chain to have the standard bureaucrat look. Five foot eleven. Two hundred, maybe two-ten. Brown, brown. Wore contacts. No distinguishing marks.

"ADD Grosskopf," Roland said, shaking his hand. "Thank you for meeting with me so quickly."

"I was curious what interaction there might be between my office and yours," Grosskopf said, noncommittally.

"I can't open up the details of the compartment; the information is highly secure," Roland said, uncomfortably.

"It's a shield office," Grosskopf said. "My SCI classification is the same as the Director's and I do more secure work. You can talk."

"In that case, I think it's a case of blue on blue, frankly," Roland said, smiling disarmingly and sitting down in the lone chair. "We have a contract with a company that is investigating some advanced concepts in crowd management. Some of the people they work with are . . . unusual people. Recently some of them had a visit from the FBI. The company contacted me to find out what was going on. I checked into it and found that it was an SCI investigation out of your office. So I'm here to try to calm the troubled waters."

"That's vague enough that while I get what you're saying, I have nothing to go on," Grosskopf said, flatly.

"It involved some officers of a corporation called Trilobular," Roland said, sliding a packet onto the SC's desk. It appeared to be a pamphlet for a corporation, and the design on the front was ... three curves forming three lobes.

There had been occasional moments in his job when George wished he could crawl under a rock and forget everything he knew about Special Circumstances. He knew he was the best guy to be sitting in the seat; he just wished he wasn't. But there had never previously been a time when he wished he could just have a stroke, right now—go out quick and not have to hear the rest of a conversation.

He was feeling that way.

There were never very many SC investigations. So he read the field reports every morning. And he had a near-eidetic memory. Furthermore, not only were the Madness killings a major SC hot spot, the description of the jewelry the "hostess" wore was strangely hard to forget. He'd read Kurt's report, including his reporting of Adept Three Everette's reactions and suspicions.

And now he had found out that the US Government, specifically the DOD, had its fingerprints all over the Madness killings.

Oh. Joy. Might as well call Chattanooga "Raccoon City."

There was only one thing to do. Dissemble.

"I can take care of that, I'm sure," Grosskopf said. "But I'll need the contract code, the SCAP box, and the name of the contracting company."

"Why?" Roland said, frowning.

"To make sure we don't stumble on each other again," Grosskopf said, smoothly.

"Very well," Roland replied. He pulled a file from his briefcase and laid it on the desk. "I rather thought you might need some of that. This is all that is transmissible for the purposes of this discussion. It's a very sensitive project."

"I understand," George said, standing up and holding out his hand. "Sorry we had this little bump."

"No problem," Roland said, all smiles. "But to be clear, there are no more issues, right?"

Grosskopf knew what he should say but he just couldn't do it.

"When you speak to the company representative, assure him that there will be no further interest from the FBI."

"That's not the same as there *is* no further interest from the FBI," Roland said, a touch angrily.

"Dr. Roland," the ADD said. "Let me be perfectly blunt. If

you do not assure the company representative that there will be
no further interest from the FBI, then you will never work in
government service again. Or as a Beltway Bandit. When it comes
to who meets the criteria for secure information, the FBI Deputy
Director is God. And in certain matters, and this is one, I sit at
his right hand. You. Will. Assure. The. Company. Representative.
If you have to give an Oscar-winning performance to do so."

"What is going on?" Roland asked, ashen.

George flexed his jaw muscles for a moment then smiled thinly.

"This is all that is transmissible for the purposes of this discussion. It's a very *sensitive project.*"

"Satire..."

"Is all I'm willing to *give* you at the moment," Grosskopf said,
now furious. "Except one more thing. The next time DARPA
decides to go *fucking around with the supernatural,* clear it with
this department *first!*"

"How did you know...?" Roland asked then paused. "What
is Special Investigations?"

"You are now beyond your need to know," Grosskopf said. "But
you can be assured that my DD will be talking to your Director
by the end of the day. Good *day*, Dr. Roland."

Grosskopf took several deep breaths after the door was closed,
then picked up the handset of his STU and hit the red button.

"Sir, we have a *serious* problem..."

Germaine looked at the secure message from the Special
Investigations Department and the added note from the Deputy
Director and sighed. He had been dreading this day. Thus far,
through careful manipulation, the Foundation had managed to
head off most scientific inquiry into the realm of the supernatural.

The frank reality was that in most cases it simply wouldn't
work. Gods and demons did not care for humans prying into
their secrets and would actively work against experimentation.
"It seems a fact that miracles can only occur in an environment
devoid of skepticism." This was held up by scientists as proof that
"believers" were simply deluded.

What scientists failed to appreciate was that they were trying to quantify something that active, thinking entities simply did not *want* quantified.

But there were occasional attempts, researchers willing to stake their reputations on quantifying "the paranormal." And they almost invariably failed. If the powers that created such paranormal events didn't ensure it, the Foundation certainly tried its best. In most cases, funding simply dried up. "Investigate ghosts? Get a real job."

The "almost" usually had to do with demons. Some researcher would find a functional summoning method and use it. And usually end up dead or possessed. It happened to poor Tesla in the end.

This, however, was something different. The psychotics in Chattanooga were not even members of the test group. And the researchers apparently had managed to avoid possession. This, in fact, was a nightmare. The entity matched nothing he, even with his vast knowledge of the occult, recognized. But there was one lead.

And there were others, a very few, with more knowledge than he. And access to even more esoteric tomes and texts. He picked up the phone.

"Dr. Carson, it is Germaine. I would like you to look at a symbol and see if you can find any information on it..."

There was another call he felt he had to make. As he talked to Dr. Carson, he pulled out his pad and started typing in a message in Attic Greek.

The language of the Vatican.

Barb was frustrated. She knew that the plague affecting the area had something to do with the Art District. But a solid hunch was not enough for a search warrant.

They'd interviewed more counselors and determined that, whatever their differences, all seven of the Madders had "anger management issues." But that was all they had. A hunch about the Art District, a trail of shell corporations and seven psychotics with "anger management issues."

"We need a break," Kurt said, looking at another set of field notes.

"We need to get a look inside those buildings," Barb said.

"I mean a break as in 'coffee,'" Kurt corrected. "Want anything?"

"No," Barb said.

As if by timing, as soon as Kurt was out of sight her cell phone rang. It was the ringtone of the Foundation: "Amazing Grace."

"Mrs. Everette, it's Augustus."

"How are you, Mr. Germaine?" Barb asked.

"Busy. This will all sound very dramatic, but bear with me. I would request that you go, unaccompanied, to Our Lady of Perpetual Help Catholic church and see Sister Mary Katherine. The sister will introduce you to a man there. You should block out at least one hour for doing so. He has additional information for you on this matter."

"Very well," Barbara said, nodding. "I take it asking for a hint is pointless."

"It is," Germaine said. "Godspeed."

When Kurt came back Barb was gone. He shrugged, set down the two cups of coffee and picked up another set of notes.

Our Lady of Perpetual Help church turned out to be a sprawling campus just off of Interstate 75 that included not just a church but a Catholic school and a large rectory. Barbara eventually found the nun she had been directed to find, and was led to a small residential building behind the main buildings and directed to a room at the end of the hall.

The man who opened the door was dressed in a pink polo shirt and green slacks and was tall, dark and handsome. Those were the three words that went through her mind along with a quick and strong stab of physical attraction. She suppressed the latter and said a very quick prayer of forgiveness. But he was just *hot* as *hell*. Latin, unquestionably, despite a definite northern US accent, bit over six feet, slender but strongly muscled with the face of a fallen angel who'd enjoyed the ride. The sole feature that was awry was that his nose had had somewhat poor reconstructive surgery. Faint scars of sutures laced the left side. And that, in fact, only added to the look.

"I'm Barbara Everette," she said, somewhat flustered. "Is this...?"

"Mrs. Everette," the man said, smiling broadly in return. Nice teeth. Nice. He extended a hand, which turned out to be heavily calloused. "I am Brother Marquez. Welcome."

"Brother?" Barb said as the man waved her into the room. There were two small suitcases and three ballistic nylon bags cluttering the double.

"Brother Karol Marquez," the monk said, closing the door. "I am the team leader for Opus Dei Special Action Squad One."

Barbara sipped some really excellent tea and watched the monk preparing his own coffee. His movements were quick and sure, but now that she was past her initial shock she could detect the sharp and semi-robotic motions of a person who had trained extensively on close-quarters battle.

"That's an interesting coffee maker," she said, wanting to slap herself for the inanity. But Brother Marquez had her thrown. She hadn't felt this attracted to a man since she met Mark in college.

"With as much traveling as we do, I find carrying some small creature comforts to be lacking in sin," Brother Marquez said, looking over his shoulder and giving her another movie-star grin. The coffee maker took small cup-like packets that made one cup of coffee or tea apiece in about twenty seconds. She made a mental note to get the name of the manufacturer. "Given that Indonesia is a coffee producer you would think you could get a decent cup. Such is not the case. And the idea of coffee that is taken from feces... There is a special circle of Hell, I am positive, reserved for people who give other people coffee made from rat droppings. Especially unawares."

Brother Marquez took a seat on the end of one of the beds and pulled a file out from under one of the nylon bags.

"Germaine made a request of our cardinal superior to have us visit this area," Marquez said, taking a sip of his coffee. From the smell of it, it made espresso seem weak. "And I cannot say that he was wrong."

Barb flipped open the thin file and surveyed it.

"There's almost nothing here," Barb said. "Nothing we don't have. The psychosis is supernaturally induced. We'd deduced that. It's not even true psychosis. They're simply dead. Soul-drained. But still vital. It has the potential to have a wider effect. Okay, we'd considered that. The source will be a demon or mystical device that will have a symbol... that's the same symbol as Vartouhi was wearing. That's just confirmation that she's involved, and I was pretty certain on that. But a mystic symbol is not enough for a search warrant."

"Indeed," Brother Marquez said. "But that symbol is why we are here. The reason that that file is so . . . sparse is that it is what you can give your FBI contact. He'll be sent a similar file though his channels, since the FBI is aware of the information. Upper echelons of the FBI are aware of . . . more. Some of it I do not have. Need to know, as they say. But some more I do. A tale I shall tell."

"Go ahead," Barb said, getting comfortable. "Does it start 'Once upon a time'?"

"Given my background, I suppose I should start 'So there I was, no shit . . .'" Marquez said with a grin.

"You were military?" Barb said, surprised.

"For my sins," the monk replied. "Or, rather, I am now in *this* position for my sins during my military service and before," he added with a shrug. "But I digress. So there we were, no shit. My tale starts with a group of French archaeologists in Syria in 1923. The proverbial shepherd boy had found some pottery fragments, which attracted the attention of a local magistrate. A small expedition visited the area. They found a city that had been destroyed, they believed, by an earthquake or possibly waters drying up or just drifted away. There were some fragmentary inscriptions of no known language. Almost everything was shattered, destroyed, gone. They only found one fragment that was of any value at all."

The monk pulled a somewhat larger file out of a bag and slid out a picture. It was a copy of an old sepia-toned photograph that showed a piece of chiseled stone. The only thing that was clear on it was the symbol the hostess had been wearing. There might have been some human figures and flowing script, but it was so worn as to be illegible.

"Unknown race, unknown religion, the lost civilization, Terra X," Brother Marquez said with a shrug. "The archaeologists catalogued their meager finds and took back the stone tablet. It was filed under 'uninteresting' in the French Museum of Archaeology, and moldered there for several decades.

"In the 1950s the Hittite language was finally deciphered, and it opened up a door into the past. A fragmentary codex of the Hittite history detailed the destruction of a race called the Osemi."

"Never heard of it," Barb said.

"That is because the Hittites were quite complete in their destruction," Brother Marquez said, frowning. "And I cannot find them wrong in that. The Osemi were, according to the Hittites, worshippers of demons. And given that the Hittites were worshippers of *Baal*, that's saying something. Let me correct, worshippers of a demon*ess*. Her name was not recorded by the Hittites, perhaps so that her name *would* be lost. But the Osemi were fanatical in her worship. And to them she gave, quote, great powers in battle. End quote."

"Define," Barb said.

"The Osemi were, apparently, the original suicide bombers," Marquez said, grimacing. "Certainly suicidal in their attacks with, quote, the strength of ten men and caring not for harm. They would push themselves upon the spear to kill the spearman. End quote."

"Ouch," Barb said. "Sounds like... Actually, that sounds like PCP zombies."

"Excuse me?" the brother said, confused.

"My FBI contact's term for the seven...afflicted," Barb said. "They act like they're on PCP. They don't have a pain response, among other things. As with any psychotic, extremely strong. Clumsy, but fast when they've got a target. And they just won't stop. One reason being that they truly *are* undead. No soul at all. If you do fight them, don't have any qualms. You're not killing anyone, you're just stopping some sort of flesh robot."

"Joy," Marquez said, frowning. "And we shall have to stop them if it comes to it. My story ends, as most do in our business, with more questions than answers. We only recently, as in today, found the link between the Osemi and the stone tablet. What the archaeologists had found was the civilization of the Osemi. But without the Hittite codex, that was impossible to determine. And ask me about the stone tablet."

"What happened to the stone tablet, she asked with wide eyes," Barb said, smiling tightly.

"Gone," Brother Marquez said, shrugging. "Vanished from the Museum. When, no one knows. There is a high-level request in to Interpol to find out where it went. We will see what they turn up. However, this," he added, pointing at the file, "indicates that someone, somewhere, knows somewhat more. We just don't get to."

"Joy," Barb mimicked, sarcastically. "We're trying to stop

this... whatever is going on, and we don't get all the information available?"

"Try pulling ops in the Rockpile in the same condition," Marquez said. "You're a military brat. You should understand need to know. Here's the important part. You were involved in the action in Roanoke."

"Yes," Barb said, sighing. "It wasn't fun."

"So you're aware that demons can control groups," Marquez said. "But they normally can only make large groups... still. They may be able to make them move in a particular direction, to shuffle out of or into a room. But they cannot direct them to fight with any real functionality. They cannot force them to kill themselves."

"I'll take your word for it," Barb said, her brow furrowing. "What's the point?"

"This demoness seems to be able to *easily* create very large groups of maniacal killers," Brother Marquez said. "And according to something in the briefing documents with no attribution, to force large groups to act in more complex ways. Even if they are not sworn to her."

"That... violates the doctrine of free will," Barb said, frowning. "The Lord gave the earth to Satan but gave man free will. She can't..."

"Well, welcome to the varsity, Mrs. Everette," Brother Marquez said sarcastically. "Sometimes it's more complicated than Catechism. I haven't seen anything in the documents I have that show *where* the information came from, but I was given it by Germaine. And he wasn't going to make a mistake that simple. She can control large groups, apparently *against* their free will. There may be a complication of which the... providers are not aware. It is possible that she or her acolytes can only control these flesh robots. But that's the nature of intelligence. You go with what you have, not what you'd like."

"Do I get to read the thicker file?" Barb asked.

"Yes," Marquez said, handing it over. "But it's not for your FBI contact. He's simply not cleared for it."

"And I am," Barb said, bemusedly. "What fun."

The thicker file didn't have much more than Marquez had given her. Very little was known about the demoness or the Osemi, only the sparse data from Hittite records. And for some reason it was "a known fact" that she could control "groups equal to or greater than thirty" in complex actions. From the combination of "known" facts it was "highly probable" that a larger group could be turned into "directed or undirected" psychotic killers. Joy.

"Says here Kali can't even do this," Barb said. "And she's thoroughly bound, right? A greater goddess of murder can't turn large groups into psychotic murderers, and this minor demoness *can*?"

"That appears to be the case," Marquez said, getting another cup of coffee. "Most such groups were definitely under the influence of drugs or simply in high-combat state. Berserkers with our newfound friend Frey, thuggees with our unquestionable foe Kali. Possibly the Jaguar Warriors of Quetzalcoatl."

"And it violates free will," Barb said. "I don't buy that. Free will is... If there is no free will..."

"Free will is not... absolute," Marquez said. "A tale I shall tell thee."

"Another one?" Barb said, smiling faintly. "How many do you have?"

"Only my confessor knows that," Karol said, smiling. "But this one touches on such questions. Once upon a time a young man came to America from Colombia under pressing circumstances."

"How pressing?" Barb asked, taking a sip of tea.

"Very," Karol replied, frowning. "A matter of a money dispute that turned quite ugly with a cartel. Blood was shed. Not that blood had not been shed *before*; that was what the money dispute was about. The young man felt he was owed more than he was paid. The buyer of his services disagreed. The buyer was a member of the cartel. One does not kill one's clients. Especially if they are members of the Cali cartel."

"I see," Barb said, her eyes wide.

"The young man decided that enough was enough with such things and went to work, very much under the table, for a lawyer in New York," Karol said, looking into the distance. "The lawyer was an immigration lawyer and asked very few questions about background. The young man was paid for various services, none of which involved bloodshed. Translation: Looking up people who were in areas that angels would fear to tread. Fortunately he was not an angel and had no issues. Suchlike. And he was happy. He continued his schooling. He hoped to become a doctor or a history professor someday. Possibly an immigration lawyer like his friend. The lawyer worked in the Twin Towers."

"Oh," Barb said, her jaw working.

"The young man went to an Army recruiter in New Jersey on September 12th, 2001," Karol said, taking a sip of coffee. "If you don't mind, I shall make another cup. Would you care for a refresher?"

"Please," Barb said, holding out her cup.

"The Army recruiter, like the lawyer, asked few questions," Karol continued, making coffee and tea clearly on muscle memory. "Later, more were asked. It is a funny thing about getting a security clearance. As long as you are absolutely truthful, under current laws, nothing that you say can be held against you. A polygraph can be a very refreshing experience. Better in many ways than a confessional. So many people hold things *back* in the confessional. Honesty is good for the soul and a polygraph requires quite complete honesty. I have made a recommendation to the Holy See that polygraphs be required for confessionals, but I doubt they will see it my way. I digress again. The young man joined the Army. He was trained as an infantryman. He went to airborne school. He joined the Fourth Infantry division. Two months after joining his unit, he was in Iraq. He got quite a reputation since he sustained the most strikes from IEDs of anyone in his unit without being medically evacuated. Also a few minor scratches here and there."

"The nose?" Barb asked.

"He was, in fact, shot in the face. And two other places. Scratches, as I said. He, however, came to the conclusion that driving around as a mobile IED magnet was not the life he preferred. However, there were hajis…"

"Hajis?" Barb said.

"Pardon my descent to colloquialism," Marquez said. "Insurgents. There were insurgents that needed killing. However, a better place might be in a more elite group. So he requested a transfer to the John F. Kennedy Special Warfare Center for training as a Special Operations weapons technician. It was as a member of the United States Army Girl Scout Brigade that he experienced a life-changing event. There are some very strange things going on in Afghanistan, Mrs. Everette. Very strange indeed. And occasionally when such things come up OCONUS—outside the continental United States—the designated red-shirts to support the local versions of FLUF are the US Army Girl Scout Brigade or similar groups." He handed her a refilled cup and shrugged.

"I see," Barb said.

"This forced him to consider the state of his immortal soul," Marquez continued. "To wit, if there be demons, then there was a hell. In that case, given some of his actions over the years, he was in deep doo-doo. You have no clue, I'm sure, Mrs. Everette, how many Hail Marys contract killings cost. Also, that there were aspects of his personality that he had always considered to be ... psychological that might not, in fact, be mundane. And he found that despite the many positive things he'd done in the military over the years, it was not the best place for repentance. Temptations of the flesh are high around military bases, and he had always had a bit of a weakness in that regard. So he got out. Reluctantly, in many ways. But he ended his term of service.

"That left him with the question of where he could spend a great deal of time repenting for his many ... many ... *many* sins. After talking about it with a couple of understanding priests, he decided that the best place was as a monk."

"Jesuit?" Barb asked.

"Heaven forbid," Karol said with a laugh. "Those leftist panty-waists would pee themselves if they ever saw a demon. No, Cistercian. Nothing like spending eighteen hours a day on your knees in prayer to catch up on those Hail Marys. A small cell and a lot of time on his knees was his lifelong goal."

"So what happened?" Barb asked.

"A bishop came to visit," Karol said, looking into the distance again. "He did the usual rounds of glad-handing, and then sat down with a certain monk and questioned him at length and in detail. The bishop was strangely knowledgeable in the area of military operations, and especially close-quarters battle. It turned out later that the bishop had been one heck of a swimmer in his day. The bishop then explained that the monk had a 'skillset' that the Holy See needed more than they needed a bunch of Hail Marys and Our Fathers. Anyone could pray. Very few could kill a man at two thousand yards. And that there were certain rituals he was going to need to go through before being fully prepared to serve the Lord. And thus the former infantryman ... among other things, became a member of Opus Dei."

"This has a point, right?" Barb asked.

"Part of the rituals were to find and eliminate every trace of demons in the soul," Karol said, turning to look at her finally. "More people are possessed than you can *possibly* imagine, Mrs.

Everette. By and large their demons are minor creatures, wills with a life of their own. Anger, lust, gluttony, all the usual sins. Vanity. So, *so* many vanity demons—and greed. Any suburban mall is awash with them. A person with an interest, a hook, is subject to being caught by one and pressed towards more sin and more. And once they are in, they are *very* hard to get rid of. All the confessions, all the prayers, all the benedictions had not rid m— the young man of his demons. It took multiple exorcisms to do so. And a great deal of will.

"Such demons can be resisted. But think of cases of major possession. Where, then, is free will? You, Mrs. Everette, are an example of the rare case of a person without hooks. You were rid of original sin by your baptism and you have lived a life avoiding sin. You know you are proud and you work against your pride. You know you are beautiful but strive against vanity. You have a temper and control it through prayer and good works, despite the many frustrations you find in your life."

"And this has *what* to do with free will?" Barb asked.

"*Everything,*" Karol said. "A person who has let demons into their soul has already *made* the choice. They have chosen Satan over God. And to the extent that they wrestle with a demon, it is usually over something they fear in the mundane world. Don't kill a person or strike them, because you will be arrested. Not because it will damn your immortal soul. For anything less than that, most people go at it with abandon. Lust, envy, hatred. Vanity again. Pride. Being holy is not about going to church on Sunday and spitting on people the rest of the week. It's not even about being under the sacrament of priesthood, as has been *clearly* shown. One must be as free of sin as it is *possible to be* in this fallen world to truly be in a state of grace. How many people do you know who are *totally without sin*, Mrs. Everette? How many in this town can cast the first stone?"

"All seven of the afflicted had 'anger management issues,'" Barb said. "Were bullies in school, two of them were abusers of their partners. Do you think that had something to do with it?"

"Well, let's see," Karol said, shaking his head. "We have a demoness of anger, hatred and murder who has placed her seal upon this town. And we have people who already had anger management issues suddenly becoming violently and homicidally insane. I don't know, do *you*?"

"So you're here as what?" Barb asked.

"Backup," Karol said, handing her a bracelet. The silver charm bracelet had only a cross hanging from it. "Pull the cross off and it activates a signal and a homing beacon in the bracelet. We'll be there within a minute though the hosts of hell stand between us. And you can be assured my brethren will not be susceptible to the siren call of a demoness. Unlike the mundane security of this town. On that level, we are accredited with the Federal Government as special contract personnel on an undercover anti-terrorism task force with authorization to use due force. All the rest is paperwork. I've been trying to convince the bishop that doing paperwork should be counted as penance but he's so far resisted my blandishments. Ring-knockers."

"So what do *I* do?"

"Find her lair," the monk said. "Find her place of worship. Then call us. We will be close."

Chapter Seven

"Where the hell have you been?" Kurt asked when Barb sat down across from him.

"You wouldn't believe me if I told you," Barb said, sliding the file across to him. "And I can't tell you anyway. But based on that, we'd better figure out a way to get a good look inside those buildings up at the Art District. This looks to be a worse problem than we'd thought."

"I got the same thing," Kurt said, giving it a cursory glance. "And something else," he added, sliding an envelope across to her.

"What's this?" she asked, pulling a card out of the envelope.

"An invitation," Kurt said. "To a charity function being held in the Art District. Not in the Bluff View buildings. Nearby, though. And check out the name of the hostess."

"Vartouhi Cass," Barb said. "Same lady?"

"Same lady," Kurt said.

"Who is Thomas Reamer?" Barb asked.

"Old Chattanooga family money," Kurt replied. "One of the architects involved with the newer additions to the Art District, like the Hunter Museum. I checked up on the place where they're holding it. He built a *house* on top of an *office* building he owns. It's about three blocks from Rembrandt's. Vartouhi is his . . . friend. The housing issue is now explained."

"Girlfriend?" Barb asked. "Lover?"

"Why don't you ask them in person? It's black tie. I hope you have a nice dress."

"Mrs. Barbara Everette," Kurt said, handing over the invitation to an unsmiling man in a black suit with an ear bud. There were two more flanking the elevator lobby, and all three had bulges at their waist on the right side. "Special Agent Kurt Spornberger."

"Yes, sir," the security officer said, glancing at the card. He pressed the button on the elevator, leaned in as the doors opened, swiped a black card over a blank spot on the indicators and hit the button for the top floor. "Have a good evening, sir, ma'am," he said, handing the invitation back.

"Nice," Kurt said, looking around the elevator.

The elevator was paneled in what Barbara sort of recalled was called "fumed oak." And unless she was mistaken, the accents were in actual gold. She suspected it *wasn't* gold leaf. And in the corner, oh-so-discreet, was a tiny surveillance camera.

"He didn't wand you," Barb said.

"What am I going to do, start shooting the muckety-mucks of Chattanooga?" Kurt asked as the elevator opened.

The elevator opened onto a foyer, even more sumptuously decorated, with six or seven people standing around holding drinks. There was more security there, dressed to fit in in tuxedoes but wearing full headsets.

"Special Agent Spornberger," Kurt said, holding out the invitation. "Mrs. Barbara Everette."

"Yes, sir," the lead officer said, nodding. "Welcome to Reamer House. Feel free to make yourself at home."

"Shall we, Mrs. Everette?" Kurt asked, holding out his arm.

"Lead on, Special Agent Spornberger," Barb replied, hooking hers through.

The exit to the foyer was a set of stairs, arched above and flanked on either side by winged stone lions. Both walls of the short stairway consisted of friezes depicting men in conical helmets and scale armor riding horses. They appeared to be hunting something but their prey was out of sight.

The main room of the home was quite large, easily able to hold the forty or fifty people gathered there. And it was laid out in a strange fashion, almost triangular, with doors leading out at six points to other rooms.

Barbara had brought one of her nicer dresses. However, she immediately realized that her conception of "nice" was somewhat below the majority of the party-goers. She also realized she hadn't known how much money there was in Chattanooga. She stopped trying to price the gowns she saw on the women at the party. Most of them looked like Paris originals.

However, there was a very definite feel to the crowd that they did not normally dress that way. A tugging of waists and bustlines was noticeable. As was the fact that most of the women didn't normally wear heels. And despite the early hour, most of them were buzzed if not drunk. Most of the women were hanging onto the arms of their dates less because they were besotted with love than because they'd topple over if they didn't.

There was nothing so déclassé as a buffet line. Instead, waiters in white tuxedoes circulated with trays of tiny hors d'oeuvres and drinks.

"Do you need anything, sir, ma'am?" one of them asked.

"Pepsi if you've got it," Kurt said.

"Coke, sir?" the waiter said with a pained expression.

"I guess," Kurt replied.

"Same for me," Barbara said. "What was that about?"

"I sort of did it on purpose," Kurt whispered. "The Reamers are Coke-bottling money. Saying the P word in this room is on the order of pounding a copy of the doctrines of Martin Luther onto the door of the Vatican."

"Be nice," Barb said. "Is it just me, or do most of these people look...?"

"It has a definite *prom* feeling, doesn't it?" Kurt said. "Just older. Heads up. Incoming."

"Mrs. Everette," Vartouhi said, extending a languid hand. "I am so glad you could attend."

"My pleasure," Barb replied. "You have a wonderful home."

"I merely have the joy of residing here," Vartouhi said, gesturing to the man at her side. "It is Thomas's home. Thomas Reamer, Mrs. Barbara Everette and Special Agent Kurt Spornberger of the FBI."

"A pleasure," Reamer said. He was small and slight with pale hair and eyes. His hand, when Barbara shook it, felt as thin and light as a bird's.

"Barbara is a missionary from Mississippi," Vartouhi said. "Agent Spornberger is originally from Chicago, if I'm recalling that correctly."

"Yes, ma'am," Kurt said. "Finest city on the face of the earth. No offense to Chattanooga, of course."

"Chattanooga was once a terrible place to live," Reamer said, his eyes lighting. "The factories poisoned the air and water. The buildings were black from the soot. It's taken many years to repair the damage and bring it into the light. You're based in the Pioneer Building. Beautiful architecture—my great-grandfather built it and did a fine job. But when I was young, you could barely see it for all the soot."

"Thomas has made it his goal in life to beautify Chattanooga," Vartouhi said. "He is a major contributor to the Aquarium and the Hunter Museum."

"Was that your design?" Barbara asked. "It's beautiful."

"No, not mine," Reamer said. "But I was involved in the construction from day one. A good design is only the start of a building. You have to stay on top of every aspect of the construction. You wouldn't *believe* how people try to cut corners. You're a missionary, Mrs. Everette? To Chattanooga?"

"I'm actually a consultant to the FBI," Barbara said. "My missionary work is separate."

"They are working on the Madness cases," Vartouhi said.

"Oh, are there any leads?" Reamer asked. "I don't know why I bother to ask. The problem is the poisoning of the land, foul emanations of the bygone days surfacing to rot the heart and mind. There are still many who cannot understand the importance of clean air and clean water. The Goldheims—"

"Darling," Vartouhi said, putting her hand on his arm.

"I can't talk about an ongoing case, sir," Kurt said, shrugging.

"You're Kurdish, Ms. Cass?" Barbara asked. "Vartouhi is a Kurdish name."

"Actually, I'm from Summerville," Vartouhi said with a laugh. "A small town just south of here. My parents named me Vartouhi because they liked the name."

"I would have guessed Middle Eastern from your looks," Kurt said.

"Actually, Irish and Native American," the woman said, smiling. "It's a common mistake. People with some knowledge of the world sometimes guess Italian or French. More commonly these days, people assume Hispanic. Few note the Kurdish name," she added with an interested glance.

"I'm something of a student of the Middle East," Barb said. "Ancient history. The Hurrians are related to the Hittites."

"I don't recognize either group," Vartouhi said, her face blank.

"Hurrians are Kurds," Kurt said. He grinned at Barb's look of surprise. "Anthropology degree. The Hittites were a branch of them that at one point conquered most of the Middle East. I notice that your entry has some Hittite elements. The double archway. The intervening friezes..."

"Hittites stole most of their architecture from other cultures," Reamer said. "Good stone workers, but if you observe their pre-conquest architecture, it's fairly simple Neolithic stuff..."

"Darling," Vartouhi said, placing her hand on his arm again. "I doubt that they want to hear a lecture on architectural development."

"Actually, I find it fascinating," Barbara said. "I've heard the same theory before. I'm under the impression they were most influenced by the Sumerians."

"It's unlikely," Reamer said. "Most of their later motifs incorporated *some* Sumerian motifs. But there is an unexplained jump in technology..."

"Darling, the Kincaids are here," Vartouhi said. "We need to say hello to them."

"Oh, yes," Reamer said. "Of course."

"Enjoy yourselves, Special Agent, Mrs. Everette," Vartouhi said. "Live for each moment."

"In this life I am dead, Ms. Cass," Barb said, nodding. "I live for the hereafter."

"What in the hell...?" Kurt said as the pair drifted away.

"Don't," Barb said. "Not here."

"So what do we do now?" Kurt asked.

"Mingle?" Barb said. "Talk?"

They stayed an hour. Most of the talk was of the Madness cases, and when it became known that Kurt was working the cases he got used to saying "I can't discuss an ongoing case." Finally, when it seemed they'd been there long enough to be polite, they left. The guards at the elevator performed the same pantomime with the security keys, which meant that nobody got to *leave* the building unless they were allowed out.

They descended to the ground floor in silence and stayed that way as far as the car.

"Okay, give," Kurt said as soon as they were in the car.

"Not here, either," Barb replied. She started up the car and drove out of the parking garage, then stopped on the street facing the building. "Notice anything?"

"No," Kurt said. "It's an office building."

"You're the FBI agent," Barb snapped. "Use your eyes. The elevator was marked for seven floors, a basement, a mezzanine and the penthouse. Count the floors."

"Seven," Kurt said a moment later.

"Where's the mezzanine floor?" Barb asked.

"Sometimes that's built into..." Kurt said, then looked again. "There's no way to fit one in."

"So where does the mezzanine button go to?"

"Where now?"

"The office."

"Now give?" Kurt asked when they were back in the offices.

"You notice anything about our conversation with Vartouhi and Reamer?"

"Like she kept cutting him off?" Kurt asked. "I'd love to have an hour alone with him in an interrogation room."

"And you're not going to get it," Barb said. "He'd have a very high-priced lawyer present, at the very least. More than that."

"Like she knew who we were, where we were from, what we were working on?" Kurt said. "Yeah. Noticed."

"Most of that stuff she can get from public sources," Barb said. "Credit records. Ownership background."

"Stuff *we* can't access without a special finding," Kurt said bitterly. "But, yeah, I know."

"But that we're working the Madness cases is privileged information," Barb said. "Right?"

"More or less," Kurt said. "It's not special compartment like SC, but it's not commonly available."

"So she has access to that from some source," Barb said.

"Could be any number of ways she'd get that information," Kurt said. "Like I said, it's not compartmented information. Through Reamer, she's obviously tied into the business and legal structure in the town. Secretaries talk. Bureau secretaries talk to legal secretaries at other firms. Lawyers golf. If it's not SCI, there's no reason that it wouldn't come up."

"In casual conversation?" Barb asked.

"You saw how much interest there is in the cases," Kurt pointed out. "But that's not all. You were nervous as hell in there."

"On the rest, I'm not sure how much I can talk about," Barb said. "There are indications that this case has something to do with a civilization the Hittites destroyed. And there *is* an unexplained jump in Hittite architectural development. If I remember my reading right, Hittites were primarily a warrior race, and they absorbed various aspects of culture from other races, mostly by enslaving them. Gods, art and architecture. But there's one strain of architecture that has never been adequately explained. And there's not much known about the civilization that's connected to these cases except that the Hittites wiped it out. Coincidence? I don't think so."

"What the *hell* does architecture have to do with psychotics?" Kurt asked, grabbing his head.

"Watch your language, Agent Spornberger," Barbara said. "The architecture of the entryway is similar to Hittite, but... Look, I've been doing some really weird reading as part of this job. Stuff I never thought I'd have to read up on. But that doesn't make me an expert by any means. The thing is, I don't think that entryway is Hittite. I think it's ... something else. There is something nagging at me, though."

"What?" Kurt asked.

"I can't place it," Barbara said, grimacing. "I wish I was more of an expert at this. The house, there's something weird about the architecture."

"Well, there's the missing floor," Kurt said.

"Something else," Barb said. "Can you get blueprints at this time of night?"

"For tactical reasons the Bureau gets copies of all new building permits and their schematics," Kurt said, firing up his computer. "So ... yes."

~

"There," Barb said, shuddering. She pointed at the screen. "Do you see it?"

"Shit," Kurt replied, nodding. "That building looks *just* like the symbol Vartouhi was wearing the other day."

"Three lobes," Barb said. "I think that 'house' is laid out as a temple. And *nobody* should know what that kind of temple looks like."

"Who in the hel . . . heck are you talking about?" Kurt asked.

"Uh . . ." Barb said, then shrugged. "Need to know. The powers that be determine who has need to know."

"Your powers that be?" Kurt asked, angrily.

"*Yours*, actually," Barb said.

"Oh, great," Kurt said. "I've got the responsibility, but nobody's giving me the information? Why?"

"That's a very interesting question," Barb said. "But not an important one at this point. Thing is that nothing's adding up here. I'm going to sleep on it. I'll see you tomorrow, but not early. I need to talk to somebody."

"Great," Kurt said. "You go 'see somebody.' I'm going to go get out of this monkey suit and get a beer. There's not much else for me to do."

As Barb unlocked her door, a black van with tinted windows pulled up beside her.

"That was somewhat nervous-making," Brother Marquez said as the passenger-side window rolled down. "If we'd had to do an entry, it was going to be tough. We'd have to blow the stair doors and go up eight flights."

"I take it you've seen the blueprints," Barb said, crossing her arms.

"For tactical reasons the Bureau gets copies of all new building permits and their schematics," Brother Marquez said. "When we go somewhere, we get copies of their copies. Also something I'd prefer you not share with your friend Kurt. Hop in."

The back of the van was laid out as a mobile command post, and two men were watching screens as they pulled away. Barb strapped herself into a seat as Brother Marquez swiveled his captain's chair to the rear.

"The entry to the house, the entire house in fact, has architecture that I'd describe as Hittite," Barb said. "But it's not. Slight differences."

"Osemi?" Brother Marquez asked, raising an eyebrow. "Where would they get Osemi architectural data? The Hittites destroyed every trace of the civilization."

"That's a very good question," Barb said. "The thing is, I don't think that's their power center. It didn't have the feel of an active temple. I've *been* in an active temple. There's a definite . . . vibe to one. There wasn't one in Reamer's house. A slight vibe, but not anything strong. Much stronger at Rembrandt's."

"But those houses well predate any indications of supernatural occurrences," Brother Marquez pointed out.

"Which is why I don't think it's in that building cluster," Barb said, frowning. "I've got the sneaking suspicion it's *under* them. But the entrance *has* to be close. Probably under Rembrandt's or one of the other buildings. But we don't have enough information to get a search warrant."

"Who needs a search warrant?" Brother Marquez said, shrugging.

"I'd rather we try to avoid a black-bag operation," Barb said, referring to a covert entry on a building. The term went back to the early days of law enforcement when the tools would be carried in black leather satchels.

"As do I," Brother Marquez said. "But those are public buildings, no? You've never heard of a health and safety inspection?"

Barb hoped that her hair tucked up under a Chattanooga Food Safety Inspector ball cap and a matching blue shapeless coverall was going to disguise her enough. It might work as long as she avoided Vartouhi.

The buildings didn't have basements as such. Just subground levels, partially open. That was as good as it was going to get. She was tapping one of the solid rock walls when the restaurant manager caught up with her.

"Can I ask what you're looking for?" he asked, seeming amused.

"Rat holes," Barb said, shining a light under the wine racks. "Rat droppings. And structural unsoundness."

"We're on rock," the man said, with a shocked expression. "And we don't have rats, ma'am!"

"Sedimentary rock," Barb replied, glibly. "Water flow can cause sudden openings in it that lead to unsoundness. And you'd be surprised what rats will bore through to get to food."

"Oh," the manager said. "Well, I can assure you we don't have rats. I am very strict about that sort of thing. But if you need anything, just holler."

"I will," Barb said, tapping at the walls with a stick until he was gone. Then she opened her Sight and tried to get something from the surroundings. There was still the feeling of otherworldliness. But now that she was in the basement, it didn't seem... malevolent. She realized it was more just... power. Not even really power she could use. Just raw power, like the hum from electric lines. You tended to get nervous around it, even fearful.

She started as her phone rang with Germaine's ringtone: "Danse Macabre."

"Yes, sir?" Barb said.

"I understand you're at Bluff View," Germaine said.

"Yes, sir," Barb replied. She wasn't even going to bother to wonder how he knew.

"I have arranged a meeting for you at Tony's in ten minutes. Ask for Mrs. Arquero. I believe you shall find the conversation... enlightening."

Tony's was a fairly high-end restaurant for Chattanooga, and Barb felt rather out of place in her coveralls.

"I'm looking for Mrs. Arquero?" she told the maitre d'.

"This way, Madame." The maitre d' may have found the coveralls a bit underdressed, but *nobody* in the restaurant industry was about to piss off a health inspector.

"Mrs. Everette." The speaker was "a woman of a certain age." Barb placed her as anywhere from thirty to sixty. Dark hair, short, wearing a suit that probably cost more than Barb's entire wardrobe. "Christina Arquero. I believe Germaine called you?"

"Yes, he did, Mrs. Arquero," Barb said cautiously, sitting down at a wave.

"My husband and I are the owners of Bluff View," Mrs. Arquero said. "And we are of course quite concerned about a health and safety inspection from such an eminent inspector." She gave a slight smile.

"It's a...fascinating place," Barb said. "Very...fascinating."

"It's a labor of love," Mrs. Arquero said. "We took a bunch of run-down and honestly unsafe apartment buildings and old houses, and turned it into a place of beauty and repose."

"The food is excellent," Barb said. "I really love Rembrandt's. It almost tempts me to gluttony."

"Almost," Mrs. Arquero said. "Do you speak Spanish, Mrs. Everette?"

"One of the languages I never learned," Barb said, wondering at the change of topic.

"*Arquero* is generally translated as 'The Archer,'" the lady said, taking a slight sip of wine. "However, the etymology is complex. It is also the term, in what Americans call soccer, for a goalkeeper. This etymology comes from its Castilian definition, which is 'a guardian at the gates.'"

"Ah," Barbara said.

"The reason for Augustus's call becomes more clear," Mrs. Arquero said, giving a very slight chuckle. "We have lived in the South for many years, and I must admit I am sometimes given to Southernisms. If you will permit the indelicacy, you are barking up the wrong tree."

"That...yes," Barb said. "The problem being, I really don't have another tree to bark up."

"Tell me what you know," Arquero said.

"Janea was attacked," Barb said, carefully. She avoided the word "mystic." "When she was found, she was wet as if she had been in the river. This place is across the river and had a certain...air."

"Indeed it does," Mrs. Arquero said with what was an almost unladylike snort. "One has to be...extremely mundane to ignore it."

"But...I realized as I was working, not exactly a...negative air. Nor...positive."

"Neither," Mrs. Arquero agreed. "Quite, quite neutral. As neutral as a hurricane. Yet an air that is...workable. Useable. And many come here to install, as it were, wind turbines. Some less neutral than others. While others act as...windbreaks. My husband and I are not the only such. There are at least nine. And perhaps twice as many groups involved in wind generation. Fortunately, those who act as windbreaks are generally stronger than those tapping the wind. Generally."

"And now?" Barb asked. "If Janea didn't come from here...?"

"As you noted, your friend had been...attacked," Arquero said. "She was, therefore, in not the best of conditions. Had you considered the strength of the Tennessee River? To swim across is difficult in the best of conditions. It is, however, quite possible to float."

"Float?"

"Have you considered what is on the *other* side of the river?"

"Kurt," Barb said, walking up to his cubicle. "What do you know about Girls' Preparatory Academy?"

"Oh, God!" Kurt swore. "Not them! *Please*, not them!"

Chapter Eight

O kay, other than about the ugliest uniforms I've ever seen in my life," Barb said, "I'm not really seeing anything different about this school compared to, well, any number of all girls' schools. Been there, left with scars."

"Didn't get along?" Kurt asked.

"Not particularly," Barb said. "Japanese ones were the worst. There is no more arrogant, stuck-up bitch than a billionaire's granddaughter who can trace her lineage back to the founding of the Empire of the Sun."

"That would be . . . ?" Kurt said.

"Two thousand years."

"Ah. Talk about old money."

"Akio considered the Medici nouveau riche," Barb said, distractedly. "We compromised. She didn't piss me off, I didn't break her arm by accident. Again."

"Very Christian of you."

"It's actually when I truly found Christ," Barb said. "He was . . ."

"Behind the couch the whole time?"

"Exactly. Actually, on the couch. Took me a while to notice. But being the only Christian in a school made me realize I could be the ugly American or witness for Christ. Witnessing, as in being the nice girl and showing them how a Christian ought to act. Turned out Jesus was right there waiting the whole time. Nothing special here. Okay, their internal network is called 'bruisernet.' That's not so good. Their colors are, you can't make this stuff up, black and blue."

"Hey," Kurt said.

"Found something?"

"Sort of. Girls' Preparatory Academy. GPA. Grade point average, right?"

"Yeah."

"It's lower than Bluff View, so that would be low GPA."

"Kurt..."

"Returning to work. Really high rate of busts for cocaine possession."

"Inverse rates of successful prosecutions."

"Might have something to do with...hello. DA's wife went to GPA. Daughter goes to GPA. So do daughters or granddaughters of half of the city council and county commission. Court judges either graduates or family attending or graduates..."

"That doesn't spell Special Circumstances," Barb pointed out. "You're just talking about a small town that's turned into a medium city. I'm not exactly seeing the Kabala or pentagrams."

"I'm starting to agree," Kurt said. "I'm looking at the website and just not seeing Satanic cult here."

Barb pulled up the website and paused.

"Okay, we've got a problem," she said.

"What?" Kurt asked, rolling over.

"Look at them," Barb said.

"I have been," Kurt said. "Other than the uniforms..."

"No, I mean *look* at them," Barb said. "This is *not* normal."

"Rich girls. Prep school..."

"They're *all* smiling," Barb said. "In perfect unison. Mechanically. Like...You ever hear about that case in Connecticut...?"

"I read the report in background prep. Holy..."

"Not..."

"*Stepfords,*" they both said, simultaneously.

"Stepfords *and* zombies?" Kurt said. "Houston, we have a problem."

"It can't be a Stepford cult," Sharice said, wearily. "Okay, they look like Stepfords. But there's too many of them. A Stepford ritual requires very high-end magics, powerful channels and multiple blood sacrifices. Find me the Ted Bundy, times ten, and I'll agree that it's a Stepford cult."

Sharice had been napping on one of the couches in the parlor. Barb had checked on Lazarus, who was out cold on Janea's chest, then reluctantly woke Sharice up.

"How many blood sacrifices?" Kurt asked.

"Nine for each Wife," Sharice replied. "Of 'good station,' generally meaning innocent of major evils themselves. For Stepfords, the average crack addict is insufficient. Don't ask why, you're getting into occult quantum physics. Let me point out that I spent last night in the astral plane, which is not exactly sleeping. Can't you just Google this?"

"Please, Sharice? I heard you were . . . involved . . . ?"

"One of my first major cases," Sharice said, sort of sitting up. "The key was finding Bundy. Bundy was their collector. The sacrifice doesn't have to take place under the dark of the moon in a temple, simply be a sacrifice by a collector using certain minor rituals. Fortunately, I'm a fairly good Seer and I know Florida."

"Wait," Kurt said. "You . . . ?"

"How many girls in this school?" Sharice asked.

"About six hundred," Barb replied. "And I've looked at a few of the ones around town. They're definitely . . . something. I've never actually seen a Stepford, but their auras are . . . awful. Not demonic, just awful."

"Still doesn't track. Six hundredish girls. Even if a third were Stepfords, you're talking about the ritualistic killing of more than two thousand women between the ages of puberty and about twenty-five by a *single* channeler. *Then* you have to remove the *ka* of the Wife."

"Which you do how, exactly?" Kurt asked, continuing, "he asked without really wanting to know the answer."

"Which is fortunate, because it's SCAP and you don't have Level Eight access," Sharice said.

"Wait . . ." Barb said. "You *do*?"

"In general, it can be voluntarily surrendered," Sharice said, ignoring the question, "but it usually has to be removed by force. Either one is a rather serious ritual that *does* require the dark of the moon. I don't see even a third of these girls being . . . those creatures. There's not that many serial killers murdering basically decent young women running around. More than are generally recognized, but not that many."

"Not in the US, anyway," Kurt said.

"Yes," Sharice said. "Don't ask about Congo and Moldova. Fortunately, there's a group of Asatru covering the Caucasus. Led by a demon-possessed former SEAL. Good story . . . I could write a book. Too tired."

"Any real-world terminology you can inject here?" Kurt asked, flailing for the shores of sanity. "Like, what's the effect of soul-death in . . . I hate to call it 'reality,' but . . ."

"There are two types," Sharice said, yawning. "The death of the *ba* and the death of the *ka*. The . . . PCP zombies are *ba*-dead. True walking dead. The effect of that, with an infilling force is, well, what you've seen. Without specific direction, you get homicidal psychosis. Without an infilling force they are, well, dead as a stump. Stepfords are *ka*-dead. Often diagnosed as sociopaths. There's more around than just Stepfords, by the way. The only thing they can feel is the pain of others. Generally, psychological pain. So they get off on inflicting pain and dominating everyone around them. They are . . . soul-suckers. Succubae, sort of."

"More shit I wish I didn't know," Kurt said. "Sorry for the language, ladies."

"You did ask," Sharice said, stretching out on the couch. "If there's nothing else, I need to rest my old bones."

"Thanks, Sharice," Barb said. "Get some rest."

"If you haven't got your health," Kurt said.

"Did you just make a *Princess Bride* reference?" Sharice said, chuckling. "I didn't know you had it in you."

"Hey, I can watch movies," Kurt said. "I didn't realize till I read the file *The Stepford Wives* was based on a real event."

"*The Exorcist*," Barb said. "*House on Haunted Hill* . . ."

"Seriously?"

"*Gilligan's Island*," Sharice muttered.

"You're making that up," Barb snapped.

"Check the secure files at the Foundation," Sharice said. "There's a reason they never got off the island. The Harlem Globetrotters story was an in-joke, though. Good night. Afternoon. Morning. Whenever it is . . ."

"Sharice?" Kurt said, pausing at the parlor door.

"*What?!*"

"Isn't the problem with Miss Grisham that she had her *ka* . . . Pulled out? Sort of like . . ."

"Shit," Sharice said, sitting bolt upright. "There is no fool like an old fool!"

"Let's think about this," Barb said, grabbing her head. They'd been going around in circles for nearly an hour.

"Sleep deprived," Sharice said. "Exhausted. You think."

"This isn't possession," Barb said.

"Wait, *what* isn't possession?" Kurt replied. "Let's get back to the point. We're investigating the *Madness* cases. Not Stepfords. If they even *are* Stepfords."

"They're Stepfords," Barb said. "Or something similar. And the Madness cases are related. Either that, or Janea's a hell of a coincidence. Sharice, I know you're tired, but just . . . tell me about Stepfords."

"They're seen as the perfect wives and mothers," Sharice said, sipping tea. "Perfect homemakers, perfectly dressed, perfect hostesses. Honestly . . ." she said, then paused.

"They look sort of like me?" Barb said, grinning.

"That, yes," Sharice said. "The truth is that they wrap their families in a web of control, both mundane and mystical, and slowly suck the life out of them. Husbands tend to get promoted, often well above their ability, because anyone who stands in their way gets run over. Generally personal tragedies, child dies, generally of some lingering fatal disease, often death, suicide. Murder–suicide is a favorite. 'He was such a nice guy with a great future ahead of him. I don't know why he killed his whole family and himself. I guess Ron with the bitch wife gets the promotion.' And woe betide the husband who tries to escape. You do *not* divorce a Stepford. Death is a blessing when it finally comes. The same goes for their children. Who are almost invariably basket cases for life unless they drink the Kool-Aid themselves."

"So they're control freak wives and moms," Kurt said. "What else is new?"

"And then there's the secondary effects," Sharice said. "Leukemia clusters around them. Accidents. The 'nice guy' down the street who turns out to be the serial killer who's been kidnapping and raping girls or boys. Generally, if you find some nice mundane community that suddenly is experiencing tragedy after tragedy, look for a Stepford and you'll find the source. Only the families of other Stepfords are immune. Specifically, they become cluster points for various malevolent entities."

"Sounds swell," Barb said.

"Oh, and they are *very* hard to kill," Sharice said. "I'm not into the 'whole kill them all, God will know his own.' I prefer things like walking the Moon Paths. The Stepford clearance I would have enjoyed, were it not quite so...So. Turns out they're pretty much immune to poisons; don't bother trying tear gas as the seventies version of HRT did. Heal in the blink of an eye, too, which turned out to matter when the only thing that worked was head shots and sometimes not even that. You pretty much have to put a stake through their hearts or cut off their heads to kill the little bitches. And that perfect skin is as thick and tough as a rhino. And if you pull the stake out too soon...Don't. Just... don't. Leave it. They sort of wake up...really annoyed."

"That doesn't explain the Madness cases," Kurt pointed out.

"Let me repeat," Sharice said with a sigh. "*If you find some nice mundane community that suddenly is experiencing tragedy after tragedy, look for a Stepford.* They, personally, are all about power and control."

"Through men, though," Barb said.

"Remember, the case was at the beginning of the feminist revolution, and up to that point, the power was *always* through men," Sharice said. "I'm not sure what a feminist Stepford would be like. *I'm* a feminist, and the thought makes me sort of shudder. And I'll repeat. Again. This isn't Stepfords. This is something else."

"They're all about power and control," Barb said. "More circumstantial. Kurt, the drug cases."

"GPA alums and attendees are all through the power structure in this area," Kurt said.

"Common in smaller cities and towns," Sharice said.

"My point, but there's *something* here," Barb said. "I Looked at some of those girls, Sharice. They're not possessed but they're also not...normal. Kurt, known associates of the victims in the Madness cases?"

"No commonality," Kurt said. "I mean, some overlap but no major common associates."

"Can you find out how many of their girlfriends or female friends were GPA girls? Not the same girl, the same school?"

"There's an app for that," Kurt said, grinning. He pulled out his smart phone and started tapping. He paused, then grinned mirthlessly. "Every single one had dated a GPA girl."

"Had?" Barb asked.

"If I'm reading this right, they were all *ex*-girlfriends. Reasoning in advance of data, I think if we poked into it, they'd have all dumped a GPA girl prior to going zomb."

"You don't divorce a Stepford," Barb said. "You especially don't dump one."

"Stepfords can do a lot of harm," Sharice said. "They could *not* strip a *ba* without an additional major ritual, which the victim had to be present for, nor could they then infill them. Both you're talking *heavy*-duty hoodoo, and animating a corpse is such high necromancy, there's only a few necromancers who have succeeded. At least succeeded and survived. Oh . . . *crap*. I hate to do this . . ." She pulled out her phone.

"Do what?" Barb asked.

"Phone a friend," Sharice said. "Augustus, I'm putting you on speaker."

"Very well," Germaine said. "Go ahead."

"We're pursuing a theory that a local girls' private school is the source of the Madness cases."

"I take it you're talking about GPA," Germaine said.

"You know, it would help if we had a *full* briefing," Kurt said.

"Agent Spornberger, a full briefing on the mystical underworld of Chattanooga would take several hours, which . . . I do not have. Be silent. Go on, Sharice. The last I checked, GPA was simply a dark power center. There are . . . four in Chattanooga and some seven in Hamilton county."

"Barb believes they may be Stepfords," Sharice said. "Or something similar."

"On what basis?"

"Gut," Barb said. "And some circumstantial evidence. Item A. Your friend suggested that I bark up the tree."

"I would not describe her as a friend," Germaine said. "More of a colleague. And GPA is . . . Paris to her London. Minas Morgul to Minas Tirith might be a more current referent. Go on."

"Stepfords are addicted to wealth and power. GPA girls are addicted to wealth and power."

"A common failing. Go on."

"All of the victims in the Madness cases, the *ba*-ripped, were former boyfriends of GPA girls. You don't dump a Stepford."

"*All* of the victims?"

"Yes, sir," Kurt said then gulped.

"I see that the evidence builds. And Janea's *ka* was functionally stripped, also a Stepford trait. Stepfords do not strip the *ba* nor infill. They do not create . . . zombies. Which is why you called me, Ms. Rickels."

"Yes . . . sir," Sharice said.

Barb looked at her quizzically. She had never heard the old witch use the "s" word before.

"My, we tread lightly, do we not," Germaine replied.

"My after-action analysis was that the Stepford ritual originated somewhere in the Hellenistic region," Sharice said. "But that is one of the three most common regions. And the best I could do at the time was Persian."

"You wish to know more about the infill ritual," Germaine said. "I had deduced that. Yes, it is broadly Persian in origin, as well. Probably earlier. Possibly Assyrian, from some of the oldest texts. Give me a moment."

Why does Germaine . . . ? Barbara mouthed at Sharice. Sharice just looked at her coldly.

"I support your theory, in general," Germaine said after what seemed a very long fifteen seconds. "I hypothesize thus. First, for Agent Spornberger. Zombies, as you call them, are not originally houdoun. African witch doctors learned the technique from Arab wizards, who learned them from Persian sorcerers. Among the Persians and those regions Persian-influenced, the Hellenistic regions including Judea, the term you may have heard is 'golem.'"

Barb slapped her forehead lightly and shook her head. "Golems," she whispered. "Of course."

Golems! Why'd it have to be golems? Kurt mouthed, rolling his eyes.

"Golems, zombies if you prefer, are known for their anger and violence. That is because they must be fed. And not upon brains, Agent Spornberger. The necromancer must continually fill their . . . beings with, not the souls of victims, but the power of the soul. Thus, the necromancer must have a continuous supply of sacrificial victims. And golems are quite perfect for gathering them, if you can control one. Or more. Elsbeth Bathory had at least five in her control at one point or another: the origin of the Frankenstein myth.

"If the necromancer does not so supply the golem, the golem turns upon its creator. And as the golems are very hard to kill, absent strong mystical aid, the creator rarely survives. Your golems do not require such a supply. Thus I had, falsely, struck golems from the list of potential phenomena. They do, otherwise, quite resemble them. However, the most ancient known rituals are... quite clearly hacks of some still-older ritual."

"Hacks?" Kurt said, then clapped his hand over his mouth.

"If one has studied the occult as thoroughly as I have, you know when someone has been copying and pasting bits of other rituals, Agent Spornberger," Germaine said. "Hacks. I have read your reports. Given that we appear to be dealing with a pre-historic cult that may be tied to the origin of the Stepford and golem rituals... it is possible that they have found the original rituals. How they create the golems, how they create Stepfords or something similar without the necessary sacrifices... shall wait to be determined. I have calls to make, and you have a girls' school to check out. Carefully. For both mystic and mundane reasons. They are, as you pointed out, tied into a rather wider-based power structure than you are aware. Tread lightly, absent definite indicators."

"As long as I don't have to wear a uniform," Barb said.

"Ooooo..." Kurt muttered.

"Stop *right* there."

Chapter Nine

*I*t was sunset by the time that they left the safe house, and traffic was heavy on 27 crossing the river.

"I hate commuters," Barb said, weaving past a slow-moving vehicle in the left lane. She let out a cry, though, as the traffic suddenly slowed to a halt in a sea of brake lights.

Kurt looked over, a tad nervous since her normally terrifying but flawless driving seemed to be less than flawless, and was surprised to see a look of shock on her face. She was staring wide-eyed at the mass of lights.

"Did we forget something really important?" he asked.

"No," Barb said in a strained voice. "I just forgot to turn off my Sight."

"Your . . . what?" Kurt asked.

"Sight," Barb said pointedly. "Second Sight. Crazy psychic sh— stuff. Ability to see into the other world. I just started getting the, hah-hah, 'Gift' of Second Sight before this mission. Never had to deal with it before. I used to not *mind* going by graveyards. I'd forgotten to push it back after we were in the safe house. Which, by the way, is a *really* safe house. Which was why I was using it."

"So . . . what?" Kurt asked, unhappily. "Demons?"

"Angels," Barb said, as the traffic started to move again. "Lots and lots and *lots* of angels spread their wings when the traffic slammed to a halt. Think white light ten times brighter than all the brake lights. Blinding."

"Seriously?" Kurt asked, peering forward. "It's just normal evening traffic."

"To you," Barb said in an annoyed voice. "In Second Sight it's cars, people, angels and demons. Lots of angels but plenty of demons as well. In all the readings I did before I got this gig and since, in the list of things about angels, one of the characteristics *not* listed was being *pests*. Leave me *alone*! Yes, I know you're there! I've got a *mission* to perform! Don't you?"

"Barb," Kurt said. "You're talking to the air."

"When I reacted I think I started to radiate," Barb said as a car swerved *out* of her lane and out of her way. "In fact, now I *know* I am. All the cars don't have guardian *angels* in them. *That* one got out of my way for *another* reason."

"Reason being...?" Kurt said, looking at the Mercedes. The driver was a normal enough looking guy. Lawyer type, one each. On his cell phone, of course.

"Demons," Barb said. "Lust, greed, envy, a couple I can't identify. When the angels spread their wings, I sort of let go the cover I was under in surprise. And every demon in the mass wants to get the hell, literally, out of my way. And all the angels who aren't involved in keeping their charges alive in traffic are swarming over to say hello. Yes, hello, yes, I see you. I'm trying to *drive* here...Gah. I have *got* to get this under control."

"Want me to drive?" Kurt asked. "In fact, I'd really prefer to drive."

"Once we get off 27, I'll pull over," Barb said. "And, yes, until I can get my Sight back under control, you'd better drive."

"You really see angels and demons?" Kurt asked, looking around. It was bugging him that the consultant "saw" stuff. On one hand, it was making him wonder about her sanity. On the other hand, the whole point of this investigation was making him wonder about his. And the Bureau's. So far, all he'd really seen was a woman in some kind of coma and what looked like a multinational involved in neurological experiments. There had been a complete lack of *visible* demons, werewolves or vampires to stake.

"Everywhere," Barb said. "More than I've seen before. I think it has something to do with the traffic. But I dunno. This is all new to me."

They pulled over after they got on Manufacturers Road and changed places.

"They call it a 'Gift,'" Barb said as Kurt pulled out. "Capital and quotes. So far it's just been a royal pain in the patootie." She closed her eyes and concentrated on closing down and cloaking.

"What do they look like?" Kurt asked.

"Which?" Barb replied.

"Either? Both?"

"Angels look like a bad special effect," Barb said. "Just sort of clouds of sparkly light. I'm not into science fiction, but I've watched a couple of *Star Trek* episodes. There was one where there was some sort of mist that sucked out people's blood...?"

"Saw it, too," Kurt said.

"Sort of like that but more sparkly and whiter," Barb said. "Except, as it turns out, when they spread their wings. And even then the wings don't really look like wings. More like gossamer strands of light with white stuff in between. Really bright gossamer strands. I'd never seen them do that before, but I haven't had my Sight working in traffic before. Demons generally, to me, look snakelike or like black mist. Best I can say. Again, this is all new to me. I was told that angels can fly and demons can't. Apparently you can sometimes see demons hitching rides on planes, since they need something to travel long distances."

"You're joking," Kurt said.

"It's what I was told," Barb said. "I haven't seen it, but I haven't traveled on a plane since I got my sight except the Foundation one. And as you can guess, *it* wasn't infested."

"And here we are," Kurt said, pulling up to the entrance to the school.

"Dang it," Barb said. "I just got my Sight turned off. Now I have to open it up again."

"I sort of wish I could see what you see," Kurt said.

"No," Barb replied. "You don't. And...I don't see anything."

The entrance had de rigueur brick pillars and a large sign. The road curved around the main entry building. From the maps and satellite photos, they knew there were several buildings in the compound with a "quad" in the middle that was entirely enclosed.

"No demons?" Kurt asked.

"They're generally associated with people," Barb said. "I've never seen one schlepping down a street. And there's a distinct lack of people here."

The school was closed and there weren't even any cars in the parking lot.

"So we get out and poke around?" Kurt said.

"There is never anything interesting in the front of a building," Barb said. "Let's take the road around."

"Public road," Kurt said. "No problems there."

"Public?"

"It goes to a subdivision sort of behind the school," Kurt said. "High-end condos."

The road curved around the school, under a bridge and down to the river. Behind the school there were athletic fields, more buildings and a dock on the river.

"Good a place as any to start," Barb said.

"Why couldn't we have checked it out when the girls were around?" Kurt asked.

Lazarus suddenly lifted his head off of Janea's chest and hissed.

"Familiar?" the young witch said, looking around the room. There were no apparent threats.

The cat stood up and hopped to the floor, then scratched at the door urgently. He had gotten up a few times before, mostly when the rest of the team was awake, to eat and use the catbox. But this was something different.

The witch let him out, then followed, more or less at a run, as the cat bounded down the stairs to the front door and started pawing at it frantically.

"I wish you could talk," the witch said, opening the door.

The cat darted past the startled security guards and down to the road, turned right and started running.

"Should we follow him?" one of the guards asked. "I mean, we were told the cat was one of our protectees."

"Cats such as that can look after themselves."

They got out by a large concrete-block building that was apparently the support building for the athletics department. The bottom was mostly open, surrounded by chain-link, and appeared to hold the boats for the crew team.

"I'm seeing a distinct lack of goat's blood," Kurt pointed out.

"Ever see a building like this with a large fireplace?" Barb asked, pointing at a massive chimney. "I mean, one that was made after 1920?"

"And the significance of a chimney is...?" Kurt asked.

"Heck if I know," Barb said. "But it's odd. Burning the bodies?"

"And there's a distinct lack of bodies," Kurt pointed out. "We probably should have parked up by the school buildings. Any psychic read?"

"I wish you'd quit asking that," Barb said. "I've got Sight. I'm not a psychic." She paused and turned her head from side to side. "On the other hand..."

Kurt's phone buzzed and he pulled it off his belt to check the message.

"What was the 'on the other hand'...." Kurt asked, curiously.

"Something's...happening," Barb said. "I mean...I don't know. Something. What, I'm not sure."

"The reason I ask is the message," Kurt said. "I set up a query to Headquarters on anything related to GPA. We don't have Carnivore access, but cyber teams track certain open-source information on the Web. Mostly looking for predators, but they keep track of other stuff. And they picked up an indicator."

"Which is?" Barb asked, trying to look over his shoulder at the phone.

"Apparently several open sites, Facebook mainly, are reporting that 'GPA girls are skinny-dipping off McLellan Island.' There are even photos being circulated, which was what triggered the alert. Technically, they're child porn. Good thing I'm exempt from the statute or I'd be in violation of federal law just looking at this stuff. What are you getting?"

"Basically...I guess you'd call it the feeling you get right before a lightning strike," Barb said. "This area is a current of energy as strong as the river, and something's pulling at it. Something nearby, but I can't tell even which direction. I'm not *good* at this. Where is McLellan Island?"

"Right there," Kurt said, pointing to the apparently deserted island in the middle of the river. The bridge they'd gone under passed over the river and the island.

"Then that's where it's going down," Barb said.

"What is going down?" Kurt asked. "More zombies?"

"I don't know," Barb replied. "But . . . my spidey senses are saying that it's about time for you to run for the hills."

"There are boats headed for McLellan Island," Kurt said, pointing. "Looks like a waterborne flash mob situation."

"Party on McLellan Island," Barb said. "Figure that is going to be mostly males. And as the climax of the party, everybody gets turned into zombies."

"If it's GPA girls who are doing it, and we still don't have a good read on how," Kurt said.

"Then I guess it's time I went and found out," Barb said. "The question being, how do I get to the island?"

"Well, you can rappel off the bridge," Kurt said. "If you've got rappelling gear. Or you can swim. I think you'd probably *float* okay . . ."

"Not in body armor, I wouldn't," Barb said. "We need a boat. Now if I just knew how to use one of those crew boats."

"I guess I am going with you, then," Kurt said.

"Like heck."

"Do you know how to scull?" Kurt asked.

"No. Not one of my skillsets. I don't even use a rowing machine to work out."

"Then I'll have to scull you over."

"You know how to scull?" Barb asked, looking at him askance.

"I had a rowing scholarship," Kurt said. "Doesn't mean I'm gay. It's not like it's male gymnastics or something!"

"Seriously?" Barb asked. "You?"

"I'm a man of many parts," Kurt said, looking at the chain and lock that secured the chain-link. "Just one problem. FBI agents, despite what you see on TV, are not routinely trained in picking locks. Got a pair of bolt cutters?"

"No," Barb said, sighing. "But I've got something that will work. On the other hand, it's practically blasphemy to use it."

"Where?" Kurt asked.

"In my bag."

Cats are sprinters, not long-distance runners like dogs. And while Lazarus didn't really have a concept of distance, he did know he had a long way in cat miles to go. Which meant he needed a ride. One he could control.

Dean Jensen was, all things considered, a fairly nice and inoffensive fellow. He contributed both time and, when he had it, money to various causes. He liked animals. (That was about to change.) He did his duty as a steward of Earth by not littering, contributing to environmental awareness and, alas, riding a bike as his primary form of transportation.

It was simply bad luck that had him pedaling down East Third Street when Lazarus needed a convenient and controllable form of transportation.

Jensen's first inkling that his evening was going awry was when claws sank into his back. He let out a rather girl-like scream and swerved so badly he nearly ran into traffic.

"What the hell?" he shouted as the claws climbed up his back. He started to pull over and was thoroughly raked for his troubles, the claws, which had now sunk into his neck, pulling him from side to side. They stopped when he was pedaling, so he just hunkered down and hoped for the best.

When he came to Hawthorne Street he started to make a turn and was clawed again. Clearly, whatever demon was on his back wanted him to go straight.

He kept pedaling. After a couple more rakes he pedaled faster.

"Nice setup," Kurt said. "I'd wondered about what was in the bag."

"This'll cut it," Barb said, drawing the katana.

"Okay, yeah," Kurt said. "It will and, yeah, it is blasphemy."

"And while you get the boat ready, I will start rigging up."

"Just keep your weight centered," Kurt said as Barb carefully boarded the quad scull. "I got the biggest boat I could manage on my own, but all that weight is going to be an issue."

"I'm not fat," Barb said. "And I have excellent balance."

"It's not *your* weight," Kurt said. "It's the body armor, rifle, pistol, sword and ammo that's the issue."

Barb carefully took a seat as Kurt pulled away from the dock.

"As soon as we hit the shore you are out of here," Barb said, clipping a radio onto his belt. "I brought you a spare tac set. I'm on four-one-five-eight. It's encrypt...Oh...*drat*."

"What now?" Kurt asked.

"I really *should* have made this call before we pulled out," she said. She reached for her phone and hit Send.

"Phoning a friend?" Kurt asked.

"Something like that," Barb answered.

"Marquez."

"I'm pretty sure whatever 'it' is is going down," Barb said. "McLellan Island. Do not fall for feminine wiles. They're Stepfords."

"Now?"

"If you please," Barb said. "The only way to get there is by boat or rappelling off the Veterans Bridge. Which would be pretty noticeable. When you get there, I'm on four-one-five-eight."

"Four-one-five-eight, aye. Ten mikes. Out here."

"Who was that?" Kurt asked.

"The mystic version of HRT," Barb said.

"Is that who you've been secretly meeting with?" Kurt asked.

"Yep," Barb said. "And I'm secretly glad they're here. I think this is going to get real interesting."

"We'll have to insert off the Veterans Bridge," Friar Mills said. Shaun Mills was redheaded and still somewhat prone to the anger management issues that his former demons had used to great effect. With a mis-set nose and scarred knuckles, he looked like what he had once been; a street hooligan and thug for the Irish mob. "Rather public. We'd best be activating a wee diversion."

"I really had hoped not to have to use this," Brother Marquez said, sending a text. "Get the team ready for abseil insertion."

"Should be a lark."

"Torquemada," Brother JD "Homer" Hughes said. "That's the code."

"I sincerely hope that the Holy See can cover us on this," Friar Jackob Okai said, pressing the detonator. In the distance there was a dull boom.

"They provided much of the funding for building the plant," Brother Hughes replied. "What's one Passat more or less?"

⁓

Sergeant Alex Teach looked up from his alana rus at the "all units" ping on his computer and shook his head.

The code 8000 was for an explosion. Location: the new Volkswagen plant. Secondary codes indicated possible terrorism. New codes started popping up, indicating that the explosion was in the finished vehicle parking area.

"Car bomb," he said, stuffing the rest of the sandwich in his face and hitting the blue lights. "Ap a car p'anp. Gre'ph. There goes *my* night."

"You're going to have to go over the side," Kurt said. "You can't really land one of these things. Carefully."

"Got it," Barb said, counterbalancing to enter the water. It was only up to her hips. "Now git."

"Hazmat," Kurt muttered. "Hazmat. I need to provide some cover for this anyway. Not sure what to say."

"Call Garson and tell him to keep everything away from McLellan Island."

Kurt's phone started beeping urgently and he pulled it out to look.

"That shouldn't be too hard," Kurt said. "There's apparently been a terrorist attack at the VW plant. A car bomb. At a car plant. Everybody and their brother is headed that way."

"Funny coincidence," Barb said, wading ashore. "You probably should head up to the bridge just in case anyone bothers to pay attention to oddities on the island."

"What if something happens to you?" Kurt asked.

Barb locked and loaded her AR-10, then did the same with her H&K .45.

"I'm what happens to *other* people, Kurt."

Chapter Ten

*B*arb ghosted through the heavy brush of the island towards the eastern tip where they'd seen the boats gathering. The island was an Audubon preserve, based on the really clear "No Trespassing" signs. She felt oddly perturbed that, in addition to black magic, the girls were violating a nature preserve. All things considered, it was minor, but irritating nonetheless.

In the twilight she could see that a fire had been lit, and hoped that she wasn't, for the second time, overreacting. The whole Lazarus thing was a good reminder that she might be a warrior of God but not a perfect one. This time, however, she could feel currents of power being used. Something mystic was happening on the island and it certainly didn't *feel* godly.

Sliding up through the undergrowth, she used her Trijicon tactical scope to observe for just a moment. As advertised, the small clearing was filled with naked girls. They were not, however, skinny-dipping, but clearly engaged in some sort of ritual. The ritual appeared to be a complex dance, possibly on the lines of the Trilobular pattern. At the center of the pattern was a small stone altar surrounded by fire.

Circling the girls were a collection of mostly young men standing stiff and still. Barb, from her range, couldn't tell if they were simply held—glamoured was the usual term—or had been soul drained.

"Dei," Barb whispered into her tac set.

"Go," Marquez replied.

"Just west of the bridge," Barb said. "You'll see it from up there. The girls are the targets. Stepfords or something similar. High regen. Resistant to penetration..."

Barb was slammed forward by what felt like a lightning bolt right in the kidneys. The pain was blinding, but she rolled forward, then up, bringing the AR-10 up and targeting the figure in the darkness behind her. She gave the trigger a slight squeeze and was rewarded with a *click*.

"Capable of rendering your weapons useless," Vartouhi said, raising her hand and sending another levin bolt at Barb.

Not even sure what she was doing, Barb raised her hand and deflected the bolt. Again she felt a surge like electricity. But it wasn't, it was clearly mystic.

"That all you got, *bitch*?" Barb gasped. She felt as if she'd been pushed through an industrial wringer by the first bolt. But what didn't kill you...

"No," Vartouhi said, waving her hands and chanting.

"Try to get *this* to misfire," Barb said, releasing her AR and drawing the katana.

Before Barb could move forward, Vartouhi made a drawing motion, and Barb felt as if someone was sucking the air out of her. For a moment.

"Oh, you are *not*," Barb said, laughing. "You really think you can draw the *ka* of a Warrior of *God*?" She released the sword with one hand and held it out. "Lord, please send to me the power to explain to this foul sorceress the extreme and absolute *error* of her ways."

Barb could feel the mystic channel that Vartouhi was using to pull at her *ka*. What she sent down the channel was a tithe of the full power of God, but it was more than enough.

Purity and godliness exploded into the soul of the sorceress, who let out a scream of pain and terror.

"Time to meet your demoness," Barb said, stepping forward, sword upraised.

Vartouhi stumbled backwards into the brush. As Barb started tracking her, she heard more movement behind her. Turning around, she found out that the guys who had been gathered around the ritual had, in fact, already been turned. They were crashing through the brush toward her, eyes flat and dead in the firelight.

"Zombies," Barb said, shaking her head. "This is going to get ugly."

There were about thirty of the zombies, and Barb quickly determined that the most important thing was to keep them from grabbing her. The best way to stop that was also the ugliest; take off their arms.

Sword combat is poorly understood in modern times. Fencers dance around, touching each other for points. When the sword was the height of killing technology, nobody tried for "touches." The point was to render your opponent incapable of further combat. The best way to do that wasn't to hack at their body, but at their *limbs*. Casualty analysis of medieval combat showed that some sixty percent of the casualties were due to loss of arms or legs. Then all you had to do was let them bleed out screaming.

As one of the zombies reached for her, Barb came across in a picture-perfect Nanameburi, the razor-edged katana neatly taking off the zombie's arm. Which didn't even spurt blood. And equally didn't slow the zombie one bit.

"Seriously?" she muttered, taking off arm after arm as the zombies swarmed her.

Acting on some instinct, she whipped the sword behind her and bounced away an incoming levin bolt.

"*Bitch!*" she shouted, dodging behind a tree to put some cover between herself and the apparently recovered Vartouhi. That just put her in line with a zombie. This time she didn't aim for the arm, but took off its head.

That dropped one.

She dodged in and out among the trees in near darkness except for the firelight, playing tag with the zombies.

"Karol, *now* would be good!"

Dean pedaled furiously onto the Veterans Bridge. He wasn't sure where this cat—he was pretty sure it was a cat—was heading, but it was firm in its intentions. It made clear when he needed to turn by pulling on one of his ears with its claws.

"I'm wearing out, okay?" Dean gasped. "I mean, can't you grab a car or something?"

What with everything else that was going on in his life at the moment, the sight of a bunch of SWAT guys tying lines to the Veterans Bridge and apparently getting ready to go rappelling wasn't anywhere near the top of the list of weird shit. But it was close.

"What the hell is going on?" he gasped.

The claws indicated he should pull in where the four vans were parked, and he hoped his misery was about at an end.

He pulled to a stop as one of the group of heavily armed troopers lifted a gun and pointed it at him. He didn't know from guns, but the barrel looked as big as a cannon.

"Halt," the masked man said in a thick accent.

"I want to!" Dean wailed. "But you're going to need to kill this cat first!"

As he said that, he felt the cat leap off his shoulder. He got a quick flash of it running down the railing, then it launched itself into space.

"Hopefully it *drowned*," Dean growled.

"Oh," the cop said, pointing his gun at the ground. "I see. Very well. Go away now. And you probably shouldn't talk about this. Nobody will believe you."

"What the *hell* is going *on*?" Dean asked.

Dean found himself looking down the barrel of the gun again.

"Using foul language at this time and place is not a good thing," the cop said. "Go away. Do not discuss what happened here."

"Okay, okay," Dean said, picking his bike up and turning around. "I'm out of here. Just don't shoot me, please!"

"God speed your travels," the cop said. "You have done God's work this night though you knew it not."

"What the fuck ever, dude," Dean muttered as soon as he was pretty sure he was out of shooting range.

Barb had managed, by much dodging and hacking, to take out six of the zombies. But the bitch kept throwing power bolts her way, and dodging both was getting tiresome. She needed to take out Vartouhi. The problem being, the sorceress apparently knew the island much better than Barb and was proving decidedly hard to corner. And the zombies were getting so turned around, Barb kept running into them in every direction. Most of them appeared to be lost when she ran into them, but that didn't make them less dangerous.

One of them finally managed to snag her, dragging her in and sinking its teeth into her arm. It couldn't penetrate her tacticals but it hurt like fire.

"Cock*sucker*!" Barb swore. She managed to retain her sword

with one hand and drew her tanto with the other. She jammed it up through the zombie's jaw, driving it into the thing's brain. As the now fully-dead zombie released its bite, another appeared out of the darkness, stumbling towards her.

She backhanded the katana and took off its head just as another levin bolt came in. This one scored, and she was slammed back into a tree, then slumped down, half paralyzed.

"Not...good," Barb muttered. She reached over and wrenched the tanto out of the zombie's skull and waited. She could hear the zombies thrashing around in the darkness, but at the moment they didn't seem to know exactly where their quarry was.

She heard a stealthier movement and waited. This time she felt the gathering energy and caught the expected levin bolt on her katana. And in the flash of mystic light she spotted that bitch Vartouhi.

The tanto flew straight and true. But instead of it hitting center of mass, the bitch dodged, and it just caught her in the arm.

Barb surged up and charged forward, but Vartouhi vanished again into the darkness. And she apparently could call the zombies, because they started closing on Barb's position.

"Fine," Barb said, spinning in place and taking another zombie's head off. "As long as it's *only* whack-a-zombie, I'm *good.*"

"I hit her with *three bolts,*" Vartouhi gasped, wincing at the pain of the knife in her flesh. "Any of them should have killed her. She just shrugged them off. She *deflected* five more. And *don't* try the Akasa ritual. Whatever she sent back at me nearly killed *me.*"

"She's only one woman," Reamer said, angrily. "Misty, Buffy, Ashley. Each of you take a group of the Osemala. Corner her and destroy her."

"Yes, Master Kom," Misty said. "*We'll* teach her the power of Osemi."

"Just kill her and send her soul to hell," Reamer said. "And get back here before the ritual is complete. You don't want to be outside the pentacle."

Barb went up the side of a tree, then leapt off, flying over two zombies and taking off both their heads in a really elegant

Swan Passes Over River Under Moon maneuver. Her landing, however, was based far more on Master Ti Kwan's "action movie" techniques. It was a surprisingly useful form, she'd discovered, for fighting zombies in near darkness in a heavily forested island covered in logs and stumps.

"Thank you, Seigun Kwan," Barb said, grabbing a sapling in one hand to swing around and take off the head of another zombie. "And now I'm pole dancing. Janea would love this."

She scrambled up the sapling until she'd reached the leafy part, then leaned out. The tree bent under her weight and she slowly drifted down towards the ground. Hooking her legs onto the tree permitted her to reach down and take off the head of another zombie from *just* out of its reach.

"Interesting," she said, flipping off of the tree and landing on the body of the zombie. "Clean-up on this is going to be a *bitch*." She backhanded, hard, and cut all the way through the torso of the zombie stumbling up behind her. "And I'm going to have to spend some serious time sharpening."

Two levin bolts came out of the darkness and she managed to deflect both. They were much lighter than Vartouhi's, but two was a bit much.

"Oy vey," she said, charging down the line of one of the bolts. She caught sight of one of the GPA girls running away and wasn't about to let her get away. However, as she closed through the woods, a zombie reared up in her way.

There was not much technique to the body check she sent its way. The zombie, totally uncoordinated, fell backwards. She stabbed down, then had to wrench the sword out of its skull. Which wasn't particularly easy.

As she was tugging and twisting, *three* levin bolts came in from various directions. She deflected two, but the third hit her square in the face like a punch from a professional boxer.

"OW!" Barb bellowed, ripping the sword out of the zombie's head. "I am *so* going to kick your spoiled *asses!*"

"What does it take to *kill* her?" Ashley wailed. "I hit her in the *face!* She should be *dead!*"

"Bring in all the Osemala," Misty said, nervously. "Go gather them up. We need to swarm her."

"Okay," Buffy said, then screamed as a cat attached itself to her face.

Lazarus didn't have any special cat martial arts training. But he didn't really need it. When twenty pounds of tom are trying to scratch your eyes out, you're effectively out of the fight.

"Aaah!" Buffy screamed. "Get it off!"

Misty grabbed Lazarus, but he was tightly attached to Buffy's face. Except for his teeth, which he managed to turn around and latch onto Misty's hand.

"Get back!" Ashley yelled. "I'll get it off!"

Misty let go of the cat, then went "Noooo!" just a bit late.

Ashley managed a perfectly placed levin bolt, again, which hit Lazarus in the back.

The cat let out a yowl and bounced off of Buffy. Who dropped stone dead.

"You idiot!" Misty screamed. "*You killed Buffy!*"

"No problem," Barb said, taking off Ashley's head. "She won't make that mistake again."

"Wait!" Misty said, holding up her hands. "Time out!"

"Time . . . out?" Barb said, wonderingly. She spun in place and took off another zombie's head, then turned back to face the junior sorceress. "Seriously? Time . . . *out*?"

"I didn't want to get involved with this," Misty said, whimpering.

"I'd say tell it to the judge," Barb said, taking the girl's head off. "But it's sort of a judge, jury, executioner thing."

She looked over at Lazarus, who was licking the burned patch on his back.

"Would you *try* not to get yourself killed?"

"Kabala field," Mills said, holding up a crystal. It was sparkling blue.

The team had rappelled down through the trees with some difficulty and were now in an assembly area just east of the ritual point.

"D . . . ash it," Marquez muttered, slinging his M4 and drawing a machete. "Why the See can't come up with a reliable counter I don't know."

"Cold steel, boyos," Mills said, pulling out a basket-hilted claybeg. "Zombies, witches and cold steel. Feels like old times."

"At least it will be quiet," Marquez said, stepping forward. As he did, a zombie, completely lost, stumbled up through the woods. He hacked it in the neck, then, as it grabbed him by the harness and pulled him in, he sawed and hacked at it until he'd taken the head off. "Quietish."

"And bloody bloody," Mills said ferally. "Right, let's go chop up some naughty schoolgirls."

Barb bounced off of two trees, taking out three zombies in a combination of Floating Iris On Wind-Tossed Water and another Heron Over Mountain. She landed with a slight stumble and realized that the combination of repeated hits from levin bolts and just hacking up zombies was starting to wear her down.

"Gotta get more PT," Barb muttered as she stepped into the clearing.

She wasn't sure exactly what the ritual was supposed to do. From her perspective it was just one more cult trying to raise some ancient evil.

"I wish these groups would learn already," she said.

She could see Reamer and Dr. Downing in the group. No surprise. The rest appeared to be of an age to be members of GPA, with a few older women. About half of them were continuing to move in a complex pavane while maintaining a high chant. The other half were turned to face Barb and, emerging from the woods on the other side, the Opus Dei team. Most of the girls were holding fencing swords, and they were *not* protectively tipped.

"You know," Barb said, pointing at the nearest foil, "That's a terrible safety violation."

One of the older women raised her hands and began to chant in counterpoint to the group of ritualists, then made a casting gesture at the Opus Dei team.

"Won't work," Marquez said, flicking blood off of a machete. "We cannot be made your servants. We are protected by the hand of God. I hereby state, as a licensed contractor of the Federal Government authorized to use due force, that you are in violation of United States Federal Codes Eighteen Sixty-Three A, Use of Black Magic, General; B, Performance of Black Magic for the Purposes of Raising Demon, Demons, Demoness or Demonesses; L, Use of Black Magic for the Removal of Souls; R, Use of Black

Magics for the Purposes of Control of Others; and T, Use of Black Magics for the Purposes of Casting of Spells of Unweal, as well as moral laws of most major religions. The penalty is twenty-five years to life in a Federal Corrections Facility for each separate violation. Failure to desist shall result in the use of deadly force."

"You want deadly force," Dr. Downing said, cackling. "*This* is deadly force!"

He raised his hand and threw a levin bolt at Marquez. The former spec ops trooper raised something that looked like a small shield, and the levin bolt grounded on it.

"Thank you," Marquez said, hefting his machete. "That allows us to open up the whole can of whoop-ass."

Barb and the Opus Dei team charged forward at virtually the same moment, and the scene descended into a maelstrom.

Barb was in the unfortunate position of having seven of the Stepfords on her side of the ritual. Three were wielding epees, and the other four foils. She knew very well that a good "touch" from any of them would put her out of the fight, probably dead. Just because they looked like toys didn't mean they weren't dangerous.

"Laz, do *not* get near the swords," Barb said, then stepped forward.

Barb danced around the seven for a bit, feeling them out. Fortunately, only one of the girls using an epee appeared to be well trained in fencing. She quickly concentrated on that one, blocking the others as she needed to keep alive. The girl was good, and more than willing to put the others to the front to retain her ability to dash in on Barb when there appeared to be an opening.

Barb brought her katana across, blocking a thrust from one of the foils, then up and across, taking off the Stepford's arm. The girl shrieked and backed away, her stump spurting. However, the bleeding stopped almost immediately and the girl simply picked the foil back up.

Another slash took off an arm at the shoulder and had much the same result. Scream, stop bleeding, get back in the fight.

The expert epee wielder had circled to Barb's left and rushed in, going for a thrust to the chest. Barb performed a desperate Sparrow Circling Flowers, taking the head off of one of the Stepfords and the hand from the epee wielder. Cutting off the Stepford's head did not, however, have the effect she expected.

The girl's body began to stumble around until it could bend over and pick up the head. Then it set it back on.

"Oh, you did not," Barb said.

"You cannot kill us," the epee wielder panted. "That wound will heal in moments. We are made invincible by the power of our Goddess."

"Really?" Barb said, blocking a foil. She rammed the katana into the mouth of the foil wielder and called upon the power of God. A surge of power went down the blade, and the girl twitched and dropped. "My master is the One True God, *brat*. And I'm here to explain to you, permanently, the error of your ways. Prepare to be spanked like your momma should have long ago."

She dodged out of the forming ring and came in on the beheaded girl's flank. The katana slid up through her ribs like butter. With another surge the Stepford dropped, fully dead.

Dodging again, she crashed directly through the group, blocking epees and foils on either side, then into the ritual.

"Nooo!" Reamer screamed, throwing a frantic levin bolt.

Barb blocked it and took two heads off of the ritualists in two quick slashes.

She turned back to the group of sword wielders, blocking more thrusts and taking off arms with abandon, figuring if they didn't have any arms, they couldn't use swords.

She had seen, in her brief crossing maneuver, that Opus Dei was barely holding its ground. She wasn't sure that they could call God's power in an offensive manner. She'd been told that was, to say the least, unusual. Which meant killing these Stepford bitches was mostly up to her.

One of the foils finally managed to plink her in her left arm, which hurt like hell. She adjusted her chi to fight the pain and wondered if God was willing to send some healing her way. Or some energy since she was starting to flat wear out.

Levin bolts. Foils. Epees. One of the remaining zombies. At one point Barb ended up stumbling over a flopping and apparently still-alive arm. The hand latched onto her boot for a moment until Barb cut down, close to her body, and took it off at the fingers. She retained it as the oddest image of the really weird entire night: Clutching pink fingernails with yellow French tips. It was a *horrible* combination. Barb wanted to track down the manicurist and cut *her* head off.

Most of her blocks and cuts were hair-close. She was spinning and slashing so fast she was well beyond technique. It was just a dance of death, with the air so full of spraying arterial blood the whole clearing smelled of smoke and iron and roasting pork.

She had more cuts than just the plink on the arm at this point. Frankly, her tacticals were so cut up, she was starting to feel half naked.

She finished off the last of the sword wielders on her side and waded into the group continuing the ritual. She expected, given the amount of time they'd been at it, that whatever demon they were summoning would have appeared by now. Barb was, in fact, sort of looking forward to it. Generally, if you took out the demon, the acolytes ended up running or going mad. At the moment it looked as if she was going to have to kill them *all*. Which was just work, work, work.

The ritualists were unarmed, but that didn't mean they went down easily. Some of them were, unbelievably, able to block the katana with their *hands*. Rhino. Tough. Skins. Barb had started to cut their heads off then kick them aside. That kept them out of the game for a while at least. She managed to punt one bottle-blonde all the way to the river.

"Marquez! How you doin'?"

"I'm going to apply to the See for a pay raise after this one!" Marquez yelled. "How do you *kill* these things? Oh, good Lord Jesus..."

Barb looked across the clearing as one of the Opus Dei team surged back to his feet and began lurching towards Marquez.

"Go with God, Brother Sutphin," Marquez said, taking off his head with the machete.

"God damn you all!" Barb screamed, suddenly losing all technique. She began wading through the group, katana slashing in a butterfly. The blazing sword, finally carrying the full weight of God's fury, was no longer simply "hurting" the Stepfords. At its touch they were dropping in severed and quite dead bits.

Technique dropped away, thought dropped away, time dropped away. At that moment, it became simply the dance of the sword. Blood and limbs flew through the air like fleshy butterflies as Barbara Everette, Warrior of God, brought His judgment down upon the coven.

Reamer finally ran, and Barb paused in her slaughter just long enough to draw another tanto and put it squarely in his back. He apparently didn't have the same resistance as the Stepfords; the tanto sank into his back and straight into his heart.

With Barb's berserker charge, the Stepfords all started to flee, scattering in every direction. They were, however, on an island, and Barb wasn't done by any stretch of the imagination. It took the group of God Warriors, with able help from a tracking cat, about twenty minutes to finally clear the island.

Barb found Vartouhi and Dr. Downing boarding one of the boats on the eastern end.

"I don't think so," she said, leaping aboard.

"You can't *do* this," Dr. Downing said, holding his arms over his head as if they were going to stop a sword. "You can't just go around *killing* people! There are laws!"

"More like guidelines," Barb said, tiredly. "And there's no such thing as angels, demons, supernatural, zombies, and the Vatican doesn't have special-operations troops. *You* can, at this point, surrender. You'll be given a very quick and very unfair trial and incarcerated in a very special holding facility."

"What about me?" Vartouhi asked. Her arm was completely healed.

"Stepfords are classified as a special form of undead," Barb said. "Executive termination, absent retention for examination, which means dissection, by the way, is authorized. In other words," Barb continued, bringing the katana across and taking off the thing's head, "kill first, ask questions *never*."

"You, on the other hand, doctor," she said, "are going to be asked a great *many* questions..."

"I suppose the real question is, what do we do with this?" Barb asked, holding up a tablet. She'd tried wiping some of the blood off her face, but her arm was even more coated.

The center of the ritual had been a rough stone altar. Really nothing but some river rocks piled up in a makeshift fashion. On them, however, had been an obviously ancient clay tablet. The tablet felt absolutely malevolent and actually seemed to be sucking in the blood off her hand. "Take it to the Foundation?"

"You put it in the bag," a man's voice said from behind her. She spun in place, katana at the ready, and paused. There were two people who had *somehow* gotten behind her, a short man with dark curly hair in a frumpy overcoat carrying an old-fashioned sample case, and an equally short redhead who looked a bit like a younger, punkier version of Janea. Given that Barb was keyed to the max, nobody should have been able to sneak up behind her, but she checked the impulse to behead both of them. Despite the fact that the redhead was carrying what looked like... a ray gun?

"Whoa, sister!" the redhead said, holding up her unweaponed hand. "Friends! Friends! Nice job on the slice and dice, by the way. Best use for prep girls I can imagine."

"You put it in the bag," Brother Marquez said, walking over. "Hello, Artie. Long time."

"Karol," Artie said, putting on a pair of purple rubber gloves and pulling a Mylar bag out of the sample case. "Cairo... right? Cairo? Just put it in the bag."

"Why?" Barb asked.

"You're holding that with your bare hands?" the redhead asked. "Your bare hands. Seriously?"

"Mrs. Everette could probably hold anything in the Dark Sector," Artie said. "In her bare hands. Just put... put it in the bag."

"Why not?" Barb said. "And why am I putting it in the bag, and, more to the point, who *are* you people?"

"So what's so special about her?" the girl asked.

"We're the people telling you to put the artifact *in* the bag," Artie said.

"We're the people that handle artifacts," the redhead said. "And what's so special about her?"

"Artifacts?" Barb asked, still unsure if she should just give up a symbol of evil to rather odd people she'd never even heard of.

"Secret Service," Karol said. "They handle static items. Artifacts. Power symbols. That sort of thing. FBI, well, *we* handle nonstatic items."

"What are *non*static items?" the redhead asked. "If it's chopping up oh-my-gods, I'm your girl!"

"You don't want to know," Artie said. "Now *put it in the bag.*"

"You aren't, in fact, our sort," Karol said, smiling to relieve the blow. "You, Claudia, are much more a Warehouse type. Trust me on this."

"But what's the other type?" Claudia asked.

"People who can deal with nonstatic items," Artie said. "In. The. BAG!"

"Alright already," Barb said, dropping the "artifact" into the bag. There was a brief flash of purple light and the feeling of malevolence dropped to nearly nothing. "What is that?"

"None of your concern," Artie said, putting the bag in the sample case. "We really *ought* to take that sword as well."

Barb went to immediate two-handed cat stance.

"Whoa, whoa, sister!" Claudia said. "Friends! Friends! I'm sure he was just kidding, right? Kidding. Right, Artie?"

"I'm sure we'll end up with it eventually," Artie said with a sigh. "Although where we'll find the room..."

"See you next time," Karol said.

"Drinks?"

"Murphy's?"

"Friday?"

"Rome. There's going to be sooo many reports about this one."

"Have your people call my people. We really need to get together more often."

"Ciao."

"But what *are* nonstatic items...?"

"What warehouse...?"

"Ask Germaine," Karol said, looking around at the mess. "He's a Regent. And we really should check on your cohort."

"Janea!" Barb said. "Just let me...take a dive in the river, I guess."

The Maiden's Tale

Chapter One

Doris shook her head and looked around the room. For a moment it was like she'd just woken up from a nightmare. There had been pain, so much pain. Then she was here. Wherever "here" was.

It was a large room with medium-height ceilings, brightly lit. It clearly was in a big structure, maybe a hotel. There were various exits and signs, none of which were really penetrating right away. People were entering from a door behind her and going past her in twos and threes, most of them talking excitedly. From somewhere in the room a song was booming an electronic beat.

> Today is your birthday
> But it might be the last day of your life
> What will you do if tomorrow it's all gone?
>
> You won't be young forever
> It's only a fraction to the sum
> You won't be young forever
> Nor will anyone

She had to think. It was like her brain was filled with cotton wool. She was...

She had a plastic bag in one hand and a backpack over her

shoulder. Looking at the bag, it said DRAGON*CON on the front, with some sort of a symbol. It had . . . some books and papers in it. There was a sign across the room HYATT HOTELS WELCOMES DRAGON*CON!

So . . . Sure, she was at Dragon*Con. Of course. Bob had told her she could find "people like her" there. People who didn't think she was weird or ugly or strange.

Come to think of it, some of the people *did* look sort of strange. The music—she could finally find its source—was coming from over by some tables halfway down the room. The people gathered around them, setting up some sort of booth, certainly fit the bill of "strange." Uber-Goths with bright-colored hair and black clothes. The girls' hair was mostly an almost-fluorescent red that bordered on purple, while most of the guys had black. One of the guys had a skater cut with dreadlocks, black eyeliner and a weird, slumped look. Strange. Stranger than her. Not . . . her sort. Not that there *was* her sort anywhere.

"Miss, people are trying to walk here," a heavy-set man said as he dodged around her. He wasn't impolite about it, just sort of informative.

"Sorry, sorry . . ." she answered and moved to the side. He'd almost bumped her.

She hugged the wall and looked around. There was a sign that said "Women" down the same wall about halfway across the room. She stayed by the wall and carefully crept into the ladies', trying not to be noticed.

She finally found the refuge of a stall, slid the bolt and sat on the toilet, trying not to panic. There were just too many people, too much chaos even though the large room had had barely thirty people in it. It was just like school. People meant bullies, boys *and* girls. The cheerleaders and the football players. The Names and the In-Crowd. The people that made sure she Knew Her Place every single day. And her place was right square at the bottom.

Doris . . . She knew that much. And Bob had said to go to Dragon*Con. That there were people "like her" there. But most of the rest of it was a blur.

Okay, take stock. She was apparently at Dragon*Con. That was in Atlanta. She had a badge pinned to her shirt. It said "Doris Grisham."

That was better. Okay, sure. Doris Grisham. She'd grown up

in Mt. Union, Alabama. Her dad was a lumber cutter, worked for Weyerhaeuser 'til he got hurt, then mostly just sat in the trailer and drank. Which was what momma did *all* the time.

She'd gone to Hill Crest High. She knew that much. She'd learned her place fer sure in Hill Crest. The only place she was safe was the library. She'd *lived* in the library as much as she could.

Nearsighted, too ugly to get a date, too dumb to pass a class. That was Dumb-ass Doris. She was a total loser. A nobody. She Knew Her Place. It was to marry some redneck as dumb-ass as her and push out another passel of useless kids that'd cut wood 'til *they* got hurt and lived the rest of their life on assistance.

But that was then. Whenever *then* was. Who was she *now*? And why couldn't she remember, when Hill Crest was clear as day?

She opened up the backpack and rummaged through it. Some cheap T-shirts, mostly thin as paper from much washing. Granny underwear that wasn't much better. The baggy jeans she was wearing had holes, and they weren't stylish holes at all. Worn running shoes in "guy" colors. A T-shirt three times too large for her. Most of the ones in the bag were XXXL, for that matter.

There was a toothbrush in the bag, and a tube of lipstick. Rolling it out, Doris knew instinctively it would make her look like she had some sort of lip disease. It was completely the wrong color. So was the dusty, dry, and unused-looking pack of cheap eyeliner. Contacts. Contact solution.

All the way at the bottom of the bag was the one thing that wasn't totally generic. It was a brooch or a barrette, it could probably be used for either. Made of steel, it had a figure carved out in relief of a woman in armor driving a chariot drawn by cats. It was remarkably intricate work. Doris suspected if she had a magnifying glass, she could pick out the details of the woman's face. But it really didn't tell her much about who she was or why she was sitting in the stall, so she carefully put it away.

She checked the pockets of the jeans. A crumpled twenty and a couple of ones in her front pocket. In the back pocket, though, was a driver's license! Hallelujah!

Doris Grisham. Female. Check.

Birthday: 9/3/1984. Okay. So it really was just about her birthday.

5'9" tall. 'Bout right.

110 lbs. Huh. Liar.

Eyes: Green. Have to check a mirror.

Hair: Red. Yep.

Address: 200 River Road, Chattanooga, TN 37405.

Okay. *That* was something. She now knew she lived in Chattanooga, TN, although it really didn't ring a bell at all.

"Okay," she said, definitely. "I'm Doris Grisham. I'm from Chattanooga. I'm at Dragon*Con. I'm here to find people like me or something. How the hell, though, do I get home?"

"Honey, if you're practicing a secret identity, you might want to keep it down," said a voice in the stall next to her. "And if you're talking to your voices, take it from me, it's a bad idea. That way they'll never shut up."

"Sorry," Doris said meekly, as there was a flushing sound from the next stall.

"So which one was it?" asked the voice as the door to the next stall opened. "And if you're not gonna use the john you might as well come out. I don't bite. Mostly."

Doris cracked the stall door and looked out.

A short, darkly tanned woman was leaning up against the sinks. She was wearing a bolero jacket, a black button-down shirt, jeans, black cowboy boots and a fedora. She probably would have been pretty, if not beautiful, if a teenage case of acne hadn't left scars to shame a smallpox survivor. But button-black eyes glittering with humor somehow drew the eye away from the skin.

"I'm Mandy," the woman said, holding out her hand. "You're Doris. Or at least that's your secret identity."

"No, I really am," Doris said, desperately holding out her license. "I've got ID. I'm from . . . I live in Chattanooga."

"So you were just grounding," Mandy said, handing the license back unlooked at and taking Doris's unresisting hand to shake it. "I get it. Been there, done that, burnt the shirt. Sometimes you just got to make sure it's you talking and not the chorus. Let me tell you, Aripiprazole helps. You wouldn't want to know me if I hadn't gotten on the prescription drug wagon."

"Okay," Doris said, eyes wide.

"Not that I'm on aripiprazole," Mandy continued, turning around to wash her hands. "I finally convinced the county shrink that I was ADHD with PTSD, and not bipolar, which is what it *looks* like. Been a wonderful world lately being almost normal. I can enjoy a con and not drive everybody around me nuts. Con virgin?"

"Huh?" Doris asked, confused by the rapid changes in subject.

"Is this your first convention?" Mandy said slowly. It was clear that she wasn't doing it to make Doris sound stupid, just slowing her own patter down for the benefit of the listener.

"Uh...yes," Doris said, almost certainly.

"So who's your con-buddy?"

"Uh...?"

Doris sighed.

"Con virgin *and* no con-buddy? *And* twenty-something hot female? Honey, you could get away with that at some place like Liberty or ConStellation, but Dragon's a bit much. Let me guess. You heard about it from somebody and just drove down."

"Something like that," Doris said. *Did she have a car?*

"I've got a fair share of human charity, but," Mandy said. "The *but* being that I'm here to enjoy myself, I'm already riding herd on Traxa, and there are places you're not going to want to go that I'm headed. Not from the look of you. But if you got some decent clothes and makeup, I'd say you'd not only fit in, nobody would look at *me*, so you're *definitely not* going."

"Okay," Doris said, ducking her head.

"But that's later, and Traxa is trying to find the dealers, so I'll take you under my wing for a bit. Come on."

Doris obediently followed the woman out of the bathroom and back into the large room.

"Registration, which you just went through," Mandy said, waving to the left. "They moved all the band stalls down here since it was getting crowded upstairs. That's the Cruxshadows booth."

"Crue-shadows?" Doris said. "The Shadow of the Cross?"

"Got it in one, not bad," Mandy said. "Not a Christian myself, but doesn't mean I don't like the music."

"I like what's playing," Doris said, timidly.

"Their single, 'Birthday.' Kind of repetitive, but it's got some interesting lyrics."

"*Then tell me what really matters. Is it the money and the fame? Or how many people might eventually know your name? But maybe you touch one life, and the world becomes a better place to be. Maybe you give their dreams another day, another chance to be free,*" Doris whispered along with the song.

"Rogue kind of strikes at the heart of things," Mandy said as they passed the booth with the Goths still setting up. "Like, you are what you do. Now, me? I've got enough on my plate just trying to keep my shit together. Most I can do is maybe help a con virgin get her feet on the ground."

"Thank you," Doris said quietly as she sidled to the side to avoid being bumped again. There were a bunch of people around the escalator, and she parked in a corner by the booth, waiting for a hole to open.

"Hey, Doris," Mandy said, waving. "I've been there, like I said. But you're not going to get beat up for getting on the escalator. And if you think you can wait until it's clear, well, it will be for about twenty minutes at five AM. And you're gonna be pretty hungry and thirsty by then."

Doris still waited until there was a little gap, then darted onto the escalator. She was nearly touching a very heavyset guy wearing an Avenged Sevenfold T-shirt. His look automatically made her think of bikers, and that triggered something unhappy. But she managed to avoid being noticed and got off the escalator at the next floor.

It was much the same as the lower level but there was natural light coming in from somewhere behind the escalator, and a restaurant, currently closed, on the left wall. She realized she was in traffic and looked for a corner to get into.

"Come on, one more level," Mandy said, taking her arm. "That's the back patio where most of the smokers, and the smokers' friends, and about half the con, it seems, on Saturday night, hangs out. But since there's still not many people, we're going up to the cigar terrace."

"Not many people?" Doris squeaked. It was too crowded for her already.

"Honey, on Friday, Saturday and Sunday night it's going to be more crowded than a club," Mandy said, maneuvering her onto the next escalator by the simple expedient of hip-checking a skinny guy with a T-shirt that said ALL I EVER NEEDED TO LEARN I LEARNED FROM D&D out of the way. "Sorry."

"No problem," the kid said. "Hey, can I take your picture?"

"Maybe when we get to the top, if security doesn't stop us," Mandy said. "And no taking pictures of my butt on the escalator."

The escalator debouched into an enormous lobby. The building from there up was entirely open-plan with a bank of glass elevators on the south side and multi-story windows on the east. In the middle was a modern-art sculpture that stretched all the way to the roof, and thinking about it, Doris realized it went down into the basement area where she'd met Mandy. People in a variety of dress, from normal streetwear to costumes, were wandering around the lobby, many of them greeting each other.

At the top of the escalator, Mandy got out of the way of the traffic and struck a pose.

"Go for it."

The guy fumbled with a digital camera for a second, then snapped a photo.

"Would it be okay if I . . . took one of your friend?"

"Uh . . ." Doris said nervously.

"You can do it," Mandy said, firmly. "Stand here, do the same thing I did."

Doris stood up straight, got a frozen rictus of a grin on her face and tried not to panic as the kid took her picture.

"Thanks," the gamer said, grinning happily. "Thanks."

"Why did he just take our picture?" Doris whispered as they walked towards a bar.

"That's what guys do at Dragon*Con," Mandy said. "Well, and game and party and drink and go to panels hungover and talk and . . . Well, that's what guys do at Dragon*Con, take pictures of costumes and pretty girls and especially pretty girls in costumes. The one with the most pictures of hot babes wins."

"So why did he take *my* picture?" Doris asked.

"The one with the most pictures of hot babes wins," Mandy repeated. "I'm just wondering why he took *mine*. Probably so I'd talk you into getting yours taken, come to think of it."

"Oh," Doris said, still puzzled. "What do girls do at Dragon*Con?"

"Oh, all the other stuff," Mandy said as they got near the bar. "And see how many guys take their pictures. The one that gets the most pictures taken of her wins."

The bar was separated from the lobby only by a two-story wall and was already starting to fill up. Doris stopped in shock as a Wookiee came around a table and, with the help of a friend in street clothes, slowly negotiated his way onto the main lobby floor.

At the bar was a stormtrooper, his helmet sitting on the bartop, drinking a Guinness and talking with a guy in Jedi robes while a rather heavyset woman in a Princess Leia slave-girl outfit listened in. Two of Monty Python's knights were sharing a beer at a table, Bedevere constantly having to lift his face-shield to take a sip.

A slightly overweight and -age Fantastic Four were at another table, Mister Fantastic fumbling with a floppy arm, trying to pick up a drink while the other three ignored him. Wolverine, on the other hand, was pointing a claw and laughing from not far away.

There were at least five times as many people in street clothes as the costumes, but it was definitely the costumes that stood out.

"Fun, huh?" Mandy asked. "Seen enough? We're going that way," she added, pointing to the glass back wall.

Glass doors led to a twenty-by-twenty partially covered patio where a couple of groups were already gathering to smoke. One was parked in a corner by the door and had not only seized most of the tables but all the chairs.

The members were mostly in their thirties or forties and seemed to be centered around a man wearing a pair of shorts and a fishing shirt.

"Mandy hath arriv'ed," the man said. "And she brings new blood. Quite pulchritudinous blood, I might add."

"Be nice, Folsom," Mandy said. "She's a con virgin. Her name's Doris. She's from Chattanooga."

"Ah, the Mountain City. Almost lived there once," Folsom said, his brow furrowing.

"Almost lived there?"

Doris wondered for a second who had asked the question and then realized it was her.

"Yes," Folsom said. "Almost moved there. Not sure quite why I didn't, but water over the bridge, as they say. And what is your quest at Dragon*Con, my dear?"

"Oh, not a quest," Doris said, shifting her feet uncomfortably. The attention was starting to scare her.

"The lady needs a chair," Folsom said, gently. "And a drink, methinks. Nonalcoholic, for the nonce," he added, pulling out a twenty. "The surrenderer of a chair does not get the drink."

A bearded man smoking a pipe stood up and waved for Doris to sit. Another took the twenty and went inside.

"Everyone is on a quest," Folsom intoned. "Always. People say that they have no goals. Pish. Everyone has goals they just haven't looked closely enough at themselves. Mandy's goal is to get her shit straight, although I think she underestimates herself. Todd's is to become Bill Gates or somesuch, whether he internalizes that or not."

"And yours?" one of the group asked, grinning.

"To have people say 'Harry who? I'm dying for the next Folsom Duncan book to come out,'" Folsom said, grinning disparagingly. "An unlikely goal to attain, I'll admit, but a worthy one nonetheless. Forget trying to find an old bone or two, seek the damned Holy Grail! You may fail, probably will based on historical record, but you'll fail *grandly*! And undoubtedly find an old bone somewhere on the way. So, what is your quest, young lady? What do *you* want from Dragon*Con? Think before you answer, take a deep breath and expound. We are muchly ears."

He pulled a thin cigar out of a breast pocket, lit it and leaned back unthreateningly. He seemed to be actually interested in the answer.

She thought about it for the first time. Really thought about it. Why was she here? What did she want from the con? Well, practical first.

"I need to find a ride home," she admitted.

"Alas, I don't know anyone going to Chattanooga," Folsom said. "And it would have to be a trusted source. That problem shall be solved in time, I'm sure. But what do you want from the *con*? Why are you here? Not how are you to leave."

"I want to find people like me," Doris said.

"Ah, now we get to some really interesting answers," Folsom said, happily. "Because they beg more questions. Todd, throw me a question to that answer?"

"Uhm...Who are you?" Todd said. "I mean...To find people like you, you need to know who you are?"

"Exactly," Folsom said. "Ever read military science fiction?"

"I don't think so..." Doris said, uncertainly.

"Interested in the military?"

"Not really."

"Know a platoon from a company?"

"No."

"Then we are not people like you," Folsom said. "That is not rejecting you. Far be it. I do so desire lovely ladies around but, alas, few of my books appeal to the fairer sex in large numbers. I misdoubt that you will remain long in our company, not because you shall be cast out, but because you will find your own path.

"However, we might help to put your feet upon it. To show you the beginning of the yellow brick road to both who *you* are and who are *your* people. Both, I assure you, can be found at Dragon*Con. The Dragon has something for everyone, even the occasional mundane that wanders in. To do so would be a corporal work of mercy, and I need those to my credit. So we must find your needs, wants and desires and perhaps steer you in an appropriate direction. But I do have one suggestion of an interesting *true* quest, if you will. One that, from my reading of your personality, would be a far jump on that yellow brick road."

"Yes?" Doris said, totally confused.

"Have you, perchance, looked at the cover of the program book?" Folsom said, grinning.

"No?"

"Might I suggest you extract it from the bag and do so," Folsom replied.

Doris pulled out the program book, a thick, magazine-sized booklet, and looked at the cover. The cover art was of a red-haired girl in a green bodysuit, leaning against a mirror. Behind her was what looked like the leg of a gigantic monster. On the face reflected in the mirror were either three tears or a tattoo of them.

"Okay," Doris said. "I looked at it."

"Like the young lady on the cover, have you looked in a mirror lately?" Folsom said, gently.

"I don't look *anything* like *her*," Doris insisted.

"Au contraire," Folsom replied. "The difference is a bit of makeup and a costume. I have never seen such a perfect example of a potential Dawn contestant in my life. You are, my dear, her spitting image. To actually win the contest, of course, requires also a suitable costume, poise and a bit of acting ability. But the potential I see before me is astounding. Seek the Grail! You may pick up a few bones and whatnot. Know anything about costuming?"

"No?" Doris said then paused. "I can sew, though." She didn't know where that bit of information came from, but it was certain.

"You're ninety percent of the way there, then," Folsom said. "Or so I'm told. To the cobbler his last. I avoid the entire track like the plague. I'd suggest, however, if you have any interest, that you consider hanging out around the costuming track. Fellow that runs it appears to be a bit of a letch, but he's mostly bark. But he is more than willing, as am I, to spend a bit more time on a lovely young lady than your average costumer. A lovely young lady who can sew would make his heart go pitter-pat."

"I still couldn't do *that*," Doris said, looking at the cover.

"Could not or would not?" Folsom asked softly. "If you *choose* not to dress that way, for your own purposes, for your own personality, that is one thing. If you choose not to participate because of fear or shame or the pressure of society, that is another. To find 'your people,' you must first know who *you* are. Are you a person who hides behind a mask of oversized clothing from an innate prudishness? Or someone who hides her person to hide herself? You won't be young forever. Who do you want to be before you die?"

"Those are the words from the song playing downstairs," Doris said.

"Rogue and I are friends," the man said. "He strikes to the heart of many questions. Who are you, Doris Grisham, and more to the point, who do you *want* to be?"

"Folsom, you have a panel," the man with the pipe said.

"Damn and blast," Folsom said, standing up. "I just get to chatting up an exquisite example of the fairer sex and they make me work. Anyway, Doris, I hope you enjoy the con. You'll often find us out here on the terrace or downstairs slowly killing ourselves with alcohol, tar and nicotine. Feel free to pop in and tell us how your con is going."

"Okay," Doris said as the group broke up. A couple of the men appeared torn between following Folsom or staying with the pretty girl, but they all eventually left.

"So what to do with myself now?" she asked as if expecting an answer.

The answer was her stomach rumbling. Okay, food.

She thought about her limited funds and frowned.

"Okay," she muttered. "*Cheap* food."

One look at the prices in the restaurant put her off of that. She couldn't even afford the buffet. There was a food court attached to the hotels, but the prices there weren't much better. With the few bucks in her pocket she might get two meals.

She knew she'd been short on food in her life. She wasn't sure when or why and was curiously disinterested. It was as if the life before arriving at the convention was a dream, that only the convention was real. But her hunger was real enough and affecting her concentration.

Asking questions was out. There was an information booth setting up, but even asking people whose job it was to answer questions was out. She could barely make her way through the crowds, and it was beyond imagination that she could ever show herself as openly as Duncan had suggested.

On the other hand, she had program books in the bag she was still carrying. She found an out-of-the-way corner and opened them up.

They were strangely cluttered with information, some of it useful and some not. She found the information about the "costuming" track, but only a brief description of the track itself, and most of the panel descriptions were confusing. What, for example, was an "appliance"? It raised strange thoughts in Doris's head.

However, while poking around in other features of the con, she found out that there was something called a "con suite," that it was open twenty-four hours a day and that, glory be, it served food.

A goal. A quest. And, as it turned out, it had been right around the corner from where she'd been talking to Duncan.

Now to find her way *back*. Where was that map?

"Eat, you greedy gluts!" a resonant voice boomed as Doris made her way into the con suite.

The suite, a large set of rooms on the second floor of the Hyatt, was crowded. Doris tried very hard not to make contact with any of the people in the room, most of them kids even younger than her, but it was nearly impossible. It seemed that sixty or seventy people must have crowded into the room as soon as the food was put out.

By the door were piles of cups and large containers of ice. Then a drink dispenser with various soft drinks. Arrayed against the far wall, the target of most of the people crowding into the room, was a set of tables piled with hot dogs, buns and a large crock pot of chili.

"Feed your maggoty bellies from the largesse provided by your loving con! Fill your bottomless pits. Feast, feast, you ravenous hordes!"

The voice was produced by a tall, handsome black man wearing an incongruous Star Trek uniform. Parked towards the back of the room, he seemed to subtly bend the attention of the entire room around him. There were several people standing nearby, many of them apparently trying to get his attention, but he appeared to know what most of them were going to say before they said it.

"More rolls, less hot dogs," he said, sending one of the minions into the throng. "The Coke's already running low." Another darted off.

A heavyset blond man came out of the back room bearing a pile of trays. He looked at the gathered group in annoyance.

"These need to go in the other kitchen," he said, and was roundly ignored.

"I'll get them," Doris said. "Where's the other kitchen?"

"Far room," the guy said in an aggrieved tone, then went back in the kitchen.

"'Kay."

Doris carried the trays through the throng, glad to be doing something that would make her unnoticed. Nobody noticed you if you were working.

She found the other kitchen and dropped the trays on the sink, the only open surface. It seemed every other surface was covered by food or the makings thereof.

Instead of getting in line she went back to the group gathered around the black man, wondering if she should help out more. As far as she could tell, the group gathered around the leader was supposed to be working, but nobody seemed to be actually doing anything.

"Peter!" the man boomed, looking at the tables. "Peter!"

"What?" the blond man said, coming back out of the kitchen.

"Where is the coleslaw? There is a distinct lack of coleslawness!"

"That's because there's a distinct lack of roominess in this refrigerator," the blond man said in an aggrieved tone. "It's in the other kitchen. I've been trying to get someone to get it for the last thirty minutes."

"Peter, Peter, Peter," the black man said, taking him gently by the shoulder. "If I have told you once I have told you a thousand times. The minions of the con suite are zombies. You must treat them as such."

He spun in place and grabbed one of the group by the shoulder, turning him to look into his eye.

"Thomas," he intoned. "Thomas, you shall obey my every command."

"Yes, master," the boy replied. "Unless it's something sexual, in which case, screw you."

"Of course. Thomas. You shall lurch your way across the room to the far kitchen. There you shall open up the refrigerator—it is the large upright box against the wall. You shall remove from it the coleslaw and place it upon the table at the far end, where the heavyset kid in the Miskatonic University T-shirt with the forlorn expression, probably due to a lack of coleslaw, is standing. Place it upon the table. Remove the coverings from the coleslaw. Stand back lest you are eaten by the ravenous hordes. Then lurch back here for more tasks."

"Yes, master," the boy said.

"Do not eat any brains on the way," the man noted.

"Yes, master," the grinning boy said and turned, arms out, to lurch into the crowd.

"Lurch faster!" he boomed, then turned back to his assistant. "There, Peter. That is how to control your minions. Mind control is the best control."

"Got it," Peter said, frowning.

"I took the trays over to the kitchen," Doris said, getting a word in edgewise. "Is there anything else you need?"

"And who is this who performs tasks in my con suite yet bears not the lanyard of staff?" the black man asked. "Speak to us, O lady of beauty and worth!"

"Uh," Doris replied.

"I see thy name is Doris," the man said. "Shane Gomez is my name, and *I* am the *master* of the con suite, the *feeder* of the hordes, the *supplier of provender* to the faceless masses. God of Feasting!

"Thank you," he added, in a much gentler tone. "I appreciate the assistance. And while I'd take you up on your offer to help more, alas, we are required to put anyone on staff through the mandatory training courses where their brains are removed and replaced by straw so that the zombies—the other zombies, that is—don't eat them. Since your brains are clearly not straw, I must regretfully decline more assistance for your own safety. Besides, right now I've got enough people. But feel free to grab a bite to eat before it's all gone. In fact..."

He took Doris gently by the elbow and walked to the head of the line.

"This is Doris," he said to the kid who was next up to the table. "She has performed service beyond compare to the good of the con and to the good of the con suite. In doing so, she lost her place in line. I, as master of the con suite, do now place her in front of you. Problems?"

"No problem, Shane," the tow-haired kid said, sticking out his hand. "Looking good. How you doing this year?"

"Too soon to tell, really," Shane replied in a much more normal voice as he shook the proferred hand. "But it looks good so far. Take care, man."

"You too," the kid replied, waving Doris in front of him. "Eat up. Most of the good stuff will be gone before you know it."

Doris snagged a hot dog, chips and coleslaw, then went back around to get a drink. She found a corner that wasn't occupied and filled her stomach, then considered her situation.

Food was covered. She wasn't sure where she could sleep, though. She didn't have enough money for a hotel room, and from passing conversations she'd overheard, she knew all the hotels were full, anyway.

Cross that bridge when she got tired. Right now she had to think. With some food on her stomach that was actually a possibility.

She pulled out the program book again and read it more carefully. All the programming track stuff started tomorrow. So she had until then to think about what she wanted to do. Who she wanted to be, as Duncan had put it.

The nice thing about the con, she realized, was the anonymity. Nobody knew her, she didn't have any defined place, nobody was really paying her any attention at all. She realized in a flash that she could be *anybody* she *wanted* to be. She didn't have to be Dumb-ass Doris. She could create a *new* Doris.

She looked at the cover of the main program and frowned. She wasn't sure she could be the person on the cover, but it had a certain allure. It wasn't as if she didn't want to be noticed, didn't want to be liked. She just didn't want to be harassed because of it. If you were pretty, guys took pictures of you. They didn't stuff you in a locker because you'd pissed off their girlfriends.

She could be anybody she wanted to be. So *who* did she *want* to be?

Chapter Two

*M*s. Rickels," Germaine said. "This is Lady Lithram, our local contact."

Janea had been moved to a safe house not far from the hospital. The neighborhood was seedy, and Sharice would normally consider the location not particularly secure. However, Germaine had also arranged for four "executive protection specialists" from Atlanta to maintain security around the clock. In addition, there were nurses monitoring Janea at all times and an on-call MD. On the mystic side, the house was owned by Memorial Hospital, a Catholic hospital. Sharice felt mildly out of place only because the defenses of the house, which were *formidable*, were so clearly Christian.

When Germaine made certain phone calls to certain people, things could get done very quickly.

"Lady Lithram," Sharice said, shaking her hand. Lady Lithram was stocky, with short blonde hair, blue eyes and a figure that spoke of manual labor. Her hands were roughly calloused. "I'd prefer traditional rites. No skyclad."

"Of course, madame," the Wiccan priestess said, nodding. "And may I introduce my husband, Lord Korgan?"

"Lord Korgan," Sharice said, shaking the man's hand. Lord Korgan was quite short, slender, and unusually for Wicca, black. He was dressed in jeans and a flannel shirt, but had ceremonial robes over his shoulder. "I'm glad to see that both poles are represented."

"The universe is balance," Lady Lithram said. "Light and dark, male and female. Only molds don't need balance, and who loves mold?"

"Indeed," Sharice said, grinning. "You're a gardener."

"We're landscapers," Lady Lithram said. "Which mostly means cutting grass to the level it would be shorn by grazers. But I do a nice flowerbed."

"I suspect they're better than the owners realize," Sharice said. "Tell me about the local powers."

"Very bad," Lady Lithram said. "Very negative."

"Negative or dark?" Sharice asked.

"Negative," Lord Korgan said. "We have walked the dark paths. This is . . . different."

"There are at least three long-term demonic residents," Lady Lithram said. "And a very large body of supporters. Satanists," she added, nearly spitting.

"They perform their black rites in Chickamauga Park," Lord Korgan said, tiredly. "We oppose their powers as well as we can, but Wiccans . . ."

"Don't fight well," Sharice said, nodding. "Some, anyway. If we have major demons in the area, why weren't we called in earlier?"

"They are generational possessors," Lady Lithram said, frowning. "They live in families, some of the more powerful in the area. Chattanooga is a very strange place, one of the few medium cities that is still 'owned,' if you will, by a handful of families. Some of those, not all, are generationally possessed. They keep the city small and manageable because it suits their purposes. Then there are more outside the powerful inner circle, but controlling towns in the area. Again, we do what we can to turn aside their more evil essences, but the Madness killings have been long coming. Something is rising, perhaps by their action, perhaps against their wishes, but definitely linked to them."

"We're supposed to be here," a loud voice boomed from the front of the house. "Check the damned list."

"Ah, I see Hjalmar is here," Sharice said, smiling. "Asatru."

"We can deal," Lady Lithram said, grinning.

"The reinforcements are here," Hjalmar said, hefting his ceremonial axe. He was accompanied by another man, short, thin, black-haired and -eyed, and covered in tattoos.

"Hjalmar," Sharice said, smiling. "Don't tell me you're going to join a circle?"

"The sacrifices I make for Frey," the massive, blond, bearded man said, giving her a spine-cracking bear hug. "But I'm going to stand outside the circle. This is a very nonviolent coven; I'm afraid I would create a disturbance in the Force."

"You *are* a disturbance in the Force," Sharice said. "Drakon."

The adept shook her hand abruptly and nodded sharply.

"I am here to assist as you need," he said. "Please continue your conversation."

"And the Lady-damned Satanists do not help," Lord Korgan said, sighing again. "We cannot prove it, but we believe they have begun true blood rites using homeless. It's possible some of the Madness killings are linked to them as well. They certainly perform animal sacrifice. There are times when parts of Chickamauga park are filled with the bodies of dead animals. No black cat is safe. And they try to pass themselves off as pagans!"

"Where we're going is liable to be dangerous," Sharice said. "Especially with that sort of spiritual atmosphere. Keep on your toes."

"Wah-Keng will watch over me, Lady Darkfire," the adept replied. "I should not require assistance."

"Hopefully," Sharice said.

"You're Lady Darkfire?" Lord Korgan said, his eyes wide.

"Only when I put on a robe," Sharice replied, grinning. "Until then I'm just Sharice. We need two more. Then we must go to your power center."

"They're on their way," Lady Lithram said. "You know Wiccans..."

"Herding cats is easier," Sharice said. "Well, let's get on our game face. We've got a soul to save."

"Doris, right?"

Doris turned and was surprised to see Folsom Duncan. She had been hanging around the cigar terrace half in anticipation of running across the only group she'd interacted with so far. But none of the people she recognized had been around. But it was still just past sunrise, so that wasn't surprising.

"Sleep okay?" Duncan asked.

"Didn't sleep at all," Doris admitted. She could feel the fatigue tugging at her, but sleep hadn't even been close to a possibility.

She'd spent the whole night in one corner or another watching the congoers. It was more or less how she'd spent high school, watching all the kids socialize around her and never being able to break in.

"That will catch up with you, quick," Duncan said, yawning. "My sleep schedule is totally off. I was up late and I should still be in bed, but it was not to be. Have you had breakfast?"

"Yes," Doris said, quietly. The con suite had donuts and coffee.

"Well, let me get you a mocha or something," Duncan said, leading her to the coffee shop in the corner of the hotel. "Given any thought to how you want to spend the con? I'll admit I probably came on too hard. You can do anything you want, it's your con, not mine."

"I gave it a lot of thought," Doris admitted. She'd had hours to think about it.

"I'm not sure it was worth a lot of thought," Duncan said, laughing gently.

"No, it was," Doris said. "I know who I am. I know why I am that way. I'm not sure it's who I *want* to be. Or even who I *should* be. Does that make any sense?"

"Yes," Duncan admitted. "People come to the Dragon for various reasons. Most come to have fun. Some come to see people, minor celebrities..."

"You?" Doris asked.

"I don't classify myself that way," Duncan said. "Some come to interact with friends they've made at previous cons. Costumers come to show off their talents. But a few, a special few, if you will, come to find who they truly are. They have been hammered into a certain mold, and it's a mold with which they are uncomfortable. To the Dragon they are all one. They are all the children of the Dragon: the stormtroopers and the Leias, the Dawn contestants and the guys taking their picture are all equal in the eyes of the Dragon. There's a song, probably before your time, about masks. The Stranger. *We all have a face that we hide away forever, and we take them out and show ourselves when everyone has gone. Some are satin, some are steel, some are silk and some are leather. They're the faces of the Stranger but we love to try them on.*

"What some find from the Dragon is that the face of the Stranger is *theirs*. In your sleeplessness do you have any idea who you want to be?"

"Yes," Doris said, pulling out the program book. "You were right. I want to be her. But you see that suit of armor behind her?"

"The one that she seems to shrink from or possibly draw upon?"

"Yep," Doris said, looking at the cover. "I want to kick its ass. I'm tired of being afraid. I'm tired of being...who I was. I want to be somebody better. Somebody stronger."

"Then fortune may have sent you to the right corner of the con," Duncan said as they reached the head of the line. "When you're actually ready to start kicking ass, look me up. I have friends who can aid you there. I'll take a venti mocha, no whip. Doris...?"

Sharice looked up at the blast of a car horn and darted across the road, making it to the sidewalk safely.

"Odin's Eye," Hjalmar muttered. "I think the spell went astray. This does *not* look like the Moon Paths."

The threesome had manifested on a city street. On their side was the back of a large building with a vehicle pull-through. Some people were filtering out of doors at the back of the building and heading down to cross the street. On the far side of the street was a large Hilton hotel.

"Dragon*Con," Drakon said, looking at the marquee for the Hilton. "We're behind the Marriott. Downtown Atlanta. Wonder which day it is?"

"Dragon*Con, huh?" Hjalmar said. "Always wanted to get there. So are we on the Moon Paths or not? Or did we shift in space and time?"

"It's the Moon Paths," Sharice said. "I think it's a metaphorical representation. An interesting one. I'm not sure who is generating the metaphor. It *might* be Janea. If so, I'd like to know why."

"May be hard to find her," Drakon pointed out as a statuesque redhead in high heels and a schoolgirl outfit walked past. "With the Dawn contest, there are about six *thousand* redheads at Dragon*Con."

"Janea stands out in any sort of crowd," Sharice said, biting her lip. "But that's not the tough part. We need to figure out the rules of this place. Let's go find someplace to sit down and consider."

The hotel was already a bit crowded, but they found a comfortable conversation set of chairs and a table on the main floor of the hotel.

"I've been thinking," Sharice said.

"That sounds ungood," Hjalmar opined. "Do you think we can get a drink or something? I wasn't expecting to be thirsty on the Moon Paths."

"That's the sort of thing I was thinking," Sharice admitted. She had a purse and opened it up. "Any of you got any money?"

"Thirty bucks, more or less," Drakon said, pulling out a leather wallet on a chain. It had a Chinese dragon embossed on it, to no one's surprise. "And a driver's license. That's about it."

"'Bout two hundred," Hjalmar said, going through the pockets of his cargo pants. "And a driver's license, Visa check card, and a room key in a pack with the room number on it. I'm here in the Marriott. 2738."

"I've got about five hundred, a Visa and an American Express," Sharice said. "Also a room key, 2739."

She got up and walked over to a nearby ATM, used it and came back.

"And I've got five thousand in my account," she said, sitting down. "Okay, interesting."

"Power equals money?" Hjalmar asked. "Relative power is about the same. That's a pretty simple metaphor."

"But one that works in this environment," Sharice said. "But we're not going to want to get into any fights."

"That sucks," Drakon said.

"Because if we do, we get hauled to jail?" Hjalmar asked. "What happens then?"

"I'm not sure," Sharice said. "But I think getting stuck on the Moon Paths is the least of your worries."

"So who are all the people?" Drakon asked. "I hadn't expected the Moon Paths to be so...crowded."

"At a guess?" Sharice said. "The staff are representatives or one or another of the gods. The leaders of each department may be gods themselves. But this has to be some sort of a neutral zone and I'd guess the police and security keep it that way. That's why we don't want to get into any fights. The rest of them? Sleeping people caught in dream. The deceased who are stuck in a sort of limbo. Christian purgatory? Demons and spirits of one sort or another. Angels, for that matter. We're going to have to *think* our way through this."

"Blast," Hjalmar said. "Maybe you should bring someone else."

"I just have to hope there's a reason we're all here," Sharice said, biting her lip. "So you're stuck."

"Speaking of which, how do we get back?" Drakon asked. "Normally you concentrate on your silver cord."

"You can see it if you open to it enough," Sharice said. "Hang on."

She closed her eyes and a moment later started to yawn.

"I tugged at the connection and got tired," she said. "I'd guess that when we sleep we'll go back."

"Isn't that sort of backwards?" Hjalmar asked. "The astral plane is the world of the *ka*, the sleeping mind. The world of dream. We go back by dreaming?"

"Which is the dream and which is the reality?" Sharice said, grinning. "But that's not getting us anywhere. We've got money, power, and a mission: Find Janea. Let's get to it."

"There's just one problem," Drakon said.

"Which is?"

"Are we preregistered?"

"Thor's left testicle," Hjalmar grunted. "Would you *look* at that *line*?"

Just as the Marriott had backed on the Hilton, the Hyatt backed on the Marriott. And running down the entire block was a line of people. Since they had been directed there to go to registration, they were apparently supposed to get in the line.

A police officer was directing traffic between the two hotels, and as he waved for people to cross, they headed over to the line.

"How long do you think it is?" Hjalmar asked.

"Long," Drakon said. "One of the reasons I always prereg. Let's go find the end."

The end, as it turned out, was around the block, down the end, and nearly to the front of the hotel.

"Dude, I'm *so* going to preregister next year," said the guy in front of them, a sallow kid in black clothes.

"Like, totally," agreed his companion, a shorter guy with a dozen piercings. "Or come in on Thursday."

"It's been like this since last night when we opened," a tall, dark-haired man wearing a headset said, handing them both tickets. "And this *is* the prereg line. Also day passes. That's your place in line in case you have to go to the head or something. Line's about three hours long. You'll get there eventually."

"Thanks," Hjalmar said, looking at the ticket. "I hope that the number on here isn't our *actual* place in line. It's in the millions."

"Doubt it," Drakon said, chuckling. "There's not *that* many people here."

"How, by Odin's eyes, are we going to find Janea in all this?" Hjalmar asked.

"I've been to Dragon a couple of times," Drakon admitted. "Thing is, the way the hotels are laid out, just about everyone comes down the back steps to the Hyatt at one point or another. Most of the programming is in the Hyatt, especially the evening stuff, and it's where all the parties are. Sooner or later, Janea's going to pass that point. The thing is…"

"We're going to have to watch it like a hawk," Sharice said. "Take shifts. Someone's always got to be there."

"That is going to be buckets of fun," Hjalmar said. "I'll take first watch."

"You got it," Drakon said. "I'll take second. By midnight or so it's pretty pointless. We can crash then and get back to the mortal realm to find out what's happening out there."

"Since we've got the tickets," Sharice said, "Drakon, go in and find a program so we can get some idea where Janea might turn up. Hjalmar…"

"Go stand by the back of the hotel and watch for Janea," Hjalmar said.

"Right," Sharice said as the line crept forward. She pulled out a twenty and handed it to Drakon. "Get us some drinks while you're at it. I'll hold our place in line."

"Yes, Mistress," Drakon said, grinning. "I know one place we're definitely going to find her, though."

"Where?" Sharice asked.

"The Dawn contest," Drakon said. "It's got a thousand-dollar prize. That's power she can use. And she's a natural."

"But it's not until Monday," Sharice said. "The question is, can she survive 'til Monday?"

As Folsom entered the restroom, a massive black man in a Blade costume nearly ran him down coming out.

"Whoa," Folsom said. "Nice costume."

The man paused and nodded as if in thanks, then leaned forward and sniffed several times. He surveyed Folsom for a moment longer, turned to look outwards as if peering through the walls of the bathroom, then nodded and walked out.

Folsom lifted one arm and sniffed. He'd showered no more than an hour ago...

"Hmmm..." he said, looking towards the door. "Try Costuming."

Doris knew she should be tired, and in a distant way, she was. But mostly she was interested. She'd gotten over to the Hilton early and then sat through four hours of programming on costuming. She was even starting to understand the lingo. An "appliance" was an accessory to the costume: a mask, for example. Raiding was digging stuff out of dumpsters. Since just about anything could be turned into a costume, raiding was an old and accepted practice.

And she knew more about uses of hot glue than she'd ever wanted to know. One of the panelists had at least a hundred suggestions for how to use hot glue. It was like she was hot-glue obsessed.

Most of the panelists were the same people, and by the end of the third panel, she had worked up the courage to go up and ask questions.

Bran Carlson was the head of the track, and while he was only "on" the first panel, she'd spotted him coming in and out of other panels. He came into the meeting room at the end of the third panel, so she screwed up her courage and walked up to him.

"Hi, I'm Doris," she said, trying not to sound like a frightened newbie.

"Well, hello, Doris," Bran said with just a shade too much familiarity. "And what can I do for you?"

"I'm not sure if you *can* do anything for me," Doris said. "But Folsom said I should talk to you."

"I must remember to thank him," Bran said, grinning. "What's up?"

"I'm...a newbie," she admitted. "Con and costuming. But so far, three people have told me I should enter the Dawn contest. The thing is..."

"All you have are street clothes," Bran said, his grin dying. "Right?"

"Right," Doris said, trying not to wince. The people in the panels, both the panelists and most of the attendees, had clearly spent years, and thousands of dollars, building up their stock of costumes, materials, tools and appliances. What Doris was asking was for someone to simply step in and for no good reason help her out.

"Besides the fact that you're pretty, why did Folsom suggest I help you?" Bran asked, all trace of flirtatiousness gone. He wasn't rejecting, he was just suddenly immensely professional.

"I don't really know," Janea said. "He's been talking about, well, finding myself, I guess. It sounds stupid, I know, especially with something like the Dawn contest. He says it better."

"Oh, God, he didn't trot out that horrid old Billy Joel song, did he?"

"Something about faces and masks?" Doris asked. "Yeah."

"The man needs to get a life," Bran said with a sigh. "But he has a point. The problem is . . . the problems *are* . . . Anita!"

"Yo, Bran?"

The woman was the hot-glue fanatic and on her way out the door, having shaken off the last questioner. Medium height, blonde and pleasantly plump, she was wearing a multi-colored, fur-trimmed robe and a pair of antlers.

"Folsom has seen fit to present me with a challenge," Bran said. "This young lady is a newbie. A costuming newbie and a con newbie. She has no materials nor tools. She has, I suspect, very little in the way of available funds. Folsom wants me to get her ready to win the Dawn contest. In addition to running this madhouse of a track!"

"Are you going to?" Anita asked.

"Depends on how much help I can get," Bran said. "Up for a challenge? Question . . . Doris. There's a rather substantial prize involved. Are you planning on spreading the wealth if you win?"

"Of course," Doris said. "I mean, I need enough money to get a ride home, but you can have all the rest."

"Wouldn't want that much," Bran said. "But I do this professionally. We'll come to an equitable arrangement. You in, Anita?"

"Maybe," Anita said, walking around Doris and inspecting her like a prize steer. "She's got the looks, I think. Hard to tell under the clothes. Attitude: two. Major work there. Doing Dawn takes a ten attitude. And then there's the question of costume. The easiest would be..."

"No costume is no costume," Bran said. "Disqualification."

"Excuse me?" Doris said. "What's that mean? I can't wear street clothes?"

"You could, but you'd never win," Anita replied. "What Bran was saying is that occasionally a contestant simply wears *no* costume. As in nothing. *Au naturale. En dishabille.* Naked. Gets a hell of a round of applause, but it's a disqualifier. Security also gets involved."

"Uh..." Doris said, blushing. "I don't think I could..."

"There have been Dawn winners that were clothed so fully you could barely see they were female," Bran said. "But they had costumes that were, well, too elaborate for any reasonable chance we could make them in the next couple of days. Not to mention the cost. So one thing you're going to have to get your head around is that you're probably going to have to walk out in front of eight thousand strangers, if not nude, then damned close. If you can't consider that, we might as well quit now."

Doris thought about that and shivered involuntarily. The thought terrified her and at the same time, honestly, thrilled her just a bit. She wasn't sure where that tendril of exhibitionism was coming from. In her heart she'd always wanted to be the pretty one, the noticed one. She hid because every time she tried to be noticed it had meant pain—mental, generally, but occasionally physical. But a part of her...

Was that what Duncan had been driving at? Was that her Stranger? And was it a Stranger or her true self? Could she get up in front of thousands of people, how was it Bran put it? Damned near nude?

Yes, she could. She *would*. She would do it. Because she suspected that strain of exhibitionism was more "her" than the shrinking wallflower she was now. And if she didn't, she'd never know.

But the truth was...

"If I had to do it tonight, no," she said. "But I will do it for the contest. I *can* do it. Will do it. I just need..."

"Don't say time," Anita said. "Or you're just stalling."

"No, I need practice," Doris said. "I need to work up to it.

Look, I'm just getting over my fear of crowds, okay? I'm going to have to get used to being...damned near nude around people. Fast. Or you're right, it won't work."

"So now you need more than *one* costume," Bran said, frowning.

"Hey, we're experts," Anita said. "In for a penny and all that. But here's the question. Do you have any skills in costuming at all? Or do you expect us to do all the work?"

"I can sew," Doris said. "I can sew really well."

"That is music to my ears," Bran said, grinning. "Because we may lay out the costume and do some of the appliances, but the big time-eater will be the sewing. If you can *really* sew, this is doable."

"Okay, you need a costume for tonight," Anita said, walking around her again. "And that, we *don't* have time to sew."

"Despite the red hair, let's go Oriental," Bran said. "I've got a kimono that might fit her. That's pretty full coverage up, just showing a hint of cleavage. That way you can get used to being seen without too much boob showing. It's going to be short, though."

"I can handle that," Doris said, gulping. "But...can I have a mask?"

"Hot glue is your friend, there," Anita said.

"Why did I *know* you were going to say that?" Bran asked, shaking his head.

"Thanks," Hjalmar said, taking the bottle of water from Sharice. "Any luck?"

They'd gotten registered, finally. It was nearly four by the time they were fully in place to start searching, and so far he hadn't seen Janea pass by. He'd seen two or three girls that had the same look, but none of them Janea. Three hours in the hot Atlanta sun were wearing on him but he wasn't going to stop looking. Janea wasn't just a friend, she was a gydia of his Hearth, and the Asatru did not leave a Hearth member stuck on the astral plane. He'd stand out here until he keeled over from heatstroke first.

"Nada," Sharice said. "I cruised the Marriott, then headed over to the Hilton to look through the Dealers Room and the Exhibitors Hall. Drakon has been covering the Hyatt and he hasn't seen her."

"Speaking of the Dealers Room," Hjalmar said. "Are you absolutely certain we're not going to get into a furball here?"

"I hope not," Sharice replied. "There's security everywhere. Mystically, if I'm getting the metaphor right, that means that if you don't toe the line you're going to get stuck in a lower plane. Hel or Niflheim, in your case. There are places on the Moon Paths like that, places where you tread lightly or not at all. Think of it as a no-PVP section of an online game. I'm not even sure you *can* attack another entity."

"So *we* are not going to get attacked and *she* is not going to get attacked," Hjalmar said. "You're positive?"

"You're not, I can tell," Sharice said.

"Call it my Viking side," Hjalmar replied, shrugging. "I'm seeing a lot of weaponry. Sure, most of it is totally costuming. I don't know what the reality of a plastic stormtrooper blaster is in this metaphor. But somebody used one hell of a lot of astral energy to get her stuck here. And Janea wasn't going to take that sort of thing lying down. She's a second-level adept and an Asatru, not a fluffy bunny hugger. She went out fighting, guaranteed. So... I don't see them, whoever *them* is, just leaving her alone. And why here? What's the significance of us being here? Of *her* being here? Not only the 'here' of Dragon*Con, but this particular section of the astral plane."

"You *really* want me to get into a discussion of astral synchronicity and potentialities?" Sharice asked.

"Uh...no," Hjalmar admitted. "I leave that up to you Wicca types. We are more the 'Can I kill it, eat it or screw it?' types."

"Okay, short answer," Sharice said, frowning. "Janea was stuck in a hostile zone. She was under attack. We managed to stop the attack and push her out of the hostile zone into one where she's not under some sort of constant attack. The nature of this metaphor might be generated by Janea or it may be a standing metaphorical zone. Given the number of gifted people who go to Dragon*Con, it's possible that it is maintained virtually constantly through dreaming. Time probably is different than the outside. An hour here may be seconds and it may be days. We won't know until we return. Did they intend for her to end up here? Probably not. Does it have anything to do with the plans of the unknown 'them' working the mundane side? Hmmm...Possibly. Quantum synchronicity would call for it."

"Okay, you just said *quantum*, at which point my brain turns off," Hjalmar said.

"Heh," Sharice replied. "Think of the otherworld as being a giant web with thousands of interconnected threads. Kick Janea out of the hostile zone in which they'd put her, call it the place of spiders, and fate, the Norns if you prefer, could put her anywhere. But she was in opposition to those unknown 'them.' That... keys her to try to fight on this side. Thus she is going to be in harmony, synchronicity, with a thread that places her still on the battlefield. Hmmm..."

"Okay, so now you're starting to use logic to go with my gut," Hjalmar said, nodding.

"You're right, but it should not, given what I'm seeing, be an actual physical battle," Sharice said, frowning. "The battle should be a metaphorical one..."

"And if the other side starts to lose?" Hjalmar asked.

"They would have to be desperate to engage in combat in this zone," Sharice said, her brow furrowing. "But if they were..."

"Smackdown time," Hjalmar finished. "Since they put Janea here, they presumably don't want her active in the mundane realm."

"With Barb taking over, their problems have increased tenfold, whether they know it or not," Sharice pointed out.

"Given," Hjalmar said. "But they're going to want to keep Janea out of play, stuck over here. So when we find her, they may try to prevent her from leaving."

"Or there may be a deeper reason she's here," Sharice said. "Synchronicity."

"Either way, they're going to try to stop her from winning, for values of winning," Hjalmar pointed out. "So..."

"You just want to weapon up," Sharice said. "Admit it."

"I'm Asatru," Hjalmar snapped. "Being without a weapon is the closest thing we have to sin!"

"What do you want?" Sharice asked.

"I want to cruise the Dealers Room and the Exhibitors Hall. If this is a true metaphor of Dragon*Con, everything I need is going to be in one of those two places. *Every* major sharp-pointy-thing dealer comes to Dragon*Con. The problem is..."

"Money," Sharice said. "Power. You'll have to trade power for sharp, pointy things."

"And I don't think I have enough," Hjalmar said. "I mean, to an Asatru there is no such thing as *too* much sharp, pointy weaponry. But I specifically don't have enough money to buy what I consider a minimum if there's any possibility of us getting busy over here. So, is the cleric willing to cough up some cash to armor up your fighter?" he added with a grin.

"Only if he avoids gaming metaphors," Sharice said. "How much do you need?"

"Around or over five hundred," Hjalmar said. "But if I use it all, I'm flat. I don't think that is wise here."

"Agreed," Sharice said. "Okay, I'll get Drakon to take over the stakeout and meet you in the Exhibitors Hall. The better weapons vendors were there. We should be able to leave it in our rooms and pick it up when we come back."

"Works."

"By the way, when we shut down the stakeout, meet me in the bar in the Hyatt."

"Shouldn't we have *started* in the tavern? I mean it's meet up in the tavern, listen to rumors, buy equipment... We're doing this all backwards!"

"Do you *want* your sharp, pointy things or not?"

"Shutting up now."

Chapter Three

The kimono was, indeed, short.

"The nice thing about a kimono is that, well, one size doesn't fit all but it does fit most," Anita said, holding the yellow silk robe up to Doris's back. "This one is going to be tight, I'll admit. But that's all to the good. Tight will definitely be noticed."

They were in Bran's room, but he'd made himself scarce after showing Anita where the kimono was. He was unquestionably busy, but Doris was pretty sure it was to keep her from being freaked out.

"You're going to need makeup, though, and hairpins," Anita continued. "And slippers. Makeup we'll need to scrounge. Ditto the hairpins, although if I can get some bobby pins, we can fix them up nicely. Actually, if we can get a couple of lacquered chopsticks, that might be enough...Try it on."

"Uhmmm..." Doris said uncomfortably.

"Go in the bathroom if it makes you feel any better," Anita said, shaking her head. "You're seriously going to have to work on your attitude if you're planning on winning Dawn."

"I will," Doris said. "But right now I'll try it on in the bathroom."

She came back out, tugging at the bottom, then at the top, then at the bottom again.

"Short, all right, but legal," Anita said. "Barely. Those are *much* better legs than I expected. Do you dance?"

"Yes," Doris said. "I love dancing."

"There may be hope," Anita said. "Right, kimono fits, barely, which is the best way. Now for the appliances. We need to scrounge...which here means by cell phone. Do you know anybody at the con at all that you can borrow stuff from?"

"Just Folsom," Doris said.

"He's not going to have makeup, trust me."

"And...Mandy. She's one of his friends."

"Mandy will have makeup. Right..."

"Quite a change, I like it," Mandy said, as Anita let her in the room. "I brought what I could scrounge up. You want to go full geisha?"

While Anita had been running down makeup and "appliances," Doris had been working on slippers. Bran had a very old but sturdy sewing machine. By taking several layers of cloth and, yes, hot-gluing them together, she got a sole for the slippers strong enough to last at least the evening. The uppers were easy enough to sew, then she attached them to the sole with more hot glue. They probably wouldn't last more than a day, but that was all she needed.

By the time she was finished with the slippers, Anita, Mandy and her daughter Traxa had fixed up a set of bobby pins into "jeweled pins" by gluing—superglue this time—plastic "gems" onto the ends.

"Now for the mask," Anita said, pulling a cheap mask out of a bin.

"That's not going to go with the outfit," Mandy pointed out.

"Absolutely not," Anita said. "Give me that hot-glue gun and the dragon brooch."

Traxa was wearing a metal dragon brooch that was about six inches long. Anita first, gently and over some protest, heated it up then laid it into a styrofoam form that looked as if it had once been used as packing material. The brooch left a nearly perfect impression of the dragon, which she touched up with the tip of the hot-glue gun. When it was done, she filled the mold with more hot glue.

"And now we wait a few minutes for it to cool," Anita said. "Okay, we've got pins, the kimono...Anything else?"

"I think I should wear this," Doris said, digging into the bottom of her pack and pulling out the metal pin of the woman in the chariot.

"Interesting," Anita said, examining the pin. "Nice craftsmanship. Doesn't really go with the outfit, but if we use it to pin up your hair it will be less noticeable. Okay, hot glue's done enough."

She removed the still-warm form and held it up.

"Voila, one dragon mask."

"I don't get it," Traxa said.

Traxa was a taller, teenage version of her mother, wearing a black bodice, black leather wings and demon horns. Doris had already determined that the outfit matched the personality. "Friendly as a prickly pear" were the words that came to mind.

Anita laid more glue onto the paper mask then pressed the dragon onto it.

"Now to form it," she said. "Put it on."

The glue was still warm, hot even, but Doris dutifully put it on.

"We gently form it to the face," Anita said, pressing down carefully on the still-malleable glue, "and we now have a form-fitted dragon mask to go with the kimono."

"A hot-glue dragon mask," Traxa said, shrugging. "It's ugly."

"And we take it off," Anita said, sharply, "and put it on a dummy. Then we spray glue it," she continued, spraying the mask and, incidentally, the dummy, "then we cover it in gold glitter."

When complete, the mask was a gorgeous replica of a golden dragon that fit Doris's face as if made for it. Which it was.

"Total cost? Maybe three dollars," Anita said. "And it's pretty much the same thing a Hollywood costumer would make for a TV show. They might use foam latex instead of hot glue but the principle is the same, and the outcome, for an appliance like this, is about the same."

"I never would have thought of that," Mandy admitted.

"That's because you haven't been doing this for *years*," Anita said.

"And I'm not a hot-glue addict," Mandy pointed out.

"Agreed. So, we have kimono, slippers, mask, pins and a nice barrette. I think you are set."

"Except for makeup and posture," Mandy said, pulling out a large box. "And *that* is *my* job."

When she was done, Doris was the perfect model of a Japanese geisha. With red hair.

"I camp moob my pace," Doris said.

"That's the point of the makeup," Mandy said. "Geisha smile very minimally but continuously. No teeth, they generally had awful teeth. They barely part their lips to speak. Don't try it, just pose and look beautiful. Speaking of posing, we need to work on your body language. Small, dainty steps. Hands folded. Head tilted..."

Over the next thirty minutes Doris was given a crash course in presentation as a geisha.

"Tis is s'upid," Doris said.

"*Beee* the geisha," Anita said, waving fingers in her face. "*Liiive* the geisha."

"You look like a Japanese hooker," Traxa said.

"That's what a geisha is, sort of," Anita replied.

"Traditionally geisha were considered far too valuable to actually engage in sex," Mandy argued. "The level of training they went through meant that their managers weren't about to risk them getting pregnant and unable to work."

"Tea-house girl, then," Anita said.

"Okay, tea-house girl," Mandy agreed. "More the look, anyway."

"Wha' 're 'u 'alking abou'?"

"Think of yourself as a Japanese hooker trying to act like she's an important lady so she can get higher tips," Traxa said.

"'Kay," Doris said. "Not."

"Attitude adjustment," Anita said. "You want to do the Dawn or not?"

"Yes," Doris said.

"With this outfit, you get to be the little wallflower *and* get noticed," Anita said. "Being noticed while *still* a wallflower is the *essence* of geisha. And when you put your street clothes back on, between the makeup and the mask, nobody will know it was you. So get out there and strut it, Doris."

"Well, not strut," Mandy said. "Geisha never strut. Tea-house girls don't either."

"Metaphorically speaking," Anita said. "I have a late panel so I got to get going."

"And I have an eighteen-or-older party to attend," Mandy said. "But you need a con-buddy. So... Traxa is going to be your con-buddy tonight."

"Says *who*?" Traxa snarled. "I wanted to go over to the Hyatt lobby."

"Says yo' mama," Mandy snapped. "That way I know you're not getting into *too* much trouble. Which is way possible in the Hyatt. Stick to the Hilton. All the serious costumers are over here, anyway, along with the serious picture-takers. You two... don't really match, but you mismatch well. I bet you get pictures taken of you galore."

"I don't want pictures taken of me," Traxa said. "Damned perverts."

"Then tell them no pictures," Mandy said. "Seriously. You are going to con-buddy with Doris tonight. End of story."

"In another week you won't be able to take that tone," Traxa promised.

"I know," Mandy said, sighing. "But that's in another week. Tonight you are going to con-buddy with Doris."

"Yes, Mother," Traxa snapped. "Okay, Doris, ready to go?"

"'Ure," Doris said. "Af'er 'u."

"You know," Sharice said, "if we could wait until the last day of the con we could probably get a big discount on some of this stuff."

Half the booths in the Exhibitors Hall had some manner of "sharp, pointy things" but most of them were cheap fantasy blades. Hjalmar normally made his own weapons and armor, but he couldn't exactly do that on the astral plane, no matter how much it looked like "reality." Thus he had to buy some. However, having made weapons a good part of his adult life, he knew what to look for and from whom. Cheap junk fantasy blades from China were not on his shopping list. On the other hand...

"I can't believe that there's a Forged Steel outlet on the astral plane," he whispered, perusing the weapons and armor on display.

Forged Steel was a well-known company in the mundane world among people who collected sharp, pointy things. And the guy running the booth was the spitting image of the mundane partner who normally sold at conventions.

"Do I know you?" the man asked as Hjalmar hefted an authentic Frankish throwing axe.

"I think I might have seen you around," Hjalmar admitted. "Svar Kellogg, right?"

"Yes," Svar said, smiling. A tall man with black hair and a widow's peak, he had the build and cut of a guy who seriously worked out *every single* day, and a faintly Slavic accent. "I can't place the name, but if I remember correctly... Asatru, right? Sorry if..."

"No, that's me. Hjalmar."

"That's right," Svar said, nodding. "You got a tower-shield from me a couple of years ago."

"Great shield," Hjalmar said, grinning. "Surprised you remember."

"Custom shields are rare," Svar said. "Custom shields sized for a guy who's nearly two meters are rarer. Enjoying the con?"

"So far it's been...interesting," Hjalmar remarked. "Thing is, I've got a need to do full Viking costume for most of the con. Problem is..."

"I make a lot of money," Svar said, smiling. "Well, let's see what we can do to shave my profits without putting me in the poorhouse."

The negotiations went on until after the Exhibitors Hall was closed, but finally they got down to a price that Hjalmar and Sharice could afford.

In the end he got a buckler, a seax, a mail shirt, and a Norman helmet with nose-piece; tunic, and trous. The kicker was the main weapon.

"I dearly love this hand-and-a-half," Hjalmar said, hefting the nearly five-foot-long sword. Contrary to myth, the sword was not particularly heavy, barely four pounds. But in use, due to its length, most people used two hands. With Hjalmar's height and strength he could easily wield it with one and still use his shield. "But it's just as dearly priced."

"Not much more than the Beowulf, and it comes with the baldric," Svar pointed out.

"This is getting way over five hundred," Sharice pointed out. "Are we sure we're going to need this?"

"If I need it, you're going to want me to have it," Hjalmar replied.

"Point," Sharice said. "In for a penny. Get it all."

"Done," Hjalmar said. "And there's no way I can carry it all in my hands. Got a changing room?"

"In the back."

"Ah, that's more like it," Hjalmar said was he walked out of the back. With the exception of the sword, which wasn't quite period, and his work boots, he was now the model of a Viking soldier.

"Remember to keep it peace bonded," Svar said, handing over some red cords. "You can have the cords gratis."

"Thank you *so* much," Sharice said, smiling and considering the considerable sum of money—power, in other words—she'd just transferred. "Can we go now?"

Drakon was tapping his foot impatiently when the two got back. "No luck?" Sharice asked.

"Lots of redheads," Drakon said. "No Janea. Nice threads."

"Thanks," Hjalmar said as a large black man in a Blade costume stopped by him and looked him up and down.

"Everything okay, friend?" Hjalmar said, blandly.

The man looked him up and down again, snorted faintly, and walked across the street towards the Marriott.

"What was that all about?" Drakon asked.

"I have no idea," Hjalmar said.

"And why do I think I recognize him?" Sharice asked. "I think I'd remember a guy *that* big and *that* black. Seven feet of pure Nubian is memorable. But I'd swear I recognize him."

"Me, too," Hjalmar admitted. "But whatever. I feel I can stand sentry peacefully now."

"You look anything *but* peaceful," Sharice pointed out. The sun was starting to go down and she wondered how long they should keep up the stakeout. "We'll stay until local time of midnight, then meet up in the Hyatt bar. Hjalmar..."

"I'll take over sentry duty again," he said, smiling. "I've got some bottled water."

"I'll bring you a sandwich, man," Drakon said. "After that I'm going to cruise through the Hyatt again. Janea's going to be making a splash one way or another."

"Even with all these redheads she has *got* to stand out," Sharice said as another one walked by in the "thermal bandages" outfit from the movie *The Fifth Element*. "I'm almost positive."

"Are you hiding?"

The person asking the question was a short, slightly plump brunette who was maybe twenty. She was in a beautiful blue-and-black pirate outfit complete with a massive hat.

"Sort of," Doris said. Traxa had said she had to go "talk to somebody" and had disappeared nearly an hour before. Since then Doris had been watching the goings-on from halfway behind a potted plant.

The lobby of the Hilton was the venue of choice for serious costumers. While more people gathered in the Hyatt in the evenings to show off their costumes, and bodies, the Hilton was where the people who cared primarily about their costumes tended to gather. And the amount of photography occasionally rivaled an assault by paparazzi. The current favorite was a guy in a *very* authentic Spiderman outfit who was just about a dead ringer for the actor in the movie. He had about twenty people taking pictures of him at a time.

"You can come out, it's okay," the girl said. "Nobody bites. Not here, anyway. They do in the Hyatt sometimes."

"Really?" Doris asked, taking a tentative step out. Making up your mind to go out in public in what amounted to a very tight, nearly paper-thin robe was one thing. Doing it had turned out to be another.

"Some of the girls can be real bitches, if you'll pardon my language, if they think you're getting more attention than they are," the girl said. "I'm Daphne."

"Doris," Doris said, shaking her hand. "That is a *gorgeous* pirate costume. You must have worked on it for months."

"I bought it, to tell you the truth," Daphne said. "Then I had it fitted. But I thought I needed at least one really good costume for Dragon. I love yours."

"It's really just something that some friends threw together for me," Doris said, shyly.

"It looks really good on you," Daphne said. "What's with the mask? Planning on robbing a Japanese bank?"

"If I wear a mask I can pretend I'm not me?" Doris said.

"Got to get over that sometime," Daphne said. "But maybe not tonight. Right?"

"Maybe not tonight," Doris admitted.

"Can I take your picture?" an Asian man said. Unlike a lot of the people, he was carrying a fairly professional digital camera setup.

"Certainly," Daphne said, grabbing Doris's arm. "Thank you."

"That's the way to do it," she whispered between shots. "You're out here to show off, but be polite about it. Some girls aren't, but

the question is, do you *want* to be a bitch? I mean, why even costume and show skin if you're going to be a bitch about pictures?"

By the time the guy was done with two or three photos there
was a crowd of people taking enough pictures that Doris found
herself blinking myopically.

"I'm not used to all this attention," she muttered through her
masklike makeup.

"But do you enjoy it?" Daphne asked.

"Yes," Doris said. "I guess I do."

"Then let's just enjoy it," Daphne said. "Smile."

"Geishas don't show teeth," Doris said.

"Tea-house girl, surely."

"Also don't show teeth."

"You realize your nipples are standing up and you can see
them through the kimono?"

"What?"

"It *probably* won't be noticeable in the pictures, but it's sure
attracting the guys. Just go with it."

When the picture-taking had died down, Daphne gestured
out into the lobby.

"You can't just stand in one place. You need to promenade."

"I'm perfectly comfortable hiding behind my plant. Especially
now that I know...what you said."

"Then why are you here?" Daphne asked.

"To learn to get over it," Doris admitted. "I'll go if I can stay
with you. Sorry to be so silly about it, but I'm just learning to
get over it. Baby steps."

"Then let *us* promenade," Daphne said, linking her arm into
Doris's and striking a pose. "I know how you feel. I was the same
way the first time I came here, which seems like yesterday. Given
some of the stuff... Never mind. I shall be the pirate and you
shall be my captured Japanese maiden. And, no, I don't swing
that way."

"Fine," Doris said as they started out into the lobby. She nearly
stopped and hid again as she noticed a simply huge black guy in
a Blade outfit watching her. But he gave her a curt nod and then
looked away. "I'm supposed to take little, dainty steps."

"With the length of your legs compared to mine, your dainty
steps are a stride for me," Daphne said, dragging her out into
the open.

They didn't get far.

"Excuse me, can I take your picture?"

"Are we sure she's here?" Hjalmar asked when he walked into the Hyatt bar.

"She's here," Sharice said, biting her lip. "What I don't know is where she's hiding. We've been looking *everywhere!*"

"Well, if there are forces at work against her, perhaps she's hiding from them," Drakon said. "Whatever the case, we need to return and find out what is happening on the mundane side."

"Agreed," Sharice said. "We'll drop off Hjalmar's gear in the room then return to the world. But we're coming back tomorrow, damnit. She must be going without sleep, and a person can only go so long that way. We need to get her out of here before we lose her forever."

"That was fantastic!" Doris burbled as Bran opened the door. "I had *so* much fun!"

"Glad to hear it," Bran said, rubbing his eyes.

"I'm sorry," Doris said, immediately apologetic. "I woke you up."

"I've got early panels tomorrow," Bran said. "No problem, though. Hey, a beautiful lady knocking on my door in the middle of the night is nothing to complain about."

"I'll get my things and get out of here," Doris said, sliding past him. He was dressed, to her surprise, in pajamas.

"If you want to talk I'll be awake for an hour or so," Bran said, sitting down on the end of the unused bed. It was more or less covered in costuming material.

"No, I'll let you get back to sleep," Doris said, grabbing her bag and heading into the bathroom.

When she came back out, Bran was still sitting on the end of the bed looking, if anything, even more wide awake.

"Seriously, people generally want to talk about something like their first costuming night," Bran said.

"If you're sure," Doris said, grabbing a chair. She'd changed back into her "street clothes" and felt mildly uncomfortable in them. As if even as street clothes they weren't what she'd choose to wear. "Well, Mandy sent Traxa down with me but she took off almost immediately. Which left me hiding in a corner."

"I hope you climbed out," Bran said.

"I did," Doris said, dimpling. "With some help. I ran into a girl named Daphne..."

"Pirate costume?" Bran asked. "Big hat? White feather?"

"Yes," Doris said.

"Did that costume," Bran said, smiling.

"You did that?" Doris asked. "It was awesome!"

"Hey, I do this for a living," Bran said, shrugging. "Lots of pictures?"

"Oh, everybody loved it," Doris said, pulling the pins out of her hair. She'd taken the time to get most of the makeup off in the bathroom. "Daphne convinced me to climb out of my corner and it was just picture city. She made like I was her captive and everybody just ate it up. We stayed in the Hilton and just talked and got pictures taken until, well, now. It was great! I never thought I'd enjoy attention so much!"

"It's called ego-boo," Bran said. "Ego boost. Duncan can lecture on it for hours. It's about status, basically. If people are giving you positive attention it feels like a rise in cultural status. Generally it means there *is* a rise in status. I'll let Duncan complete the lecture and go on about how the gene is selfish."

"The one thing that kept throwing me was that there was this *enormous* black guy in a Blade costume that, like, followed us around. He wasn't acting...stalkerish. He didn't actually spend that much time watching *us*. But every time I looked around, there he'd be, usually with his back to us. Actually, it sort of looked as if he was watching out *for* us. Which is weird. And he totally ignored people taking his picture. If *we* moved, *he* moved, pictures being taken or not."

"Yeah, that would be weird," Bran said. "Going to do the same costume tomorrow?"

"I could," Doris said, frowning. "I don't want to put anyone to any more trouble..."

"But you'd rather do something else," Bran said, nodding. "Makes sense. Come to the panels tomorrow and we'll see what we can come up with. You should think about showing more skin. You're probably going to have to when the Dawn contest comes, and you need to get used to it."

"After tonight I think I can get my head around that," Doris said. "One guy did try to grope me. I don't *think* his wrist is broken."

"Glad to hear you're getting some assertiveness," Bran said, yawning. "You're going to need it. Now, if you don't mind, I'm actually getting tired again."

Doris smiled and then shrugged.

"I was half expecting a come-on," she admitted.

"You're . . . not really ready for that, unless I'm mistaken," Bran said. "Maybe later in the con."

"Until then, then," Doris said, standing up.

"Have a good rest of the evening."

Doris knew she should be tired; she hadn't slept at all last night and it was after midnight, but she was still charged up from the evening. She wandered down to the lobby of the Hilton, but most of the costumers had packed it in and everything was closed up. The Marriott wasn't much better.

However, the Hyatt was still going strong. She flashed her badge to the security on the back steps and found that the "smoking area" outside the back door was just about packed. There were still vendors out there but she wasn't going to spend her limited amount of cash on drinks.

However, besides the various people, in various clothing ranging from street clothes through corsets and miniskirts and schoolgirl outfits to one guy in a leather thong and body paint, there was a group of people banging on drums down at the far end. And girls doing belly dancing in the middle.

Intrigued, she walked over to watch. The rhythms were catchy and pulled at something in her. She knew she liked to dance, she just wasn't usually someone to do it in public. Her dancing was all done in her room to the radio. This was different. Different dancing and a completely different environment.

Could she, maskless, walk out there and join in?

No, but she didn't have to be maskless. She considered her location then walked to the nearest ladies' room.

"Is that her?" the woman asked.

"Yes," the man at her side answered. "We should kill her, I tell you."

"And risk the penalties?" the woman asked scornfully. "She doesn't know who she is or where she is. She is no risk to us."

"Her friends search for her. They're gone now. But when they find her, that is a much larger issue."

"She has to win the crown to defeat us. There is no chance that that dormouse can beat me."

"Let's hope so. I am tired beyond words of this prison."

"I'm tired of these losers. Let's go find a party."

"You just want to find someone to torment."

"That's what we do, precious."

Once in the ladies', Doris entered a stall and pulled off her shirt. Going shirtless was out. That, she couldn't quite handle yet. But it was an old shirt and worn. And she had a small pen-knife in her bag.

Five minutes later she walked out. It wasn't a great costume but she at least could be a tad anonymous. Call the costume "The Dread Pirate Roberta." She sort of remembered a movie with a character, 'The Dread Pirate Roberts,' who always wore a black mask. The sleeves were gone from the ratty old shirt, and it was now a midriff shirt. The lower part of the shirt was the mask.

All the girls in the circle were in such beautiful costumes, she didn't want to get in there in her holey jeans and beat-up running shoes. So she chose a quiet corner off to the side and started dancing.

Just the hips at first, warming into the rhythm. What was that line about "Dance like nobody is watching?" She knew almost from the first that, ratty clothing or not, people were watching. Men were watching.

And she liked it.

Chapter Four

*H*ave you had any sleep at all?" Duncan asked as Doris sat down at his table in the restaurant.

"Nope," Doris replied, grinning. "I've been having too much fun."

"Is that a faint sheen of glow about you I detect?"

"If you mean am I pregnant, no!" Doris replied, hotly.

"Horses sweat, men perspire, and women glow," Duncan said. "You appear to glow. Your hair is wet."

"I was dancing," Doris said, shrugging.

"This early?" Duncan replied, chuckling. "Shouldn't you at least wait until the sun is over the yardarm?" He paused and looked at her. "You don't mean you were dancing all *night*?"

"Until about an hour ago. The last drummer gave up, the loser."

"Good God, woman!" Duncan said. "Pace yourself. No sleep, and dancing all night? Were your shoes on fire? What happened to the little wallflower?"

"I am the little wallflower," Doris said, shrugging. "Until I can put on a mask. Then I get to be the mask."

"Well, seriously, you need some rest," Duncan said. "Food, at least. My treat."

"I accept," Doris said. "I feel sort of bad about the fact that I'm living on charity. But I sort of got over it, partially, last night. Guys kept giving me bottles of water."

"I hope you only took those that were sealed," Duncan said, signaling for a waiter.

"I was careful," Doris said. "It sort of bothered me at first. But they seemed to like it and they really seemed to like my dancing. One of the drummers asked if I was going to be there tonight. I said probably. I know I have to sleep sometime, and I'm tired, but not the kind of tired where you can go to sleep. You know?"

"Yes," Duncan said, nodding. "But you have to rest sometime. And, frankly, you could probably use a shower after dancing all night."

"Do I smell?" Doris asked, looking panicked.

"No," Duncan said, grinning. "But you still could probably use a shower. Am I right?"

"Yes," Doris said.

"I'm not using my room for the next couple of hours," he said, handing her a key. "Feel free to avail yourself of it. Get some sleep if you can, wash up if nothing else. Remember the rules of the con. Drink, Eat, Sleep, Game. Or costume, in your case. What are your plans for today?"

"More costuming panels," Doris said. "Then I'm going to see if I can figure out how to make a harem-girl costume for tonight. I don't think I can. There's too much involved. And I need to figure out what costume I'm going to do for the contest."

"If you'd like another suggestion...?" Duncan asked.

"Sure," Doris replied. "You've been on the money so far."

"Don't spend all your time in costuming. There are a thousand things to do at this con. No person is all one thing. Or if they are, they're called obsessives. You might try looking in on some other panels. I'm going to a demonstration by a friend of mine at one, over in the Marriott. You might want to look that up."

"Damn, you're up early."

Doris looked up, then up again, at a tall, thin man with a straggly beard and long, frizzy hair.

"Ah," Duncan said, grinning. "It's Kelly. Kelly Lockhart, Doris Grisham. Doris, Kelly. Join us for breakfast?"

"Don't mind if I do," Kelly said, grabbing a chair. "It's not often that I get to eat breakfast with a beautiful lady."

"I won't tell Star you said that," Duncan said, chuckling.

"Young lady."

"Or that."

"Redhead."

"There you go. Foot nicely extracted. Doris, Kelly is a feature of Dragon*Con I don't think you've yet had the dubious pleasure of experiencing."

"Oh?" Doris asked, puzzled.

"I'm the court jester," Kelly said. "Which means that since nobody takes me seriously I can get away with things that would otherwise be outrageous."

"And people just say 'Oh, it's Kelly' and shrug."

"There you go."

"Such as the fu . . . screw-up fairy?"

"Don't remind me," Kelly said, wincing. "Okay, there are some lines that shouldn't be crossed."

"The problem is not crossing a line," Duncan said. "It's jumping across it butt naked. Or, perhaps, in the screw-up fairy costume."

"You have all these in-jokes," Doris said.

"Danger of an inbred community," Duncan said, smiling. "The fu . . . screw-up fairy . . ."

"Tech-ops says that whenever something goes wrong, it's the . . . screw-up fairy," Kelly said, by way of explanation. "So one year I decided to come as the screw-up fairy."

"Imagine yon large—hirsute, I might add—male in a size triple-XL Tinkerbell costume."

"Technically it was Texas small."

"Oh," Doris said, grimacing. "Brain floss!"

"Yes, yes," Duncan said, grinning. "We *all* wanted economy-size brain floss."

"With condoms hanging from the belt," Kelly pointed out. "Doesn't make any sense, otherwise. I mean, it'd just be a guy cross-dressing if I didn't do that."

"And there is far too much of that at Dragon*Con, anyway," Duncan said.

"I saw a great big fat bearded guy in a Sailor Moon outfit last night," Doris said, shuddering.

"Sailor Moon cosplay should be outlawed," Folsom said, nodding. "Seriously. There ought to be laws with stiff penalties. Hanging on first offense, with successively higher penalties." Duncan frowned as his breakfast was served, and pulled out his cell phone to check the time. "This is fun, but I think it's throwing my schedule off. I'm not sure I'll be able to make Ed's demo. Kelly, Doris is going to avail herself of my shower. After that, do you think you could be a friend and get her over to Ed's demonstration?"

"Sure," Kelly said. "I don't have any plans."

"I'm going to wolf this down and then scoot," Folsom said. "Doris, don't let this trickster lead you astray. He's renowned for it. Kelly, actually *get* her to the demo, okay?"

"You just say that because you love me," Kelly said, grinning.

"Or something like that," Folsom replied.

"Eh, this is too effing weird," Hjalmar said, looking at the crowds below. "If I'm getting this right, this is the next day, in the morning. And we were away for, what, two hours?"

"We were here for one day in this reality and out-of-body for two," Sharice said, biting her lip. "There's a rule going on here that I can't define. Time is way skewed. I came right back because I was afraid we were going to miss the entire con if we stayed away. Instead, we're right back where we should be starting again."

"Rules of game?" Drakon said. "We rest and we restart at the proper time?"

"But who is running the game?" Sharice said. "And what are the other rules? *Most especially*, who is running the game? Because if it's certain entities, then it's going to be rigged."

"Rigged or not, it's the only game in town," Hjalmar said as he threw on his mail. "What's the plan? I take it I'm getting sentry again."

"Where have we missed?" Sharice asked.

"It's a huge con," Drakon said. "We haven't really hit the gaming areas. I covered the lower levels of the Hyatt yesterday. Ran into a fascinating guy in the anime room. He knew, like, every anime ever created and every martial arts movie ever. Even met Bruce Lee a couple of times."

"Costuming," Hjalmar said, waving at his armor. "There's a whole huge track on that over at the Hilton. And we didn't really hit the Hilton much at all."

"Drakon, you take gaming," Sharice said. "I'll take costuming. Link up with Hjalmar at two. I'll spell Hjalmar so he can get some food and rest. Then we roam again."

"Works," Drakon said, shaking his head. "Gaming. Why'd it have to be gaming?"

"Would you rather sit through lectures on period fabric making?" Sharice asked.

"Come to think of it, I *really* want to check out the gaming room..."

"You look refreshed," Kelly said as Doris exited the elevator.

"I feel refreshed," Doris said, heading to the lobby.

"Let's take the tubeway," Kelly said, gesturing in the opposite direction. "This time of day it's not too crowded, and it's closer."

"I haven't been this way before," Doris said as they headed into the skyway. "I didn't even know this was here."

"There are a half-dozen ways to get back and forth," Kelly said. "Trust me, I know them all. And you can watch the crazies from up here," he added, gesturing down to the street. "Like the guy in armor who looks as if he's a sentry."

Doris stopped and considered the guy in period Norse costume.

"He looks familiar," she said.

"That's common," Kelly replied, taking her arm. "And we're walking..."

"Lots of people in costume already," Doris said.

"This is when the con really gets going," Kelly said as they proceeded on their way. "Most of the day registration is on Saturday. Which is why the day-reg line is so long. Tomorrow will be busy, too, what with the concerts and the Dawn contest."

"I'm going to do that," Doris said, shyly.

"Dawn?" Kelly said, surprised. "Well, you're a natural for looks, but... What's your costume?"

"I haven't really decided yet," Doris said. "It's going to be limited."

"Hmmm..." Kelly said, frowning. "Dawn's not something to just jump into. I mean, not if you're serious. It's become almost a masquerade lately. People work all year on a costume for it. Just throwing something together? Good luck. And why Dawn?"

"I'm trying to find out who I really am," Doris said. "Dawn is about as far from who I am now as I can imagine."

"Then maybe it's not who you really are," Kelly said. "Maybe something like gaming is more your style. All that takes is brains and skill. You've clearly got the brains; all you need is the skill. And you can pick that up fast. If you just want to win something to prove something to yourself, well, one of the gaming contests is more likely."

"Hmmm..." Doris said, doubtfully.

"Or, well, you've been doing costuming, right? Maybe something like the Iron Costumer contest. I wouldn't suggest masquerade, that's also something you work all year on. But there are more places to prove yourself, to find yourself, at Dragon*Con than Dawn. Just a thought."

"I'll think on it," Doris said as they exited into the food court. "Oh, I have been this way. I found the food court my first day. But I've mostly been eating in the con suite."

"Shane appreciates that, I'm sure," Kelly said. "He goes to a lot of trouble to come up with solid meals even though his budget is really small for all the people he has to feed. And he never has enough staff. Most people aren't willing to sell their souls to be con-suite zombies. But to get to the Marriott we go this way."

"I offered to help out," Doris said. "In the con suite. But he said I had to have my brains removed."

"It's not a con rule, it's his," Kelly said. "All con-suite staff must be zombies. I think it's an African hospitality thing."

Doris giggled at that and then looked around in surprise as they entered the Marriott. "I never would have found this way if you hadn't shown it to me."

"There are signs, but they're more harm than help," Kelly said. "There are a thousand paths around Dragon*Con. I like to try them all."

"Duncan said you can go anywhere."

"Dragon*Con is really about fifteen cons rolled into one," Kelly said. "Media con, derivative con, anime con, lit con, fetish con. And each of those cons has dozens of little cliques. I try to fit in with them all."

"I imagine you mediate a lot," Doris said.

"Heh," Kelly replied. "I'll *fix* things from time to time. 'Mediate' would be a stretch. Most people would say the opposite."

"So are you staff?" Doris asked as they headed down the escalator. She didn't notice in the crowds the small woman in robes exiting the back of the hotel.

"I used to be a director," Kelly said. "These days I just run the battlebot tournament. And occasionally MC. And whatever else strikes my fancy. And in here," he continued, leading her into a ballroom, "we have Edmund's demonstration about to start. I'd better introduce you quickly."

He led her to the front of the crowded room where an older man, balding and blocky, was laying out a collection of edged weapons. They ranged from small punch daggers up to halberds with just about every major type in between. A stocky, dark-haired woman with a friendly face was helping him with the layout. She glanced over her shoulder and grinned.

"Edmund, it's Kelly."

"Hello, Kelly," Edmund said, neutrally. "To what do we owe the honor?"

"I come bearing gifts," Kelly said.

"I'll check my wallet," Edmund replied.

"Seriously. Duncan asked me to lead this lovely stray over and introduce her. Doris Grisham, Fig and Edmund Wodinaz. Ed and Fig, Doris. My work here is done." With that, he wandered off.

"Hey, Doris," Fig said, shaking her hand. "Folsom mentioned you. Want to help out?"

"Love to," Doris said.

"Well, grab some blades and start putting them up."

Hjalmar watched the old woman coming across the road and sighed. She was heavyset, pear-shaped, and not short. But the reason for the two canes was clearly some sort of serious movement disability, not to mention age. She'd started at the front of the pack crossing the road, and by the time she was halfway across, the policeman stopping traffic was watching her with a baleful eye, as she was the only one still in the road.

She finally made it to the steep, long stairs, took a look up from her hunched position, sighed, took both canes in one hand and grabbed the railing, preparing to hoist herself up.

Hjalmar just couldn't take it anymore.

"Ma'am," he said, walking over. "If you don't mind, I can carry you up. If you can take a fireman's carry."

"I accept," the woman said after a moment's pause. "I'd take the 'handicapped' entrance but it's nearly as bad. And longer."

"This won't take a second," Hjalmar said, bending down and getting the woman across his shoulders. She was *much* heavier than she looked, and she didn't look light.

He carried her up the stairs and then set her down, carefully. He managed not to groan as the enormous weight came off.

"Got your feet?" he asked.

"Got it," the woman said. "Thank you. May Frey bless you."

"You're Asatru?" Hjalmar said, surprised.

"No," the woman said, laughing. "*You* are, silly. I'm of a *much* older religion than *those* upstarts."

Hjalmar nodded to her in a puzzled fashion and went back down the stairs to take up his sentry post.

"Nice of you," the security guy said. It was the same guy who had handed them their tickets the first day.

"I just couldn't stand the suspense of not knowing if she'd make it or not," Hjalmar said, half ashamedly. He preferred a tough-guy image, frankly. "And I really wanted the image of her rolling back down out of my head."

"Al Mater is old, but she's sturdy," the security guy said, shrugging. "She's been making the con since it's been around and will probably be making it when everyone else has quit."

"Al Mater?" Hjalmar said, puzzled.

"Con name," the security guy said, shrugging. "I don't know her true name. Don't know anyone who does. Like I said, she's been around for a looong time. Got a question for you."

"Shoot," Hjalmar said, spotting and dismissing another redhead.

"You were here pretty much all day yesterday."

"Yep."

"And you look to be settling in today. Nice threads, by the way."

"Thanks."

"So what's up?"

"Looking for a friend," Hjalmar said. "We're worried she's in trouble. She doesn't have a cell. We figure everybody has to come by here sometime. The other two are cruising the con. I stand here and look for redheads."

"More or less what I figured," the guy said, extending a hand. "Ryan, by the way."

"Hjalmar."

"Here's the thing. Since you're going to be standing here anyway, why not join security?"

"Excuse me?" Hjalmar said, surprised.

"You're going to be here anyway. If you're here as security, we can free up one body. All you've got to do, in addition to looking for your friend, is check to make sure everyone has a badge. You'd be surprised what kind of people try to sneak into the con without paying. They'll pay you back for your membership, and instead of your friends having to bring you drinks, we get powerups delivered."

"Powerups?" Hjalmar said, tilting his head.

"Sandwich, PowerAde bottle, vitamins and a PowerBar," Ryan said. "All you gotta do is go up to Room two-twenty-two—that's con-ops and security—explain the situation, and you're in. If they've got questions, tell 'em to call me."

"Hmmm…" Hjalmar said. "I may have to take off in a hurry."

"Go to room two-twenty-two."

"I'll wait 'til I get relieved, then go," Hjalmar said. "We're serious about finding this friend of ours. Two-twenty-two."

"Two-twenty-two."

Edmund's demonstration was a solid hour. The first thirty minutes covered, in brief, each of the weapons and their common forms of employment. Then fifteen minutes were a demonstration of axe, war hammer and long sword against various forms of armor. Pig shoulders, mail, and plate were expertly chopped and diced. He may have used a cane, normally, but put a sword in his hand and he came alive. The last fifteen were questions and answers.

Doris's part was to be the pretty assistant. She was initially surprised that when Edmund began discussing a particular weapon she could pick it out immediately. But just as Edmund seemed to change with a sword in his hand, so did she. It was more than "the pointy end goes at the bad guy." The feel of a sword awakened something in her that she hadn't known was there.

When the demonstration was finished, she and Fig started collecting up the weapons while Edmund answered still more questions. She lifted one of the swords and sighted along the blade. It wasn't a period weapon; Edmund referred to it as a "fantasy sword" based on a falchion, but it was the most perfect weapon she could imagine. At least for cutting flesh. Long and curved with the blade thickened towards the end, the balance was beautiful. She waved it slightly then flipped it in her hand, a motion that Edmund had demonstrated, but also demonstrated was difficult for a beginner.

"You look as if you were made for that sword," Fig said, smiling.

"It's beautiful," Doris exclaimed. "I don't care if he says it's a fantasy sword. If there wasn't someone, somewhere, who used one like this in battle, there should have been."

"You seem familiar with the pieces," Fig said.

"I guess," Doris said. "I certainly like them."

"Could you give us a hand getting these up to the room?" Fig asked.

"Absolutely."

The collection was a huge mass, but between the three of them and a baggage cart, they managed to get them all up to a room in the Marriott in one load.

"Thank God that's over," Edmund said, settling into a chair.

"Are you okay?" Fig asked.

"Just short of breath," Edmund said. "I'm getting old, honey."

"You're never going to get old," Fig said. "You just get better."

"I get better with young lovelies around, that's for sure," Edmund said, winking at Doris. "Thank you for helping out. It was more help than you realize. I owe you."

"You don't owe me anything," Doris said, still holding the falchion. She flipped it again and shook her head. "Someday I'll be able to afford a sword like this."

"Well, you can borrow it if you need to," Fig said. "But for the time being, try this."

She pulled out what was almost the sketch of the same sword made from sections of wood bound together at both ends but slightly separated in the middle.

"Those are my new training swords," Edmund said. "They have the same heft and balance as a live blade, but you don't have to worry about leaving your arm lying on the ground."

"Why not rattan?" Doris asked, doing a sweep. He was right, it was the identical balance.

"Hand it over," Edmund said. When he had it in his hand he popped her, hard, on the butt. "That's why."

"That barely hurt," Doris said, taking the sword back. *Not nearly as much as a hickory switch*, she thought.

"Rattan would have left a bruise," Fig said. "With these, all you need for live fighting is a face mask and helmet. They're even better than wrapped rattan or PVC. You can hit somebody on an unprotected joint and it won't cause any damage."

"Since you like the falchion so much, take that one with you," Edmund said. "I have others. There's a scabbard."

"Thank you," Doris said as Fig loaded her with a scabbard and baldric. "I can't thank you enough."

"I'm sure you will find a way to use it well," Fig said.

Barbara felt bad that she hadn't been able to stop by the safe house before. But she'd been busy. Now she laid a hand on her friend's shoulder.

"Come on, Janea," she said, drawing on the power of God and channeling it to her friend. The fact that an Asatru worshipper of a fertility goddess was one of God's children in His eyes was proven simply because she *could* send her friend power. "I need some backup. This FBI guy is getting freaked by invisible demons. I need somebody to take his mind off of them. You'd be perfect."

There was not a flicker on the monitors, but Barbara hoped the power would help out.

When Hjalmar got back from his break, Sharice raised an eyebrow at his new badge and lanyard.

"Security?" she said.

"I'm here, anyway," Hjalmar said. "All I have to do is check badges."

"Hjalmar," Sharice said, pulling him to the side. "Try to remember this is the astral plane."

"I do," Hjalmar said.

"You're joining security for a sector of the *astral plane*," Sharice said. "I know the whole 'maintaining' thing is ritual for you, but...this could be a *serious* complication."

"I told them what's going on, that we're looking for a friend. And that I have to leave by midnight, and that I may have to leave in a hurry. They didn't have any problems with it."

"Try your silver cord," Sharice said.

Hjalmar closed his eyes, then yawned.

"Thanks," he said. "Now I'm tired. It'll be fine. And if one of you guys can cover for me here from time to time, I've got access to all sorts of areas now that we didn't have before. I doubt Janea is in any of them, but if we get a sniff I can look."

"Okay," Sharice said, doubtfully. "I'm going to go check out the Hyatt. Good luck. Hopefully, wherever Janea is, she's not getting into *too* much trouble."

"Bran, I need to apologize," Doris said.

"I can't imagine what for," the director said as people shuffled out of the panel.

"I need to pay you back for the materials I used," Doris said. "I feel like such a fool. I knew there was no way I was coming to a con with no money."

"And you remembered..." Bran said, smiling.

"I put it in my backpack," Doris said, ducking her head. "I had *plenty* of money with me. What a ditz!"

"You didn't use hardly anything in materials," Bran said. "Seriously, don't worry about it. Are you going to costume tonight?"

"Yes," Doris said. "I knew what I wanted to do but I just couldn't figure out how to make it. Not in time, and the materials would have been expensive. I'm going to do the belly-dancer thing."

"Good for you," Bran said. "That's a nice step up."

"And I get to wear a veil," Doris said. "Now, where do I look?"

"Dealers Room or the Exhibitors Hall," Bran said. "Try stall 938. Heki does great costumes. Have fun."

The Dealers Room was downstairs from the panel rooms, but the Exhibitors Halls were on the same level. She headed that way and was somehow unsurprised to run into Kelly.

"Hey, Kelly," Doris said. "I'm going shopping for harem-girl outfits. I'll probably have to try on *several*. Want to come along?"

"Be still my beating heart," Kelly said, grabbing at his chest. "I thought you didn't have any money?"

"I found some in my backpack," Doris said, shrugging. "I guess I forgot I put it in there. Anyway, time to get busy on a costume for tonight."

"Lead the way, fair maiden," Kelly said. "Fortunately, my wife is a director and busy in the Hyatt, two hotels away. And, of course, nobody *ever* gossips at Dragon*Con. I should be safe."

"I can't wear this in public!" Doris said, holding up the harem-girl pants. They were, essentially, transparent.

"Well, maybe not with a thong," Kelly said. "Unless you're willing to *really* let it all hang out."

"I don't w...I don't ha..." Doris stammered. "I can't wear this in public! I thought it would have more coverage than *this*!"

"You're thinking *I Dream of Jeannie*." Heki was a short woman with a lined face and black hair shot with white. "That would look fabulous on you, dear."

"Kelly, I'm sorry I dragged you along," Doris said, shaking her head. "But I can't try this on. Not and let anyone see it."

"If you don't let anyone see it, you're not going to wear it tonight," Kelly said. "It's not *that* bad."

"I dunno..." Doris said.

"If you really want, I'll shut my eyes," Kelly said. "And there's always gaming. You're dressed for that. If baggy shirts and jeans are what you *want* to dress like, you don't have to wear a harem-girl outfit. Don't let people pressure you into doing something you don't want to do, being somebody you don't feel comfortable being."

"That's a good point," Doris said, frowning.

"You want to think about it?" Kelly asked. "I know where there's a Magic tournament."

"No," Doris said, her face hardening. "I'm going to do it."

"Up to you," Kelly said, indifferently.

A few minutes later, Doris came out of the dressing room. She'd had to ask Heki to help her out with a few of the fittings, and there'd been a certain amount of giggling and bell ringing from the dressing stall.

"What do you think?" Doris asked, uncertainly.

"I take it back," Kelly squeaked.

"Take what back?" Doris asked, worriedly.

"I take back what I said," Kelly squeaked, then cleared his throat. "You should wear that all the time. I mean, *All. The. Time.*"

"Kelly, my eyes are up here," Doris said after an uncomfortable delay.

"I've made my decision."

The outfit was complete, from slippers to pink gauze pantaloons to mildly opaque red vest with gauze sleeves and silver bells to headdress with more bells. And included a totally opaque silk veil.

"I can't do this."

"You look great."

"Then quit undressing me with your eyes!"

"I don't have to undress you with my *eyes*, Doris."

A crowd had gathered by the simple expedient of the first guy who glanced to the side and stopped, stunned. He, in turn, was bumped by another guy who looked the same way. At this point there were at least a dozen males all gazing at Doris, slack-mouthed. And about half as many female companions glaring at her.

"That's it," Doris said. "Not gonna do it."

"Doris," Kelly said. "Seriously. You should. You look like a million dollars, and with the veil, nobody will know it's you."

"Everybody's *staring* at me!" Doris whispered.

"Honey," Heki said, sighing, "that's the *point.*"

"Doris, up to you," Kelly said. "Gaming's still an option. But I've never seen anyone who looks as good as you in one of those. And the veil is totally opaque." He paused for a moment then shrugged. "Of course, it's the only part that *is.*"

"Not *helping.*"

"Up to you."

Doris thought about it for a moment, trying to ignore the stares, then shrugged.

"How much?"

"I need better underwear," she said as they left the Dealers Room. The entire harem-girl costume fit in a very small bag, which was all that anyone needed to say about it.

"With that I will agree," Kelly said. "But it really *is* a stunning outfit."

"I could tell by the look of dead fish on all the guys' faces," Doris said, chuckling.

"Deer in headlights, surely."

"Nope, dead fish. Round, unblinking, dead eyes. And I don't think they sell underwear in the Dealers Room."

"There's a mall across the street."

"Let's go shopping."

Doris waited in the shadow of one of the potted plants, hoping for a friendly face. She'd made one more trip to Heki's shop and picked up a long, full-coverage, dark-blue hooded cloak. Which was the only reason she'd been able to step out of Folsom's room after changing.

Parked where she was, she should be able to see anyone going into the Hyatt. But she was also virtually invisible. What with the books about a certain magic school, hooded cloaks were everywhere.

She'd settle for Mandy or Kelly. Even Traxa. Anybody she knew. Fortunately, she spotted Daphne.

"Pssst," she whispered over the din of the smoking area. "Daphne. Daphne!"

"Yes?" Daphne said to the hooded figure.

"It's Doris," Doris stage-whispered.

"Doris, why are you hiding in the shadows in a hooded cloak?" Daphne asked, grinning. "Shall we promenade?"

"Maybe. Maybe not. Come 'ere."

When Daphne came over, Doris maneuvered herself so her back was to the crowd, and opened up the cloak.

"Oh my God!" Daphne said, covering her mouth and trying desperately not to giggle. "Oh my *God*, Doris! That is *shameless*!"

"But *I'm* not," Doris said, pulling the cloak back around her. Tight. "This was a *bad* idea. I blame Kelly. I don't think I can do this! I'll go change into..."

"Baggy jeans and T-shirt?" Daphne said. "If you want. Where'd you get it?"

"In the Dealers Room. I found some money in my backpack."

"Well, you've spent the money on it and it looks absolutely stunning," Daphne said, frowning. "*I* could never wear it. But you wear it very well."

"I'm not sure I can wear it in public, though."

"You like to dance, right?" Daphne asked.

"Yeah. That's why I got it."

"Could you wear it if you were dancing?"

"Maybe."

"Be right back."

"Okay, I've fixed it with security," Daphne said, coming back and taking Doris's elbow. "Keep the cloak on and come with me."

"Security?" Doris asked.

"They don't like people working for a large crowd," Daphne said, leading her into the interior on the same level as the smoking plaza.

"Aren't we supposed to go . . . ?" Doris said, sticking a hand out to gesture up to the lobby. The lower level was already fairly crowded with costumers and picture-takers.

"No pictures up there and definitely no sticking in one place," Daphne said, leading her to the back of the large room. At the back was a young man in Middle-Eastern, dress sitting on the floor surrounded by drums. Doris vaguely recognized him as one of the drummers from the previous night.

"You sure we're not going to get in trouble?" the kid said.

"I told you, I know Mike," Daphne said. "No more than thirty, forty-five minutes, and if it gets too crowded we'll have to shut down."

"What are we doing?" Doris asked.

"*You* are dancing," Daphne replied. "Wait until the drums start to take off your cloak. Right." She cleared her throat and raised her voice. "Ladies and gentlemen, come one, come all to the most amazing demonstration of dance you have ever seen in your life! She will amaze and astound you with her virtuosity and beauty! Gold is preferable," she added, sweeping off her hat and holding it out. "Silver is acceptable! Is that a copper piece I see there, young man! No copper for her! This is: the amazing *Doris*!"

The drums started up and Doris took a deep, cleansing breath, then swept off the cloak. For a moment she thought her ears were going to pop from the inhalations, then the flashes started going off. She ignored those, and the wolf whistles, and started dancing.

"I think there's, like, fifty bucks in this hat," Daphne said when security had broken up the crowd. It was a necessity, they were getting twenty deep.

"There was just something . . . right about getting paid to dance," Doris said. "I never thought I'd say those words, though."

"There's even a gold coin," Daphne said, pulling it out. The coin was so old and worn it was hard to tell what the original denomination was.

"Where'd that come from?" Doris asked.

"Death, I think," Daphne said, gesturing at the hooded figure with the scythe who was being led away by security. "Probably got it off the eyes of a dead king. You can have it."

"Heh."

"Let's divvy it up and then promenade," Daphne said. "Sinbad, you good for a twenty?"

"Works," the drummer said. "I can't remember the last time I got paid. Oh, yeah. Mosul, 1648."

"Funny," Doris replied.

"Think you can walk around in that now?" Daphne asked.

"Yeah, I think I can."

"You're a brave, brave girl," Daphne said, chuckling.

They headed upstairs, stopping every few feet for pictures, and finally reached the lobby. Despite the picture-taking ban, quite a few people were up there in costume simply to be admired.

"Whoa!" Doris said, stopping to look at one of the outfits. The woman was nearly as tall as she, with equally red hair, and wore a magnificent laser-cut leather bodice and bikini bottom that were formed like demon hands. The matching leather wings were, if anything, more amazing. The demon horns were quite unnecessary.

"That's an amazing costume," Doris said, smiling at her.

"Yes," the woman replied. "And it doesn't make *me* look like a slut."

"Excuse me?" Doris said, stunned.

"Piss off, trash," the woman said, ignoring her.

"That's Garnet," Daphne said, quietly, drawing Doris away. "I'd better warn you, that's your main competition for Dawn this year. And that outfit is just what she's wearing for her *hall* costume. I can't imagine what her Dawn costume is going to look like."

"Oh," Doris said in a small voice.

"Don't let her get to you, though," Daphne said. "She knows you're going to be in Dawn and she's trying to get to you. She's always like that."

"Well, sometimes people can be sort of prickly on the outside..."

"Don't think it," Daphne said, shaking her head. "She's a bitch all the way to the core."

"Oh."

"She's going to do anything she can get away with to make sure she wins Dawn," Daphne said. "If you let her get to you, she will. Don't."

"Okay," Doris said, nodding. "I won't. Screw her."

"That's the spirit."

She changed in Duncan's room again. The harem-girl costume fit comfortably in her backpack, but she fingered the material for a bit before stuffing it away. She had no clue the next time she'd get to wear it, but she was looking forward to it. Kelly had been right, she looked *very* hot in a harem-girl outfit. And not at all like a slut.

Looking hot, *knowing* she looked hot, had never been something she could even imagine. It felt good to be appreciated. It was amazing the changes that had been wrought on her in just a few days. The fact that she could take an insult like the one that Garnet woman had thrown at her and more or less ignore it, proved that.

But that brought up the question of Dawn. Kelly had said that it was getting to be more and more of a costume contest, and even with the money she had left from her find, there was no way she could create a really outstanding outfit by tomorrow. Which meant she needed an edge...

Hmmm...

She picked up the practice sword Edmund had given her and hefted it. Then she picked up her backpack and left the room.

There had to be *somewhere* in this gigantic hotel where she could be alone.

Chapter Five

"Hi, I'm Doris," Doris said, sitting down. "What's *your* name?"
"Hi, Doris, I'm Folsom," Duncan said, laughing. "You're looking chipper."

"Nervous energy and caffeine," Doris said.

"You haven't been dancing all night again, have you?"

"Yes," Doris said. "But this time I cheated. After I changed—thanks for letting me use your room again—I snuck into one of the meeting rooms that wasn't being used and danced by myself. Well, sort of," she added cryptically. "I was practicing for Dawn."

"I thought you were just supposed to parade out there and show yourself off," Duncan said, puzzled.

"You have up to one minute to do whatever you want," Doris said. "And at the judges' discretion, it can go longer. I read the rules carefully."

"And you're hoping for the judge's discretion," Duncan said. "That's ballsy. Ovarian, in your case. What are you going to do?"

"It's a secret," Doris said. "But thank you for introducing me to Fig."

"She's a nice lady and Edmund likes pretty girls around," Folsom said, shrugging. "I try to keep on their good side. You're really not going to tell me."

"Nope," Doris said, thinking hard. "I need to go to the Dealers

Room and the Exhibitors Hall and pick up some stuff. Then I need to find Fig and Bran, in that order. Then I'm going to be busy, busy, busy."

"Then you're going to need a good breakfast," Duncan said, signaling for a waiter. "My treat."

"I found some money in my backpack," Doris said. "I can buy this time."

"One meal won't break me," Duncan said. "Seriously. And you should save that money. I suspect you're going to need all of it."

"Feeling like a leech, I accept," Doris said.

"You're not a leech," Folsom said, smiling faintly. "I feel that I owe you, not the other way around."

"Why?" Doris asked.

"I think you'll understand someday," Folsom replied, shrugging. "Or perhaps you'll forget."

"Never," Doris said. "I could never forget any of this. It's going to be burned into my memory forever. This has been the greatest experience of my life. Do you know the best part?"

"What?" Duncan asked, grinning at her enthusiasm.

"Today is my birthday," Doris said, grinning back. "And I'm going to win the Dawn contest. Guarantee it."

Bran looked at the sketch and the list and his eyebrows went up.

"Can you do this?" he asked.

"I saw the basic dress and the shoes over at the mall yesterday," Doris said in a rush. "Assuming they're still there, yes. I've got the money to cover both. The rest of it is just sewing. I can buy the material, now."

"Don't worry about the material," Bran said. "I've got emotional investment in this if nothing else. But I don't know if some of this is necessary. And it's going to take a long time."

"I can do it," Doris said. "I have to. I'll be over in the mall for a bit, then if you don't mind, I'll use your room."

"That's fine," Bran said, handing over the sketch and then a key. "I'll be here most of the day. Good luck. I'll be sure to be at the contest."

~

"Do I look like some sort of messenger?" Traxa said as she entered the room. "Go to Fig and get this. Go to the mall and get that. I've got *other* things to do at this con, you know!"

"All I can say is thank you," Doris said, concentrating on her sewing. "Or, thank you, thank you, thank you. This is taking longer than I'd expected."

The costume she'd settled on was a modified Egyptian look. The name was "Dawn, Warrior of the East," and the dual swords gave it a nice eastern look.

"I'm not sure you need much more than the dress," Mandy said, pulling at the fabric. "That right there is an invitation to rape."

She intended to do a very sedate sword dance as part of the presentation, but it still had to be a very...mobile dress. One of the more popular shops in the mall, at least during Dragon*Con, was one that normally supplied to exotic dancers. The dress had come from that shop. As had the shoes, which were more sturdy and practical than they looked.

"You've seen the costumes," Doris said, picking up another "appliance" and sewing it on. The added parts gave the base dress a look of semi-armor. It wasn't nearly as ornate as some of the other costumes, but she was counting on the sword dance to put her over the top.

"And I don't think the veil is a good idea," Anita said, none-theless working on same. "The judges want to see faces nearly as much as bodies. Remember the rule about hair over one eye."

"I'll take it off eventually," Doris said. "The shoes match the costume match the headdress. With the sword dance, it should be enough. I just look more like Dawn than any of the other contestants, including Garnet. And is it just me, or does she look a little long in the tooth for the Dawn contest?"

"And she's older than she looks," Mandy said. She caught a glare from Anita and shrugged. "Well, she *is*."

"Garnet's ascendant," Anita said. "Getting on the bad side of an ascendant..."

"Garnet *thinks* she's ascendant," Mandy snapped. "But she cannot ascend without winning Dawn. And with all the bad blood she's been creating, if she doesn't ascend she's in for a world of hurt."

"Forgive *me* for trying to maintain some semblance of neu-trality," Anita snapped back.

"And forgive me for thinking 'neutrality' is just another word for cowardice!"

"Well, *I* remember what happened the *last* time!"

"What are you girls arguing about?" Doris said, looking up from her gluing.

"Nothing," they replied in chorus.

"You ever get the feeling you're being led around by the nose?" Sharice asked.

"I'm not being led around," Wulfgar said, munching on a sandwich. "But I get the feeling that Janea's not going to pass this point as long as I'm here. Or she only passes in the few cases where my back is turned."

"We're not being *allowed* to find her," Drakon said, walking up. "I was in the gaming areas looking for her when I ran across the old man from the anime room. And got to talking. And completely lost track of the mission. His name is Ken Suno." He flexed his jaw and shook his head. "Damn me for not seeing it."

"Seeing what?" Sharice asked.

"At a guess?" Drakon said. "Su-san-o-o. Brother of Amaterasu. *Major* Shinto god. Here he's the head of the anime track."

"Damn," Wulfgar muttered, his eyes widening. "The guy who heads up security..."

"What?" Sharice asked.

"Huge blond guy," Wulfgar said, shrugging. "Blue eyes, but he doesn't look Scandinavian or Aryan. More...Greek."

"Name?" Drakon asked.

"Mike. *Michael.*"

"Holy Mother," Sharice whispered. "*The* Michael? Transformed God of War? Patron saint of elite forces? *Archangel* Michael?"

"At a guess."

"Okay, *no* getting on the wrong side of security," Drakon said.

"I helped a little old lady up the steps the other day," Wulfgar said. "Pear shaped. Looked about a thousand years old. Guess what her con name was? Al Mater."

"*The* All-Mother?" Sharice asked.

"Ta-da," Wulfgar said, then winced. "Svar..."

"Svarog?" Sharice said. "*Tell* me we didn't just do a deal with Svarog."

"Think so," Wulfgar replied. "Hope that doesn't come back to bite us in the butt someday."

"European," Drakon said.

"Slavic god of smithing," Sharice said, shuddering.

"Not a nicey-nice god, I take it," Drakon said, nodding. "Fun."

"Gods and avatars," Sharice said, looking around at the crowds. "Lost souls and people in dream state. I said it but I didn't really *grok* it, you know?"

"Which means Odin is somewhere around," Wulfgar said, starting to grin. "And Thor."

"Thor could be rolled fully into Michael at this point," Sharice pointed out. "You might have already met him."

"Fir, surely," Wulfgar said, then shrugged. "Good enough, for that matter. But it also means there are demons," he added as a girl dressed as a succubus walked by.

"Neutral ground," Sharice said.

"I don't see Michael enforcing neutral ground," Drakon said. "I mean, I don't know much about Christian myth, but I don't see it."

"I think Barb would probably say that it's ineffable," Sharice said, shrugging. "Even demons are God's creations. They're fallen angels."

"There is *no way*," Doris said, looking around the room.

The backstage of the ballroom was packed with contestants. It was a sea of redheads in everything from elaborate fantasy costumes to a feather and two bangles. The only similarity was that there was some red to their hair, ranging from strawberry blonde to auburn, and they had three tears painted under the left eye.

"I can't win this," Doris said. "Look at Garnet!"

The previous year's winner's costume was an elaborate laser-cut leather demon complete with the talons.

"That must have cost an arm and a leg."

"More like a soul," Daphne said. "Souls. But they weren't hers. Win or lose, you are going to participate. And have you looked more closely? Most of them truly don't have a chance. They're just here because for thirty seconds, eight thousand people will be looking at them."

Now that Doris had some time to recover from her shock,

she had to admit the little pirate had a point. More than half the women in the room really would look better in street clothes. Spandex was a privilege, not a right. And even for those who had some semblance of the real "Dawn" look, most of the costumes ran to the sort of thing you got from a Halloween shop. Little Bo Peep and Sexy Cop.

That left, out of probably two hundred, maybe thirty who were contenders. Considered honestly, Doris was in that category. So those were the girls to beat.

At which point...

"I'm still not going to win," Doris said.

"Seek the Grail," Daphne said. "You may find it or not, but the value is in the search."

"Do you know Duncan Folsom?" Doris asked.

"I know the name," Daphne said. "But we've never met. We run in slightly different planes but we're aligned."

"If you're going to register, please do," the lady at the table said. She looked as if she could have been an entrant once upon a time. "We need to get this show going."

"Yes," Doris said. "I'm registering."

"Stage name?"

"Excuse me?" Doris said.

"Most people use their mystic name," the lady said. "It cuts down on the stalkers. Or you can use your mundane name. Up to you."

"Myst..." Doris said, frowning. "I don't really have..."

"Sure you do," Daphne said. "Think about it. Everyone does, they just hold it deep inside. Who *are* you, really? Doris Grisham of White Springs, Alabama?"

"Yes," Doris said. "I am. And...no, I'm not."

"The Faces," Daphne said, softly. "The thousand faces of the hero, the nine billion names of God. Who *is* the Goddess within? What name calls once from the darkness, twice from the light?"

"Janea," Doris said hesitantly. "My name's Janea."

"Good one," the lady said, writing it down on a form. "Original. Okay, you're done. Your friend has to stay. Only contestants from here on out."

"Good luck," Daphne said, hugging her. "Truth is, we're from about as far apart as anyone could imagine, but I think I've grown knowing you. Which takes some doing."

"You're . . . going to be around when I'm done, right?" Doris asked.

"Always," Daphne said, giving her a kiss on the cheek. "But when you win, I think there will be others who will want to greet you. There are some who have been waiting to see who you become. I hope we see each other before the end of the con, but that's tonight at midnight. And everyone will be gathering for Dead Dog. But I'll be with you when you hear the whisper of the wind."

"What?" Doris said.

"Just go, honey," Daphne said, pushing her into the throng. "Be the Goddess."

Doris waved as she walked away but Daphne didn't look back. She already missed the little pirate and hoped that they'd be able to meet again and get some contact information before the end of the con. She thought about the last conversation for a second and then frowned.

"Plane?"

Waiting for the contest was about the most nerve-wracking experience of her whole life. The girls had been assigned numbers at random rather than as they turned up, to keep people from gaming the system. Winners tended to be either early in the contest or very late.

Despite that system, Doris suspected some sort of foul play since Garnet's entry was next to last. Worse, Doris had somehow gotten the slot right before the previous year's winner. Which meant she was probably going to be upstaged.

And the more time she had to think, the less she liked her costume. It wasn't elaborate enough to win for the costuming value—several of the judges were serious costumers—and it was too elaborate to win her points for sexy.

One by one the contestants went out, did their little pirouette or, in rare cases, some sort of routine, and then in some cases submitted to questions from the judges. If you didn't get questioned, it was pretty clear you weren't in the running. But most of the girls weren't really there to win, as Daphne had pointed out. So most of them came back happy looking. The few that didn't were the "contenders" who weren't asked questions.

There were fewer than ten girls left and Doris started to sidle towards the front. It was no big deal. Walk out, do the quick dance, come back. Hopefully the judges wouldn't ask her questions.

"'Did you do the costume yourself?'" Doris muttered, sliding over to the wall by the stage entrance. "'Except for most of it, which I bought in a stripper shop.' 'How long have you been costuming?' 'How long has the con been going on?'"

"Now the little newb is talking to herself," Garnet said. "How quaint."

Doris had been so focused on the stage, she hadn't even noticed the woman walk up.

"Well, it's talk to myself or talk to you," Janea said. "I'll take talking to air first."

"Think you're special?" Garnet snarled. "You're nothing but a tiny little nobody in this con. You're nothing. You're worthless."

"Which is why you keep picking on me, right?" Janea said. "Because I'm so worthless you know I'm going to kick your ass."

"Really?" Garnet said, smiling. "Think so?"

Without the slightest warning, she snatched off half the barely attached appliances on the costume, ripping the dress in the process. "Not now."

"Oh..." Doris said. "You... you..."

"And next...Janea...presenting Dawn, Warrior of the East."

"Good luck," Garnet said.

Doris stood, just breathing hard for a moment, then reached up and ripped the rest of the elaborate fake armoring off the dress, ripping more of it in the process.

"...Dawn, Warrior of the East...?"

Janea strode onto the stage without even glancing at the judges or the crowd, then spun into a lotus position with her back to the crowd. She opened up the brooch on her cloak and spun it out of the way, then drew her swords and laid them, crossed, in front of her on the stage.

The music started and she stood up, took her right sword, and stuck it through the constraining material of the dress between her legs, and cut from just below her crotch to the floor. She spun up on one foot in a pirouette and the two swords lashed the remaining fabric away, the leg-length pieces flipping away through the air like butterflies. *Then* she started to dance.

Everything else fell away then. For Janea, when she was in movement the world became the dance. The crowd did not matter, the judges did not matter, Garnet did not matter. Only the dance.

There have been sword dances performed in every society that had periods when the sword was the paramount weapon, from Caucasus saber dances to Wu-Shu. Most of them had little to do with actual combat. But they mostly shared the peculiarity of performing them being a life-and-death event for the *performer*. Most styles involved moving the blade *very* close to the performer's body. The closer the blade to the body, the faster...that was the essence of the sword dance.

The dance of Janea was not one style, not one way. A watcher would see elements of Wu-Shu, Hungarian and Cossack, and even Choliya, but it maintained that single essence.

To balance on the razor blade between life and death. To trim the hairs but not the skin.

When Janea came to her feet and started dancing, her costume was already in tatters. As she danced, it became more so.

> Roll out of the bed
> Look in the mirror
> And wonder who you are
> Another year is come and gone

"Okay, we found Janea," Wulfgar said, his mouth hanging open.

He had seen Janea dance before. He'd even snuck into a club she was working at, which made him feel very much like a pervert. But he'd never seen her *dance*. Not like this.

She was a spinning dervish across the stage, the double swords flickering in and out and a veritable torrent of material flying away from her rapidly denuding body. There could be no question that the swords were razor sharp. Not only were they slicing through the fabric of the costume like paper, she was, in time with the dance and often while in the air, catching pieces in midair and cutting them smaller. She was already down to not much more than a micro-mini and a halter. She couldn't go much further without being down to "no costume."

"I think the judges are enjoying it," Sharice said dryly, as Janea flipped one of the cut bits of dress with a sword tip to settle on the head of the creator of Dawn.

"They're not calling time on her, anyway," Wulfgar said.

"I think the crowd would rise up in fury if they did," Sharice said. "Damn..."

"That is..." Drakon said, his jaw dropping as Janea somersaulted across the stage, bits of material still flying off as the swords flashed in and out. "I *would* have said that was physically impossible."

> But maybe you touch one life
> And the world becomes a better place to be
> Maybe you give their dreams another day
> Another chance to be free

Janea had carefully choreographed her planned dance. This wasn't it. What she was doing, how she was doing it, she wasn't exactly sure. She also didn't know if she was dancing *well*. But she also didn't care. There was only the dance.

As the last bars of the song closed, she dropped to a split facing the judges, slid her swords up between the veil and her face, ripped the veil away with a flick of the wrist to give it some heft, then dropped the prescribed lock of hair over her cheek. As the piece of gauze settled to the stage, it was quiet enough she thought she could hear it touch the ground. She distinctly heard the "tink" as the swords crossed in front of her.

The MC wasn't asking any questions—she wasn't sure why, but he looked too stunned or something—so she bounced twice to get some momentum, popped straight to her feet and walked off the stage.

"Beat that, *bitch*," Janea said as she walked past Garnet.

"She gets presented the Crown and the Prize in the Hyatt main lobby," Wulfgar said, pressing through the crowd. "We can probably make contact there."

"Think again," Drakon countered. "She's going to be surrounded by security. All you're going to get is blinded by camera flashes."

"It's the best chance we're..." Wulfgar paused as someone even larger than he was stepped in front of them.

"Sorry..." the guy said. He was dressed a bit like some sort of bird and was wearing an eagle mask. "But it's time for you guys to go home."

"Excuse me?" Wulfgar said. "And who are you to..."

"Wulfgar," Sharice said, carefully. "*Don't* start anything. We're looking for a friend."

"We know," the eagle man said. "Which is why I'm explaining, politely, that she's going to be busy for the rest of the convention. And that Pat says it's time for you to go home. Most of the mundanes go home after the Dawn show. You don't want to stay for Dead Dog. Mundanes who stay for Dead Dog sometimes never make it home."

"Is that a threat?" Wulfgar asked.

"No, that is information," the bird man said, tilting his head sharply to the side. "If you'd like a threat, it can be arranged."

"We're just going," Sharice said, suddenly, grabbing his arm.

"But..." Wulfgar said. It wasn't as if she could move him.

"We're going, Wulfgar," Sharice said. "Back to the room. Then we'll pack and go home."

"But..." Wulfgar said as he let himself be dragged away.

"Just shut your fool Asatru mouth," Sharice said, walking as rapidly as she could through the crowd.

"No call to be..."

"Asatru are horrible about studying other religions," Sharice said as they left the Hyatt. "So take my word for it, we are leaving."

"Malakbel?" Drakon asked.

"Ancient Assyrian?" Sharice said. "Maybe. I don't think so, though. Think...Barb."

"You mean the White God?" Wulfgar said, craning his head to look for the Eagle Man. The guy, despite being huge, had disappeared. And most of the crowd seemed to be people in mundane dress who were headed for the exits.

"Not...exactly," Sharice said. "*But those who wait on the* LORD *will find new strength. They will fly high on wings like eagles. They shall run and not grow weary. They will walk and not faint.* I can quote a half a dozen other verses, not to mention Nostradamus. I don't think *that* messenger was from any minor god you can care to name. So we are *leaving.*"

⌒•

Doris was left alone for a moment to blink at the crown in her hands. There was no way that those were actual rubies. They looked real, but it was amazing what they could do with synthetics these days...

"Janea."

The woman was probably in her forties, blonde, with a face that was not so much kind as so understanding of humanity, it had sort of gone past *un*kind to wise.

"Ma'am?" Doris said.

The past hour had been a blur. Garnet had most assuredly *not* won and security had become involved. She'd never even gotten close to Doris. Knowing what was going to happen, two guys dressed like goons had interposed themselves when she left the stage to *very* muted applause. One move towards Janea had been enough for them to wrap her up in tentacles and drag her out of the room.

The judges *had* asked questions, later, mostly along the lines of "Are you seeing anyone?" She wasn't even sure what she'd answered. Pretty much everything from when she'd picked up her swords was a blur.

Now someone else she didn't know wanted something.

"I am Regina," the woman said. "I'm the Senior Director of Programming. Since *you* are now Programming, I'm *your* Senior Director."

"Okay?" Doris said.

"Your time from now until Dead Dog is blocked out," Regina said. "First there is the formal presentation of the Crown, and the prize of course. Then interviews with select media. Then the visit to the Green Room to meet select Guests. Last, Dead Dog where you will be formally Chosen and given appropriate transportation home."

"I get a ride?" Doris said.

"Yes, dear," Regina replied, softly. "You get a ride home. You didn't know that was the actual prize?"

"No..." Doris said, confused. "Don't most people have rides home?"

"Oh, most of the regular congoers can get home just fine," Regina said, taking her arm. "You, of course, are special. I am personally pleased that you won. You've had me worried for years. You really couldn't ever reach your full potential as you were, two people sharing one soul. But even if you were still having transportation problems, it's not as if Janea or Doris couldn't find friends."

"I have found friends here," Doris said. "A lot of friends. Speaking of which..."

"You may run into a few," Regina said, leading her into one of the back corridors. "But this time of the con, it's hard to get up to the Green Room other than through the special ways."

"I thought there was other stuff we were going to do...?" Janea said. She sort of remembered it and sort of didn't. Everything was getting a bit disconnected. For example, she wondered how they got onto one of the upper floors. She didn't even remember an elevator. They were, though. From the upper walkway she could see the whole Hyatt spread below her. It was like being a god. There was an odd rainbow effect stretching down to the lobby. It looked almost like a bridge.

"Bit of a blur?" Regina said, pausing at the door of a suite. "Don't worry, it's all taken care of. And so we come to my true domain, the Green Room. Say hello to Carl."

"Hi." The guy was immense, but Doris sensed he was as kind as he was big. "My con name is Fir. If you need anything, or anybody's giving you any trouble, just say my name and I'll be there."

"Thanks," Doris said, following Regina into the suite.

The room was crowded and overheated. It also was...wrong. It must have been the size of a ballroom to hold all the people that were in it, and hotels didn't put ballrooms on top floors. It also didn't *look* that big. It looked like a normal suite.

She looked around for people that she knew, but they were all strangers. A bunch of them were half familiar, like she'd seen them in a movie or something, but she couldn't place any names.

There was music coming from a stereo, but it was being drowned out by a young guy in Renaissance dress banging on a piano. An Elvis impersonator wearing stormtrooper armor was accompanying on guitar. Doris couldn't figure out the tune, though, since they seemed to be playing two entirely different styles. Worked, though.

"I swear," Regina said, shaking her head. "Wulfie and the King are never going to get 'Nocturne for a Hound Dog' down. And this is Clark, who you'd probably get along with."

"Charmed," the man said, taking her hand and kissing it.

Doris certainly was. She'd expected a kiss on the hand to be sloppy, but it was just a touch of dry lips. And the guy was the epitome of tall, dark and handsome. He was also, as usual, vaguely familiar.

"Have we met before?" Doris asked.

"I assure you we have not," the guy said, smiling. Damn, he had nice teeth. "I would remember."

"Alas, you two don't have *nearly* enough time to get *properly* acquainted," Regina said, smiling at him. "Which is a pity. Ah, I think that you might enjoy this group."

"Look, I *asked* Pat!" a man with a wild head of hair and shaggy eyebrows said. "Pat says He *doesn't* play dice with the universe. Take *that*, Niels!"

"Al? Eddie? Isaac?" Regina said. "This is Doris. She's the winner of the Dawn Contest."

"If Pat doesn't play dice with the universe, how exactly *does* He explain wave particle duality?" Doris asked.

"He said, and I find myself troubled by this, that He did it to see how many atheist brains He could get to explode." Isaac was dressed in English period dress and wore a powdered wig. "Of course, I am troubled by any scientist discounting the obvious existence of a benevolent Creator."

"God is omniscient, omnipotent and omnipresent," Eddie said, grinning. "Clearly He is also omnihumorous."

"I rarely find him so," Isaac said. "But perhaps the joke is too subtle for my intellect?"

"Or too slapstick?" Eddie said. "Like putting me through hell inventing the lightbulb just so that comics could finally have a visual representation for gestalt?"

"So . . . quantum mechanics is a *joke*?" Doris said.

"If you think about it clearly it makes a certain degree of sense," Isaac replied with a pained expression. "But one must first accept a Creator as a given. If you fail to include a thinking being as part of your thesis, the entire universe becomes unbalanced. I have carefully examined this quantum theory problem, and a thinking being with a specific agenda is the simplest answer to the many conundrums. Take wave particle duality. Mass is undetectable at the quantum level. Yet it interacts with all things using a logic which is indefinable as well. Last, it is in everything. Omnipresent, omnipotent and ineffable. This *is* the definition of the Lord."

"I'm going to go find Niels and say...What *is* that phrase that the children are using these days?" Al said, distractedly.

"'In your face'?" Doris said hesitantly.

"That, yes, exactly..." Al said then sat down again. "But what is its *exact* meaning? To what, *exactly*, does it refer? A portion of the body? Is it, at some level, a metaphor for the constancy of problems being central to the human existence?"

"Or maybe some people who are a *bit* more grounded," Regina said, leading her over to another set of couches. Three men were engrossed in an article in a magazine.

"I keep wanting to go down to Houston and strangle the head of NASA," one of the men said. He was tall with a rangy build, bald as a cue ball and wearing a Hawaiian shirt. "There was so much *promise* there."

"It's like SFWA, really," another man said. Slighter and darker, he wore a suit that was rumpled and had papers sticking out of most of the pockets. "At a certain point, the rule weenies take over."

"I wouldn't say it's *quite* as bad as SFWA..." The third man was slight, blond and darkly tanned, with an English accent.

"Robert, Ike, John, this is Doris," Regina said.

"Ah, the Dawn Queen," John said, standing up and bowing over her hand. Unlike Clark, he didn't attempt to kiss it. "Welcome to the Green Room, charming lady."

"Down, John," Robert said, smiling at her. "What do *you* think of the modern space program, miss?"

"I think they jumped the shark with the Shuttle," Doris said. "Once they'd dug the hole they just kept digging deeper to see if they could find gold. Which was a bit like looking for it in Kansas."

"I suspect it went to an earlier point than that," Ike said, shaking his head. "One could see the future history of the program in the early control by the bureaucracy of almost every aspect. If one had a sufficiently advanced computer and a proper model, one could almost certainly predict every action that has taken place..."

"Yes, yes, if you had a sufficiently advanced computer," Robert said. "One terabyte not enough. One *petabyte* not enough? How much *is* enough, Ike?"

"Hey, I've practically got a terabyte in my *phone*."

Doris spun around at the voice and grinned when she saw Kelly.

"They let you in here?" she asked.

"I can get anywhere," Kelly said.

"Yes," Regina said, dryly. "Like crotch rot."

"Technically, I think that is only found in the cro..." Ike said then trailed off at her glare.

"A terabyte in your phone?" Robert said, incredulously. "I hate modern society. I suppose you... *text*?"

"Blackberry," Kelly said, holding up his phone. "You really need to catch up here, Robert. It's embarrassing that somebody like me can figure out something you envisioned better than you can."

"I didn't envision... ringtones," Robert said dryly. "I wish no one had. If I hear *one more* acid rock song in the restaurant..."

"Unless you're talking about Jimmy," Kelly said, gesturing over to a black guy by the wall, chatting up a blonde in a long white dress, "you're probably not talking about acid rock. Metal, *maybe...*"

"Whatever," Robert said. "It all sounds the same. And I also didn't envision phone porn."

"Got that one right," John said, holding up a finger. "But the social implications turned out to be somewhat... muted," he finished in a puzzled tone.

"*I* refused to switch to that newfangled touch tone," Ike said, proudly.

"Isaac, did you just use 'newfangled' in a sentence?" Kelly asked. "Regina, you've got things to do to prepare for Closing. Why don't I show her around?"

"I think I'd rather entrust a child to a tiger," Regina said.

"But you do have things to do, don't you?" Kelly said.

"Yes," Regina said. "The problem being, I'm trying to figure out which side of the field you're playing."

"I never play the field," Kelly said. "Astara would kill me. Seriously, I'll have her to Ceremonies on time."

"Why?" Regina said, suspiciously.

"Oh, come *on*," Kelly said, grinning. "You *know* the amount of chaos it's going to cause."

"That sounds suspiciously like honesty," Robert said.

"Yes, it does," Regina said. "Which makes me even more nervous."

"She'll be there on time," Kelly said. "And I swear on my hon... well, I swear on *Robert's* honor that she'll be fine."

"Knowing this is probably a bad idea..." Regina said, then kissed Doris on the cheek. "Truth is, when there's fun involved in the outcome, you really can trust Kelly. So I'll see you at Dead Dog."

"Okay," Doris said. "*What* chaos?" she continued, looking at Kelly.

"Oh, you know," he said, leading her away. "Angst. Jealousy. Plans ruined. Dead Dog is the official moment for all the angst built up during the con to come pouring out. Don't sweat it. It's not about you, really. It's just...get this many big egos all in one place and you end up with blood on the walls. So who do you want to see?"

"Uhm..." Doris said. So far every "guest" had been fascinating. "I don't know, who do you suggest?"

"Let's take the grand promenade," Kelly said, offering her his arm. "*Everyone* wants to meet the Dawn Queen."

"Time for Dead Dog," Regina said.

Again Doris had that moment of disconnect. She'd been wandering the Green Room for what seemed like hours but had almost no recollection of exactly what she'd been doing. She'd met dozens of people and vaguely remembered being fascinated by all of them, but with the exception of a guy in Revolutionary period dress named George, subject governmental structure and politics, she really didn't recall anything in detail.

"Has somebody been slipping me something?" she asked, looking over at Kelly. She blinked rapidly and shook her head. "When did you change into costume?"

Kelly was wearing Viking period dress, except that it was silk, which wasn't normal Viking fare, and while he looked exactly the same, tall, slim, long blond hair going gray, he had a more saturnine look than she remembered.

"Seriously, we have to hurry, now," Regina said, taking her hand. Regina was wearing what Doris first took to be scale armor, then couldn't decide if it was supposed to be just scales. Or, possibly, diamonds. It seemed to be drifting from one to the other. "It's out on the balcony."

"What balcony?" Doris asked as they stepped through the door. She thought she had been all over the suite, but never noticed that there was a balcony.

"This isn't a balcony," she squeaked as they stepped through the doorway. The Green Room must have been on the top of the hotel, because they were outside on what looked like the roof. But the roofs of hotels always had walls around them, and this one didn't.

For that matter, the con took place in downtown Atlanta. She knew that. She'd been moving around the hotels. She knew, in general, what the surrounding area looked like.

It was *not* a mountain range.

"Where *is* this?"

"The balcony of the Green Room," Regina said, her voice shifting in and out in liquid syllables. Doris had never even thought about "doing it" with a girl but the syllables went right to her insides. She also now appeared younger. *And* older.

"Okay, somebody *has* been slipping me drugs," Doris said as the mountaintop started to fill with the people of the Green Room. They seemed to be splitting into camps, and she saw Shane with his zombies gathering to one side. On the other, Fig, also wearing armor, was standing by the side of Edmund Wodinaz. Edmund was wearing Viking dress, an eyepatch, and a broad hat, and carried a spear. He looked just as elderly as the last time Doris had seen him but the term "spry" came to mind. Also "dangerous."

"No, sweetie," Regina said, her voice going melodious and liquid. "This is where you have been the whole time, in the heart of the Dragon, the place where dreams become reality and reality is, for a time, but a dream. But it's time for you to go now. You are the Chosen, sent to bring the message of the Dragon to the world. For this year..."

"I challenge!" Garnet snarled. "She has been given illicit support throughout the con. The rules have been broken!"

"She quested for allies and found them," Regina said, tightly. "She was given no support from within the convention nor by convention personnel other than that to which she was entitled. I never even spoke to her nor influenced her actions until she had won the contest, and she is *my* avatar! Such support as she obtained came from those who loved her, trusted her and supported her. She is properly Chosen. That is the one and only rule. You *had* your chance and you blew it. And if we wish to discuss rule breaking, *you* used physical violence."

"And I'm about to use more!" Garnet said, straightening up

and waving to the group gathering on the north side of the mountain. "I *shall not* be denied! My acolytes gather for sacrifice and my allies are prepared to open the way."

"Do you think you are the only one with acolytes?" Edmund said, smiling tightly and gesturing behind him. "Or allies? And I note you seem to be missing many of both. Where *is* this summoning? Where are these allies?"

"They are..." Garnet said, looking around. Her side did seem a bit... small. "This *will* not be!" She reached behind her back and a sword of black flame appeared in her hand.

"Got that covered," Edmund said, drawing a battle-axe from midair. "You're going *down*, bitch. I've had about enough of your prancing."

"I was rage and power when *your* followers were trying to make spears from *flint*!" Garnet shouted.

"*Now* she's willing to admit her age," Frig said, a shining spear appearing in her hand. "Want a shawl, grandma?"

"At least *she* still *has* followers," Svar said, drawing a blade of midnight.

"Oh, yeah?" Edmund said. "In case you didn't get the update, Michael's avatar is going through them like Garnet through a case of chocolates."

"You Aesir *bastard*...!" Garnet screamed, charging forward.

"*Ladies and gentlemen!*" Kelly said, a microphone suddenly appearing in his hand. "*In the south corner weighing in at the Hosts of Valhalla... Odin One Eye, King of the Aesir! And his lovely wife Frig! In the north corner weighing in at the Hosts of Hel... Garnet Osemala, Queen of Rage and Darkness! And her lovely consort Svar Balog, of course! Welcome tooooo... ARMEGED-DON SMACKDOWN! And I will be your host for this annual Ragnarok... Loki the Jester!*"

"And it's time for you to go," Regina said, as the two armies charged and Garnet swelled into a vast demonic form. Freya led Doris to the edge of the precipice and gestured for her to jump. "Time to Return."

"I can't jump off of that," Doris said. "I'll die."

"You'll be fine," Freya said, giving her a push. It was like being hit by a mallet, and Doris suddenly found herself falling. "And I will be with you always... my Child of Life."

"Wow," Janea said as Barb walked into the room. "You look like *you* should be in this bed."

The normally pristine Christian Adept was covered in blood, and her tacticals looked destined for the rag bin. Even her hair was a mess, which Janea had *never* seen.

"I'm heading for one," Barb said, walking over and taking her hand. "I heard you'd come out of your.... You were awake and I came right over."

"What happened?" Janea asked.

"The...usual," Barb said, frowning. "Zombies, succubae, and heroes to add to the wall. I think we shut this one down hard. I hope so. Stepfords are a nightmare. Are *you* okay?"

"I don't think I've ever been better," Janea said, taking a sip of water. "I'm sort of stiff from lying on my back and I'm having a hard time with balance but I feel...great."

"Do you remember anything?" Barb asked. "I tried to send you support when I could."

"I'm not sure," Janea said. "You're not the first one to ask. I sort of remember meeting people. And something about dancing. But other than that, not much. Apparently Sharice, Wulfgar and Drakon are in the same boat. Whatever happened on the other side, somebody doesn't want us recalling it too clearly."

"Not too surprising," Barb said, leaning over to hug her. "I don't really care. I'm just glad to have my Janea back."

"I'm glad to be back, too," Janea said, frowning. "And sad at the same time. Barb?"

"Yeah?"

"Don't make a habit of it or anything," Janea said. "But...it's okay if you call me Doris."

Book Two

Old Time Religion

Chapter One

"What do we got?"

Sonny Cribbs had been sheriff in Claiborne County since before the deputy he was addressing was born. On his return from two tours in Vietnam, he'd figured it was off to the mill for a life of cutting trees into lumber. But there was an opening in the sheriff's department and he was a veteran in good standing. That and a poppa who'd been managing the sheriff's campaigns for ten years was all it took.

Slim, dark and tanned, his wife still occasionally had to deal with nightmares of tunnels and bodies.

Back then there'd been nothing like "certification" for a deputy. You put on the badge and you got to work. By the time it'd come up, he'd been elected sheriff and nobody had asked about his credentials since.

Mostly his credentials were pushing forty years of seeing what man could and would do to man.

The single-wide trailer had seen better days. Probably decades ago. Set back in Mathis Hollow off Slate Creek Lane, its existence was marked only by a dirt road and a battered mailbox.

And now police tape.

"Two victims." Deputy Sheriff Randell Smith was what Sheriff Cribbs could not avoid calling "The New Breed." Five-seven and stocky even without his body armor, he looked like a Marine, which he had been. He'd been through all the right schools before applying to be a deputy. He came in knowing the lingo and all the right buzzwords. Good boy, but sometimes Sonny wondered if they permanently implanted a stick in officers' asses in the Academy. On the other hand, maybe it was a Marine thing. "Male, thirty-eight, one Elvis Cowper. Female, age thirty-seven, one Amy Cowper, his spouse. Missing subject is Lora Cowper, age fourteen, daughter."

"Damn," Sheriff Cribbs said, spitting out a stream of tobacco juice. "Walk me through."

"Nine-one-one received a call from the missing subject's school when missing subject failed to make the bus," the deputy said, occasionally glancing at his notes. "Phone calls to the residence were unanswered. A call to the mother's work determined she had not shown up. At which point they called nine-one-one. Officer arrived on scene at eight forty-seven AM. Door was open. Officer entered and found subjects in state of rigor mortis. Officer called for investigation team."

"And the officer was ...?" Sonny asked.

"Myself, sir," the deputy said, closing his book.

"See anything ain't in that little book, son?" the sheriff asked.

"Lots, sir," the deputy said, his face working. "And it's not easy to describe. Which is why it's not in the little book."

"Let's go," Sonny said, sighing.

The interior of the trailer wasn't neat, but Sonny had seen a lot worse. However, it was also obvious that there'd been some sort of a struggle. A table was overturned and a corner of a wall was busted.

"Looks like somebody was fighting," the sheriff said.

"That's what I thought, sir," the deputy said. "But you might want to wait on that."

Inside the "master bedroom" were the victims.

"We got us a sicko," Sonny said, walking carefully to the bed.

The mother and father were spread-eagled on the bed. The mother's nightdress was pulled up and she clearly had been violated. For that matter, the father's pants were bloody. So were their mouths, and a ring of redness was around both victims' ankles and wrists.

"Forensics still hasn't gotten here," the deputy said, swallowing. "But there's a bunch of stuff strange about this."

"Got that right," Sonny said, bending over to look in the father's mouth. "There's blood in there. Like it's all cut up. But I don't see no cuts."

"Yes, sir," the deputy said.

"And what the *hell's* that smell?" the sheriff asked, sniffing. He didn't really have to, the whole trailer reeked of it. "It ain't dead bodies. These ain't been here long enough to smell that bad. But that's what it smells like."

"Yes, sir," the deputy said, clearly relieved. "You see what I meant by this is stuff I couldn't exactly note. I'm not sure how to. And there's a couple of other things."

The daughter's room was obviously in transition from girl to teenager. There were still dolls piled on the floor, but there were more pictures of rock bands on the wall than "My Little Pony." And the window was open. The screen was pushed out.

"She get away?" the sheriff asked.

"I don't... think so, sir," the deputy said. "There are marks on the door frame like somebody scratched at it. Like..."

"They were dragged out," the sheriff said, sighing. "Real sicko."

"Knock-knock," a voice sounded from outside the trailer.

"I hate it when the FBI gets here before Forensics," the sheriff said, his face turning to a snarl. "Randell, find out where the hell Forensics is!"

"Yes, sir," the deputy said, carefully sidling out of the trailer.

"Outside," the sheriff said when he got to the door. "God only knows what we've already fucked up."

"As you say, Sheriff," one of the agents said, nodding.

Once well away from the crime scene Sheriff Cribbs took the time to switch out his chew, then nodded at the agents.

"Sheriff Sonny Cribbs," he said. "And you be?"

"Special Agent Clement Adams," the first one said, nodding back. "And Special Agent Rain Diller."

Adams was from the same block that created Randell. Medium height, light brown hair, stocky but not quite the lifter look.

More like he'd wrassled in college. Diller was slimmer, with dark brown hair, but when he took off his glasses for a second, Sonny caught a look he hadn't seen in a long time. It wasn't the look that boys back from Iraq usually had. It was more like the Vietnam Thousand-Mile Stare. Diller might be an agent, but he was a killer at heart.

"Mother and father murdered, daughter appears to be a kidnap victim," Sonny said. "The killer's a real sicko. You'll see what I mean. I don't think we're getting the girl back."

"Any idea how long?" Adams asked.

"Now that my fucking forensics team has bothered to show up, maybe," Sonny said as the he saw two of the forensics team hoofing it up the drive. "But it's been at least six hours. Rigor mortis had set in when my officer found them just before nine."

"Thirty hours and counting," Diller said, looking around. If a victim of a kidnapping like this wasn't recovered within thirty-six hours, they weren't going to be.

"Amber alert's out," the sheriff replied. "What?"

"What's that drag mark?" the agent said, walking away.

"Looks like the dad shot a deer," Sonny said, walking over. "I know it's out of season, but the family clearly ain't got a pot to piss in..."

"Look closer, sheriff," Diller said. "The brush is bent *away* from the house."

The path was broad, with not only the loam disturbed, but small saplings and bushes pressed down. If it had been a deer, it had been the biggest buck in Claiborne County history.

"Don't know what it is," the sheriff said. "But it ain't the body of a fourteen-year-old girl. Ain't a body drag mark at all. Seen them."

"So have I," Diller said, looking into the woods. "But it's also odd. Maybe a tarp with something piled on it."

"Sheriff, we're going to have to have copies of all your findings," Adams said, walking over. "If you'd like we can bring in forensics support."

"Appreciate that," Cribbs said distantly, rubbing his chin. "Don't look like the dad raked the leaves much."

"I'd like to see where it leads," Diller said.

"Randell!" the sheriff said, shouting across the yard. "Go with this FBI guy."

"Roger, sir," the deputy said, trotting over.

"Stay off the path," the agent said. "Be back."

"You're going to mess up your shoes," Randell said as they walked through the woods.

"I've done that before," the agent said, sniffing. "What's that? A dead deer?"

"Maybe," the deputy said. "But it smells like what I smelled in the house."

The agent approached the still-obvious path of whatever had been dragged through the woods, and bent down.

"It's coming from the trail," he said, sniffing around like a dog. "There's a dark discoloration."

"You want my thoughts?" the deputy asked as they started off again.

"We at the FBI always welcome input," the agent replied, looking around.

"I think this guy is a real sicko," Randell said. "I mean seriously deranged. I think he brought a dead body with him. Maybe more than one. That's the only way to explain the smell in the house."

"And it would explain the drag marks," the agent said, stopping and cocking his head. The brush and trees had thickened as they headed up the ridge, and at one point the dragged area narrowed down between two trees to barely the width of a body. "But I don't think you could drag many bodies through *that* gap."

"Tarp with leaves?" the deputy said. "The lawn didn't *look* raked."

"Maybe," the agent said. "In which case we're wasting our time. But why would someone drag leaves through a forest, deputy?"

They continued to follow the path up the hill until it stopped at a small opening in the ground. Diller bent down and held his hand to it. There was airflow coming out.

"Cave," he said. There were more signs that something had been dragged into the cave. Something large that had, somehow, shrunk down to fit. The edges had that same foul stench.

Caught on the rock was a thin strand of golden hair.

The agent rocked back on his heels and paused for a moment, frowning. Then he blanched.

"Shit," he muttered. "Son. Of. A. *Bitch*! I'm an *idiot*."

"What?" the deputy asked. He was standing well back to avoid contaminating a possible crime scene.

"Nothing," Diller said, standing up and backing away from the hole. "Fuck me, fuck me, *fuck* me."

"Sir, what's wrong?" the deputy asked, looking around for the threat.

"You used to be a Marine, right?" Diller said, pulling out his cell phone.

"Shows, huh?" Randell said.

"Then understand this, Marine," Diller said, turning around and pulling off his sunglasses. He looked the Marine straight in the eyes while dialing from memory. "You did not see anything unusual about this. We didn't take this walk. If called to testify about *anything*, you will be as uncommunicative as a *stone*. Do you understand me?"

"No, sir," Randell said, his eyes wide.

"This is Agent Diller," the agent said into the phone. "The Claiborne case has Special Circumstances."

Chapter Two

Janea knew she shouldn't enjoy shocking the hell out of the poor FBI agents she worked with. Among other things, they generally had the life expectancy of a gnat. But they were so *mundane.*

Besides, appearing to be a giant invitation to have sex was her Calling. It was a form of worship, as was the frequent, lustful and giving sex in which she engaged.

So she made a performance of getting out of the rented Taurus. One long leg out, slow and sensual, then the next, then roll to her feet with a little bounce to get the boobs jiggling. The agents clearly weren't used to spike heels, a short, flirty miniskirt and a midriff top at a crime scene. Nor the sway as she walked over.

"Doris Grisham," she said, holding out her hand to the stocky one. "Call me Janea."

Janea was taller than either agent—at least with five-inch heels on—busty, curvy and redheaded. A former stripper and high-dollar call girl, she had found her Calling in the service of Freya, the Norse goddess of fertility and love.

The Foundation for Love and Universal Faith had, in turn, found her through Asatru connections. Since then she'd been working her way up through the Foundation and was now listed, just last week, as a Class Three Adept.

"Yes, ma'am," Agent Graham said, clearly in shock.

"I understand you called for SC," she said, posing. "Here I am!"

"Yes, ma'am," Graham said, still in shock.

"Ma'am, we have a serious case here," Diller said, breaking out first. "I'd like to brief you in."

"Go for it," Janea said, dropping the pose. "Two dead, kidnapping. Why SC?"

"This," Diller said, walking over to the dragged patch. "This goes up to a small—very small—cave on the hillside. There were hairs there that appear to be from the kidnap victim. And there's a smell..."

"Ichor," Janea said, squatting down and suddenly all business. "Not demonic ichor, though. At least none that I've smelled. Can I get a sample here?"

"Yes, ma'am," Graham said, going over to the FBI Forensics team that had taken over the investigation.

Janea knelt and sniffed at a dark patch, then shook her head.

"That *definitely* doesn't smell like demonic ichor," she said, frowning. "Are the victims still at the crime scene?"

"No, ma'am, they're being moved to Quantico at this time," Diller said.

"Here's a scoop," Graham said, handing her a scupula and a bag.

"Thanks," Janea said, taking a sample of the ichor patch and handing it over to the agent. "Get that sent to Quantico as well, please. Mark, tag and photo. I'd prefer not to go hiking; any pictures of the cave?"

"Yes, ma'am," Diller said, laying out the photos on the hood of her Taurus. "The pictures of the victims..."

"I quit puking a few investigations ago, Special Agent," Janea said, smiling. She leafed through the photos and nodded. "These aren't even bad. Picture of the girl? Maybe a personal item? I'll need to touch it with my bare hands, so it's going to be useless as evidence."

"Yes, ma'am," Graham said, walking off again.

"Going to try to get a psychic reading?" Diller asked.

"That didn't even sound sarcastic," Janea said. "I rarely can, I'm not that kind of Adept. But I sometimes get something, so it's worth a shot. It will be forwarded to real psychics who will try harder. But mostly it was to give him something to do, since he's clearly freaked out by me."

She kept leafing through the photos, back and forth, concentrating mostly on the marks on the victims' arms and wrists.

"What in the hell is this reminding me of?" she said musingly. "Why did you guys call SC? And who called it?"

"I did," Diller said. "When I realized that the victim had been dragged by something that was...amorphous? And dragged into that tiny cave opening."

"Anyone gone in?"

"It's too small," Diller said. "I think the victim could barely fit. Now that you're here we'll think about getting in there. But that was the other part..."

"It's like HazMat," Janea said.

"Ma'am?" Diller asked as Graham came over with a doll.

"If you're not trained you don't even think about entering the area," Janea said. "First rule of HazMat, right?"

"Yes, ma'am," Graham said, clearly regaining his composure. "I don't know if this was her main doll..."

"Understood," Janea said, taking the doll and concentrating. "Nothing. Send that to FLUF in North Carolina, though. Maybe they'll get something. Okay, we need to go caving. But I don't know a damned thing about spelunking."

"We've got a team on the way," Graham said.

"More spear carriers," Janea said with a sigh. "Okay, first your in-brief on SC. I have been on four live SC investigations. Quite often what looks to be SC turns out to be something else, so I've done way more regular investigations. But on *every single* SC investigation so far, the agent working with me has *died*. I don't like that. Not one damned bit. I *really* don't like that they die the *same way* every time. They try to be heroes. I like heroes. I'm Asatru; we're all about being a hero. I'm mortally certain that they went to Valhalla. I still don't like losing them. I get to know them, I get to like them, they play hero and they *die*. Gentlemen, I'd like to break that streak if you don't mind."

"All for it," Graham said, his face white.

"Be nice," Diller said, taking off his glasses.

"Here's how we break it," Janea said. "Be cowards. Be complete and total cowards. If something seems freaky or creepy, run like ever-loving *Hel*. Most especially, leave me behind. It's *my* job to handle this stuff, *not yours*. If I say 'run,' then run fast. If *I* run, run *faster*. If I say 'Don't touch the glowy thing,' don't touch the glowy thing. If I say 'I need to go in there by myself,' don't *follow me*! If I get taken out, don't try to stop whatever took me out! If

I can't, *you* sure as Hel can't. Either one of you really incredibly firm believers in any god?"

"No, ma'am," Graham said.

"Not anymore," Diller said.

"Interesting answer," Janea said. "Okay, Number One: Be cowards. Number Two: Don't think I know everything. I don't. I've been *told* I didn't get one agent killed, but I *feel* like I did because I underestimated the threat. I'm not always right. Number Three: Ah, Hel, it's all the usual stuff. I want to know what you think. I'm an Adept, not an FBI guy. Sometimes this stuff overlaps in ways you wouldn't believe. Tell me what you think. That's about it."

"Run like hell and don't trust that you know what you're talking about," Graham said. "That's a hell of a way to run an investigation."

"Sorry, it's truth," Janea said. "An item on the second one is that I have not a *clue* what this thing is. There's loads of evidence and I've got a funny feeling I should. But I don't. Talk to me. Seriously, I need thoughts."

"Uh," Graham said. "Okay. Well. If this was a thing that carried off the victim to the cave . . . It's at least as large as a big cow or a bull."

"And it can change shape," Diller said. "This track is six to seven feet wide in most places. The cave entrance is only two-and-a-half wide and less than a foot high."

"So something like an amoeba?" Janea said, nodding in thought. "More?"

"There are no indications that there were restraints tied to the bed or any surrounding object," Graham said. "I don't know what that means, but there's usually marks."

"I hate to say this," Diller said.

"This is brainstorming," Janea said. "Everything's on the table."

"Tentacles?" Diller said.

"Amoeba-like . . ." Janea said. "Tent . . . Oh, shit!" she added, slapping her forehead. "I am such a *moron!*"

"What?" Graham asked, his eyes wide.

"It's not a demon," Janea said, nodding. "It's an Old One."

"Old One?" Diller said.

"You guys can feel free to think of them as demons," Janea said, relieved. "They've got, from your perspective, a lot of the same attributes. They can instill control over a subject, they can instill fear better. Actually, they freak people out on first sight and tend to induce insanity. The big question is, what kind? Is this a Great Old One or one of its minions?"

She paused and considered the path.

"Not too big, Old Ones can get really huge. Tentacles. Drags along the ground. Shit. Shambler."

"And a Shambler is...?" Diller asked.

"Uh..." Janea said, thinking. "Basically, it's nothing but a mass of tentacles. The victims weren't raped and they weren't tied. They were held and fed upon. The Shambler stuffs its tentacles in every orifice and sort of sucks the life force out of a person. The victims are going to be a godsend to the SC forensics guys; there hasn't been a Shambler attack since the advent of modern forensics."

"Ma'am," Graham said, blanching. "We have a kidnap victim."

"Which is probably a snack," Janea said, her face falling. "It's unlikely we'll get her back, and even if we do, she's probably going to be permanently insane. Bad news: The Shamblers are sometimes called the Night Hunters. This is *not* going to be the last attack. The attacks are probably going to be at night and it's probably using the cave system to get around. They can go out in light but they don't like it. Good news: I'm going to have to get somebody to do some research for me, but they're not that hard to kill. They're not susceptible to mundane weapons but fire does a number on them. I don't think anyone's ever hit one with a grenade, but it would probably dispel it back to where*ever* they come from. But the easiest way is to control them with certain words of power and dispel them with a mystic chant. I think there's a powder or potion that works as well. Once we find it, getting rid of it should be easy."

"And we can trust that?" Graham asked, an eyebrow raised.

"It's a Shambler," Janea said, shrugging. "Like I said, I'll get someone else to research it. But this *should* be relatively easy."

Barb used her key to open up the dojo. As she flipped on the lights and they approached the mat, Yi glanced around the school. He raised one perfectly groomed eyebrow as he slid off his handmade leather loafers and glanced at the American and Japanese flags hanging on the wall. "Japanese," he muttered under his breath. Barb faced him and they bowed in the Chinese manner.

"I see you remember the courtesies, Laoshi. Let us see if you remember how to dance."

Yi looked Barb directly in the eyes, and without looking at his target or giving any indication that he was going to move, shot out a low kick to her left ankle while gliding forward and darting two fast fingertip strikes, one at Barb's left temple and one at the peroneal nerve on the outside of her right thigh. Faced with an attack on a low line, a high line, and a low-middle line, Barb moved backwards in *bei hu*, crossing her left leg over her right and avoiding the kick as she flowed through the two quick circular parries necessary to deal with the hand strikes. She allowed the hand parrying the strike to the temple to follow the line of the attack and extend it, moving Yi's arm along the line and exposing his ribs, then, twisting out of the cross-step stance to a front stance, she threw a vertical fist punch to Yi's unprotected short ribs.

Yi's left hand flickered like a hummingbird's wing and his palm flashed under the armpit of his extended right arm to slap Barb's punch away. His right arm folded in as his stance and weight dropped low, and the point of his elbow arrowed toward Barb's ribs.

Barb's palm slapped it away, and for a bare instant they stood, looking almost like mirror images of one another, then they flowed backward simultaneously and both assumed the *ao bo* reverse stance.

Yi's lips curled in a slight smile and his eyes sparkled. "Very nice. But your knees are too stiff." He inclined his head slightly and, with his eyes lowered to the floor, launched into a *tam twei* jump kick. As Barb deflected the kick, she dropped into a low side stance, and was just starting to launch a side kick when Yi disappeared.

As her left foot came up in the powerful sidekick, Yi landed from his jumping kick and his legs scissored as his weight dropped, bringing his head below the level of Barb's waist. His right foot was behind Barb's left leg, and she fell and rolled backwards as he shifted his weight forward, smacking the inside of her thigh with his knee.

On the way down, she deflected one open-palm strike aimed at her bladder. As she desperately tried to roll away, Yi seemed to float forward, moving sinuously across the mat like oil on a mirror, and his hands were everywhere as they executed the myriad open-hand and fingertip strikes that were a hallmark of Wah Lum. The master of mantis moved impossibly quickly and struck at vital targets from seemingly awkward angles of attack.

Barb continued her roll. She had parried two strikes while

rolling and thought she had avoided at least three more due to her movement. There was no way that this could continue, and she knew it. Yi was going to hit her—a lot. As she rolled backwards and somersaulted to her knees, she decided she had two options: get pummeled by a barrage of strikes that she could not hope to counter, or do something that would be so outside of a conventional response in this situation it would be almost stupid to try it. It would either work or leave her completely open. Stupid it was.

She brought her knees together and folded back on her heels until she was sitting in the Japanese *seiza* posture. By dropping to her heels, she narrowly avoided being struck twice by Master Yi. As soon as her butt touched her heels she breathed out and moved forward, her left arm blasting forward through the maelstrom of Yi's hand movements to take his right arm and push it across his body. Her left leg came out and her body angled as she began to turn herself and Yi in the beginning motions of the aikido throw *shio-nage*. As Yi rotated his spine to begin a counter and his left hand snaked toward her head, Barb reversed her turning motion and brought her other hand up to assist as she executed the aikido wrist turn throw *kote gaeshi*.

Rather than being thrown and possibly joint-locked or choked, Yi followed the motion of the wrist twisting, and rotated his trapped wrist in three dimensions while leaping to his right. He hit on his shoulder and seemed to levitate to his feet. Barb spun on her knees and rose to face him.

"Aikido?" he asked. "Tch-tch-tch."

Barb waited for the scornful lecture on the true nature of unarmed combat, or the scathing rebuke to remind her that she had asked Master Yi to work with her to polish her Wah Lum skills, not Korean arts. Instead, Yi merely slowly walked toward her. This was bad, very bad.

Yi was completely relaxed as he strolled toward her. Barb moved into a bow stance, a traditional Kung Fu ready posture. Yi stopped in front of Barb, just in range of a hand strike to the body, and stood looking at her. Barb shifted her weight and moved laterally, then rapidly diagonally and backwards. Yi mirrored her moves, seemingly floating across the mat. His hands were folded in front of him, held at waist level. Barb slid forward and threw two punches, one at Yi's face and one at his groin.

Yi did not parry or block, but merely stepped back out of range and immediately stepped back to his prior position as soon as Barb's second punch began its retraction.

Barb shifted her hips to start a kick, and Yi was suddenly the center of a very disturbed universe of punching, kicking motion. His left foot slid into place beside and behind Barb's left ankle as strikes whipped out toward Barb. The first strike was to Barb's ribs, and she deflected it with a downward block as she used the back of her other wrist to ward off Yi's strike to the femoral nerve complex on the inside of her right thigh.

Yi's third strike was delivered as he twisted his body and used the spiral motion of his turn to twist his left leg into Barb's, disrupting her balance. The palm strike was blocked by Barb's forearm, but Yi snaked his arm around the forearm and drove a traditional Wah Lum relaxed fist into the brachial nerve in her armpit. Yi's left leg slid forward and drove against Barb's right knee while his right hand delivered a light fingertip strike directly between her eyes to her "third eye." Her head snapped back as she started to fall, her balance completely gone.

Yi hit her with a downward elbow and three fingertip strikes before she could hit the ground. As she hit the ground, off balance and in such pain that she barely had the ability to fall properly, Yi slapped a palm against her shoulder while seizing her arm, flipping her to her stomach. Blinding pain constricted Barb's heart as Yi's fingertips forcefully struck the *lingtai*, spirit platform, cavity between the thoracic vertebrae. As her vision began to go gray at the edges and her heart went into arhythmia, Yi rolled her over on her back and looked down at her.

"I told you that your knees were too stiff," said the Master as he pressed on her lower abdomen, and then his fingers did a dance along her nerve meridians to "unseal the heart" and stop the muscles around the organ from contracting and shutting down its vital function. "If your knees were supple, you would have flowed with my force. If you flowed with my energy, you would not have been off balance. If you had not been off balance, you would not have fallen. If you had not fallen, I could not have killed you, as I just did. As the ancient scrolls of Wah Lum teach, 'The mighty landslide is begun by the action of one pebble.' You neglected to see the pebble, Laoshi."

The Master helped her to her feet and said, "Shall we try again?"

Before the word "again" was formed, Barb was airborne. Her left foot snapped out at Yi, and, as he countered with a forearm and began to slide back, she rotated her body in midair and whipped her right shin downward in a round kick that smacked Yi's arm and opened his centerline. As she landed and squatted down on her heels, her right leg shot between Yi's legs and slid against his front leg, while her elbow whipped up toward his undefended groin as her spine contorted to provide power for the strike and her body began to rise.

BARBARA EVERETTE!

It was not her name that she heard but her essence, the entire syntax of her soul fitted into a single gestalt. And it hurt. It was unvarnished and unquestionable. Every sin of her life was part of it, a dark fire that seared with coldness. Even those parts of her life which were clearly and unquestionably positive were a raging fire, the sun suddenly implanted in her body.

She had looked upon demons without fear and spoken to angels both in dream and awake. She now knew why it was said that you could not look upon the naked face of God and not be blinded. "Hearing" His voice, unfiltered and direct, was right on the edge of death.

No wonder He usually spoke through a burning bush or something. Direct contact would kill most people.

GO TO THE PRIESTESS OF LOVE.
SHE REQUIRES AID.

Yi deflected the elbow and launched a seemingly offline relaxed fist strike for the bridge of Barb's nose. He stopped the strike as he noticed that she had gone rigid. Grabbing her shoulders, he lowered her gently to the mat, and his fingers flowed up the blood-bearing and nerve pathways of her body, seeking any residual damage to Barb that may have been caused by his techniques. Her chi was almost overwhelming, a raging power he had never before felt or even imagined. Satisfied that she was physically healthy—breathing, if shallowly—but that her spirit was occupied elsewhere, he dropped into a lotus posture, placed her head in his lap and meditated.

About five minutes later her body gave a strong twitch and she started breathing at a more normal pace. Then her eyes flickered open.

"I need to call Janea," Barb said, blinking rapidly. "That *hurt!*"

"Pain is weakness leaving the body," Master Yi said, holding out his hand.

"That's not a Zen saying," Barb replied, sitting up. She took a deep breath and stretched. "Ow."

"I have a fondness for movies."

Janea picked up her phone, looked at it askance, then hit the send button.

"Yo, Wonder-Barb," Janea said.

Agent Diller looked over at her and then back at the road, grabbing the dashboard futilely as she swerved into the next lane, then back.

"Miss Grisham..." Diller said. "Janea! Pull over and talk or let me drive!"

"Oh, hang on," Janea said, pulling over to the side of the interstate. "So to what do I owe the call from Soccer-Momasaurus?"

"Where are you?" Barb said.

"Why?" Janea asked. "You want to come along for the ride? Why this time, Barb? Huh? I've had three, count 'em, three FBI guys die on me since the last time we *spoke*. Three. One of them left a wife and four children. Where were you then, Mrs. God-Strike? Playing housewife?"

"I was in Chattanooga even if *you* weren't," Barb said. "When it's time, it's time. And this is time. I need to know where you are and I need to get there before you do anything.... Just wait for me to get there."

"What? Foolish?" Janea snapped. "What's so important *this* time? It's a lousy little Shambler. I can dispel one in my sleep."

"I don't know," Barb said. "But I do know that I have to be there. And I'd suggest you don't do anything until I get there."

"How do you know?" Janea asked sarcastically. "God tell you?"

"Yes," Barb said.

"Wait," Janea said. "I was joking. Are we talking about the White God? Or just, you know, a messenger?"

"God," Barb said. "Not the Holy Spirit. Not an angel. Not Jesus. God. In person. And it's not an experience I'd prefer to repeat."

"And He told you...what?" Janea asked, fascinated. She'd felt the power of Freya many times, but once, through Barb, she'd gotten a touch of the power of the White God, and it was the difference between a firecracker and a nuclear weapon. She had never had a direct god call, but she'd heard that even with minor deities they could be unpleasant. She didn't want to think about what a direct call from the Big Guy would be like.

"To go to the priestess of love," Barb said, sarcastic in turn. "How many priestesses of love do I know?"

"Really?" Janea said, grinning. "The Big Guy said that? About me?"

"Actually, it's not words, you know that," Barb said. "It was more like…'seek she who gives love greatly.' Maybe 'quest for.' It's… But, hell, He included a picture. It was you."

"God *knows* me?" Janea squealed.

Agent Diller had been trying to ignore the conversation, but at that he turned his head and frowned.

"God knows everybody, Janea," Barb said. "Now where are you?"

"On Interstate 75 near Knoxville," Janea said. "We're going to meet with a cave rescue team."

"Why?"

"Because somebody needs rescuing from a cave?" Janea said.

"Don't go into the cave until I get there," Barb said. "Seriously. Don't."

"We won't," Janea replied. "When can you get here?"

"I've got to get the kids dropped off and make arrangements," Barb said. "Then I'll get on the road. I'll be there by morning."

"There's a girl's life at stake here, Barb," Janea pointed out.

"God knows everyone, Janea," Barb replied. "And He knows the fall of a sparrow. Don't. Go."

"Roger," Janea said. "Barb, seriously, glad to have you back."

"I'm not sure I am," Barb said. "But I'm back for this."

"So…what was that?" Diller asked as Janea pulled back into traffic.

"That was Soccer-Momasaurus," Janea said.

"Who is?"

"Barbara Everette," Janea said. "She strongly suggested, more like ordered, that we wait to penetrate the cave until she gets here."

"That was the part about 'There's a girl's life at stake.'"

"Yes," Janea said. "And if Barb says wait, we wait."

"There's a girl's life at stake," Diller said.

"Remember my thing about 'Don't be a hero'?"

"Yeah," Diller said, angrily.

"Well, that's the way I am with Barb," Janea said. "If Barb says wait, or run, or duck, or squat, I run or duck or squat."

"Why?" Diller asked.

"Because..." Janea said, then paused. "Okay, think of me as a hand grenade. I can take out, well, a Shambler easily enough. I took on a pretty serious incubus, and despite the fact that his powers and mine... overlapped, I managed to avoid his temptations and destroy him."

"Okay," Diller said, frowning. "Sorry, but this stuff is still..."

"Yeah," Janea said. "I know. That was the one where I lost the poor bastard with the wife and kids. Incubi and succubae are the same thing, they just... morph. I told him to run."

"I remember the lecture."

"Well, if I'm a hand grenade, Barb is a nuclear weapon," Janea said. "A big one. A city buster."

"Oh. What was that thing about 'God knows me'?"

"That's why she's a city buster," Janea said, pulling off at the exit. "Barb gets her power from what we Asatru call the White God. The only member of FLUF who does."

"You mean the Christian God?" Diller asked, sarcastically. "Big beard, floating in the sky?"

"Right," Janea said. "The Big Guy. Mr. Beard."

"Well, I'll believe that one when I see it," Diller said. "God doesn't drop down and help out. That I *know*."

"Oh, He does," Janea said, pulling in at the hotel where they were to meet the rescue squad. "He just chooses His time and His methods."

"And what are His time and His methods?" Diller asked, still sarcastic.

Janea took off her sunglasses and turned to look him in the eye.

"Wherever Barbara Everette is."

Chapter Three

*W*ell, look what the cat dragged in," Janea said, rubbing her eyes as she opened the door.

"I hope like hell you have two beds," Barbara said, brushing past her, setting down the cat bag and letting Lazarus out. She looked around the room and shook her head. "*How* long have you been here?"

"I got here this . . . yesterday morning," Janea asked, looking around in confusion. "Why?"

Janea had a number of habits that Barb found mildly irritating. She couldn't drive very well. And while Barb understood that sensuousness was part of Janea's calling, there were times when she took it a bit too far.

But while Barb had recalled those on the very long drive, she had somehow managed to forget what sharing a room with Janea was like.

Although it had taken her less than twenty minutes to pack, Barb knew where every single item was in her suitcase. She had grown up as a military brat, and packing was very close to breathing as a skill. If she needed a pair of running shoes, she knew they were at the base of her larger bag, upright, held in place by two pairs of jeans. If she needed pumps, they were in the same bag, left side, middle. Barb had two clothes bags, the larger case and a folding hanging case for dressier wear.

Janea, on the other hand, had a *special* method of packing. When she was going on assignment she would grab a pile of whatever was closest and reasonably clean. She would then throw it in up to ten bags along with shoes, makeup at random, and whatever else struck her fancy, including various "toys." When she needed something, she would then tear through most of the bags trying to find it, tossing everything in her way in random directions.

There were clothes hanging from wall sconces. Not neatly on hangers, but because that was where they landed. There were clothes on the table, both beds, every horizontal surface including the *entire* floor. And not just clothes. Adjusted as she was to Janea, and worldly as Barb was, some of the things that were scattered around the room made her blush.

"Never mind," Barb said, dragging her cases into the room and finding a spot with not too much in it. She dumped the pile of clothes on the bed onto the floor and shook her head. "It was a long drive. Talk in the morning?"

"Suits," Janea said, climbing into bed. "Given who your God is, I won't ask if you've considered switch."

"Don't start, Janea," Barb said, pulling out her toiletries and heading to the bathroom.

"I'm just saying," Janea said, raising her voice. "Cleaving only unto should only be for guys! Girls are just, you know, comfort!"

"He knows where you live, Janea!"

"Hey, I'm on the side of light!" Janea shouted as the shower started. "This is like *praying* for me! It's holy worship! I'm just talking snuggling, *honest*!"

When there was no response Janea snorted and turned off the light.

"Teach her to run out on me..."

Mike Argyll, the leader of the cave rescue team, was not the smallest person Barb had ever seen, but that was because she had once met a midget. He was under five feet in height, but burly and hirsute with shaggy black hair and beard to match.

"Now that our second outside consultant is here," the team leader said, "can we actually do the *brief*?"

Although Barb and Janea were still based down by Knoxville,

the FBI had more or less taken over a motel near the crime scene as a base station. Still forty-five minutes from the trailer, it was the closest hotel with facilities for meetings. The "Cave Examination Team" was gathered in one of the meeting rooms, going through a hasty brief before the penetration.

"Go," Graham said, taking a sip of coffee.

"Okay, I'm told that this penetration has special issues," Argyll said. "But caves are caves. Caves can and will kill you if you let them. The answer is to not let them. The biggest thing is simply safety. Caves have sudden drop-offs that, despite your lights, you're going to tend to miss. That's why I'll be leading the penetration."

"Nope," Barb said, sucking at her own coffee. She needed it. "I'm going to have to take point."

Lazarus was curled up on the table in front of her, watching the briefing with what certainly looked like lively interest. At the insertion by Barb he mewed as if in agreement.

"I'm sorry," Mike said, wriggling a finger in his ear. "Did you just miss what I said?"

There were dozens of cavers in the local area, and once the word got around that it was possible the "perpetrator" had taken the girl into a cave, all of them wanted to help out. But the FBI, due to the "Special" nature of the investigation, had called in a group they worked with that was national quality. The team consisted not only of Mike but of two assistants, either one of whom could have broken him in half. They also clearly felt she had not been listening.

The problem being that although it was an FBI team, it was not cleared for Special Circumstances, and higher-ups wanted it to stay that way.

"As you said, this case has special issues," Barb said carefully. "The perpetrator of these crimes has special combat abilities. Believe it or not, Janea and I are the people that the FBI considers *most capable* of handling those abilities. A cave *might* kill you. This perpetrator *will* kill you. Which is why I have to be point. If you doubt my abilities, I'll be happy to throw you, or either Mongo One or Mongo Two, around the room."

"Okay," Mike said, "You have to take point. But there are more issues than safety. Restrictions can be a stone bitch. I looked at the one on the hill. That's what we call about a three. It's tight, but you can go straight in. Restrictions go up to seven. At about a five, you've got to suck in your breath and then go through something that looks like a corkscrew. Please forgive me, ma'am, but you are...well built. Just those...issues alone are going to make any restriction over a four an issue for you. If I go first, I can usually figure out a way for big people to fit. If not..."

"I get stuck and you pull me out," Barb said.

"Restrictions can be long," one of the helpers said. "You might be too far in to pull out. That's the point. We know when to back out. You don't. And, yes, people die that way."

"If there's a serious restriction issue, we may have to turn over point," Barb said reluctantly. "By the same token, if you think you are near the perpetrator, you need to get out of there as if all the hounds of hell were on your tail. Do you absolutely and positively understand me?"

"Listen to the lady," Graham said.

"I hear you," Mike said, looking puzzled. "But you're not really telling me why."

"Because you don't get to know why," Diller said. "You just have to get the ladies to the perpetrator and then get the hell away." He looked at the team leader and frowned. "Look, if I was leading the penetration, that would be how *I'd* handle it. Cut and run. These ladies may not look like it, but they are professionals at this. You get them to the perp, let them handle it from there. And if you have any questions afterwards, don't ask them."

"Including 'where's the perpetrator?'" Graham said. "The perp is unlikely to be coming back. And that *does not* leave this investigation."

"So what are you ladies?" Mike asked, looking askance. "The FBI's La Femme Nikitas?"

"If we near the perpetrator, there will probably be a foul stench, like rotting bodies," Barb said. "If you smell it particularly strongly, back off. Then let us take over."

"He keeps his bodies in the cave?" one of the assistants asked.

"We'll probably be able to track him by the smell," Barb continued.

"Which is good because caves go every which-a-way," Mike said. "And we both asked questions."

"Which she is ignoring," Agent Graham said. "What else do they have to know?"

"We'll brief them in on lights and gear at the site," Mike said, shrugging. "You want to go all super-spook on us, fine. But what you ladies have to worry about is the cave."

"That is correct," Barb said. "But what *you* have to worry about is what is *in* the cave."

"These ought to fit you."

Mongo One's name turned out to be Thane Dale. Twenty-six, brown hair and eyes, and six foot four inches, he was a college student at University of Kentucky where Mike Argyll was a geology professor. Mongo Two, six two and blond, was Cedar Blackburn, a geology grad student at same.

The suits Thane was holding out looked something like wet suits with a slick exterior. And far too small.

"That's going to be *really* tight," Janea said, holding it up. "Tight is fine up to a point, but..."

"That's the point," Cedar said. "They are supposed to be constricting. They're going to, sorry, flatten you two ladies out. They do the same for beer guts."

"I don't know if I can get that flat," Barb said, holding up the suit.

"Try," Argyll said, coming around the back of the van. He was already suited up. "If you can't, you're barely going to be able to make it through the exterior restriction. And we're going to have to brief on climbing, rappel, and belay. Not to mention lights, lines and various other issues. So if you could *kindly* get ready."

It took about two hours to get fully prepared for the penetration. Besides the helmet light, Barb had been issued four more. Three lights was considered a minimum, five was about right. Thane carried seven as well as backup batteries. Cedar was burdened with ropes, climbing gear and a bag of what Barb had referred to as her "necessaries," and was carrying reels of thin line so they could find their way back. All of them were in the slick suits, hard hats with lights, and pads on elbows and knees.

"You want to try this?" Argyll said, pointing at the hole.

Barb was already sweating up a storm in the suit, and the hole looked far too small to fit through. But...

"I might as well start learning now," she said, getting down on her knees. "Any suggestions?"

"Turn your head to the side, stick your arms in and pull," Argyll said.

Lazarus gave her a look like "what's the problem" and walked into the hole.

"That cat your familiar or something?"

"Something like that," Barb said, then did as she was told and slid into the hole like a reversal of birth.

"Ow," she muttered as she entered a slightly larger area. The smell was distinct but not strong. The Shambler had gone deeper.

"What happened?" Argyll asked.

"Scraped my cheek on the rock," Barb said. "There's enough room in here for you and me. I think."

"Plenty," Argyll said, sliding past her and looking around. There was a faint light from the exterior but his helmet light lit it like day. "Two openings," he added, using a handlight to point them out.

"Restrictions," Barb said, sliding over on her belly. There was no standing in the cavern; the ceiling was less than three feet.

She sniffed at the one to the right but didn't smell anything except, possibly, a faint animal musk. There were some small bones on the floor, and she realized they were probably in a bear's winter den.

The one to the left, however, had some distinct drag marks. She realized it was going to be hard to track the Shambler based on ichor because, surprisingly, the walls of the cave were black. Lazarus was standing by the opening as if wondering what was taking her so long.

"I thought these were limestone," she said, pointing to the wall.

"That's a slime mold that covers just about every cave wall in the world," Argyll said. "That's how you know it's a pristine cave, it's got black walls. But something's been through here," he added, pointing to the drag marks.

"And that would be the way we have to go," Barb said, looking at the restriction. It was tighter than the entrance, but shining her light in, she could see an open area beyond. She tilted her head back and forth.

Lazarus looked at her again and just walked into the cave ahead of her.

"Get on your back," Mike said, shining his light in. "Head to the side again. I'll brace your boots. Grab on and pull up and to the left as you're looking, my right. Yo, Cedar! Next victim!"

Barb had been slithering and poking and sliding for what seemed like days and was, in fact, four hours when she finally got to a spot where she stopped.

"I can't fit through that," she said.

Barb's impression of caves, she had realized, came from the mine in Snow White. Caves were supposed to be high things where you walked through going "ooo" and "ah!" at the pretty stalactites reflecting the light from your torches.

Caves were not supposed to be barely negotiable, narrow, dark and nasty tunnels. They had slid through mud twice, ducked under a "sump," which was a restriction filled with water, and only been able to stand upright in two caverns. And those had neither stalactites nor happy, singing dwarves. And now this.

The irregular opening was barely a foot across and high. Or so it looked.

"Eh, you'd be surprised," Argyll said, cocking his head from side to side. The cave before the opening was no great shakes, being barely two feet high, but it was wide enough the entire team had crowded in. "What I don't get is, who the hell *is* this guy? He dragged this girl through all this? Why? How?"

They'd found not only more scraps of hair but bits of clothing along the way. There was no question at this point that they were on the trail of Loren Cowper. But Barb didn't expect to find her alive and had made that very clear to the party.

"Hope you don't find out," Janea said. "You seriously think we can fit through there?"

"I've gotten through worse," Thane said. "Want me to show them?"

"No, I've got it," Argyll said. "I'll make sure it's doable, then you ladies can follow. Better tie me off, though."

Shane reached forward and slid a rope around the team lead's ankle.

"Ready to yank," Shane said.

Lazarus looked at her and yowled.

"Professor," Barb said, looking at Lazarus. "If it's doable, maybe I should go first. Heck, maybe Laz should go first."

At that, Laz yowled again as if saying, *"Not on your life."*

"No. It's fine. Right," Argyll said, folding his shoulders inwards. "You ladies are going to have to do this different, but...gimme a push."

Cedar grasped his ankles and slid him forward, and the geology professor slid into the hole like a piston.

"Right, pull me out, this is a reverse entry," Argyll said after a moment. He slid out, then flipped on his back. "We're going up again."

Cedar slid him back into the hole to the maximum extent of his arms, then pulled back out.

"Right," Argyll said, his voice muffled. "Gonna have to wriggle this one. Ladies, the way that you're going to have to do this is..." He paused for a moment, then screamed as the rope started flying through Thane's hands.

"What the hell?" Thane shouted, grabbing on. But it continued to slide through his gloves.

The screams sounding from the hole echoed through the cave and were magnified until they cut off abruptly. There was a crunching sound from above and then a stream of blood gushed onto the floor of the cave.

"Oh, my God," Cedar said, rolling to the side and retching.

"I think we found the perpetrator," Barb said, looking at the hole. "I'm going to need my necessaries."

Chapter Four

"Now, you understand these things don't respond to the normal God stuff," Janea said worriedly.

"The Lord has dominion over all things, seen and unseen," Barb replied, looking askance at the opening. The much smaller professor had barely fit. She wasn't looking forward to trying to slide up the slot. Much less fighting at the top. Or possibly not even at the top. "I'm more worried about sliding up that damned hole. Refresh me on cold steel."

"Shamblers can normally be cut," Janea said. "But they regenerate tentacles like mad. Cut one, you just get ichor all over you for your trouble."

"Thane, I need my bag. Then there's this chant thing."

"*A-ku-surgo, ka-ka-gree*," Janea repeated gutturally. "You've got to get the inflection on the *gree*."

"Sounds like demon Tongues to me," Barb said, looking over at the assistant. Thane was pressed against the back wall of the cave, wide-eyed. Cedar had disappeared, probably halfway back to the entrance. "Thane!" Barb slid across the slick floor and grabbed the assistant's face, pulling it to look at her. "Eye contact! I need you to focus for me!"

"Sure . . ." the student said, his eyes still wide. He was shaking from head to foot.

"I need my bag," Barb said. "You are sitting on it. You sure power of light won't stop it?" she added to Janea.

"With you, no," Janea said. "But generally you can throw

239

Bibles and holy water at these things all day and nothing happens. They're not strictly demons. They're, like, some sort of remnant being. Maybe they were demons for dinosaurs. Who knows? But they sort of predate gods."

"God created the world and all in it," Barb said, taking the bag from the student. She slid towards the opening and slid the bag open, considering her choices. First she pulled out her H&K and buckled it on. It would make moving up the hole harder, but she wasn't going to face this thing without a gun at least available. Then she pulled out two wakizashi, short, slightly curved Japanese folded steel swords. Last she pulled out a tanto knife of similar design.

"Except yours, I guess," Janea said. "But don't count on God helping you with this one. He rarely gets involved with Old Ones."

"Ladies, are you talking about what I think you're talking about?" Thane asked.

"That's why *I* was supposed to be taking point," Barb said, flicking both of the sheathed swords to the side so the sheaths clattered against the wall. She took one in either hand, and a deep breath. Closer to the hole she could smell the stink of the Old One. The professor must have been so caught up in his role of expert he hadn't noticed. Or was it getting...?

"Is that a...slithering sound?" Janea asked.

"Looks like we get to depend on *your* pronunciation," Barb said, backing up. "Now would be a good time!"

The creature emerging in the helmet lights was pure nightmare. Its very form was hard to determine. Mostly a mass of writhing tentacles, there were suckers and pseudopods extending in chaotic order, and everywhere there were eyes that were oddly human. The color was not black but a nauseous, leprous green that shaded to black and purple in places as if the entire being was one mass of gangrenous corruption.

Janea hefted the battery-powered sprayer and showered the mass with a yellow powder.

"*A-ku-surgo, ka-ka-gree!*" Janea shouted triumphantly, then grimaced. The tentacles were continuing to creep into the room. The thing, fortunately, wasn't moving fast. As if it wanted to maximize the terror.

"Isn't working," Barb commented, still backing up. There wasn't much more to back to.

"I noticed," Janea said. "*A-ku-surgo, ka-ka-gree!*"

"Right," Barb said, flipping onto her back. "Let's try this *my* way. Lord, send me Your aid in battle against evil and I will in Your name kick some unholy ass!"

With her back on the floor, she pushed off of a notched spot in the ceiling and slid towards the monster on her back, wakizashi crossed.

Over the years Barb had studied practically every form found in the East. Traveling from place to place, the one constant was that as soon as they arrived, her father would use his contacts as an FAO to find not only a martial arts studio but the very best that would take a female. As time went on, and Barb's ability improved, the word would usually precede them.

But there was never, or rarely, the *same* style available at the *best* facility at the next posting. Hong Kong, it was Wah Lum; Singapore, Mantis; Thailand, kickboxing and krabi krabong; Japan, bushido and karate; Okinawa, tuete, and so on. All of them had combined into a personal style that Barb mentally dubbed Barb-do-kicki. Which translated as: "whatever works."

Fighting a multitentacled demon from nightmare was never part of *any* of the training. But she'd fought up to six students of centipede who were used to working together, so it was close. The position was centipede, the sword work krabi krabong, the swords Japanese. Barb-do-kicki at its essence.

The only problem being that the swords bounced right off the tentacles.

"Janea, find another chant or something," Barb said, spinning around and slamming a tentacle with a round kick. The tentacle tried to grab her leg but slid off of the slippery suit. Spinning again, she slapped two more away with the swords and flicked a point into one of the thousands of eyes. That, at least, sunk home.

"God, now would be a really nice time to prove the Priestess wrong," Barb said, concentrating on her channel. Finally, she felt a surge of power. "Thank you, Lord," Barb said, slicing a tentacle off at the tip.

The thing keened a loud cry and redoubled its efforts to get through the spinning swords and legs. It pulled itself fully into the chamber, revealing a bulbous body at the center that was no more pleasant than the rest of it.

Janea was chanting a series of prayers, some of them in languages Barb actually recognized.

"Was that Tibetan?" Barb asked.

"Yes," Janea said, desperately. "I don't know what this thing *is*! If I don't know what it is I don't know which dispel to use!"

"Fine," Barb said, her eyes lighting as the swords began to glow. "We'll do this *my* way."

She slid forward again, the wakizashi crossing in a butterfly pattern and shredding tentacles as she went. They did regrow, and were covering her in pumped ichor, but the important thing was that they were opening up a hole to get to the body of the creature.

One finally managed to wrap around her arm, but she countered by rewrapping multiple times, reeling herself rapidly into close quarters with the Old One.

Once there, a single stab of a glowing wakizashi drove deep into the amorphous body of the creature. As the sword reached its vitals she felt a massive wave of power pass through her, and the thing exploded like a pus-filled water balloon, drenching the chamber in ichor and an unholy stench.

"Ack!" Barb said, rolling onto her stomach and blowing out ichor. There was more in her nose than her mouth, but it was foul either way. And it stung the eyes like acid. "Yuck! Ptui!"

"Okay, so I guess The White God *does* get involved with Old Ones," Janea said, shaking the ichor-covered mass of papers in her hand. "And... *yuck!*"

"Lord," Barb said, rolling to her knees and bowing her head. "Thank you for Your assistance with defeating evil this day. May Your Name be glorified in company with Your Son, Jesus Christ. Bring comfort to the soul of Professor Argyll and take him into Your arms. Whatever his sins of this life, he died in battle against evil in Your Name. Amen. Okay, Thane, how do I..." Barb paused and shook her head. "Sugar."

The student was back against the wall, his eyes wide and unseeing. A line of drool was hanging from his open mouth and the only noise he was making was a faint mewing of terror.

"Well, Freya does get involved, as it turns out," Barb said, flicking the swords to clear them of ichor.

"How?" Janea said, somewhat bitterly.

"You're not totally insane," Barb said, gesturing at the student. "That makes three bodies we're going to have to extract."

"You're *really* going to try to go up there after the girl?" Janea asked.

"Of course," Barb said, looking at her in surprise. "How else? I'm also going to have to get the professor."

As she said that, Lazarus came out of the far opening a bit sheepishly.

"Welcome back," Barb said. "And next time I'm going to listen to you."

"Barb," Janea said, eyeing the hole. "Look, let's try to drag Thane back, then get some more professionals. I'm not even sure I can find the way *out*."

"There's a li . . ." Barb looked towards the exit and stopped. "Where's the line?"

"Cedar took it with him," Janea said, shaking her head. "I'm really unsure about finding our way out."

"We'll figure it out," Barb said, sliding over to the opening. "I'm gonna need a push. Oh, and I suppose we need to tie me off in case I get stuck."

"Aaaruck!" Barb snarled as she finally cleared her hips from the hole. "That felt like being born again."

"Should work fine for *you*," Janea said.

"Christian jokes," Barb muttered, rubbing her hip. It turned out that bringing the pistol in a holster was impossible. She'd ended up sticking it in her belt on her front. She'd had a wakizashi in either hand, though. One up, one down, unsheathed and being *very* careful. "It's more open up here."

The cavern was a chute climbing upwards at about a sixty-degree angle to the north. At about six feet wide and more than ten feet high, it was one of the more open areas they'd passed through. She could see where it leveled off again about twenty feet up, and possibly an even more open area at the top. Getting up it was going to be a chore, though. The floor was slick with slime, ichor and blood.

"Professor's not here," Barb said. "Safety first," she added, sheathing the swords.

She got down on all fours and tried to climb up the chute, but she kept sliding down. The second time, her leg slid into the hole to the lower chamber, nearly breaking it.

"This is impossible," she said, sitting down. Then she noticed that the rope that ascended up the chute. Presumably still tied to the professor's ankle, it was tucked to one side in a slight cleft that ran along the chute.

She pulled it out and flicked it to the side, trying her weight on it. Wherever the professor was now, he seemed to be solidly stuck.

"This is a bit morbid," she said, pulling on the rope, then carefully climbing up the chute hand-over-hand. About halfway she slipped and fell on her face, bruising her chin, but she was able to get enough purchase with her feet to make it to the top.

As she neared the top, she stopped and sniffed and listened. The smell of ichor was overwhelming but there was no sound from the chamber beyond.

"How's it going?" Janea shouted.

The voice boomed through the cavern and Barb suppressed an ungodly curse.

"Quiet," she hissed, listening again. Still nothing.

She pulled herself over the opening and drew her pistol, triggering the SureFire flashlight on it in addition to her helmet light and quickly shining both around.

The cave was, for once, high and wide with the traditional stalactites and stalagmites. It was still dark with the slime mold, and in places there were deep pools of ichor. It definitely looked like the creature's lair.

She followed the rope to a crack between two of the stalagmites where the professor's body was wedged. All the body except the head.

"That explains the blood," Barb said, pointing her pistol around until she spotted the head. It had apparently rolled into a corner of the cave. "Okay, that's the professor."

But search as she might, she couldn't find the kidnap victim.

"That's odd," she muttered, getting down on her knees and shining the light into every crevice.

By dint of much searching she found three openings off of the cave. All of them had signs of being used by the creature but none of them had traces of the victim.

"Ssssh . . . sugar," she muttered.

She went back over to the entrance and called down.

"Janea. Found the professor. No sign of the victim. Three exits, all used. At this point, we need to call it."

"Got it," Janea said.

"I'm going to try to stuff the professor down the chute," Barb said. "I'll roll you his head first."

Lazarus walked out of the cave and then over to a patch of brush, and started rolling in the leaves as if trying to rub something off his fur.

Barb pulled herself out of the opening, then pulled the body of professor Argyll through. She'd gotten good at that over the last few hours.

"You'd think there'd be somebody waiting for us," Barb said, shaking her head. "Give me Thane's hand."

Getting out of the cave had been nearly as much of a nightmare as fighting the thing in it. Fortunately, every time the two agents got lost, Lazarus had directed them to the right course. The major problem had been maneuvering the stiffening body of the professor and Thane. Thane could and would perform minimal functions—would crawl when they told him to crawl—but getting him through the restrictions had been a special pain. And any time the light started to go away, such as the one time Janea's helmet-light battery had given out, he would start to howl.

As the student exited the cave he started to mutter, a precursor to a howl. Night had fallen by the time they exited the cave and apparently the light from Barb's helmet wasn't enough.

"It's okay, Thane," Barb said, pulling him to his feet. The FBI was still clearly investigating the area around the trailer, and there were Klieg lights set up. "Go to the light, Thane. It's okay, I'll be with you."

Randell looked up as a tall figure stumbled into the light and collapsed right on top of an evidence marker.

"Watch where you're . . ." he said before recognizing the lost caver. "Holy shit!"

"Watch your language, Special Agent," Barb said, holstering her pistol as she walked into the light around the trailer. She was dragging the body of the professor by one wrist. His body had stiffened into a slight U, which had actually helped with most of the restrictions. "Area's cleared but we couldn't find the girl."

~•

"Trying to give a cat a bath in the shower is a baaad idea," Barb said, toweling her hair as she walked out of the bathroom. Lazarus darted past her, yowling.

The agents had wanted to question them immediately but they'd given in to the argument that both needed a shower badly. So the foursome had returned to Barb and Janea's hotel. Barb and Janea had driven in a different car by mutual agreement with the agents. Their rental car now smelled like rotting skunks.

"Cedar said you were all dead," Randell said. "At least what we could get out of him. He's nearly as bad as Thane. All he'd do was scream about blackness and repeat that you were all dead."

"Which was why there wasn't a welcoming committee," Janea said. "O ye of little faith. Actually, that's *exactly* what ye are."

"So what was it?" Graham asked.

"Not sure," Barb said.

"It wasn't a Shambler," Janea said. "Underestimated the threat again. It didn't respond to the Jagana spell or the Jugu powder, which a Shambler would have. And Shamblers don't have those eyes. I'm going to have to call a researcher at the Foundation to see if they have a clue. But the good news is, it's dead. Which, I suppose, explains why you got the Calling. If I'd gone in there expecting a Shambler we all *would* be dead."

"The professor is," Barb said, shaking her head. "I should have listened to Lazarus."

"No sign of the girl?" Randell asked.

"There were three openings off of the lair," Barb said, tightly. "All used. We had a dead team member, one who was catatonic, and neither Janea nor I were cave experts. I turned the penetration at that point."

"In case it sounds like we're being ungrateful," Graham said, looking at Randell sharply, "good job on taking out whatever that thing was. And thank you for recovering the professor and Th—" He paused as his phone beeped, looked at it, and flipped it open.

"Agent Graham . . . Yes, sir. You're sure. Yes, sir, right away."

He closed the phone and looked at Barb with a flat expression. "You're sure this thing is dead?"

"All are not dead that sleeping lie," Janea said, her brow furrowing. "But it's as dead as anything like that can be. Why?"

"We've had another attack."

Chapter Five

"Your creature has been identified," Augustus said over the video link.

Janea had sent a report to FLUF before heading to bed, and the next morning she and Barb had headed back to the FBI forward base after a brief stop to drop off the rental car and pick up a new one.

Graham had headed to the site of the new attack, so it was Barb, Janea and Randell receiving the call.

"The creature is a *skru-gnon*."

"A child of foulness?" Janea said, her eyes wide. "Oh, no, no, no..."

"And what is a...*skru*..." Barb asked. "That's Tibetan again, right?"

"A *skru-gnon* is an unholy mating of human and Old One," Germaine said. "It is a way for Old Ones to enter into the world."

"And more," Janea said, her eyes closed. "The children of the foul are..." She paused and opened her eyes, slitting them slightly. "The children of the foul are the children of *gar gyi dbang phyug ma*, the mother of all demons."

"Tiamat again?" Barb asked, exasperated. "Doesn't she *ever* learn?"

"No, *gar gyi dhang phyug ma* is not Tiamat," Janea said, shaking her head. "It was assumed at one time that they were the same but they're not. The Gar is an Old One, not an Old God. It was said that it was banished—or vanished, the translation is tricky—from this plane before the first civilization of man arose. It was the creator of the Shamblers, they were of its essence but separate..." She paused as she saw the looks Randell and Barb were giving her.

"Okay, look, this is pre-science," she said. "And it's all legend. Tibetan and Incan and some from Basque, of all places. But this is the best guess on the part of the researchers. The Old Ones do not reproduce sexually. Most of them don't reproduce, period. The Gar, though, can. It mostly reproduces asexually, fissioning off creatures like Shamblers. But the Shamblers cannot reproduce. All of the remaining Shamblers that haven't been destroyed were created from the essence of the Gar."

"So what's a *skru*..." Barb asked.

"*Skru-gnon*," Janea said. "A child of foulness. The Gar can, somehow, induce reproduction in human females. Only humans, not animals. Through them it can produce a mixture of Old One and human, an unholy union, as Augustus said. They are much more powerful than Shamblers or any of the other creatures it produces by fission. They may be the souls of Old Ones brought to this plane."

"So that...thing," Barb said, closing her eyes.

"Was born out of the body of a woman," Janea said, her face firm. "The worst possible sort of rape, the highest violation of the credo of my goddess. If Freya had a fraction of the power of the White God, she'd be turning up in *person* to kill this Old One."

"The worst part is that they can, in turn, reproduce," Germaine said. "They can only reproduce by...the term means 'breaking selves,' which is assumed to be fission. But that means they are able to once again flood the planet with their minions. And the *skru-gnon* are, of themselves, powerful and fell creatures. However, there has not been a child of foulness found on earth since the very dawn of history. There are indications that, yes, the Old Gods battled the Old Ones for power on this planet and won in the very dawn of man. Gods versus the Titans is the most commonly known myth. If so, there should be *no skru-gnon* on earth: they would have never allowed them to remain. But now there appear to be at least two."

"Which means that someone has managed to bring the Gar

back," Janea said. "And if so, we are all in serious trouble. That means that the stars have aligned: the Old Ones are returning."

"We need to figure out where these things are being produced," Barb said.

"That's pretty tough," Randell replied, thoughtfully. "Okay, I'm trying not to get totally weirded out by the conversation, but here goes. Let's say that this was your run-of-the-mill serial killer."

"We could wish," Janea said.

"They're bad enough," Randell replied, darkly. "But this is about that sort of investigation. We'd look for specific clues as to the person's identity. DNA, trace materials like fibers, car tracks."

"Well, the thing makes tracks," Barb said. "Problem being, you have to follow it through caves. I'm not sure how many more cave teams I want to lose."

"At one level, I'm thinking as many as it takes," Randell said. "But that's not the point. The point is, there would be clues as to where they came from. Who they are. Where they live."

"But with these things..." Janea said.

"Yeah," Randell said. "They don't have fingerprints. They don't have ID. They don't use cars. I think we're just going to have to go through as many cave teams as necessary to find the lair."

"Maybe not," Barb said. "Look, Janea, what do we know about the Gar?"

"Not much," Janea said. "And I'm working off of rusty memory. I'll get Chao Lin to send me a full download on it. But...It's large. I mean *really* big. The size of a mansion or maybe even a factory. It's going to be noticeable if it's above ground."

"Does it eat?" Barb asked. "Drink? Defecate?"

"I'm not sure if it defecates," Janea said, smiling slightly. "But it eats. That's one of the things that is mentioned. It was mostly fed captives but it is generally carnivorous. Very carnivorous. One of its alternate titles translates as something like the Stomach That Walks."

"So it has to be getting food from somewhere," Barb said, musingly. "How did it get here?"

"That's a puzzler," Janea said, shrugging. "There's a summoning spell in *De Voco Turpis*, but I know it doesn't work. It's been tried, trust me."

"Who would try to summon something like this?" Randell asked, angrily.

"Who would kill a dozen, a hundred, women?" Janea asked. "The Gar gives its earthly acolytes power. Power over others, money, you name it. Anyone crazy enough and ambitious enough. And smart enough. There have been attempts to summon the Gar for centuries. Someone finally managed."

"They'd have to have some pretty serious occult knowledge," Barb said, crossing her arms and looking at the far wall. "That's the point. The Gar doesn't exist in a vacuum. It was summoned by someone with serious occult knowledge and access to some pretty obscure texts, at a guess. That's the first point. Second, they've got to be somewhere in the vicinity. These things didn't travel here from California. Third, it has to eat. A lot of food, probably meat, is going to nowhere."

"Okay," Randell said, nodding. "Now we're cooking. You're getting to our meat, if you don't mind the pun. So we need to start looking for large food stocks going nowhere, who has been accessing obscure occult texts in this area and who in this area, has that sort of occult knowledge."

"And I'm thinking that the ichor might tell us something," Janea said, musingly. "I mean, it's biological trace material. There's all sorts of things you guys do with that these days. Right?"

"True," Randell said, then frowned. "The good news is, I know who the samples got sent to. We've got our own local lab, which isn't normally the case. And our blood sample guy is a real wizard at anything along the lines of biological samples."

"Your body language is screaming that there's bad news," Janea said, smiling.

"Yeah," Randell said, grimacing. "The bad news is, it's Stan."

"Stan, tell me you have something," Randell said as the three-some walked into the lab.

Most FBI offices, even regional offices, which Knoxville was, do not have a major forensics department. Knoxville was unusual for two reasons. The first had to do with its proximity to Oak Ridge. During WWII, keeping German spies away from the Manhattan Project was a major priority for the FBI. And during the Cold War the priority was nearly as high.

With the thawing of the Cold War, it would have only made sense to dial back on some of the facilities in Knoxville. However, a combination of bureaucratic finesse and long-term congressmen had kept the Knoxville office at nearly the level of its heyday.

The second reason was less political and much more mundane. The University of Tennessee, also based in Knoxville, had one of the premier forensics departments in the United States. The Knoxville office could, therefore, draw upon top-flight students from the UT department and worked as a cross-pollination point with UT forensics.

The Knoxville FBI forensics department was, therefore, second only to Quantico in its level of knowledge and skill. And it arguably had a slight advantage in pure biologicals.

Unfortunately for the field members of the local office, the advantage rested mostly on the slightly stooped shoulders of one Stan Robertson, PhD.

"What complete moron sent this foul stuff to *my* lab?" the lab tech shouted, waving a vial in the air. "Blood, yes! Epithelials, of course! Saliva, urine, body parts, naturally! But it would take a moronic Republican—oh, sorry, oxymoron!—It would take a Republican to send this idiotic hodge-podge to me! And I note that the sample bag is signed by one Special, as in 'I took the short bus to school, Agent Randell Smith!' So you would be the moron, *ey*?"

Stan Robertson was five foot seven, sixty-ish, with thinning light-brown hair going gray and a lean, muscular figure. His face also turned beet red when he was angry. As he was much of the time.

"That would be me," Randell answered evenly. "So you don't have anything?"

"What is this stuff?" Stan shouted. "It is not, let me make this plain, any of the above, ey? It's not even degraded human biologicals. Nor any mammal. I haven't gotten through the full spectrum of reptiles, fish and amphibians, ey?"

"We were hoping you could tell us," Randell said. "By the way, Stan Robertson, PhD, Mrs. Barbara Everette and Doris Grisham. Dor... Miz Grisham prefers to be called Janea."

"Whatever," Stan said. "There are two distinct samples. Very distinct. If I was to make a bet, they're two different *species*! The DNA is just *bizarre*. The cell structure is as alien as anything I've ever seen."

"There are cells?" Janea asked.

"Yes, there are cells," Stan snapped. "If you can call them that." He walked to a monitor and flipped up an image. "You want to tell me what that is?"

The cells on the monitor were stellate in shape and appeared to be almost jet black.

"That was in this junk," Stan said, waving the vial again. "Then there's this!"

The second picture was of more cells, but curved like a banana. The only similarity was that they were, again, black.

"That was from the first sample I got," Stan said. "And those were really weird. They were reproducing like mad. I was afraid I had a pathogen on my hands but they weren't infectious in any normal test. But as long as they had a food source they continued to reproduce. They would consume just about anything, proteins, agar, sugars, but they had a real fondness for potassium enhancements. Don't get me into doctrine of types, I'm not a Christian whack-job, but they went crazy over banana. Continued to reproduce down to minus one hundred degrees Celsius, and they don't degrade until four hundred degrees Celsius. Getting complete clearance of them is going to be a job, let me tell you."

"Internal cell structure?" Janea asked.

"Which one?" Stan asked. "The banana cells are less odd. They actually *have* mitochondria. There are some structures that might be equivalent to Golgi bodies but for the rest I'm stumped. They have DNA but not nuclear DNA. The star cells are semi-viral—that's the best I can do. They don't have mitochondria, and how they process oxygen without mitochondria is a good trick, they don't have nuclear DNA, they don't even have bacterial *ring* DNA, and they don't seem to have any internal structure at *all*. They're closest to a coronavirus but they're *not* coronaviruses. I don't know what they are. Alien is the best I can do, and that's as good as you're going to get."

"That's from the second attack?" Janea asked. "The stellate cells, that is?"

"Second sample, yes," Randell said. "You know what he's talking about?"

"Uh-huh," Janea said, distantly. "That means it's probably not a *skru-gnon*. Interesting."

"What in the blue blazes is a shu-gnon?" Stan yelled. "What

is this..." He paused as one of the machines started beeping urgently and walked over.

"Now that's odd..." he said, rubbing the back of his head. "That's... Okay, that's impossible."

"What?" Janea asked, walking over to the machine.

"The banana cell," Stan said, gesturing at the readout. "It has human DNA."

"I thought you said it *wasn't* human DNA," Randell said, walking over and looking at the readout.

"It's not," Stan snapped. "Anybody but a moron would know that! But it has *some* human DNA and that sounds really really stupid. Wait... this is *impossible!*"

"It's a match," Janea breathed.

"It's *not* a match," Stan shouted.

"Okay," Janea said, her voice tight. "It's a *near* match."

"What?" Randell said. "Would either one of you make some sense?"

"None of this makes sense," Stan shouted. "It can't be... It's..."

"Would you hit the link, please?" Janea asked, pointing at an icon. "Or do you want me to do it?"

"Fine," Stan said, hitting the icon.

The image of a young black woman appeared, a mug-shot photograph. Thin and with a worn face, probably from heavy drug use.

"Lorna Ewing," Randell said. "Street name, Fantasy. Missing person, Louisville, Kentucky, probable foul play. This thing's... related to her?"

"Sibling or child," Janea said. "Let me be clear. Child."

"Oh, dear Lord," Barb said, shaking her head. "I had hoped you were wrong."

"Okay," Stan said, calmly. "I am missing pieces of information. I do not *like* to be missing pieces of information. I cannot do my job if I'm *missing pieces of information!*"

"Are you going to shout about 'impossible' and 'morons'?" Janea asked, sweetly.

"Not to mention, what was it? Christian whack-job?" Barbara said, tightly. "Because I do not enjoy being shouted at. But the Lord tells us to take people as they are instead of, oh, throwing them through a wall."

"You and what army?" Stan said, angrily.

"Stan?" Janea said, still sweetly. "You really don't want to ask that question. Because I've seen her when she gets mad. You don't want to be the one she gets mad at."

"I would never harm a human who was not intent on harming others," Barbara said. "But can you please just calm the tone a bit? And if you would like the other information, we will give it to you. But your first instinct will be to shout 'morons' and 'religious nuts' and other similar insults. And then the only person you have to blame for not being able to do your job is you."

Stan looked at Barbara, then looked at the screen. Very faintly he started quivering. He looked at Barbara, then looked at the screen. More quivering. It wasn't fear, it was just his body trying to tell him to go away. From the thought of what they'd said as much as anything.

"The term you're looking for here is 'cognitive dissonance,'" Janea said, trying not to laugh. "I take it you're an atheist."

"No one can be a scientist and *not* be an atheist," Stan said firmly.

"Feel free to hold as true to your beliefs as I hold to mine," Barbara said, mildly. "But you're also looking at something that is plainly impossible. And we have given you a rational—for values of rational—explanation. However, it is an explanation that is entirely at odds with your beliefs. Thus the cognitive dissonance. May I make a suggestion?"

"Please," Stan said.

"You do not have to think of this as metaphysical," Barbara said. "Think of it, instead, as a very advanced form of science. One for which we do not have the theory, yet. Feel free to work on theories for it in your back brain."

"There's a body of scientific literature on this, actually," Janea interjected. "I've read some of the papers. Most demons that manifest have what is called transform DNA, which is basically DNA made up from scratch. Some don't have any DNA at all, but those have no capacity for reproduction with humans. These appear to have something different, again. This is the first I've seen of this sort of approach. Makes sense since it's Old Ones and not demons. They're assumed to come from completely different backgrounds. This is sort of a proof of that hypothesis."

"Demons have cellular structure?" Stan said, blinking.

"Manifested ones do," Janea said. "Mammalian, primarily. Those with DNA appear to have no senescence coding, thus the 'immortal' aspect. And there appears to be no cellular turnover. How that works is being very quietly studied by a group of SC scientists."

"Why don't *I* know about this?" Stan asked angrily.

"Because if you don't *have* to know about SC you don't *find out* about SC," Randell said. "And once you do find out about SC you wish you *didn't* know."

"Think of it this way," Barb said. "You can now do the first and only paper on the biological structure of Old Ones. You're the world expert."

"But there's only about five hundred people in the world who can read the paper," Janea said. "And only about fifteen who will."

"You being one of them?" Stan asked.

"I'm not a biologist," Janea said. "I'll read the abstract and the conclusion and skim the rest because I won't understand half of it. But I'll get the important bits that I need to know the next time I run into an Old One. The first and most important being, how do we kill these things?"

"Well..." Stan said, turning back to the screen with a huff. "The first sample was a...sku-gnon?"

"*Skru-gnon*," Janea corrected. "I'll leave you the spelling."

"Certain poison gases might work," Stan said musingly. "The hyperproduction of cells explains the regeneration. Fire...would be mostly useless unless it's *very* hot. Thermite or something like that. Cold? Impervious. You could hit this thing with liquid nitrogen and it wouldn't blink. *Might* die if you immersed it in liquid helium, but good luck on that. I don't know anything about the rest of its structure. I don't suppose you could bring one back alive?"

"Not even going to try," Barb said. "These are a crime against God."

"And on the part that you don't like to think about," Janea said, as Stan started to get worked up again, "they have a psychological impact on the unprotected that is severe. You don't want to be in the same room with a live one."

"Just their cells are driving me crazy," Stan said, grabbing his hair.

Barb looked at Janea, her eyes wide.

"Uhm, Stan," Janea said, her face tight. "Just how crazy are you feeling?"

"What?" Stan asked.

"One of the aspects of the Old Ones is that they tend to induce panic and insanity," Janea said. "Just how crazy are you feeling?"

"I'm..." Stan said, collapsing in a chair and grabbing his head. "I'm not feeling good, that's for sure."

"Okay," Janea said, patting him on the shoulder. "Feeling obsessive?"

"I'm OCD," Stan said. "Obsessive is normal for me."

"More obsessive than normal?" Janea asked.

"Maybe," Stan said, still not looking up.

"Voices?" Barbara asked.

"What are you, my psychiatrist?" Stan asked.

"Seriously," Barb said.

"No," Stan said. "But I am feeling more frantic."

"*More* frantic?" Randell said.

"Stop," Barb snapped. "And?"

"I'm not normally a violent person," Stan said. "I shout, but I don't feel violent. Angry, yes. But not violent. But I've been feeling very violent since I've been studying these samples. And...Yes, crazy. I am neurotic, not psychotic. I am beginning to manifest traces of what I would diagnose as psychosis."

"There's not enough material for emanations," Barb said. "And I don't feel any at all. Do you?"

"Not a twinge," Janea said. "A fundamental aspect?"

"How?" Barb asked. "How could it be a fundamental aspect?"

"Arachnophobia," Stan said.

"Non sequitur," Janea replied.

"Arachnophobia," Stan repeated, finally raising his head. "Arachnids induce fear and panic in a large number of people. The theory is that they are so unworldly, so unlike any normal creature, that it induces an automatic 'other' response in many humans. It's been studied because of the possibility that there would be a similar response on the part of anyone encountering aliens. Ladies, I don't think that we are dealing with something... metaphysical," he said with a spit of distaste.

"I think that these are extraterrestrial. So, yes, a higher form of biological science. Perhaps with other abilities that are beyond our current understanding. My reaction is, therefore, a reasonable one. My psychological issues with it are a function of that response and there are appropriate medications to relieve some or all of the response. I will immediately consult my psychiatrist. I don't know how, exactly, I will explain that something I am studying is driving me insane, but I will explain it as best I can and avail myself of the appropriate medications. I'm thinking Haldol. It will slow my thinking and make me marginally less functional, but I will be able to continue to study this phenomenon without, in fact, becoming insane. Hopefully, once I've finished the study I will be able to resume my normal medication schedule."

"It's possible you won't," Janea pointed out. "These things tend to put people in the loony bin. Maybe you should just put the samples away until we figure out a way to study them without resorting to antipsychotics. I know this sounds sort of Catch-22, but I think that continuing to study them is a little crazy."

"I am a scientist," Stan said, standing up. "It's what we do."

"That is pretty much the same thing Victor Von Frankenstein said," Janea replied.

"He was a fictional character," Stan replied, firmly.

"Bet you a dollar?" Janea said. "Seriously, we've got what we needed. Drop it."

"Not on your life," Stan said.

"It's not your life I'm worried about," Barbara said. "It's your soul."

Chapter Six

G raham," Barbara said unhappily, looking at the house that was the site of the second attack.

The two-story house was in a small neighborhood near the town of Goin, Tennessee. Brick front, vinyl siding, two-car garage. It looked enough like Barb's house to be a twin, right down to the holly hedging.

At the trailer she had managed to avoid, to the greatest possible degree, thinking of the victims. The horror that they had experienced she now clearly understood, and if she sunk too far into sympathy it was going to take the edge off her deadliness.

With this set of victims, she suspected empathy was going to be unavoidable.

Local police were keeping the news media well back, but they were staying nearly as far away. The forensics van was from the FBI, as was everyone on site at the house.

"Two dead, two missing," the special agent said without preamble. "Dead, father Wilkerson Boone, age thirty-two, Jason Boone, age nine."

"Oh, Lord," Barb said, taking a deep breath.

"MO of deaths is slightly different," Graham said, looking at her oddly. "Both were strangled. The marks are...strange."

"I bet," Janea said. "Sucker marks?"

"Yes," Graham said, blinking.

"We've got some updated information," Randell said. "Keep going."

"Missing, Wendi Boone, mother, age thirty-one; Titania Boone, age thirteen."

"These things are gathering hosts for the Gar," Janea said.

"*More* hosts," Barb replied, tightly.

"The what?" Graham asked.

"I'll update you in a second," Randell said, holding up a hand. "Trail?"

"Similar trail leading up the hill to a cave," Graham said. "The cave is known in the area. A local kid got lost in it a couple of years ago and a rescue team had to find him. Attack occurred approximately two AM."

Barb looked at the horizon, where the sun was already falling below the mountains.

"If this thing recognizes that there is more prey here, it might come back," she said, frowning.

"That's what's got me worried," Graham said.

"Okay," Barb said, nodding. "We need to clear the forensics people by sundown. I'd like to get the FBI to take over holding back the media. Hopefully get rid of the media. Can we get the other houses cleared?"

"Not without some sort of serious cover story," Graham said. "Washington is getting really exercised. They want to know what you're going to do about this."

"There's only two of us," Janea said, angrily. "There are, or were, at least two of these Old Ones, and now we're pretty sure there's a major Old One involved. That means there could be *dozens*. These caves go all through this region, and that's the natural environment of the Hunters of the Dark. I'm not sure we can get in there and comb them out one by one. I'm pretty sure that it would be suicidal to *try*."

"We have to do something," Graham said, waving his hands.

"We'll wait for this one tonight," Barb said. "It may use the same exit, looking for more prey. We need another cave team, but this time, no civilians."

"You're civilians," Randell pointed out.

"You know what I mean," Barb said. "Send out an urgent message. There are bound to be cavers in the military. Get us a team of people who know how to survive *and* know how to cave. Get them here, and all the gear we're going to need, fast."

"You don't want much, do you?" Graham said.

"How many more do you want to die?" Janea asked. "You asked for our answer, that's it. We need a team of fighters to go into the caves and find these things. On their own turf, which is a bit like fighting a leopard in the brush. But leopards aren't the size of a water buffalo, stronger than a gorilla, invulnerable to most weapons, and able to drive you insane if you look at them. Hopefully find out where they're coming from. And, you know, survive."

"And we're going to want military-grade weaponry," Barb said thoughtfully.

"Why?" Graham asked. "I thought you said these things weren't vulnerable to normal weapons."

"We don't know that," Barb said. "The *skru-gnon* wasn't, but the other beasts might be. And when people fought them before, they were using spears and clubs. I would personally like to see what a grenade does to one. And if we fight them aboveground, a rocket launcher would be nice. You have to see these things to understand."

"But if I do see them, they'll drive me insane," Randell said. "Great."

"Hey," Janea said, "that's what Thorazine is for."

"So we're going to sit here all night?" Janea asked.

The hillside was covered in secondary growth, mostly poplar and pine with scrubby undergrowth. Barb had carefully pointed out the poison ivy to her less-than-outdoors-oriented partner. She'd found a clear spot above the cave opening with a good view of it and the rest of the hillside, and settled down for a long stalk.

The cave opening was larger than the one by the trailer, irregularly shaped, again, but nearly the size of a manhole cover.

"Unless we get a visitor earlier," Barb said, taking a sip of coffee. She was on short sleep from the night before, she'd had some very vivid and really awful dreams, and it had been a long day. It was working up to be a longer night.

"I don't sit still very well," Janea pointed out.

Especially with Janea around.

"Try," Barb said.

"Fighting these things in the dark is going to suck," Janea said about five seconds later.

"That's what night-vision systems are for," Barb said, holding up a set of thermal goggles.

"Yeah," Janea said, picking hers up and turning them on. "Cool. You can see the FBI guys standing over in the shadows."

"That's because they pick up on heat sources," Barb said.

"Which means they might be next to useless with these things," Janea said, setting her goggles down.

"Huh?"

"We don't even know if they're exothermic," Janea pointed out.

"Exo...?"

"Hot-blooded," Janea said. "They could be, you know, like insects. They don't give off heat. We don't really know anything about them."

"How's it going?" Graham said over the radio. Both women were wearing tactical headsets.

"It would be fine if Janea could understand the basic premise of hunting," Barb said. "Which is to be quiet. For that matter, if you keep asking me every five minutes, I am going to come down there and take your radio away."

"We need regular commo checks," Graham said.

"Agreed," Barb said. "Nominal."

"Out."

"You really are way too into this," Janea said. "I'm starting to agree with Stan. We need to study them."

"The problem being that anyone who studies them goes insane," Barb pointed out.

"Maybe do it like 'The World's Most Dangerous Joke,'" Janea said.

"What?"

"You never watch Monty Python?" Janea asked, surprised.

"I tried to watch that...what was it? *The Meaning of Life*?" Barb said. "I didn't get it. I don't get most British comedy."

"Aesir shit!" Janea said. "How the Hel did I get you for a partner?"

"Language."

"Oh, I'm sorry," Janea said. "Let me rephrase. Fecal matter of a Great Old One. How in Niflheim did I get a stuck-up, prissy, doesn't-get-British-comedy person like you as a partner?"

"Because you know more about this stuff than I do and I'm better at killing things than you are," Barb said. "Now this is supposed to be a stakeout. Which means we need to be *qui-et* so that they won't know we're *here*."

"Barb."

"Yes?"

"We're two reproductive-age females," Janea said. "We're not a stakeout, we're *bait*. You probably survived that *skru-gnon* because it *wanted* you alive."

"You put the most pleasant spin on things," Barb said.

"I just thought of it," Janea said. "I think we should have waited for the rocket launcher to do this."

"Master Sergeant," Major Esgar said. "Sorry to get you out at this time of night. Please sit down."

Master Sergeant Scott Attie, five foot nine inches, one hundred and ninety-five pounds, brown hair and eyes, was a fifteen-year veteran of the Special Forces. As such, he was used to callouts at *any* time of night. But this one was different. Just as he was getting to bed, on his first real downtime in five years of constant deployments to Afghanistan, he'd been told to report to an office at Joint Special Operations Command, wear civilian clothes, and be prepared to be TDY—on temporary duty—for an unspecified period.

His wife, who had been wearing a negligee that left nothing to hide at the time, had been less than amused.

"Yes, sir," Attie said, taking a seat and trying not to sigh. He enjoyed his job, but he'd really been looking forward to some downtime. Maybe heading over to the Cape for some fishing.

"All of the following is Top Secret, Special Compartment Intelligence," the major said. He looked tired, as if Attie's brief was just one more item to be checked off in a very long day. "There is a priority need for someone with combat experience and experience working in caves for a rapid-deployment mission. Your bio states that you have extensive civilian caving experience with additional military experience in Afghanistan. The mission will be undercover, civilian clothes, has a high risk of loss of life, and will be in CONUS."

"Uh, sir?" Attie said, looking puzzled. "Posse Comitatus?"

Posse Comitatus was an act passed just after the Civil War that prohibited the military from being used within states of the United States for anything other than disaster relief and suppression of rebellion. It was holy writ in the military that you did not violate Posse Comitatus.

"There will be a more complete briefing," the major said. "But to cover that, there is a formal and secret determination by the Supreme Court that in matters of Special Circumstance, Posse Comitatus does not apply."

"Special Circumstance, sir?" Attie said, realizing he was getting out of his depth.

"There was a reason I told you to sit down."

"Janea. Wake up."

Janea, despite Barb's mostly monosyllabic replies, had chattered fairly constantly for two hours and then fallen asleep on Barb's shoulder. She was clearly having nightmares at a couple of points, but Barb couldn't believe she'd fallen asleep at all. Given where they were and what they were waiting for, tired as she was, Barb could not imagine sleeping.

But when she started to hear stirrings from within the cave, it seemed like a good idea to wake up her partner.

"*Freya hjelpe!*" Janea muttered then came awake. "Freya aid, that was a horrible dream."

"Quiet," Barb whispered. "I think we have company."

"That's just what you were *saying*," Janea said, shaking her head. "I *am* awake, right?"

"Just grab your axe," Barb hissed.

Barb recognized the major aid that she was receiving from the Lord was simply to be able to look upon these horrors with some degree of calm. But as the tentacles slowly crept into the moonlight, she had to hold hard to her sanity. They were causing flashbacks to the battle in the cavern, the *skru-gnon* questing for any opening to flow into. There was a special horror to it as a woman. She'd never been raped, but what the *skru-gnon* did was beyond any rape by mortal being or even demon.

She slowly drew her katana, as quietly as she could, then slid to her feet. She had borrowed an MP-5 from the FBI, and she'd use it if it turned out to be effective. But she already knew that, with God's aid, the katana would work.

"Ready?" she whispered as the monstrosity came fully into view.

"Wait," Janea said, holding her arm.

The reason for the pause was apparent as a second entity wriggled from the ground. The two stopped in the area in front of the cave, their tentacles writhing and twisting together in what might be silent communication.

Then a third joined them. And a fourth. And a fifth.

As a sixth started to emerge, one of them turned its attention uphill. And they all began to climb towards the two women.

"Uh-oh," Janea muttered.

"Graham!"

Graham's head came up at the sound of Barb's voice. Except for a regular "Nominal" it was the first time she'd communicated all night.

The FBI team had been augmented by more personnel from area offices. The investigation was beginning to have all the aspects of a war zone. Washington had admitted that, given the level of threat, they were considering calling in the military, at least covert portions thereof. The problem being that every cover story they could come up with was almost as bad as the reality. Clearing four hundred square miles of American territory and having a mini-war with an alien, or possibly metaphysical, army was going to require quite the cover story.

But at present they had twenty special agents on duty, both to keep the press away from the crime scene and as potential backup.

He got the feeling from the sound of the normally unflappable Mrs. Everette's voice that they might be a bit short.

"Go," he said, waving to Randell to turn on a speaker in the command van.

"We are headed down the hill!" Barb said, then cut off. *"Sorry, I tripped. This is Old One large force. Say again, large force. At least eight Old Ones are in pursuit! FLIRs seem to reduce the horror aspect. Recommend all agents don night vision gear and prepare for assault."*

"And please don't shoot us!" Janea added. *"We're the ones with legs running away!"*

"Shit," Randell said, grabbing his M-4 and piling out of the truck. "We have incoming hostiles! All agents, form a perimeter behind the house! Friendlies on the way in. Don night vision gear! Do *not* look at these things with your naked eyes!"

"We've got you covered," Graham said, calmly. "Come on in."

"Damn," Janea said as she tripped and bounced off a sapling.

"Come on!" Barb shouted, grabbing her hand and pulling her to her feet. "We don't have time for your horror-movie antics!"

"I'm figuring all I have to do is stay ahead of *you*," Janea said, sprinting down the hill.

There was a seven-foot wooden privacy fence that separated the lawn of the Boone household from the forest beyond.

Janea hit the wall and grabbed on, frantically scrambling at the slick wood to try to climb over.

Barb boosted her over then took a running jump. Grabbing the top, she somersaulted over and landed on both feet.

"Show-off," Janea said, running across the lawn to the line of agents.

"Lazy butt," Barb panted.

"Where are they?" Randell asked as the two skidded to a stop.

"You know those nightmares where something's right behind you chasing you, and if it catches you, you die?" Janea asked.

"Don't have them," Randell answered.

"Well, that's where they are," Janea answered, pulling around her MP-5.

"No, they're not," Randell said.

"Listen," Barb said.

It was a rustling, nothing more. Randell had hunted deer before joining the Marines, and to him it sounded, at first, like just a big herd of deer.

But if so, it was a *really* big herd.

Then the security fence started to rattle as something pulled at it, pushed at it, thumped along a thirty-foot section. And then planks started coming down.

What flowed through the openings was hard to see with infrared. The things were the same temperature as the background. Perhaps fortunately, because even what he could see made something in the back of his head start to gibber. Tentacles and eyes and mouths all flickering in movement as the things, in awful silence, glided across the lawn.

"Oh my God," one of the agents muttered. "Oh, dear God in heaven."

Another screamed and pulled the trigger, and then the whole group opened fire.

Barb fired short, controlled bursts from the MP-5 and watched in fury as they seemed to have no effect.

There was an effect; even with the FLIRs, she could see ichor flying through the air, but the wave of blackness was barely slowed.

"These aren't heavy enough!" Barb said as she ran through the end of her thirty-round magazine. The things were nearly on them, and she flipped the MP-5 over her shoulder and drew her H&K, firing carefully targeted single shots into the creature closest to her. Which shuddered to a halt and began to deliquesce.

"Larger rounds!" Barb shouted. But by then it was too late as one of the agents was yanked off his feet, screaming.

Barb holstered the pistol and whipped out her katana, taking a cat stance.

"Lord," she muttered. "I think we're going to need a little help here."

Randell continued firing burst after burst into the monster that was closing on him, backing up as he realized he was coming in range of its tentacles. But the high-velocity 5.56-millimeter rounds didn't seem to have any effect.

As he ran out of his second magazine he, too, drew his sidearm, an issue .40 Sig Sauer, and began pumping rounds into the beast. Finally, it stopped.

"Right again," he muttered, dropping the magazine and inserting another. He stepped forward to try to help the other agents, when his FLIR suddenly blazed in white-out.

Barb waded into the mass of creatures, the five-hundred-year-old katana slicing through tentacles, eyes, mouths and bodies like a blender.

Two agents were down, one of them clearly dead. Wondering why the firing had stopped, she charged across the lawn to the fallen agent and sliced the creature that was on him in half, narrowly missing the agent himself.

Spinning in place, she saw that most of the line was shielding its eyes and backing up.

"Lord help them," she muttered. "I hoped the FLIRs would work."

Hers was working fine; the backyard of the house was lit like midday. Which was why she saw Janea dragged off her feet and towards the cave by one of the creatures.

Janea was trying to hack down one-handed with her axe, but the thing simply wrapped her arms and legs in tentacles and carted her off on its back.

"Oh, that ain't happening," Barb said. "*Shoot* these things!"

But the remaining creatures clustered around her, blocking her way, no longer attacking the FBI agents and concentrating entirely on her. She suddenly found herself beset by a flood of the monsters, tentacles closing in from every direction.

"Fine," she said. "Let's dance."

Randell ripped off his FLIR, despite knowing that it was probably going to mean Thorazine for the rest of his life, and looked around.

The reason for the flare-out was immediately apparent. In the middle of the lawn, surrounded by beings out of nightmare, was the "soccer mom." She was glowing a white so bright it was hard to look at with his bare eyes, and turning the monsters around her into sushi. Strangely enough, as horrible as the things were, he felt an immense peace and comfort. He just didn't *care* that they were monsters from beyond any nightmare. He wasn't sure the feeling would *last*, but it was good enough for now.

"Take off the FLIRs!" Randell shouted. "There's light! Switch to forty caliber!"

Randell chose one of the monsters, and by emptying a full magazine into its center of mass, he managed to kill it. As other agents joined him they slowly reduced the crowd around Barb.

"Thanks for the help," the ichor-covered Mrs. Everette said as the last of the creatures fell. "Gotta go."

"What?" Randell shouted as the housewife sprinted for the back fence.

"One of them's got Janea!"

It wasn't until then that the agent realized the redhead was gone.

"Shit," he muttered, sprinting after her. "ALICE," he shouted, using the acronym for post-battle cleanup. "Take care of it!"

As he cleared the fence, he heard one of the agents saying, "Was she *glowing*?"

By the bright light that was coming from somewhere, Barb could see the thing that had Janea. And it was nearly to the cave.

She sped up, dodging through trees with a grace she normally used for heavy traffic.

"Oh, no you don't," she said, actually using Janea to bound over the thing and block the way to the cave.

"Nice to see you," Janea said. She was tapping at one of the tentacles with her axe and looking thoroughly pissed. "Sort of. You're doing your glowy thing and it's whiting out my goggles."

The thing was clearly in a quandary. It had a bunch of its tentacles wrapped around Janea, and more were necessary for propulsion. It tried to free up some of the ones holding Janea, and the redhead was able to nearly struggle free. Then it tried to use some of its ground tentacles and it nearly toppled over.

"Uff," Janea said as she was tossed through the air.

All of those tentacles free, the thing attacked.

"Thank you," Barb said, cutting off a half-dozen tentacles at once and driving the glowing katana deep into the belly of the beast. "Eat God's power, you hell spawn."

"You know," Janea said, sprawled out on the ground. "It's not exactly a sin, but it's extremely embarrassing for an Asatru to get captured."

"Be glad that's all that happened," Barb said. "Did you get any of them?"

"Two," Janea admitted. "Not that I want these things as my servants in Valhalla. Freya, please note, I'd *really* prefer not to have these things as servants in Valhalla."

Chapter Seven

*Y*our little firefight woke up the neighbors. We're already getting queries from CNN, and it's the middle of the night. The Director is not going to be a happy camper tomorrow."

Assistant Deputy Director George Grosskopf was, for his sins, the FBI official in charge of managing Special Circumstances. What he was currently trying to figure out was how to manage the cover-up on this one.

"This may be too big for a cover-up, alas," Germaine said over the videoconference. "And please note that the Great Powers are in agreement on maintaining confidentiality. It is possible that They may intervene to prevent a widening hysteria. But we cannot depend upon that. Their ways are ineffable."

"Seismic sounding," Janea said. "I just thought of it on the way over to the trailer. There's a kind of seismic sounding system that uses a series of explosions, sonic something or another. Trot out a geologist to spin it as a way to map the cave system."

"We need to clear this whole area," Barb said. "There are probably more of these things. And what's the word on our caving team?"

"The military has found a few personnel who are able. And willing to keep quiet about it," ADD Grosskopf said. "They're also bringing special weaponry. Refresh me on the thing with the rounds. The rifle didn't work as well as a pistol? That sounds backwards."

"Well, sir, the M-4's not a real killer, sir," Randell said. "Never has been."

"I've been thinking about it," Barb said. "And I have a theory. But that's all it is."

"Go," the ADD said.

"These things are mostly a mass of tentacles with a very small body," Barb said. "And they regenerate like mad. Even if you hit the body, you don't kill them unless you break it up. And the same goes for the tentacles. You have to do a lot of damage. High velocity rounds kill and wound primarily through hydrostatic shock. These things don't respond at all to hydrostatic shock. You have to really chop them up. The sword actually worked better than my pistol, you just have to get way too close for comfort. Bottom line is, the bigger the round, the better. Coupled with the more rounds you can put on target, the better. I'd suggest that the SF bring a *really* good forty-five SMG with them."

"I'll pass that on," Grosskopf said. "The only one that comes to mind is a Thompson. There are some newer ones but most of them aren't all that great."

"I'd hate to have to work a Thompson through the caves," Barb said with a sigh. "But if that's what we have to work with, that's what we'll have to work with. God's ways are, as Augustus said, ineffable."

"Any thoughts on something that will allow us to clear the entire area and *not* be worse news, or as bad as, an invasion of demonic entities?" the ADD asked. "So far we've floated a meteor strike, radioactive release, and a spill of poison gas that was on its way to be destroyed. None of them are considered politically palatable enough. The Powers That Be would rather tell the truth than any of the above."

"Yeah," Janea said, nodding thoughtfully. "And it would kill several birds with one stone. You're going to need some briefed-in experts who are willing to lie their asses off, and create a bunch of false data, but it just might work."

"This is CNN in Goin, Tennessee, where the federal government has just announced a major threat to not only the local area but the entire region...."

"Methane gas?" Barb said incredulously, rubbing her hair with a towel.

"Hey, it worked," Janea said, yawning. It was just after dawn, and that afternoon they were headed back into the caves to try to find the lair of the Gar. They were going to need sleep. "Methane gas builds up underground all the time. All it needs is one spark, and *boom*! There've been four instances of major methane explosions in known geological history. The geology is totally wrong for it in this area, and there's no way that it would affect as large an area as they're clearing. But it gave us a reason to get civilians out of danger, a reason for Professor Argyll's death, *and* people are buying the bogus seismic charges story, so we don't have to explain a major firefight in a sleepy neighborhood. The neighbors are now complaining about not being warned about the charges and being awakened in the middle of the night instead of insisting it was a firefight. You know people are buying it when they're complaining about the wrong things. *I* deserve a pat on the back."

"I'm starting to think you've got the wrong goddess," Barb said, crawling gratefully into bed. "Ever considered Athena? No, not devious enough. Hera?"

"Bite your tongue," Janea said, putting her hands behind her head. "Like I want to be the spider in the web. Give me someone who wars with gusto and lusts with passion. I spent a little time with a cult of Ishtar when I first got into paganism, but it was too 'love is the answer.' Love's great right up until someone needs their ass seriously kicked. You might as well be Buddhist as Astara." She paused for a moment then grimaced. "I don't want to go to sleep."

"Me neither," Barb admitted. "I'm glad to be horizontal, but I *don't* want to sleep."

"Nightmares," Janea said. It wasn't a question.

"Worst I've ever had," Barb said. "I woke up probably twenty times last night, same damned nightmare every time."

"Want to talk about it?" Janea asked.

"Not on your life," Barb said. "I just want to forget them. I've never been particularly submissive."

"Held in place by an amorphous form?" Janea asked, frowning.

"In a dark place?" Barb said, sitting up.

"Skip the rest," Janea said, sitting up in turn. "Recurrently?"

"All the time," Barb said. "I had one intervention, I think, by a messenger. But other than that, every time I woke up it was from the same dream."

"That's not a dream, that's a projection," Janea said. "Do you feel . . . a longing?"

"Repulsed and pulled at the same time," Barb said, nodding. "Like wanting a chocolate but knowing it's got acid filling."

"Any particular direction?" Janea asked.

"No, just the pull," Barb said.

"Look, I don't want to go through those dreams, either," Janea said, pulling her legs up and wrapping her arms around them. "But if, when, we do, we need to see if we can get any impression of the location. If these are astral projections, we may be able to get a feel for where we are. It's a clue and we're currently clueless."

"Not looking forward to that," Barb said, lying back down. "But it's a start."

"The things I do for this job," Janea said, still sitting up. She didn't look ready to try her own idea yet.

"God never makes a Gifted life easy," Barb said. "Get some sleep. We're going to need it."

"Ladies," Randell said as Barb and Janea entered the briefing room. For once he wasn't wearing a suit. He was in cargo shorts and a polo shirt instead.

Things had built up since the beginning of the investigation. The FBI had brought in a complete forward command center, a series of temporary trailers, instead of schlepping in a motel. Barb would have preferred the motel, but it turned out some of them were rigged as shield rooms. Since the real nature of the threat was being kept even from the vast majority of the responding units, keeping its nature secret in the command post area was going to be tough.

"We nearly couldn't get in here," Barb said. "There were a half a dozen checkpoints on the way in. Not to mention the rent-a-cops guarding the command center."

"That is what credentials are for," Randell said. "Okay, your new team. Master Sergeant Scott Attie of Fifth Special Forces group."

"Ladies," Attie said, looking at them with curiosity.

"The Master Sergeant has combat experience and has been a caving exploration leader. Sergeant Jordan Struletz," Randell continued, pointing to a tall, slender blond guy wearing thick glasses. He was looking more than a touch anxious. "Sergeant Struletz is from 319th MI group. He has some combat experience and has done extensive civilian caving."

"Ladies," Struletz said, swallowing nervously.

"Just two?" Janea asked. "We had twenty last night and we nearly got our heads handed to us."

"Three," Randell said. "Me. I've worked in confined spaces and I'm not claustrophobic. I've also seen the threat. And I'm not insane."

"Thank FLIRs and the Hand of God for that," Barb said.

"FLIRs certainly," Randell said.

"Master Sergeant," Barb said, ignoring the implied jibe. "I've got some questions that are going to sound very strange. Especially since this is an official mission."

"If I can anticipate some?" Attie said. "I was briefed on Special Circumstances and the threat. One of the reasons that there's only two of us is that most people turned the job down when it was an unspecified 'high risk of loss of life.' Most of us have been in enough situations where we're more than willing to turn something like that down. Others weren't willing to believe the in-brief on SC, while being more than willing to never mention it. I think that most of them thought it was just a test, anyway. I am not a believer, as you would term it. This has got me thinking, but that's not the same thing."

"Not at all," Barb said, nodding. "Last thing. How's your mental stability?"

"Fair," Attie said. "I've seen and done some things that bother me, but I'm one of those people that it doesn't bother so much." He shrugged. "When it's your time, it's your time. Monsters, bullets or IEDs, doesn't really matter. You're gone and that's the end of the ride."

"People like myself consider it a beginning," Barb said, turning to the sergeant. "Sergeant, frankly, I'm considering just cutting you. You look too nervous already and when we get in the caves we can't afford that."

"Yes, ma'am," Struletz said. "I can understand that. Ma'am, understand that I was unsure about accepting the briefing on SC. But when I was briefed, ma'am, I realized it was a necessity for me to volunteer. I am a believer, ma'am, Catholic, if you don't mind. I'm a member of the Society of Saint Michael, ma'am. To avoid combat with true evil would be, in my eyes, a sin. Am I afraid of dying, ma'am? Yes. But my soul is the Lord's, ma'am. I go to His arms unafraid."

Randell snorted and shook his head.

"Problems with that, Agent Randell?" Barb asked.

"No, ma'am," the agent said. "If he wants to put his trust in God, go for it. I'm going to put my trust in a good weapon."

"On that note," Barb said, looking at the Master Sergeant. "I asked for military-grade weapons."

"And we brought a good array," the Master Sergeant said, nodding. "I was given leave to draw on anything in the SOCOM inventory. But most of it's not going to be useable in the caves. Very closed space, very close-quarters battle, ma'am."

"There goes the rocket launcher," Janea said, sighing.

"Yes, ma'am," the Master Sergeant said, looking at her dubiously.

"That was a joke, Master Sergeant," Barb said. "We're both familiar with firearms. I'm better with them than Janea, but she's not bad."

"Yes, ma'am," Attie said, reaching down and putting a bag on the table. "When I was given this mission, and the mission to prepare the gear, I had to think hard about it. I'd planned on MP-5s..."

"They're not all that good with these things," Randell said. "Five point five six is worse."

"And then I got that intel in the middle of the night," Attie said dyspeptically. "Which threw a wrench in the works. The optimum was a forty-five-caliber SMG that was small, light and robust. Unfortunately, the state of the art is still the Thompson in forty-five. The problem with forty-five is recoil and muzzle climb. The traditional way to deal with that has been weight. The weight of a Thompson is, looked at that way, a feature, not a bug. And they're tough as hell."

"Tell me they've at least been reworked," Barb said with a sigh. "The last Thompson I fired was practically mint in that nobody had ever changed *anything* on it. Which meant it was a piece of... it was not a very good weapon."

"Yes, ma'am," Attie said, smiling slightly. "But then I got to thinking. SOCOM has been evaluating a new forty-five SMG. It's barely out of the prototype stage but it's been passing every test with flying colors."

He opened up the bag and drew out a small—very small—submachine gun.

The distance from the rear of the weapon to the barrel was barely fourteen inches. The extended magazine was nearly as long as the weapon. And it was very close to a square, as opposed to the longer, more tapered style of weapons. Instead of a trigger guard, there was a full hand guard around the trigger area, and a pistol forestock. Forward of the trigger/hand guard was a large boxy area that Barb couldn't figure out. And the barrel actually extended directly from where the middle of a person's trigger hand would be instead of being above it. That meant the chamber was in front of the operator's hand, which was a bit nervous-making.

Barb's initial reaction was one of disdain. The majority of the weapon's body was polymer, and she had never seen a polymer weapon that worked. And every time she'd seen the "newest thing," it had turned out to be an old thing in new, and usually less capable, packaging. And small SMGs generally shot very poorly. Trying to control the recoil was just impossible in anything that small. She'd shot a Czech Skorpion, one of the most popular "cool" guns in movie and TV "action" shows, and keeping it in the area of a human silhouette, much less any sort of actual *accuracy*, was nearly impossible. She didn't think this weapon could be much better.

"And that is?" Barb asked.

"The TDI Kriss Super V," Attie said, dropping the magazine and ensuring it was clear, then handing it over to Barb. "It's a forty-five SMG that uses a style of recoil damper that drops the muzzle climb and recoil. It's also got fewer parts than a standard SMG, so it's reliable as hell."

"Sounds nice," Barb said, doubtfully. "Sounds like you work for their PR department."

"Which was my reaction when I first played with one," Attie said, nodding. "Thing is, they're right. Little fucker..."

"Language, Master Sergeant," Barb said.

"Sorry, ma'am," Attie said, rolling his eyes. "Little sucker shoots like a rail, ma'am. Full auto or single shot. The only problem is getting used to it 'cause it feels unnatural to shoot. There's recoil, but just enough you can tell you've fired. And you keep wanting to fight the muzzle climb and it's not there."

"How?" Barb asked, interested.

"Basically, the bolt hits a metal buffer that goes *down* instead of back," Attie said, shrugging. "That shifts the momentum of the recoil and automatically fights the muzzle climb for you. Takes a couple of magazines to get used to it. After that, well, it's kind of like what you'd think a laser would feel like firing. I mean, there's some recoil, but nothing you have to fight. You can shoot it offhand, easy. And you can't say that about any other SMG on the market in *any* caliber."

"Hmmm," Barb said, ensuring the weapon was clear then targeting with it. She had to admit it was a very *smooth*-feeling weapon. Except that it just felt too damned small. Which in a cave was, again, a feature, not a bug. Unless you wanted to hit your target. "Reliability?"

"Would you like the results of the official test or the unofficial test?" Attie asked, grinning.

"Unofficial?" Barb asked.

"AWG has its own testing regime," Attie said.

"AWG?" Janea interjected.

"Asymmetric Warfare Group," Attie replied. "Don't ask. Just say they need weapons that work. They've got their own testing regime. First, they dunk a weapon in mud for three months."

"Ouch," Barb said.

"Yep," Attie said, grinning. "Then they clear out the barrel and fire four thousand rounds through it. If it doesn't break completely, they're happy. The standard is that it has to successfully fire the first hundred rounds without detail cleaning. After that, it can only be detail cleaned. If it has to be repaired, it's a fail."

"The AK test," Barb said.

"Right," Attie said. "Then there's the dust test. Dust and mud do two different things. So they put it through a three-day simulated dust storm. Same standard. Then they fire eight thousand more rounds through it. The weapon can't break during the final fire run."

"And the AWG test?" Barb asked.

"They *never* detail cleaned it," Attie said, smiling. "They only detail clean if there's indications that it's necessary due to repetitive jams. They had a total of eighty-seven jams in the whole test series, ten thousand rounds. An M-4, by comparison, has an average of one hundred and eighty jams and requires frequent detail cleaning. The only other weapon that makes the same standard is the AK, and it's a piece of..." He paused and looked at Barb. "It's robust, but not very good otherwise. This is robust, mostly because it's got very few moving parts, and one he...heck of a weapon. The Kriss is the shi...It's the best weapon to come along since the Ma Deuce."

"You're gun-geeking out on me, Barb," Janea said.

"Military fifty-caliber machine gun," Barb said, looking at the weapon in a different light. "Okay, I'm still taking my H&K, but this sounds like the right system for the mission. What else?"

"I was worried about bouncers," Attie said.

"We're not going to a bar," Janea said, frowning.

"Ricochets," Barb said.

"Right," Attie said, smiling. "So it's frangible ammo. My only question is if it's got the penetration for the threat. So we'll mostly carry frangible with ball backup."

"Okay," Barb said. "Can we use anything heavier in there?"

"Caves aren't mines, ma'am," Attie said, dubiously. "You don't want to use much in the way of explosives. Cave-ins happen."

"I'd really like to avoid that," Janea said.

"So we'll be carrying some frags," the master sergeant said with a shrug. "I don't recommend using them under normal conditions; they'll bounce all over the damned place. But if we have to use them, we'll use them. Other than that, standard caving gear. I've got combat harnesses for your stuff. We'll have to be taking them on and off...."

"And thus we get to what a lovely adventure this is going to be," Janea said. "Are we done gun geeking? Can I wake up now?"

"Just one thing," Barb said.

"Got to have some range time with it, ma'am," Attie said.

"Oh, great," Janea said. "Can't I just use an *axe* like normal?"

The FBI Command Center had come rather completely stocked, including basic materials for a range. So it had been a matter of less than twenty minutes to get in place and get ready to test out the new weapons.

The Kriss had a folding stock, which Janea had dutifully folded out and tucked into her shoulder. She took a good two-point stance, leaned into the weapon and prepared to fire.

"Ma'am?" Attie said, cautiously. "They say to always let people fire the weapon the first time their normal way. But you're lean-ing *way* too far into it."

"I've fired an SMG before, Master Sergeant," Janea said.

"As you say, ma'am," the master sergeant said. "Fire when ready."

Janea shook her head, leaned into the recoil and lightly stroked the trigger. And nearly fell on her face as the bullets drew a line from the middle of the silhouette halfway to her position. On the ground. She'd tried to fight recoil that just wasn't there and ended up barely missing shooting her foot.

"What the Hel?" Janea said, holding the weapon out and up, her eyes wide. "There's *no* recoil."

"There's not much, ma'am," Attie said, grinning. "Especially when you consider it's forty-five. Thompson kicks like a freaking mule, even with all the weight."

"That was just..." Janea said, her eyes still wide.

"Unnatural?" Attie asked.

"Good word for it," Janea said, taking another stance. This time she didn't bother to lean in, and triggered another burst. All five rounds ended up in an eight-inch pie-shaped area. Normally, one or two would have been in the circle and the rest climbing up and away. "This is..."

"The stuff?" Barb asked, taking a stance next to her. Barb didn't make the same mistake, which was why her first five rounds all ended up in the target zone. Her next five ended up in a three-inch group. Then she simply held down the trigger, expending the rest of the thirty-round magazine into a five-inch circle. "That *is* very nice."

"Yes, ma'am," the master sergeant said, blinking in surprise. His own shooting was on the same order, maybe a touch better, but he didn't expect to see that level of ability in a civilian female. He didn't expect to see that much expertise in most *SWAT* members.

Barb put in another magazine, flipped the folding stock down, then fired with one hand on the pistol grip and the other on the forestock grip. Firing that way, she put five rounds into a five-inch circle. She tried a modified two-handed grip using just the pistol grip. That wasn't particularly comfortable, but it was possible. She managed to put the next series in the same five-inch circle. One-handed, she put them into eight inches. Then she switched to left and did a bit better.

She heard a snort next to her and looked over at Janea. Who

was, in turn, looking at the master sergeant. Who was standing open-mouthed and staring.

"There's a reason I call her Soccer-Momasaurus," Janea said, laughing.

"It's *Mrs.* Everette, right?" Sergeant Major Attie asked with a tone of slight disappointment.

"Yes, Master Sergeant," Barb said, shaking her head. "And I note you're wearing a wedding ring."

"I'll go Muslim."

Chapter Eight

O n the road again," Janea sang, loudly and deliberately off-key. "Ah cain't wait to git on the road ag'in!"

She was dragging herself through liquid mud that just barely didn't cover her nose and mouth, by pulling at cracks on the ceiling of the cave.

"Janea," Barb said, sucking in her breath to get through a tight spot. "Sound carries in caves."

"Yep," Janea said. "And the sooner we run into these things and kill a bunch of them, the faster we can get out of here. I'm getting really tired of mud. And my stylist is going to *kill* me for what I'm doing to my hair."

"How you doing, Sergeant Struletz?" Barb said. She started to shake her head at Janea's reply and almost got a mouth full of mud. Not that it would have mattered much. Her face was already completely covered.

"Great, ma'am," the sergeant replied. "Loving every minute of it."

"You sound serious," Janea said, amazed.

"I am on a mission to destroy evil in God's name, ma'am," the sergeant said, happily. "And I'm in a cave. I'm good."

"Randell?"

"What was it you said?" Randell replied. "Oh, yeah. Nominal." He started laughing so hard he got stuck.

"What's so funny?" Master Sergeant Attie asked.

280

"So, last night," Randell said. "That was just last night, right?"

"Yeah," Janea said. "That was *just* last night. Trust me."

"So Mrs. Everette and Miz Grisham are staking out the cave the Old Ones used to attack the house," Randell said. "They figured the one that attacked the Boones might come back."

"Might have been," Barb said. "We'll have to wait for Stan to sort out the genetics."

"If he doesn't go mad first," Janea said, chuckling.

"So Graham would call up there every fifteen minutes for a commo check," Randell said. "'Cave One, status?' And Mrs. Everette would reply in this dry, I'm-An-Astronaut voice: 'Nominal.'"

"It's not funny," Barb said.

"That was right up until a bit after one AM," Randell said, chuckling. "When all of a sudden there's this '*GRAHAAAM!*'"

"Well, what were there?" Barb asked. "Twenty of them? And who killed most of them?"

"Oh, yes," Randell said, sarcastically. "The glorious power of the Lord God Almighty did save the day." He ended the litany in a very thick Southern accent. Which sounded natural.

"Well, it did," Janea said, cocking her head around to look back at him. "I mean, I may not worship the White God, but I recognize His power. I just think most of His Scriptures are poppycock. No offense, Barb."

"None taken," Barb said. "When it comes right down to it, most of the Old Testament is to fill out page count. People forget that. The essence of Christianity is only to be found in the words of Jesus Christ. And it all comes down to His definition of His Father: God is love. Everything else is padding. I enjoy going to Episcopalian worship. I like the pomp and pageantry and I enjoy a good sermon. But the truth is, whenever two or more are gathered in His Name, there is God. Heck, just Jordan and I count for that. You with me, Jordan?"

"Two or more are gathered in His Name, ma'am," Jordan said. "Still wish we had a priest with us."

"Priest, schmiest," Randell said. "I'm glad the master sergeant turned up these guns."

"What is with you and religion, Randell?" Janea asked.

"You picked *now* to ask?"

"I'm trying to take my mind off of sliding through muck," Janea admitted.

"Look, I saw what Mrs. Everette did," Randell said. "I get it. She's got a special relationship with God. I don't. I don't want one. I've seen what a 'special relationship with God' gets you in the end, and I don't like it."

"Gets you in the end?" Barb asked, curious.

"Can we drop it?" Randell asked.

"Sure," Janea said. "To each her religion. Or lack thereof, as the case may be."

"I did four tours in Iraq," Randell said after a few minutes of silence.

"I've done . . . seven?" Attie said. "You sort of lose count. More in the Rockpile."

"I grew up in a small town," Randell said, ignoring the master sergeant's interjection. "Pretty similar to Goin, except in Kentucky. They're all pretty much the same."

"They're the same all over," Barb said. "Choose a country."

"I was raised Baptist," Randell said. "*Primitive* Baptist, which is about as fundamental as you can get."

"That's pretty much out there," Barb admitted. "I know some. Basically good people, but . . . 'You can't point a person into heaven' doesn't seem to compute."

"But that was what I saw as religion," Randell said. "And don't get me wrong. I *believed*. I knew that God had his eye on me every single second and that there was black and white. And everyone that thought like me was right and everyone that didn't was evil. Homos deserved to be killed, screwing was total sin, hell was just the other side of dancing."

"I had a similar upbringing," Janea said.

"*Really*?" Barb asked.

"Sort of," Janea said. "My parents went to a similar church. Their actual expressions of faith pretty much stopped there."

"Thing is, I believed," Randell said, angrily. "I believed that God had a plan and a set of rules, and I had to live by them and everybody else did, too."

"And?" Barb asked.

"And when I got out of high school, I had a classic education in fundamentalist doctrine, not much in the way of learning and not a job to be found."

"So you joined the Army," Attie said. "You're not a stranger in that."

"So I joined the Army," Randell said. "Mostly for the college but also because, well...from my perspective, back then, this *is* a religious war. The kid I was then was perfectly comfortable with burning the whole Moslem world if they didn't understand that Christianity was the only way. Don't ask what I thought of Jews."

"They killed Jesus," Janea said. "Pretty much what most fundamentalist Moslems think, at a guess."

"Buddy of mine in high school had a T-shirt," Randell said. "'Say what you like about Hitler, he killed a lot of Jews.' We all thought it was a hoot. Not that he could ever wear it in public, even in *our* town."

"Every religion has idiot fanatics," Barb said.

"Yeah," Randell said. "But we knew we were right. Then I went to Iraq."

"You keep saying that," Janea said.

"First tour was okay," Randell said, ignoring her. "I mean, it wasn't fun, but it was. I was killing hajis. I was doing God's work. Just like Jordan is now."

"A *little* different, I think," Jordan protested.

"Not the way I thought," Randell said. "Second and third was more of the same, just more boring. First one was in Fallujah."

"Ouch," Attie said. "That's one hell of a first deployment."

"Like I said, I enjoyed it," Randell said. "By the fourth I was a junior sergeant, but I had three previous tours under my belt. And we had a different mission. More time with ISF—Iraqi Security Forces."

"Thank you, Petraeus," Attie said, fervently. "*Finally* a guy who understood Counter-Insurgency."

"I got detailed to work with an ISF company," Randell said. "Liaison for support and training. We were working near Ramadi..."

Nobody asked a question. Finally he continued.

"We got called to a village. Al Qaeda was sort of on the run in the whole region. The sheiks had turned on them. Regular US units were combing out most of the hold-outs, then the ISF would back-fill. One of the US units in the area had been patrolling through the area and found...the village. And they said 'It's clear' and went on. And it was."

"Al Qaeda had cleared it," Attie said.

"Thoroughly," Randell said. "Every living being in the village was dead. Men, women, children. The dogs and the donkeys. *We* got to bury the bodies. The company commander was a Kurd. Good guy, spoke a little English. I couldn't figure out how he could be so... The ISF guys weren't taking it *well*, but they were so *calm* about it. I wasn't. I was screaming to God. The CO told me I had to calm down. He was right that I was setting a bad example. But I asked him how *anyone* could do something like that? Kill everybody? Hell, even in My Lai there were troops that protected people. There was no indication of that in Al Qar. And his answer?"

"They believed in God," Barbara said.

"They believed that God told them it was not only right, it was *demanded*," Randell said. "'They believe in God. So anything that they do is right.' So you could sort of say I had an epiphany. Mrs. Everette, I don't care if it offends you. There *ain't* no God. There's only the Devil playing at being nicey-nice. God is shit. Do I believe there's something greater? Oh, yeah. And it's hell and Satan and that's the whole ball of wax. It's nothing but a giant sham to make people do stuff that no human should do to another. Allah and God and Yahweh are all just posers, the same damned—and I use that term with interest—fuckers that all need to just go away and leave us the hell *alone!*"

"Oh," Barb said.

"So if God is so high and mighty, how come we have to crawl through this stinking cave to fight these things?" Randell asked. "How come He doesn't just blast them from on high? How come people had to die so we'd even know they were there? How come those people had to die and those women have to go through what they're going through? Why, Mrs. Everette? If 'God is love,' then *why*?"

"I could give you the doctrinal answer," Barb said. "But I don't think it would make you any happier. Probably upset you more. So...You may feel as you feel, believe as you believe, and I'll believe as I believe. Suits?"

"Not really," Randell said. "But I don't think I'm going to sway you, either."

"I'm interested," Attie said. "What *is* the doctrinal answer?"

"Most people say 'free will,' but that's the children's Sunday School answer," Barb said. "Are we anywhere *near* out of this stuff?"

"Nope," Attie said, shining a light ahead. "Still a couple of hundred feet, minimum."

"Sugar," Barb said. "The actual doctrinal answer goes back to the Fall of Man. The Garden of Eden thing. Part of the separation after the Fall of Angels was that they weren't confined to *Hell*, they were confined to *Earth*. One of the reasons for the fall, according to some pretty good Apocrypha, was that God had created Man 'in his own image,' which was what caused that particular rebellion. There were three or four Falls, depending on which texts you believe. But there's a lot of debate about what 'in His own image' means. The fundamental answer is, God is a great big fat guy with a beard. Or at least human looking. The more logical explanation, and the one that fits the translation of the word 'image' best, is probably sentience. That is, humans can think, plan and make decisions completely on their own. They can choose to do good or ill. Thus 'free will.'"

"So what about angels?" Janea asked, fascinated.

"Angels seem to be more like AIs," Barb said. "Same with demons. They're programmed to do certain things and that's that. The more complex they are, the higher in the hierarchy, the more things they can do. But they *don't* have free will. If we ever get to the point of being able to actually study them, and I hope we never can, I think that's what they'll find. That angels are simply very complicated computer programs. Seen that way, the Fall was something like a corrupted program or a computer virus."

"That's not a very believer approach," Attie said, surprised.

"Depends on how much of a thinking believer you are," Barb said. "Nothing in that violates *any* of the Scriptures. It's just a more advanced way of translating them. Possibly not advanced *enough*, but probably closer to the truth of the reality. The people who were first trying to understand the Fall didn't have our level of technology. They couldn't conceive of a thinking engine like a computer. The point is that both demons and Man were put on earth. God's apparent intent was to let Man rule the earth, possibly even over demons. Maybe get them back in shape or something."

"Okay, now," Janea said. "*That's* very weird."

"Fits with the scriptures," Barb said. "Angels are not a *higher* form. Neither are demons, which are simply corrupted angels. *Man* is the next highest form after God. Angels are lesser than we, because we have *souls*. We have sentience. They don't. The Creation in the Sistine Chapel got that just right. Angels are *lower* in the mural than Man. *Man* is the next creation after God."

"So what happened?" Attie asked.

"Well, the apple thing," Barb said, laughing slightly. "Women messed it up, according to the accepted texts. Basically, humans rebelled. God said, 'This is your paradise and all you have to do is not eat of the fruit.' There's big debate about what 'eating of the fruit' really means. Did we invent agriculture? Writing? Philosophy that rejected the notion of God? But, whatever we did, we upset Him. To the point where he threw us out of the Garden and onto the Earth. Which was the province of demons. So we're stuck here with the other rebels. This is our Guantanamo."

"So I was right," Randell said. "This is Hell."

"If it were hell, there would be no chance for redemption," Barb said.

"The thing being that, by our actions, by our faith, and through the intercession of his Son Jesus, we've got a chance to get off of this plane of sorrow and bask in His light for eternity. Through love and good works by some choices of faith. Simply by being and not being terrible by determinism. Through confession and being in a state of Grace, according to Jordan. I'm of the informed opinion that if you sufficiently worship your weapons, keep them well, protect the innocent, do not let fear overtake you and die well in battle you're okay, too. For that matter, 'an firstly do ye no harm' seems to work, as does Buddhism, which isn't even a *religion*, and the more positive aspects of Hinduism. I have met people that God clearly has touched who come from faiths so divergent from, well, Primitive Baptist, it's hard to see the connection. Janea is the priestess of a goddess of *sex*, and God has given her power through my connection to Him. God is love. All the rest is dross. And to find Him all you need to do is truly love. And whenever two or more are gathered in the name of Love, which *is* His name, then He is *there*. Janea could probably argue that two people having loving, joyous sex are worshipping God."

"I was just about to point that out," Janea said.

"God is on my side," Randell sang sarcastically. "Still doesn't explain the demons."

"But free will does," Barb said. "Demons, or these Old Ones that I will admit have some non-demonic aspects, need the intercession of humans. God gives us that choice. We can choose to be good, we can choose to be evil or we can do what most of us do, which is muddle along in the middle. But the reason that

God does not strike these things down from on high is that He expects His followers to take care of things. Which is exactly why we are here. Humans brought these things into being, and humans, with the help of God—as the evil humans had the help of demonic agencies—are to set things to rights. God helps those that help themselves, if you will. Or would you rather a God who held your hand while you sucked your thumb in a corner?"

"Point," Randell said.

"The *actual* point is, Special Agent, that even if you reject *God*, God does not reject *you*. If you love and do not hate, if you live by His basic precepts, the Golden Rule, if you will, then you are *good*. His forgiveness, even for rejecting Him, is infinite."

"So you're saying that if I live a good life I'm doomed to play a harp for all eternity?" Randell said. "No, thank you."

"The harp motif is *so* fourteenth century," Janea said. "Back then most people worked hard from sun to sun and died young. Sitting around all the time and not having to work for their food was the only thing they could *imagine* as paradise. Valhalla isn't playing a harp. We Asatru are called to battle. I mean, like I told Barb, I tried out Astari, which is all nonviolent and whole-grain goodness, and got *really* bored. Which is why I'm Asatru. Give us a harp and we'll try to eat it. Give us a *battle* and stand back. The afterlife is what you are *called* to. I know a person who's pretty certain it's the chance to meet and talk with people like Da Vinci. Although I think the line of geeks is going to be sort of long."

"So all I've got to do is live a blameless life and I'm in?" Attie asked. "No church, no singing?"

"In my opinion?" Barb said. "Yes. Love and do not hate. Treat other people with love and respect unless they have clearly given themselves to evil. And even then, understand and forgive them if you can. But that doesn't mean you have to let them *live*, mind you."

"Hmm," Attie said. "So what if you've sinned?"

"Sin is such a big word," Barb said. "And it's a really narrow concept. I'm not saying that it's all shades of gray; it's not. But there's a really easy way to define sin. Do you have any sort of conscience? I know some very good warriors who don't. They have to just fake it."

"I know the kind of guys you're talking about," Attie said. "But, yeah, I've got a conscience."

"Anything you've ever done you *really* wish you hadn't?" Barb asked.

"Couple," Attie admitted.

"Can you forgive yourself?" Barb asked.

"That's a tough one," the master sergeant admitted.

"God can," Barb said. "But it helps if *you* can. People seek forgiveness for that sort of thing in a lot of ways. The doctrine of Confession is the traditional Catholic method. I...know someone who has a lot of forgiveness to seek. He's seeking it through... good works. I, frankly, wish he was with us now."

"I thought you said *good* works," Randell said.

"By certain definitions of good," Barb said, chuckling slightly. "Killing demons? Good. Counts for a *bunch* of rosaries, or so I'm told."

"Oh."

"Others seek it through self-examination," Barb continued. "Mostly, though, people seek it through the normal sort of absolutions. Owning up to it to the people that they've hurt. Seeking to redress the damage. Doing things that counteract the evil they have done. My friend's approach is...idiosyncratic. But sincere. And, again, unquestionably in there with God. He had some *actual* demons to throw off of his soul. But once he did, he's pretty much in as much of a state of grace as anyone I've met. And what he does is kill demons. *And* their worshippers."

"That gets back around to where I have issues," Randell said.

"I wasn't planning on getting Jesus in a cave," Attie said. "But you're a very good missionary, Mrs. Everette. And you can shoot. That's a benefit."

"Think about what you just said," Barb said. "'Getting Jesus.' *Getting* has several connotations in English. It means 'receiving,' which is the meaning I think you meant. But it also means 'understanding.' Which is equally the case. This is how to 'get' Jesus.

"All that Jesus really asked is that we love our fellow man and care about him. Why on *earth* are you in this cave if not for *that*, Master Sergeant Attie? Adventure? You're far too experienced a warrior. You're here to save lives. Jesus dragged a cross up a long hill while stones and food and spit were hurled at Him, was nailed to that cross, suffered, and died a most painful and horrible death to *prove* to His Father that we poor humans were worthy of being forgiven for *whatever* Adam and Eve did to tick God off. *He* died so that *we* might live in eternity, period. If you die in this cave, open-eyed and willing to die to save others, do you *really* think that Jesus is going to reject you? He's a guy who got *nailed* to a *cross* to save *our* souls. Yeah, He has enough forgiveness for you, Master Sergeant. And He is going to appreciate someone who's willing to die to save others. Been there, done that."

"You know," Attie said, thoughtfully. "If you'd been my preacher when I was growing up I might have stayed with the church. Baptist, too, by the way."

"I know a few very good Baptist ministers," Barb said. "I also know more who are total pricks, pardon my French."

"You're making *me* think about converting," Janea said with a laugh. "But I love sex too much."

"Mary Magdalene was a prostitute," Barb said. "There's *no* other way to interpret Matthew. So was her sister, Martha. Which made Lazarus, who Jesus *raised from the dead*, their pimp. God may be a little down on it, but Jesus has no issues."

"Speaking of whom," Janea said. "Where *is* Laz?"

"Probably finding a drier route," Barb said with a chuckle. "He took one look at this passage and clear as day said 'Blow *that!*'"

"Well, we've got an open area up ahead," Attie said. "Finally."

"Might want to let me go through first," Barb said. "The last time I let somebody else take point it didn't turn out well."

"I think it's okay," Attie said. "Unless your Old Ones have green cat eyes. He apparently found a drier route. Little bastard."

"Language, Master Sergeant."

Chapter Nine

"Well now, this is interesting," Barb said as she emerged from the mudhole.

The immediate area around the opening to the mudhole was more or less triangular and about thirty feet high. The room continued onwards into the cave through a very odd passage.

The passage was high but narrow with a smooth, flat floor. It opened outwards, broadly at the top and again, slightly, near the floor. And it clearly twisted like a snake. The walls were irregular with spines of limestone sticking out. As she shone her light on the wall she could pick out the outlines of fossilized sea creatures from ancient aeons.

"Keyhole passage," Master Sergeant Attie said, pouring a bottle of water over the Kriss to get some of the mud off. They were both covered in the thick, sticky mud, as was all of their equipment. "Called that 'cause it looks sort of like an old-time skeleton keyhole."

Barb did a rough clean on the weapon, ensured that it was still cycling well, then shone her gun-light up. She quickly realized that it didn't reach all the way into the sides of the spread-out upper portion.

"There could be anything up there," she noted, sweeping the Kriss around.

"Yep," Attie replied as the rest of the team dragged themselves out. "I've been thinking on that."

"That was just unpleasant as anything I've ever done," Janea said. "Except this one guy in Los Angeles...."

"Let's do a gear check," Attie said. "That could have been pretty rough on our systems."

The team, in pairs, spent a couple of minutes checking out all their gear. Surprisingly, with the exception of having to change a battery in Randell's radio, it was all functioning.

"Good stuff," Barb said, happily. "I do so appreciate good gear."

"I got most of it off of Navy SPECWAR," Attie admitted. "Salt water is worse than mud, and the SEALS can break *anything*. So their stuff has to be really robust. And the radios are designed with obstructions in mind. They've actually got about the best gear around for caving, just most cavers can't afford it. Or don't have the clearance to get it. Let's stay sharp. There's not only limited visibility at the top, there could be passages off of it."

"Master Sergeant?" Struletz said. "I could probably chimbley to the top and work my way along through there. That way we'd have top cover."

"And if you had to get down in the middle of a firefight you'd be vulnerable as hell," Attie said.

"I'll do it," Barb said, releasing the Kriss to draw back on its three-point harness. She jumped up and got both feet onto small projections on the wall, and then started climbing the passage like a spread-out spider. Fast. She was rarely in even three points of contact, and it looked most of the time like she wasn't in contact at all. She hardly used her hands.

"That was just...bizarre," Attie said when she reached the top.

"Benefits of a lifetime of martial arts study, Master Sergeant," Barb said, not even winded. "I had this instructor in...Malaysia? Yeah, Malaysia. He loved really bad martial arts movies. But he took some of the stuff from them, some of the stuff you're looking at and going 'Yeah, right,' and added it to his art. Stuff like fighting off of balconies and walls. He believed that the essence of martial arts was grace. It wasn't a really great combat art, unless you were fighting on a ledge, but it *was* good for learning balance."

"*Kung Pow*?" Struletz asked.

"Oh, that was minor," Barb said, laughing. "The original was worse. And there are much, *much* worse martial arts movies than *that*."

She shone her light down the passage and was pleasantly

surprised to find that from the top, she could see for nearly sixty feet. The passage, viewed from her lofty vantage, was a series of domes covering the serpentine lower portion. There were still bends, and there were spots that the light didn't illuminate; indeed, there were small nooks and crannies that were going to be hard to check out, but she could cover the team very well from up here. The only problem being that the irregular oval top portion she currently was standing in was short enough she was having to bend nearly double. But she'd be able to stand up in the next dome. At least if she did the whole thing with her legs spread across the passage. That was going to be unpleasant.

"I won't say what you look like from down here," Janea said. "But you'd better be glad you're not wearing a skirt."

Barb pulled both legs to one side of the passage, bracing on the far side with one hand, and held out her right.

"Toss me Lazarus," she said.

"You're joking," Janea said.

"He can make his way through up here," Barb said. "And he's better at spotting these things than we are."

"Okay," Janea said, coaxing the cat over then standing up with him in her arms. "I'm not very good at throwing."

"Let me," Randell said, taking the cat. Lazarus was looking notably worried but he allowed himself to be manhandled. "Catch."

Randell tossed the cat vertically, eliciting a startled "Rrow?!" but he tossed him high enough and accurately enough that Barb was able to make a fair catch.

"You've got point," she said, setting Lazarus on a more-or-less flat spot. "Head on out."

Where the domes were, the passage became, from her position, an oval tube, slightly serpentine, with a very wide crevasse in the middle. Most of the time she could make her way along in a crouch to the side of the lower passage on the slightly slanted floor. Other times she braced with one hand and moved from one side of the lower passage to the other. Sometimes she had to spread and duck-walk, especially in the short lower portions between domed areas. Those would have been the unfun portions where she couldn't see what was awaiting her in the dark nooks to either side. But then there was Lazarus.

In a similar way, but easier because he was shorter, four-legged, and, well, a cat, Lazarus was more or less trotting down the passage, his tail flicking from side to side for balance and occasionally jumping across the crevasse when one side or the other became nonnegotiable. He was, in fact, getting very near the limit of Barb's light.

"Slow down, Laz," Barb said.

"Tell *him* to slow down?" Attie said. "*You* slow down. We're barely keeping up and we're *walking.*"

"It's clear," Barb said, squatting on one foot and bracing across the passage with the other. She was in one of the narrower entries to a dome, and the crack to the lower passage was barely six inches wide. "This is a really strange formation."

"The upper passage is formed when an underground river finds a portion of softer rock," Attie said, taking a pause under her position. "That's the upper tube. Over time, it wears away at the lower rock, again finding channels through it, until it either dies, goes to easier rock to wear away, or whatever. Generally it forms something like this. They're fairly common."

"First one I've seen," Barb said. "Everybody good?"

"Except for the drying mud caked in my hair, ears and nose?" Janea asked. "Peachy."

"Good," Barb said, shining her light towards Lazarus. The cat had gone to full "Halloween cat" mode, back arched, tail straight up and bristled into a bush. "We've got company! IR mode!"

The Sure-Fire built into the end of the boxy weapon had a flipped-down cover. Flipping it up, the light apparently disappeared. In fact, it was now filtered entirely for infrared. As the whole team followed suit, the light in the passage disappeared entirely.

Dropping her FLIR down, Barb regained sight of the passage, the gun-light now acting as an infrared spotlight.

"Laz!" Barb yelled. "Get out of there!"

Her connection to the cat was something she barely understood. As far as she could comprehend it, they weren't even two different individuals. The type of soul that was necessary for Barb to resurrect the cat was an indivisible part of a human being. To bring Lazarus back to life had required sharing the soul. They were now one being in two separate bodies.

She wasn't sure what would happen if Lazarus was ever killed. But she was pretty sure it wouldn't be pleasant. The highest probability was that she would also die.

Cats rarely obey orders but they do have a certain amount

of common sense. As a tide of blackness roiled down the passageway, the cat turned and bolted for the rear, jumping lithely from side to side of the passage. However, as he passed Barb, he yowled a warning.

"We've got company at the rear," Barb said, flicking the light around to look over her shoulder. More of the Old Ones were clambering down the upper passageway behind her. "Could use some help here."

"On my way," Randell said, starting to chimbley up the passage.

"*No* time," Barb said, opening fire on the group to the front.

The .45-caliber frangible rounds poured into the mass of Old One spawn, blasting the two in the lead into a pile of ichor and goo. Unfortunately, that had forced her to clock out her magazine.

She dropped the mag, not even bothering to catch it for a reload, and slid another in, fumbling the replacement slightly due to the unfamiliar weapon.

The Old Ones had gotten into the domed area by then, spreading out to either side, with a couple coming across the roof. She took those out, and one of the ones on the walls then backed up so that they would have to come through the narrow portion to get her.

She could hear Randell firing from behind her and just hoped he could keep the mass to the rear off her back.

Master Sergeant Attie had moved to the opening below her and engaged the Old Ones above him in the domed area. His fire was solid and precise, the .45-caliber rounds shredding every Old One in sight. With the narrowness of the passage overhead, there was no way that they could get to the party from above. They had to either come at them on the floor or get past Barb to the wider portion behind her.

"I'm good," Randell said. "No more this way." He was actually perched with his back braced to either side of the passage in a domed section, so he had a pretty good view.

"And we're clear here," Master Sergeant Attie said as the last Old One dropped in a splatter to the floor.

"Shamblers," Janea said, reloading her weapon. She'd been covering the floor below Randell. "They're easy enough with the right weapons. I'm not looking forward to running into another *skru-gnon.*"

"Anybody get a count?" Attie asked.

"About seven your way," Struletz said. "Three to the rear."

"How many of these things *are* there?" Randell asked angrily. He'd slid down the passage to the floor again and reloaded. He also reloaded his expended magazines.

"At a guess, it depends how long the Gar has been manifested and how much it's had to eat," Janea said, shrugging and starting to reload her magazines from the stores they'd brought with them. "The Gar spins these things off of its essence. If it's been manifested for a short time and the food is limited, a few dozen. If it's been a long time and pretty much unlimited food? Thousands?"

"We don't have enough ammo for thousands," Struletz pointed out.

"Catch," Attie said, tossing Barb's refilled magazine to her. "That hit me in the helmet, by the way."

"Sorry," Barb said, shrugging. "I wasn't exactly going to try to reholster it under the circumstances."

"Nope, we're good," Attie said. "Move out?"

"Let's take an alert break," Barb said, thoughtfully. "That little firefight is bound to have attracted some attention. If somebody takes the other side of this dome, we're in a good, defensible position. Let's see what thing wicked this way comes."

"Any progress on finding where the Gar might be?" Janea asked, taking out a bottle of water.

"Graham's got a team coming up with lists of buyers in the area," Randell said. "We figure it has to be cattle or pigs or something, from the description of how much this thing eats. There are several animal auctions in the area and they've gotten lists of all the purchases from them. So far, nothing's standing out."

"Who buys the animals?" Struletz asked.

"You want the short class on animal husbandry?" Randell asked with a chuckle. "My dad had a small farm. Cattle, it works like this. Farmer has a bunch of cows. The cows have babies, male and female. The females he keeps. The males he sells at auction. Other farmers, that don't want to bother with breeding, buy the males and deball them. Those sit out on grass and feed up for a few years as steers. Feed-lots buy the steers and feed them up. Slaughterhouses buy the steers. From time to time the breeding farmer takes his bull to auction, sells it and gets a different one. Then he puts it to the cows, some of which are the daughters of the former bull. Which is why you've got to change bulls from time to time. So there's some minor sales of cows when a farmer has too many or needs to raise cash, a few bulls change hands, but mostly it's steers that get moved around. It's all carefully tracked because of mad-cow and other stuff. So there's plenty of records."

"So what are you looking for?" Janea asked.

"Anomalies," Randell said. "Farmers who are buying a lot of mature steers, mostly. Or a lot of cows. If you're talking at least a head a day, that's thirty head a month. Farmers don't buy thirty head in a month. They don't buy thirty *calves* a month, generally. Not in this area."

"Be back," Barb said, sliding off her perch and moving forward.

"Problems?" Attie asked.

"Just an idea," Barb said.

She clambered down the passage to the next domed area, keeping a careful eye out in case any Old Ones had lingered, then paused at the next narrow section of the upper passage.

Juggling her pack out was a bit awkward, but she removed a spool of wire from it and then put it back on her back.

She used the wire first to attach one of her fragmentation grenades to the wall, then ran a section of wire across the passageway. Last, she straightened the cotter pin on the grenade, and then carefully tied the wire into the pin.

"Set a little present for our friends in case they come back," Barb said as she settled back into her perch. "Grenade IED. Give us some warning that doesn't involve Laz spitting and hissing." She stroked the cat gratefully. "Thanks, Laz."

"That's the sort of thing *I'm* supposed to be thinking of," Attie said. "Want me to set one to the rear?"

"Trail seemed to go this way," Barb said. "The only thing to the rear is however Laz got in, and he got through presumably without running into any of them. Most of them should be to our front. Up to you, but it would just be a booby trap I'd have to get past. Not to mention Laz, who I don't think understands tripwires."

"Point," Attie said. "We don't have any movement yet."

"Think I'm taking counsel of my fears?" Barb asked.

"No, ma'am," Attie said. "Just pointing out that we're in here to see if we can find the lair of this Gar thing. Which we're not doing."

"I'd like to see what responds to the fire," Barb said. "Give it thirty minutes."

She dropped her pack again and pulled out a ration bar. "Besides, I'm hungry."

She was on her third ration bar, and the thirty minutes were nearly up, when there was the crack and *szting* of a grenade going off down the passageway.

"Heads up!" she shouted, dropping her FLIR and going to IR.

She braced against the side, pointed at the narrow opening to the domed area, and waited. And waited.

"Just a scout?" Attie said.

"No," Barb said a moment later. "Not just a scout!"

This time the things attacked from every level. They were pouring down the upper passage in a mass but more were clambering along the sides and the ground. There seemed to be hundreds.

"I've got ground," Struletz said, taking a knee next to the standing master sergeant.

"Middle," Attie said, triggering a burst into the mass coming down the passage.

"Top," Barb said, firing into the mass. Targeting any one of the Old Ones was nearly impossible. The tentacled monstrosities were writhing into and across each other, and the small bodies were nearly impossible to make out between the FLIR and the way that they chaotically moved. Chopping them apart with .45 was the only way to go.

"Take left," Randell said, appearing to her side. "I'll fire across to right."

"Got it," Barb said, retargeting to the left of the domed area. The Old Ones were soaking up the fire to get to the party, pouring through the opening on the far side of the dome.

She had nine magazines in ready pouches. She'd laid three of those out on the rocks, ready to hand. She ran through those in less than a minute, then scrabbled for more in her pouches.

The only thing that kept them alive was that the Old Ones were choked by the opening to the dome, the narrowness of the passage and the two shooters on the top. None of them even got across the domed area. But the entire area was covered in ichor and deliquescing Old Ones by the time she slid in her last magazine.

"We don't have the ammo for this," Attie said. "I've only got two hundred more rounds of forty-five." With thirty rounds per magazine, that was only eight and a half mags. One more heavy firefight.

"We've reduced their numbers, at least," Barb said, her face tight. "But you're right. We don't have any clue how many more of these things there are. We need to pull out and regroup. If we're going to do it this way, we need more people and more ammo."

"That means we have to go back in that damned mud," Janea said. She'd been unhappily covering the back door alone during the fight.

"Would you rather be eaten?" Barb asked.

Chapter Ten

"T his whole caving thing is throwing off my sense of time," Barb said as she dragged her aching body out of the cave opening above the Boone house. It was nearly three in the morning and raining.

"Ah, *clean* water," Janea said as she stood up gratefully. With the exception of the serpentine keyhole passage, the entire trip had been either crawling or on hands and knees. "I need a shower, a real meal and about two days' sleep."

"We've got all three available," a voice above her said.

"Holy Freya!" Janea snapped, raising her weapon and triggering the light.

"Ouch," the ghillie-covered man said, raising an arm to shield his eyes. "That smarts. Mind taking that light out of my eyes?"

"Who are you?" Barb asked, pointing her own light to the side.

"Just a passing stranger who wondered what might come out of the cave," the man said. "We've basically taken over the neighborhood. You can get a shower, and a meal, down the hill. Oh, welcome back, by the way. Although I just lost some money."

"Delta Force," Graham said to the first question asked when the team found him. "They've sent in a full squadron and are covering this opening as well as a couple of others. There's a battalion from the 82nd that's setting up in Goin, a SEAL team on the way from the Little Creek, and the National Guard is in the process of fully clearing the area. We've taken residence of most of the houses in the neighborhood. There's even another SC team here. You can head over to their house for showers and some rest. What happened? Did you find the Gar?"

"I don't think we even got close," Randell said. "But we were running low on ammo."

"That bad?" Graham said.

"That bad," Barb said, shrugging. "The cave was filled with them. I'm not sure how many we killed. A bunch. And I'm pretty sure there were more. We heard some scrabbling behind us on the way out."

"Look, we'll do something like a full report in the morning," Janea said. "I'm whipped. And not in a good way. Sergeant Struletz? Do me a favor and after you get cleaned up, come over to the SC house. I need to worship. Oh, wait, you'd find that a sin, wouldn't you?"

"Yes, ma'am," Struletz said, unhappily. "And I don't think that 'I figured I could just confess' would sit well with my priest."

"Master Sergeant?" she said. "Married, right. Okay, Randell?"

"So I'm third choice?" the FBI agent said.

"I could go find a Delta if you'd prefer," she said.

"Nope," Randell said, raising a hand. "Be there with bells on. I'm not planning on converting, though."

"Sharice," Barb said happily, as Barb and Janea wandered into the kitchen of the house. "I'd hug you, but you don't want to get this muck on you."

The homes in the neighborhood still held most of the furniture and possessions of the owners. They had been seized under eminent domain, but the rules were "use carefully." After the emergency was over, the owners would be back and the government would pay for any damages. Assuming the entire region wasn't swarmed by Old Ones.

The old witch, who these days rarely left the compound of the Foundation, was one of Barb's favorite people. Elderly, wise and accepting, she was also one of the most powerful Wiccans in the world. If anyone besides Barb could handle a *skru-gnon*, it would be Sharice.

"Look what the cat dragged in," Sharice said, smiling brightly. "And there is the cat," she added, looking at Lazarus. He'd stopped to clean himself, as he'd been doing repeatedly since getting out of the cave. "I have some premium cat food around here for you. Vivian!"

"Yes, mistress," a plump young brunette said, coming into the kitchen. "Welcome back, questers! Merry moon and a fair day." She bobbed a curtsey and smiled. Like Sharice, she was wearing a paisley dress, and was about covered in silver jewelry.

"Merry moon," Barb said, nodding to her. "We met in Chattanooga but I never got your name."

"Vivian Le Strange, Janea and the redoubtable Mrs. Everette," Sharice said. "Vivian is one of my protégés. Dear, if you could find a can of something for this poor stray that has wandered into the house? And then get started on something for our weary questers. They are *not* vegan. Steak and eggs?"

"Sounds great," Barb said. "And thank you. Showers?"

"Upstairs," Sharice said, standing up and waving to the door. "I'll wait for you to eat before plying you with questions."

"This is not good news," Sharice said, sipping her tea. "The Gar could not have produced so many Hunters if it was not well fed. And it must have been in existence for some time."

"We'd gotten that far," Barb said. "The FBI is trying to figure out where all the food is going."

"What you may not have considered is that the Gar is reported as continuously growing," Sharice pointed out. "If it has been in existence on this plane for that long, if it has been so well fed as to produce hundreds, at least, of Hunters . . . it must be very large. The facility to hide such a thing would be, in turn, large."

"It could be in a cave," Janea said, doubtfully. "But most of the ones around here are pretty small."

"That's a piece of data," Barb said. "One the FBI needs. Damn, I was looking forward to sleep. . . ."

"That is interesting information," Graham said, yawning. "This area doesn't have a lot of large structures. How large are we talking about?"

"A building that has at least twenty thousand square feet of open area," Barb said, shrugging. "It could be a very large barn. An old factory. A warehouse."

"Figure it's going to be a barn," Janea said. "Running a bunch of cattle or pigs into a factory is going to raise questions. If you run a bunch of cattle into a barn, nobody's really going to notice that they're not coming out."

"The problem being, none of the farms around here have been buying a lot of cattle," Graham said. "Fewer than normal. There's been a long-term drought in the area and there's a bit of a glut. The price is actually down."

"Who is buying?" Barb asked.

"Mostly feed-lots and slaughterhouses," Graham said. "And that's often more or less one operation. Most of those are over in the Midwest. There *are* a couple in the area. But a slaughterhouse is a big operation. Lots of workers. It's not a one-man thing."

"Special Agent, I got into this whole field when I stumbled upon an entire *town* that had been converted to the worship of Almadu," Barbara said.

"And we've been ignoring the slaughterhouses," Graham said, slapping his forehead. "We figured this couldn't be a whole bunch of people involved."

"I would suggest waiting until morning to check them out," Barb said. "Have they been evacuated?"

"I'm not sure," Graham admitted. "And I need some sleep, too. I'll get somebody to run up a list overnight. Get some sleep. We'll check it out in the morning."

"We have work to do," Barb said as they walked to the commo trailer.

She was tired and grouchy. Exhausted as she was when she went to bed, she had slept fitfully, her sleep constantly eroded by nightmares. There was the repetitive one, the one that she and Janea had identified as a Sending, of being held in a dark place. But she also woke up, more than once, with dreams that were memories of battling the hundreds of Hunters of the Dark. And she still suffered from nightmares of the battle against Almadu. They had eventually all rolled together.

She was starting to realize that PTSD really sucked and that she was, unfortunately, susceptible to it. Which meant she was going to have to find a PTSD therapist who either was already briefed in on Special Circumstance or who could actually be convinced she wasn't totally crazy.

And now, instead of going and finding the Gar, they had to go to a videoconference.

"This operation has gotten huge," Graham said. "Part of the work is coordination. You *have* to have it. And you two are the on-site SC experts."

"This is usually the sort of thing that Germaine handles," Janea said. "I can be... less than politic."

"I already had a brief meeting setting it up with the aides of all the bosses that are going to be in the conference," Graham said, waving to a golf cart. "I just pointed out that you ladies were the equivalent of mystical shooters and that they should expect shooter attitude."

"I think I'm a bit more polite than that," Barb said. "But I'll admit I'm not at my best at the moment. Who's going to be in the conference?"

"You don't want to know," Graham said, swallowing.

While the team had been in the cave, the operational tempo in the area had picked up. Goin had the look of a military post, with soldiers moving everywhere and several mobile command posts set up. Graham led them to a full-sized trailer with about a dozen antennas on top, and opened the personnel door.

The interior was lined by plasma screens, with workstations lining both sides. And it was occupied by only one technician.

"Bobby, we nearly up?"

"We're going live in about thirty," the technician said, waving to a set of three chairs. "Left side of the trailer and end. There's a couple of minor players I'm having to shift to right, so if you have to look at them, you'll have to spin around and everybody will be looking at the back of your head." He handed Barb and Janea headsets and pointed to the chairs. "The cameras have pretty fair depth of field, but try not to move around a lot. If you're wondering what you're looking like, these are you," he added, pointing to two small monitors at the work station.

Barb looked at the monitor and saw a very wan version of her normal self.

"I should have done my makeup better," she said, shaking her head. She looked up at the row of monitors and shook her head again. "I can't see most of these."

"Center will be NSA," Bobby said. "Right FBI, left Homeland. Spreads out from there. You can back the chair up if you need to look far to the side. Just try to stay in front of the camera. And we're going live in five . . . three . . . two . . ."

"NSA?" Janea said as the monitors went from color panels to video.

"National Security Advisor," Barb said, waving at the middle-aged man in the center screen.

Each of the screens had a tag on it so that the unfamiliar knew who they were dealing with. There was a name, but the title was always, unfortunately, an acronym, many of which she had a hard time working out.

NSA, FBID, HS, NORTHCOM, NGB, ARNGT, and on and on.

Barb spun briefly in place to look over her shoulder, and shook her head. Augustus was on one of the rear panels with the acronym USEURSCCOM under him. He smiled and nodded with a glimmer of humor in his eye. It was the first trace of humor she'd ever seen in him, and she suddenly realized that he must have a very nasty sense of humor.

"Odin's missing eye," Janea whispered.

"Uh, Janea," Graham said, wincing. "We're live."

"I'll be chairing this conference," the National Security Advisor said. "If you wish to make a comment, press the alert button and I'll bring you in. Review of the threat. As of this morning, we have the report from the SC Onsite Team that they encountered in excess of fifty of the . . . 'Hunters in the Dark' during their penetration of the Goin cave system. This is in addition to previously encountering and dispatching a . . . screw-ganon?"

"*Skru-gnon*," Janea said. "Child of Foulness."

"A *skru-gnon* in the first insertion, and in excess of twenty Hunters and a Child in the encounter at the Boone residence," the NSA said. "Mrs. Everette, is there any way to get any sort of feel for the actual threat numbers?"

"No, sir," Barb said, taking a sip of coffee. "The caves are just chaotic and you run into what you run into. My best guess is that we ran into only a fraction of the total. Every time we've gone deeper into the caves, we've run into more."

"General Cable," he said. "Any input?"

"No, sir," the NORTHCOM commander said. "If we could figure out how many people there were in caves, it would make Afghanistan a lot easier. Tactically, the only choice on the cave end is to send in a large number of shooters with ... SC support, and comb them out. Frankly, I'd be surprised if we get them all. This may be an ongoing issue."

"We need a better answer," the NSA said.

Janea sighed and pressed her button.

"Ms.... Grisham?"

"Please use my goddess name of Janea," Janea said. "It's a point of protocol, not a bitch. You would not call a Catholic nun by her given name. It's the same with a priestess. All of the information we have is from prewritten records, oral histories passed down from when humans were hunter-gatherers. So our actual information on the Old Ones is very sketchy. But the information that we have gleaned is that, even after the war against the Old Ones had been won, there were many Children left scattered across the globe as well as more numerous Hunters. Hunters, in fact, still remain in outlying areas; SC has battled remnants within the last decade. There may not be a good answer except combing them out over the years."

"A point to keep in mind, and I apologize for my breach of protocol," the NSA said. "Then we come to the subject of this... Gar? Pronunciation ... Janea?"

"*Gar gyi dbang phyug ma,*" Janea said. "The mother of all demons, or the mother of all foulness. *Progenitor* might be a more accurate term."

"The Gar," the NSA said. "We are now informed that it might be physically large. SC team input."

"Again, legends," Janea said, shrugging. "There are one hundred and fifty-seven divergent cultures that have myths of the Great Flood. What really happened? Was it the rising water from the last glacier melt? No one knows for sure. The legends of the Old Ones are the same. Most of them we get from Tibetan scrolls, which are opaque even by Tibetan standards and in many places degraded. Some were lost during the Mao years along with their information. The *gar gyi dbang phyug ma* is never properly described. None of them are, for some cultural reasons. We can only get descriptions from the names that are used for them. *Gar gyi dbang phyug ma* is her short name. Her full name translates as something like: That Which Is Fifty Elephants Covered in Cobras That Walks as a Stomach That Is the Mother of Foulness That Perverts the Mind That Walks in Dark Places That Cannot Be Harmed That Creates the Horror.... It goes on. Some of the name is missing from the scroll, and I can argue all day about various translations of the words. *Mother* could be *progenitor*, *stomach* could be *gallbladder*, things like that."

"I see," the NSA said, looking a bit stunned.

"The other thing to consider is that the Gar is one of the *lesser* of the Great Old Ones," Janea said. "You don't want to think about He Who Is Sleeping coming back. And don't ask me for the full name. You don't want the nightmares. But if someone has figured out how to bring back the Gar, it may mean that the great prophecies of the Old Ones returning are being fulfilled. This may only be the beginning. Or the tip of an iceberg."

"If it's like fifty elephants, why can't we find it?" the NSA asked, returning to the point. "FBI on-site."

"We had been dismissing slaughterhouses as a possible hide point," Graham said. "Until last night, the possibility that this might be part of a group conspiracy had not been addressed. Our next step is to check out the two slaughterhouses in the area. They have not been fully evacuated, since they had stock on site that required maintenance. Given the possibility of SC threat, we were waiting for the SC combat team to recover from their mission before checking them out. It's next on our list, sir."

"Elimination," the NSA said. "SC command."

"As Janea alluded, the Gar is mentioned as being resistant to conventional weapons," Augustus said. "However, that was in a day when 'conventional' referred to spears and clubs. The height of military technology was the atlatl. So it is possible that modern weapons may have effect. Then again, it's possible that they may not. In which case..." He paused and sighed. "In that case, we had better hope that Mrs. Everette's Christian God is willing to give sufficient aid to our case."

"SOCOM query," the NSA said. "Go."

"How can conventional weapons not have effect?" the admiral commanding SOCOM asked. The former SEAL was polite in tone, but his posture showed he was having a hard time believing the subject of the conference.

"Answer..." the NSA said then paused. "SC Onsite."

"Pass," Janea said, looking at Barb.

"In the case of demons, conventional weapons pass through them," Barb said. "But *they* can hit *you* as hard as a tank. I've got the broken ribs to show. In the case of the Children, everything we've hit them with has bounced unless there is godly intervention. Then they're easy enough to kill if you do enough damage fast enough; they regenerate like nobody's business. Simply engaging most SC entities is hard enough for the unprotected. So far, we haven't seen the sort of mind control that major demons have, but there are plenty of indications the Gar may have that ability. And the Old Ones... Perhaps as a fundamental attribute of their otherness and perhaps as part of a sending, they induce pathological psychological conditions on the viewer. It's pretty hard to hit something if you can't look at it. With the Children and the Hunters we've found, the effect is lessened under FLIR. But we haven't had anyone view the Gar. My guess is that the effect is going to be stronger. I've done some pretty horrific targets, general. This is going to be a tough mission. Even by *my* standards."

"NORTHCOM input," the NSA said.

"We need to ensure that all non-briefed persons are held as far from the threat as possible," the general said. "Both for security reasons and due to the nature of the threat. And promulgate a finding that any possibility of encountering threat requires use of FLIR, whether day or night."

"That's going to degrade our day viewing," SOCOM interjected.

"Admiral," Barb said, trying not to sigh. "SEALs are tough and tough-minded. Which is good. But if one of your SEALs or Deltas views one of these things with their naked eyes, the best you're going to get is a broken man. What you're going to get most of the time is someone who spends the rest of his days in a padded room under heavy Thorazine. Think of it as a safety measure; these things are HAZMAT for the brain."

"CJCS," the NSA said.

"Agreement with NORTHCOM," the Chairman of the Joint Chiefs said. "Order will be promulgated to *all* briefed personnel. Query: How high can we go on the weaponry hierarchy?"

"Non-nuclear," the NSA said. "If we have to go nuclear ... we might as well go public."

"To be avoided," Germaine said.

Janea started at a jerk from Barb and looked over at her. The housewife had a strange, wide-eyed expression. Janea had seen it before, though, and cringed at what was about to happen.

Barb reached out with a strangely uncoordinated hand and pressed the alert button.

"SC on-site," the NSA said, then frowned at the picture of Barb and Janea.

Janea spun in her chair to look at the screen with Augustus on it. He had his head in his hands, but she could see the grimace on his face.

"The nations of the world shall be tested," Barb said in a deep, resonant tone. Her eyes were still focused forward, wide and unseeing, and even her face had changed, becoming more solid, squarer, mannish. If the man was a triathlete. "The faith of this nation shall be its salvation or its doom. The great battle looms. May this be a sign of the end times, the ending of all things. This battle shall be but the beginning as the vanguard of Satan readies its panoply. You have this time to prepare."

Barb closed her eyes and shook her head, then looked around.

"Sorry," she whispered to Janea, closing her hand over the microphone. "Long night. I think I sort of drifted off there. Anything important happen?"

Chapter Eleven

"I just got a call from the Director," Randell said.

After the meeting had rapidly broken up, Barb, Janea, Randell and a team of Delta Force commandoes had started checking out the slaughterhouses.

There were three in the region, but only one, Conner Farm and Slaughter, that was near the site of the attacks. And its position made something like an equilateral triangle with all the encounters.

Barb and Janea had chosen to ride with one of the Delta platoons, all of them squeezed into an Expedition, while Randell had ridden with the other.

"And what did the Director have to say?" Barb asked as she got out of the Expedition.

"There's a debate about whether you should be pulled off the mission," Randell said, grimacing.

"Why?" Barb asked, angrily.

"It's mostly for good reasons," Randell said, sourly. "For values of good, as you said one time. Basically, one side of the debate is that you're clearly too important to lose. I got the feeling that a couple of the flag guys got Jesus after your little communication."

"Seeing someone actually channeling tends to do that," Janea said. "That's just the most public one I've ever seen."

"It wasn't public, though," Barb said. "God doesn't want worshippers that only worship because of miracles. The Lord wants

Believers, people who believe without miracles. If the Lord had wanted to be public, He would have channeled through someone on national TV. You said that was one side of the debate. What's the other?"

"Apparently members of the administration who were not present feel you are 'compromised' by your position," Randell said, shaking his head.

"I am a warrior of God," Barb said, confused. "What did they think I was before? Open-minded? Sort of *agnostic* on the subject?"

"This is probably taking a long time to sink in with some people," Janea said, shrugging. "With this . . . incident, a lot of people who had, they thought, a pretty firm understanding of the world are suddenly having that worldview challenged, and challenged in a very *big* way. People, especially powerful people, don't handle that well."

"I take it I'm not pulled off the case," Barb said.

"Your boss pointed out that he had authority over who does what," Randell said. "Unless he says otherwise, you're the mission commander. Speaking of which. Major Chap?"

"Sir?" the Delta platoon commander said.

"Normally I do this sort of thing with FBI," Randell said. "They know the drill. The way this goes is, I serve the warrant, we clear the area of personnel, secure them away from the building and perform a search. Absent finding anything, we apologize and we leave. If we find the Gar, we detain the personnel as suspects, fall back and call for support."

"Roger, sir," the Delta said.

"My point being, and I'm not being sarcastic or humorous, that this is not a situation where we kill everyone in the building," Randell said. "Detain for questioning."

"We do that most of the time, sir," the Delta said, nodding. "Rather more than the other way."

"Very good," Randell said, squaring his shoulders. "Ladies, if you get a sniff of the Gar . . ."

"We're out of there," Barb said, looking at the facility. "But, frankly, it's here. Somewhere."

"Really?" Randell said, puzzled. "Mystic vibes?"

"That," Barb said, nodding. "Janea and I have both been getting Sendings in dreams and the . . . feeling is very strong now. But more than that. Smell."

The suggestion was not so much hard as impossible to ignore.

The entire area just stank. Most of it was the smell of cattle manure and urine, a heavy, thick tang of feces and ammonia. Overlaid on it, under it, behind it, was a very thick smell of rot. Not normal garbage, but a smell like gangrene and pus.

"Got it," Randell said, nodding. "Smells like . . . Old One. And cattle shit. Time to serve the warrant."

The front offices of the slaughterhouse were an old, two-story farmhouse from, probably, the twenties. It had been fixed up with nice landscaping and a manicured front lawn. Over the porch was a large sign that said CONNER FARM AND SLAUGHTER.

Barb had figured that, given there were cars in the parking lot indicating people were around, someone would have been curious enough to come out front and see why a group of heavily armed strangers had pulled up in a couple of Expeditions. But nobody had so much as moved a curtain.

One platoon of Delta moved to the rear of the building while the second took up position on the porch flanking the front door. Which Randell walked up to and opened without knocking. He held the warrant over his head.

"FBI search warrant," he called, loudly. "If everyone could please stand up and keep your hands in the open!"

The door opened on a large great room with smaller rooms to either side and a staircase to the rear. There were doors at the back of the room leading to the rest of the ground floor. It had been set up as a reception area, with a receptionist's desk and comfortable chairs. On the wall were posters of happy cows ready for the slaughter and glossily unreal pieces of meat.

It was also empty of humans.

"Well, they were only keeping a skeleton crew," Randell said as cries of "Clear" could be heard from the rear of the building.

"This doesn't look good," Janea said, walking over to the receptionist's desk. There was a mug of tea on it, and she cupped it with her hand. "Warm."

"Building clear," Major Chap said as a pair of Deltas came down the stairs shaking their heads. "No occupants."

"That leaves the slaughterhouse," Randell said, waving to the rear of the building.

"I'm getting that shivery feeling," Janea said, following him out.

～

The slaughterhouse was a massive structure, five stories high and nearly a football field long. To either side were equally massive covered stock pens. Which were totally empty.

A curving sidewalk led from the offices to the front door of the slaughterhouse. There were more personnel doors to either side, and on one end, a large loading dock.

Again, the area was entirely, eerily empty and quiet.

"Not even birds," Janea pointed out.

"It's in there," Barb said.

"Oh, yeah," Janea said. "The question is, do we even want to knock on the door to check?"

As she said that, the door opened and a naked woman walked out. She was skinny and brunette, covered in ichor, with open, pus-filled wounds covering her body. Another and another followed her, each of them staring into the distance as if unable to see. In all there were nearly twenty. And many were clearly pregnant. With what, Barb really didn't want to think.

Barb recognized a few of them. Lora Cowper was there as well as Wendy and Titania Boone. And Lorna Ewing. She looked as if she was about dead, her body covered from head to foot in sores, and skinny as a rail. One of the women, a plump blonde in her twenties, was still wearing tatters of clothing. Barb suspected she was looking at the tea-loving receptionist.

The group stopped about thirty feet from the slaughterhouse and spread out, holding hands.

"*You are come,*" they said in sibilant unison. "*You shall be my new acolytes. Send unto me the beasts of the field and the maidens of your kind. I shall render you great rewards. Failure shall be punished.*"

"We are not here as your servants," Randell said, shuddering. "We are here to return these...maidens to their rightful homes and to remove you from this place."

He grabbed his head in pain and swayed as a wave of anger radiated from the slaughterhouse.

"*Great punishment shall befall this world!*" the women half-sang. "*I who once was am again! You have no power before me! Obey my commands or die!*"

"This is why you don't send unprotecteds on SC," Barb said. "We need Opus Dei. Major Chap."

"Ma'am?" the major said. His face was more set, but if he was in pain it wasn't evident.

"Each of your personnel will grab one of the women," Barb said. "They will probably fight and protest. We will then return to the Expeditions and report." She paused and breathed hard, aware of the horror of what she was about to say. There were more women than there were personnel. "Lora Cowper, Titania Boone and Wendy Boone are priority," she continued, pointing to each. Then she took a deep breath. "Other than those, the priority is . . . the most fit. Leave the ones on death's door."

"Ma'am," the Delta said. "Clear."

"Execute."

If any of the Delta Force commandoes were affected by the emanations coming from the Gar, it wasn't apparent as they sprinted across the lawn and started snatching women. And they clearly had the snatch-and-grab down to an art. All of the women fought, and although a few were in fairly good shape and fairly large, they might as well have been babies. The Deltas picked them up in a complex hold and then sprinted back across the yard.

There was a tremendous bellow, so high and terrible that even Barbara swayed for a moment, and then the walls of the slaughterhouse started to bulge.

"Run!" Barb screamed, turning to run into the house. It was the most direct route to the Expeditions.

She paused at the door, aware that if anyone could look back without becoming Lot's wife, it was herself. She still took the time to flip down the FLIR.

Under the FLIR, what was rapidly shredding the steel and concrete of the slaughterhouse wall wasn't clear at all. Most of it appeared transparent with long pseudopods crashing through the walls. She shook her head, then flipped up the FLIR.

The only thing her brain could think, besides "RUN," was of something like a four-story amoeba covered in cilia that were themselves as thick as the trunk of an elephant. The skin of the thing was covered in flickering colors, similar to a squid, but the colors were a leprous green and the purple of gangrene. She knew just seeing the thing was going to give her nightmares, and something in her brain was gibbering into madness.

After one look, she went with her lizard hindbrain and ran as fast as she could.

～

"Well, we found it," Graham said. "We've lost two teams trying to get a good look at it; FLIR doesn't seem to be enough with this thing. NRO even lost a computer system trying to get a look at it. The image processors froze. But we found it. The question is what we do about it."

"Well, I'm Asatru, but even *we* know when to run," Janea said. "I'm sure as hell not going to try to hack it to death with an axe. Maybe if I had a couple of really strong fighting bands that wouldn't go crazy or be swayed into worship. But not by myself."

"Is there any plan?" Barb asked.

"If we can get a lock on it, we can drop JDAMs," Master Sergeant Attie said. "But we can't even get a team in that can hit it with a targeting system. We lost a Predator driver, satellite systems lock up. . . . You were right. This thing is insanity on a thousand legs."

"We need to do something," Randell said. "It apparently has some concept of direction. It's moving—slowly, fortunately—in the direction of Goin. But who knows where it's going to end up."

"Where are the women and what's their status?" Janea asked.

"In Knoxville at a sanitarium," Graham said. "They still appear to be in contact. They're not talking from it at present, but they are calling for it to come to them."

"Is Goin on the route to Knoxville?" Janea asked.

"Yes," Randell said. "Why?"

"That's your answer," Barb said, nodding. "It's not going to Goin. It's going to where we have its 'maidens.' Without the maidens it can't create the Children. Is it eating?"

"Apparently," Graham said. "A team checked out the slaughterhouse when they were sure it was gone. There were a lot of bones, most of them chemically charred. And they've found a few cattle that it found on its route."

"Once it breaches the SC perimeter it's going to be Katy Bar the Door," Janea pointed out. "Somebody needs to make some decisions. Fast."

"The answer was in the Sending," Barb said. "This is a test of our faith. The only way that we're going to get rid of it is to express our faith as a nation in a really convincing way."

"That ain't going to happen," Randell said, shaking his head. "I mean, what do you want the government to do? Get the president on national television and ask everybody to pray to Jesus to drive a demon from our land?"

"Pretty much," Barb said. "Doesn't have to be Jesus. Just God in whatever form people wish to worship. God is love, remember? But I'll bet you dollars to donuts that's the only thing that's going to work."

"That is unlikely to happen until all reasonable methods have been tried," Graham said. "We've got a lot of firepower. We need to try that first."

"You just don't get it, do you?" Janea snapped. "Firepower is *not* going to stop this thing."

"How do you know?" Randell asked. "We haven't even been able to *try*."

"Because... God *said* so?" Janea said, angrily.

"God's never tried a JDAMs," Randell answered, hotly.

"Look, if somebody can explain this JDAMs thing to me and it's not too complicated, *I* can get a lock on it," Barb said. "Looking at it under FLIR at the slaughterhouse was not too bad. I *don't* want to try to tell you what looking at it with bare eyes was like. But *I* can look at it."

"We can set that up," Master Sergeant Attie said, nodding. "You don't even have to get close. And one of the systems has a built-in FLIR. Probably best to use that."

"Yeah," Janea said. "On the fuzziest setting it's got."

"You sure you want to come along?" Barb asked as they headed to the helicopter.

"I'm Asatru, and I ran and didn't even look *back*," Janea said. "I'm feeling a little weak in the goddess region. So, yeah, I want to go along. For that matter, if I can look at this thing and not go mad, I'd appreciate being the one to order down the bomb. It's sort of directing violence, which is up there for my goddess with having good sex."

"You got it," Barb said as she climbed into the Jet Ranger.

"If you ladies are buckled in?" the Army warrant asked.

"Pilot, are you briefed in on this?" Barb asked after donning headphones. "You can't get near this threat. You cannot get in direct view. If you happen to make a mistake and get too high, don't look at it."

"We're briefed in, ma'am," the pilot responded as the helo climbed for height. "Your LZ is a clearing on a secondary hilltop. The mission target is a hill that should both overlook the threat and protect us from sight. May I ask a question?"

"Go," Janea said, rereading the manual on the targeting system. "May I ask why I can't see it?"

"If you weren't told then you don't have the need-to-know," Barb said. "But don't get curious. On your life, don't get curious. I'm deadly serious."

"Yes, ma'am," the pilot said.

"Well, here we go," Janea said, looking at the woods in distaste. "Have I ever told you how much I prefer cities?"

"I've gotten that impression," Barb said, grinning. "Let's head up the hill."

"FLIR," Barb said as they reached the military crest of the hill.

"Oh, you betcha," Janea said.

The device they were carrying included a telescope. But it wasn't necessary to spot the Gar. The leprous monstrosity was slowly working its way down the road below. As Barb watched, it plowed into a house, leaving a splintered wreck in its wake.

"Oh, dear Freya aid," Janea said, softly.

"You going to be okay?" Barb asked.

"I'm not sure that's correct," Janea said. "But I'm not going insane *now*. Don't ask me about tonight."

"Let's get this set up," Barb said, taking off her pack.

The target identifier was essentially a larger version of their headsets with a laser system and a GPS. By lasing the target it got a distance, direction and change of altitude. With that information it knew the precise location of the target and would automatically communicate that to whatever system was used to bring down the firepower, artillery, MLRS or JDAMs from aircraft.

"Don't look at it with clear eyes," Barb said. "But you need to take the FLIR off to target this thing."

"Got it," Janea said, taking off the FLIR with her eyes closed and fumbling forward to get her eye on the scope. "Damn... it's a *lot* harder to look at with this thing. It's more close up."

"Still okay?" Barb asked.

"Hanging in there," Janea said in a strained voice. "Let's get this over with."

"Roger," Barb said, picking up a microphone. "Wildcat Four-Four, Wildcat Four-Four, this is Sierra Charlie One..."

"Don't look at the ground," Lieutenant Aaron Yin said bitchily. *"What kind of stupid order is that?"*

"It's an order," Captain Brandon Lovell said, banking his F-16 around to the east to keep in the target basket. "So don't look at the ground."

"Wildcat Four-Four, Wildcat Four-Four, this is Sierra Charlie One."

"Roger, Sierra Charlie," Captain Lovell said.

"Our device says it's connected, Wildcat."

"Roger, ma'am," Lovell replied. "Got a good lock on your box."

"Why Wildcat, I didn't know you cared," another female voice answered. It was a very throaty contralto, and Lovell had a sudden serious desire to meet the owner of the voice.

"We are doing target upload at this time," the first voice said with a touch of asperity in her voice.

"Roger, have target data," Lovell said. "Drop permission on file. Release." His F-16 rocked a bit as the thousand-pound bomb dropped off its wing, but he corrected automatically. He'd dropped literally hundreds of JDAMs over Iraq and Afghanistan. "Twenty seconds to impact." He watched the countdown clock, then started counting. "In ten . . . five . . . two . . . Impact."

"Roger, Wildcat. Good drop. On target. Standby."

"Sierra Charlie One, status of target," another voice asked. Lovell looked at the connection data and blanched. It read: AF Six. The Chief of Staff of the Air Force was on the line.

"Negative effect," the ground spotter said.

"Not a Freya-damned thing," the contralto added. *"This is stupid."*

"Retarget, Sierra Charlie," AF Six said. *"Wildcat, full ordnance drop on acquire."*

"Retargeted," Sierra Charlie said a moment later.

"Positive acquisition," Lovell said. "Wildcat Mission, full ordnance drop. Ordnance away."

"RTB, Wildcat," AF Six ordered.

"What the fuck did she mean, negative effect?" Yin asked over the local frequency.

"I don't know and I don't care," Lovell said, banking his fighter around and heading back to base. "Ours not to question why . . ."

He paused as there was a scream from Yin's aircraft, and looked over at it. Which was fortunate because his wingman was banking hard towards him and about to midair.

"Son of a bitch," Lovell snapped, banking into a barrel roll. "Yin, what the fuck?"

"*Wildcat. Status,*" the air combat controller called.

"Wildcat Four Two is in OOC," Lovell said, turning to look at the descending aircraft. Yin was in a flat spin and still screaming. "Tardis, punch it! EJECT, EJE..."

Then his eyes glanced to the ground.

Barbara shook her head as the spinning F-16 slammed into a distant mountaintop and exploded in fire.

"Lord, please send me the power to destroy this thing," Barb whispered fiercely. "There are many faithful in this nation. Would You ignore Your Chosen because of those few who are blind? Please, Lord, give us Your mercy."

"I don't think it's going to work," Janea said, flipping down her FLIR and picking up the target designator. "I think you're getting Stern God on this one. Very Old Testament. Jesus need not apply. Believe or be damned."

"I think you might be right," Barb said. "And I'm not sure which way we'll hop."

Chapter Twelve

There is BDA from the site," the Air Force Chief of Staff said over the video link. "Are you sure you actually hit the target? The bomb craters looked as if we were just bombing an open field."

"Oh, they hit," Janea said nastily. "But they didn't have any effect. They blew up real nice. And it didn't even slow the Gar down. It was like it wasn't there."

"If you'd been looking at it, you'd think we were bombing a hologram," Barb said. "That's a demonic effect I've seen before. Bullets just go right through, and then it hits something and destroys it. Don't ask me how it works; it's metaphysics."

"That wasn't the worst part," Janea said bitterly. "*I* was looking through the scope. It brought its captives with it. Even *they* were protected."

"How many?" the NSA asked.

"Five, I think," Janea said. "Those we couldn't grab at the slaughterhouse. And, honestly, if I'd been one of them, as I almost was, I'd have preferred the bombs worked on me. I'd be thanking you from Hel."

"You think you're going to hell?" SOCOM asked. "You're a priestess."

"Hel, H-E-L," Janea said, rolling her eyes. "It's where Asatru go that don't die in battle. Sort of like Christian limbo. Just a boring place."

"That is interesting but not getting us anywhere," the NSA said. "Suggestions."

"The faith of the nation is being tested," Barb said, tightly. "That's the bottom line. We are not going to be able to stop this thing absent God's aid. And He is being, as Janea pointed out, Old Testament. We either prove that we still retain faith in Him or we might as well be doomed now."

"I hate to ask this, but nuclear weapons?" the NSA said. "It is on the table."

"Then you'd just have a *radioactive* pissed-off Old One," Janea snapped. "You're not getting it. There was no effect. None. It's *insubstantial* to most things. But it can affect its environment if it *chooses*. I strongly doubt that plasma is going to help, no matter how much you throw at it. There are references to these things inhabiting stars. That's more firepower than we've got, buddy."

"Janea," Barb said.

"No," Janea said. "I'm tired of being looked at like a freak because I *believe*. Well, get this straight, you stupid suit bastards. Get with belief, *now*, *fast*, or this country, this nation, this continent and this world are *doomed*. Get that through your fat politician *heads*, for Freya's sake. I don't care if you believe in the White God or Odin or fricking *Vishnu*! Just get some faith, fast, or find somebody to do your job who has it!"

"Janea," Augustus said. "Your passion is understood. But try to be a bit less Asatru for a moment. NSA."

"Go," the NSA said, his jaw working.

"We need to move this discussion to the next level," Augustus said. "And I strongly recommend bringing in the SC Onsite team, passionate as one of them may be."

"I will take that under advisement," the NSA said balefully. "Break this down."

"Well, that was fun," Janea said, starting to take off her headset.

"Miss Janea," SOCOM said as soon as the other leadership was off the line.

"Yeah?" Janea answered, settling her headset back on.

"I was wondering if, assuming we get this situation under control, you might be in the Tampa area any time soon," the admiral said, his face blank.

"Is that a palpable *hit*, admiral?" Janea purred. "You're kinda cute for an older guy."

"Ahem," the admiral said, clearing his throat. "I appreciate the compliment. But actually...I'd like to talk to you about this Asatru thing. Any religion where the prime requirement is to die in battle...interests me. And all this is sort of giving me religion. Possibly over dinner?"

"Assuming we can kill this thing, it's a date," Janea said. "In fact, kill it or not, it's a date. 'Cause we might as well have *fun* while the world is consumed by evil."

"I don't get where a bunch of people praying are going to help," Randell said. "Does God need the power? I thought He was all-powerful."

"No," Sharice said. "He doesn't need the power."

There being effectively nothing to do but wait for doom, absent a miracle, the FBI agents and the cave team had gathered at the SC house. Most of the rest of the groups in the area were packing up as fast as they could. Most of them still didn't know why, but the panic was palpable in those who did.

"I'm Wiccan, but I fully recognize the power of the White God," the old witch said, taking a sip of tea. "Whether the White God was, is and ever shall be or not, He is immensely powerful. He could bat the Gar like a fly. A gnat. A mite."

"So what's with the 'the nation must have faith'?" Randell said angrily. "He's just going to let us die?"

"He might as well," Janea said, shrugging. "When Ragnarok comes, people are going to have to choose sides. If this nation can't get its act together with the threat of the Gar..." She paused and frowned.

"What?" Barb asked.

"The Old Ones are neutrals in the battle between our side and the infernal," Janea said. "And the US is the most powerful nation on earth. If your God, all the gods, are questioning *which side the US will come down on...*"

"Surely we are not so far gone," Barb said, her face white.

"This is a pretty good test," Janea said. "And if we're so far depraved that we would side with the infernal in the final battle,

He can take us out of play by giving us to the Gar. For that matter, it's probable that the infernal and the Old Ones don't get along any better than the gods and the Old Ones. It gives the *demonic* a serious thorn in their side."

"That is sick," Randell said. "See, *this* is why I hate God."

"Why?" Janea said. "I think it's brilliant. If we can't even get it together to face the Gar, we're sure as Hel not going to get it together before the hosts of the giants. This is a pretty easy and straightforward test. Can we muster enough believers to make a difference? Or are we useless to Him in the final battle? Hel, in the old days He'd have dropped fire from heaven on us for being too far gone. This time we get the Gar. How *many* Lots can America muster? There's going to be more than one family, but are there enough?"

"'And the beast shall arise from the endless depths...'" Barb said, frowning. "Actually, the Gar is sounding *a lot* like the Antichrist."

"I thought it was 'sea,'" Randell said.

"Bad translation," Sharice said. "More like 'from complete deepness.' Apparently, King James had a thing with not liking the ocean. 'From the sea' was close enough to 'from the deep,' so that's the King James version. He had about two hundred scholars working on the translation, but he had final approval on the text, and they were... aware of certain political realities. It's beautiful verse, but there's a lot of stuff like that in it. 'Suffer not a witch to live,'" she added a touch bitterly.

"What's the actual translation of *that*?" Master Sergeant Attie asked.

"That's a bit debated," Sergeant Struletz said. "It's got two variants even in the oldest texts, one of which wasn't available to King James' scholars, and you've got to remember that even *that* is from oral tradition. One variant is something that translates sort of as 'she who poisons.' But that one was written during a period when arsenic was just being widely recognized as a poison, and all the kings, and you've got to remember that it's always kings who got these things written, were *really* down on poisoners. The other is more like 'she who uses black magic to kill.' Definitely a woman. Definitely one with powers that are poorly understood. One translation is more or less 'she who is a fish.' Which makes *no* sense."

"The preferred one-word translation is 'sorceress,'" Vivian

said, raising her hands hopelessly. "But it's us witches that prefer it, so there you go. But it's definitely not witches, at least as we define witches. Which, pardon the pun, is female persons who are worshippers of the All. We're still pagans, and a few of the prophets were really down on that, too. But if it wasn't for that one word, we'd probably be able to get along with Christians about as well as, say, Hindus. But King James' scholars had to go and translate that *one word* wrong. So we're unredeemably evil in the eyes of almost all Christians."

"Catholics aren't that way," Struletz said. "Most of us, anyway. Ecumenicism and all that. We're still down on you because you're pagans, admittedly."

"So are you," Sharice said. "Ever prayed to Michael?"

"Let's not start *that* debate," Barb said. "If we can't convince the earthly powers that it's time to get God, in all his fury and glory, involved, we are in deep kimchee."

"And you may just have that chance," Graham said, plucking his phone off his belt and looking at a message. "We've got a videoconference set up at sixteen hundred."

"With who?" Janea asked. "Another group of suits?"

"I believe I asked you not to ask," Graham said.

"Mrs. Everette, High Priestess Janea," the President said.

Barbara nodded and tried not to smile. The government loved acronyms so much, they couldn't even have "President" on the screen. It had to be POTUS. The only part that surprised her was the person next to him, a middle-aged man with CJSCOTUS under his name. Then there was SHR, a pinched-faced woman who was looking decidedly unhappy at the conversation, SMjL, a middle-aged man who looked as if he was about to burst a blood vessel, MLHR, an older man who was mostly looking bemused, and SMiL, a middle-aged man who was watching Barb with a great deal of interest.

Way over to the side were minor luminaries like SECDEF, CJCS, DHS, NSA and so on. Force commands didn't make the cut, so Janea couldn't preen for SOCOM.

"The basic message is clear," the president said. "This is a test of the faith of the US by God. What I'd like to ask is if anyone knows why."

"Mr. President, I have to make an issue," the Speaker of the House said. "I feel I must ask you to refrain from bringing deities into this discussion. It is a violation of the Constitution!"

"That is, in fact, your answer, sir," Barbara said, calmly. "God is trying to find out if the US is a nation that will support the side of the holy in the Final Battle. If not, by giving us over to the Gar, which is more or less neutral and as much a threat to the infernal as to the holy, He takes the most powerful nation on earth out of play. Furthermore, the lesson of the Gar will not be lost on the rest of the world. It will increase faith in other lands. China is rapidly Christianizing. Their projected Christian population in fifty years exceeds our entire population. Those are warriors He can use in the Final Battle. That is our analysis. As best we can do, given that it is the ineffable mind of the Lord of Hosts."

"This is insane," the Senate Majority leader snapped. "I cannot believe we are even having this conversation!"

"You want insane?" Janea asked. "I got video of the Gar. Tell you what, you view twenty seconds of it and then we can have this meeting with your successor."

"I won't stand for being threatened!" the majority leader said.

"It's not a threat," Janea said. "If you really don't believe that this is happening, then *view the tape*. It is either true that this is a . . . call it super-powerful entity, which we need divine intervention to fight, or it is not. If it is not, then you can view the tape with no problems. There's nothing to fear. If, however, you *cannot* view the tape with no problems, if there *is* something to fear, then we need to get to that point now and get past the 'I don't believe this.' Among other things, while we're talking, the Gar is moving towards where I'm sitting, and I'd like to get the Hel out of Dodge. Like the White God, I am offering you a simple test. A poisonous one that I know you will fail, but an honest test. Let's hope that He has more mercy than I."

"To get back on the subject of this meeting," the president said, clearing his throat. "There is an issue."

"Praying to God for divine intervention?" the Speaker said. "You *bet* there's an issue! You've got *zero* chance of being reelected if you do!"

"That is not the issue," the President said. "And since everyone here has a security clearance and this conversation is Top Secret, it's an issue that had *better* stay in this room. The issue is this. While I have attended many services over the years and while I...don the trappings of religion for various purposes, I am not, in fact, a believer. I will admit that the reports I was made privy to about Special Circumstances have swayed me more to the side of belief, but I am not the sort of believer, well, *you* are, Mrs. Everette. The question is, does that matter? Will God still grant us intercession?"

"God does not care for the kings and princes of the world," Barb said. "Render unto Caesar the things that are Caesar's. What He cares about is the essential faith of this nation."

"I cannot believe this conversation," the Speaker said. "This conversation cannot go on. My constituents will *explode* if we start having national prayer breakfasts!"

"Oh, for a way to pick it up and drop it on Market Street, then," Barb snapped. "Get this through your head. In a few hours, the Gar will reach the town of Goin. Sometime tomorrow afternoon, it will reach the perimeter we've set up. Sometime tomorrow night, it will reach the outskirts of Knoxville. You can keep trying to keep people out of its way, it will eventually outrun you. It will convert worshippers, gather reproductive females to make Children, and *feed*. It will feed on humans, cats, dogs, cattle, anything that is brought to it. It will cast off Hunters to go forth and gather for it. It will create Children to make *more* Hunters. It will physically spread and its influence will spread. It will take first this region, then the state and North Georgia, Western North Carolina. It will spread its influence and spread its influence until, yes, there will be Hunters in *Ghirardelli Square* gathering resources to feed its essence. By then, we will have either crumbled as a nation or, my greatest fear, become a nation of its *worshippers*, feeding it an endless supply of largesse. Then with our power and might we will go forth in the Gar's name and conquer the nations of this planet. Their food and thousands, millions of handmaidens will be sent to its essence and it will *consume the world!*"

"How big can this thing *get*?" the House Minority Leader asked.

"Who knows?" Janea answered. "The people who were feeding it before were hunter-gatherers, maybe they had horticulture and early animal husbandry but probably not, and it got as big as fifty elephants. That might be a round number meaning 'it's really fricking big,' but it's *already* bigger than that. There's no indication that it has an upper limit. It is just The Stomach That Walks. My guess? With industrial food production and the fact that the US is a breadbasket with lots of cows, pretty fricking big. Like, big-as-a-city big. And millions of Hunters, thousands of Children. With enough support, billions of Hunters, millions of Children. We're currently dealing with maybe a couple of thousand Hunters, and we can't deal with *them*. Did the part about this not being the worst Great Old One get up to your level?"

"No," the President said carefully.

"The *gar gyi dbang phyug ma* isn't the worst of the Great Old Ones," Janea said with a sigh. "There are only seven mentioned in the Tibetan texts, but there are references to there being many others. The Gar is one of the few who had real worshippers. Most of the rest didn't seem to care one way or the other and were as mercurial and deadly as weather. They didn't even seem to destroy for the joy of destruction, as many demons do. They just didn't seem, in general, to notice humans."

"How were they defeated?" the Senate Minority Leader asked.

"The gods," Janea said, carefully. "Humans apparently..." She paused and looked at Barb.

"I can handle the E word," Barb said with a smile.

"Humans apparently evolved with the Great Old Ones just being part of their world," Janea said. "At some point they managed to get the gods to intercede. There was a big battle that was so far back it's not even in most religious texts, and the gods won. Then they took the humans as their worshippers, and you get Odin and Zeus and all the rest eventually. The battle with the Titans might be a reference to the battles with the Old Ones."

"So... why can't the old gods intercede?" the Speaker asked. "That would... actually be a lot more palatable."

"You want me to try to penetrate *divine politics*?" Janea asked. "I thought you were going nuts about there even *being* a God? Answer is, I dunno. I do know that they are not as powerful as the White God by a lot of orders of magnitude. They're still *there*. Many, as those the Asatru worship, side with the White God. Mostly. Don't ask me about Loki; it depends on the day. Others side with the infernal. But for whatever reason, they aren't intervening. I couldn't even get Freya to give me enough power to battle a Child. She was just hands off. I was nearly taken by a Hunter, one of her most powerful priestesses taken to be defiled, and she didn't intervene. That tells me that they are held. At a guess, because of this test of the White God."

"So God is hanging us out to dry?" the Senate Majority Leader asked. "Great!"

"No, He is *testing* us," Barb said. "This is part of the test. Can you, the leaders of this great nation, get your heads around there being a One True God and can you lead your people in His direction or will we continue to... What was that book a while back? Will we continue to slouch towards Gomorrah? Can you lead or can you only run in front of wherever the band is headed? Because this is but a *minor* test. Much greater tests are coming. I think what God is saying, getting it down to a bumper-sticker, is 'Lead, follow or get the hell out of the way.'"

"The problem being that this is a *democracy*, Barbara," the Speaker said, as if speaking to a child. "And in a democracy, that is under rule of law, we have to follow the laws. And the law says, no interaction between church and state."

"Don't argue with me, sweetheart," Barbara said, smiling broadly and then pointing at the roof. "Argue with Him if you'd like. I do."

"Is this unconstitutional?" the President asked.

"Yes!" the Speaker and the Majority Leader both snapped.

"I was asking the Chief Justice," the President said.

"There are numerous precedents," the Chief Justice said. "Presidents have often asked for national prayers. After 9/11, for example. But given the current makeup of the Court, if they were all brought in on the decision and prior decisions related to Special Circumstance, it would come down to... ideological position. Which means, probably, a five–four vote in favor. The problem being, we don't have time to debate. Which brings in the other precedent, which is 'the Constitution is a document, not a suicide pact.' I won't get into the debate about the meaning of 'respecting an establishment of religion.' We simply don't have time."

"If you do this you are going to be out of office so fast it will make your head swim," the Speaker said. "I'll enter the impeachment documents the next day."

"That's a chance I'll have to take," the President said. "Mrs. Everette, I understand that you do not have any recollection of your... message."

"No, Mr. President," Barb said. "I've seen the recording, though."

"Do you have any thoughts on the nature of the prayer?" the President asked.

"Oh, good . . . You're not asking a soccer mom to write your prayer for you?" the Majority Leader said.

"Do you mean, do you have to say 'Dear Lord God of all the Christians of this land, please destroy the Gar for me'?"

"More or less," the President said.

"No," Barb replied. "It can be ecumenical as you'd like. But it's going to have to be somewhat specific. 'Dear Higher Power, we'd sure like you to like us' won't cut it. If you'd like, I can work something up and then you can debate this while we are *running away.*"

"Mrs. Everette, I don't know if this is a divine message or not," the President said. "But the Lord seems to work through intermediaries. You are, as I understand it, the most powerful member of the Special Circumstances network. Is that right, Germaine?"

"Very close," Augustus said. "And for this, undoubtedly the most powerful."

"I doubt that God will choose to work through me," the President said, somewhat ruefully. "As such, when the prayer is given, I would like you to be available in the area of the Beast."

"Yes, Mr. President," Barb said. "I'll be there."

"And, yes, send me a rough draft," the President said. "Break this down."

"*This is Mary McCrory with CNN live from the vicinity of Goin, Tennessee. Overnight, the rumor has spread that the events in Tennessee are anything but a major methane buildup. What is going on is unclear but the area has been sealed off from entry. Our news crew has managed to slip through the cordon to a position very close to the small town that is near the center of the restricted area . . .*"

"*Mary,*" the anchor said, breathlessly. "*Can you see what might be happening?*"

"*Not exactly,*" the reporter said, ducking through trees. "*We've seen military vehicles moving out of the area all night, as if they are in full retreat. But what they are retreating from is unclear. We're trying to get to the top of a hill where we can get a better view.*"

"According to our legal correspondent, it's a clear violation of the Constitution to prevent the free movement of citizens for anything other than a natural disaster," the anchor said. *"Were you molested by the military in approaching the area?"*

"Well, the military is stopping anyone from coming in. We managed to evade several roadblocks. But this area is particularly well patrolled so we've had to go on foot for the last few miles."

"The main guess is that there's been an alien landing," the anchor said. *"Can you confirm that?"*

"We may be able to in just a moment," the reporter said excitedly. *"The trees are opening up ahead and..."*

She suddenly began screaming and the picture from the camera wobbled erratically. For just a moment it showed a swath of destruction in the distant valley and then panned towards the head of the swath. There was a brief glimpse of *something* and then the picture blanked out.

As the voice feed from the camera crew cut off, the anchor was left sitting with her mouth open.

"We're having some difficulties with our reporting team in Tennessee," she said after a moment of her mouth opening and closing soundlessly. *"We are now taking you to our legal analyst, Rebecca Shelby, for a look at the legal ramifications of forced resettlement and denying access to the area on the part of citizens. Rebecca?"*

"The President is doing his speech at eleven AM," Graham said, entering the briefing room.

The FBI team had moved back to the Knoxville headquarters. The military was keeping as many people out of the area as possible, and the investigation part of the incident was pretty much over.

"It will be to Maynardville by then," Barb said, looking at the map on the wall. It was some sort of interactive screen, and it showed the approximate progress of the Gar as well as all the major military positions.

"Yes, it will," Graham said. "Which they're evacuating. He'd prefer to wait until prime time, to get the maximum viewers, but this is going to have to do. All of the TV networks and radio stations have been informed that it is under Emergency Broadcast rules. We'll have to see what the cable channels do, but most of them are probably going to go along. And we've basically given up on the methane story after what happened to the CNN team. But the point is...we'd probably better get moving."

"Okay," Barb said, picking up her purse and gesturing to the door. "You first, Laz. And yes, you're coming along."

The cat flicked his ears, then walked to the door as if it was his own idea anyway.

"Think he'll use your script?" Janea asked as they walked down the corridor to the elevator.

"God willing."

"Ladies and gentlemen of the United States, my fellow citizens, citizens of nations around the globe, I come to you in this, our nation's hour of need to beg for your help.

"As President, I see many things that are secret and terrible. There are constant threats to the lives of peoples all over the world that never make the news, that are never known but to a very few. The threat this nation, and the world, faces in Tennessee must, for the time being, remain one of those secrets. My fellow Americans, peoples of the world, you don't *want* to know.

"However, there is one thing I must ask of all people, of all people of...faith. I do not care if you are Christian or Muslim. I do not care if you are Jew or Mormon or Sikh. I do not care if you are Vishnaya or Syncretic neo-Pagan. In this, our nation's hour of need, I need you to join me in prayer. I need you to bend your heart and your soul and your belief to ask for intercession by the Almighty, however you may choose to speak to Him, Her or It. I ask you this with all my heart, with all my soul and, yes, with my gathering belief. Now, please, I beg of you with all my power, join me in a prayer.

"Dear Higher Power, we, the believing people of this nation and of this world, ask for your intercession in this, our hour of need. Grant unto your chosen the power to destroy the fell beast which besmirches our land. Give us your blessing and aid, Lord, we ask by all your Nine Billion Names. Amen."

He bowed his head for a moment and shook it. And then clearly went off script.

"Please, God. Save us. We know we're not worthy, we know we have strayed far from Your path. But please don't do this to us. Please. Send us your power or we will fall into the blackness of everlasting night. Amen.

"And now . . . we wait for an answer."

"Sharice," Barb said, looking over her shoulder at the crackle of underbrush. "What are you doing here?"

"Wouldn't miss it for all the chocolate in Switzerland," Sharice said. "It down there?"

"Yep," Barb said. "We were just getting ready to take a peek. You don't have FLIRs."

"If the Lady isn't willing to shield my mind, I guess I'm pretty much over the hill," Sharice said. "I've seen a few things in my time. I think I'll be okay."

"That does it," Janea said, dropping her FLIR to the forest floor. "I can't be Asatru and fear. And I'm afraid. I will face the test of Fir. I shall overcome it or be blasted. Whichever way it goes, I'm not going to fear."

"Let's go, then," Barb said, pushing aside a screen of privet.

The Gar was moving through the outskirts of the town of Maynardville, leaving its usual wake of destruction.

"Is it me, or is it getting bigger?" Janea asked, her voice a little too firm.

"It's bigger," Barb said, calmly. She could feel the horror, but it was washing over her like light rain. "There was a lot of minor cattle ranching in the valley. Lord hope everyone was evacuated safely."

"That *is* rather ugly, isn't it?" Sharice said. If she was bothered it wasn't apparent.

"Yes, it is," Barb said, cracking a grin.

"I'm glad you guys think this is funny," Janea said, her voice shaking.

"Not at all," Sharice said. "But here in this place, we stand on the precipice of doom with but one roll of the dice between us and the end of all we know. It is laugh or cry, and my choice has always been laughter."

"I am Asatru," Janea said, firmly. "I am the high priestess of the goddess of love and war. I will not let this *thing* defeat me. My goddess defeated it in times past and will aid me to defeat its powers. I. Will. Not. Fear. I am Asatru."

"There you go, dear," Sharice said, smiling again. "To each her deity. Anyone got the time?"

"President's speech should be starting," Barb said, looking at her watch. "Okay, God, time to count the Lots. Do we make the grade, or should I just go home and give up the land of the free?"

"And the home of the brave, don't forget," Janea said. "There's a reason that the US has the highest number of Asatru in the world. Laz," Janea continued as the cat walked up and parked by her feet. "I'm not sure you should be seeing this."

"He seems to be taking it well," Barb said, looking at the cat. "Maybe it doesn't affect cats."

"There is nothing living anywhere near its path," Sharice said. "Were it not for his connection to you, he would be dead."

"Alive enough," Barb said as the cat stood up from its haunches and suddenly assumed a pounce position. His tail swished back and forth and he started to purr. "Very alive," she added and then stopped.

She'd felt the feeling before, like gathering static before a lightning strike. But never like this. She could feel that it was not just her being filled by the Power of the Lord, but the two priestesses by her side, the cat, the growth around her. It was a massive ball of power gathering and gathering and gathering...

"Oh, good Freya," Janea said, her eyes wide. "Uhhh...I'm not sure I can channel *this* much..." she ended on a squeak as her right arm shot outwards, palm upraised.

Barb, not fighting it but not willing it either, found herself following suit, as did Sharice. Lazarus stood up and opened his mouth as if about to wail.

And from the three outstretched arms, and one bellowing mouth, shot a beam of light powerful enough to level a city.

"This is Bob Toland near Knoxville, Tennessee," the reporter said, then lowered his microphone. "Good?"

"Sound's good," the sound man said, raising a thumb.

"Bit to the left," the cameraman said. "Better view of the mountains."

"I hope like hell whatever it was got that CNN crew isn't near here," the producer said. "President still has the airwaves. And it's dead air. People are starting to freak. Let's roll. At this rate, we might even get live."

"Right," Bob said, clearing his throat. "This is Bob Toland near Knoxville, Tennessee. As you can see behind me..." he continued turning to the northeast.

As he turned, a beam of white light shot down from the heavens. It was so bright it seemed to override the sun, bright as a magnesium flare in darkness. It blinded him for a moment and he could feel a prickle on his skin. For a moment, he thought the President had dropped a nuke, but it wasn't that. Just light. The purest, most white light he had ever seen in his life or could even imagine.

"Good God," the producer whimpered, his hands over his eyes.

"Yeah," Toland said, blinking and hoping that his vision would return. "I think that might have been exactly what that was. Tell me you got that."

"I got it," the cameraman said, lowering the camera. "I've got a burned-out CCD chip, but I got most of it. Damn."

"I think you might want to watch your tongue there," Toland said, looking up and blinking. "Seriously. Be careful how you speak."

"Thank you, Lord," the President said, his hands clenched together and tears streaming down his face. "Thank you for protecting us with Your divine hand. I pledge that this nation stands by Your side through all the trials ahead.

"And to the people of this great nation and all the peoples of other lands who joined us in prayer. Know that we have faced a great test and have shown that this nation stands by the side of the Powers of Good. Great trials face us in the future, but know that if we stand by our deity, whatever name we choose to use, that the power that watches over us will never fail. Thank you for your prayers, and God bless you all."

Epilogue

*M*aster Sergeant Attie wasn't too sure why he got stuck as point on this particular recon, and he'd just as well have foregone the pleasure. But here he was, driving through downtown Maynardville anyway.

"Damn," Struletz said, pointing to the left. "I think we've found where it *was*."

The large building, probably an old factory, was partially demolished. Partially. About half of it was flattened by something, Attie was pretty sure what, but the rest was still standing.

"No real evidence of what got it," Attie said, trying to make something out through the FLIR. "It's just...gone."

"Got a heat source on the right," Struletz said, pointing. "Across the road. Looks human."

"Go check it out," Attie said, stopping the Humvee. He'd seen Struletz drive. "Command," he continued, thumbing the mike on the long-range radio. "We appear to have survivors. Checking it out."

"Target?"

"Target appears to have been neutralized," Attie said. He could see the human figure Struletz had pointed out, and he or she appeared to be waving. Struletz had also stopped.

"What do you got, Jordan?" Attie asked.

"I've got one human female," Struletz said over the squad comm. *"She says there's four more. They don't know where they are,"*

they don't know how they got here and they don't got no clothes, Master Sergeant."

"Roger," Attie said. "Wait one. Command. Survivor is human female. Report of four more. Absent clothing, don't know their location or method of arrival."

"Roger," the TOC said. *"Wait one. Determine if subjects are currently pregnant, over."*

"Jordan, any of them pregnant?" Attie said.

"Say again, Master Sergeant?"

"Any of them *pregnant*," Attie said. "As in carrying the Devil's spawn."

"Oh, right. Stand by. Uh, that's a negative, and they're pretty pissed at the question. Any chance of getting some clothing up here?"

"Command, negative on the pregnancy query. We need some clothing and a medical team."

"All of the girls who were in the sanitarium are totally recovered," Randell said, shaking his head. "As are the five the recon team found. No bruises, no sores, the ones who were pregnant with *skru-gnon* aren't. No psychological effects. Even the systemic effects from long-term malnutrition are gone. Some of them are a little underweight but that's it. And none of them can remember anything about their experiences. The ones who were apparently kidnapped by the cult remember that, but nothing about the Gar or what happened to them. The doctors are openly using the term *miracle*."

"Because it is," Janea pointed out.

"Then there's the bad news," Graham said. "The teams have made it all the way up to the slaughterhouse, and a team has started an analysis of the material there. The actual reports are going to take months, but the hot-wash is bad enough."

"How bad?" Barb asked. She knew that after channeling that much power, she should be a physical basket case. But instead she felt as if she had been reborn, a tingling throughout her body like a heady, pure wine.

She also knew she wasn't the only one. Most of the people she'd run into on the way back to headquarters were walking around with grins on their faces. She wasn't sure if it was just people in the region or across the nation or the world. But people had clearly been touched by God.

"Pretty bad," Graham said. "The Gar had been growing for nearly three years. The slaughterhouse was bought by a new owner who summoned it and then fed it. He'd replaced most of the workers over time to keep it quiet. But it had been producing Hunters and Children for nearly two years. By a year ago, the company wasn't actually producing meat. But they kept their trucks. And they were making deliveries."

"Children," Janea said.

"Hundreds," the agent acknowledged. "Scattered all over the country. And then there are the ones in the mountains."

"That's a huge operation for one slaughterhouse," Janea pointed out. "Where'd they get the funding?"

"We're looking into that," Graham said. "It wasn't the owner. The slaughterhouse had been on the ropes until about two years ago when it was bought by an offshore company. That's a nest of shell corporations. One did stand out, though."

He pulled up a file on his phone and showed it to Barbara.

"Look familiar?" he asked.

Barbara blanched at the symbol.

"Trilobular?" she asked. "I thought that was shut down, hard, after the Osemi operation."

"It was," Graham said. "But it was involved in the purchase of the slaughterhouse. You can rest assured that there is going to be some high-level interest in the rest of these corporations."

"So the fight isn't over," Barb said, shrugging. "No big surprise that there's some sort of big corporate backing to the Other Side. We've got the same. Doesn't matter. We know, now, that God is with us as we are with Him. His hand will protect and guide us. Compared to the trials that are coming, a few *skru-gnon* and corporate pirates are nothing. But we will prevail. God is by our side."

"Amen," Randell said. "You preach it, Miss Barbara. You go."

"That sounded sincere," Janea said, smiling.

"You know what they say," Randell said, shrugging. "Comes a point when you just gotta give in. I've seen hell. Maybe there really is a heaven. Figure I'll get me some of that Old Time religion."

"Good enough for me," Barb said.

Lazarus looked between the two of them and, for just a moment, appeared to shake his head.

"Mark?" Barbara asked as she came into the house. It was midafternoon and Mark's car was in the garage. Unusual, to say the least.

She set her bags by the door and walked into the living room. No Mark. Kitchen. No Mark. No surprise.

She was halfway down the hallway when she knew, distinctly, where Mark was from the sounds from the bedroom. Just to make sure, she opened the door. And paused at the surprised expressions. Then quietly shut the door, walked to the dining room and sat down at the head of the table. Normally Mark's spot. She steepled her fingers and waited. It took about three minutes for Mark to arrive.

"Barbara..." he said, in a choked voice. "You're...home."

"Yes," Barbara replied, in a voice so totally mild it was slightly terrifying.

"Barb," Mark said, carefully. "I...I just want to point out I have *never* cheated on you...with a woman."

Author's Afterword

*N*ot a eulogy.

This novel has been a work in progress for a looong time. And during its writing real-life stuff has changed. Most of that relates to Dragon*Con which is, I assure my gentle readers, the most fun you can have with your clothes on. (And in some of the room parties, that's optional.) During the day the con is aggressively PG-13 and I've been bringing my daughters since they were quite young. They've always loved the swirl of color and fantasy that goes on day and night. At this point the con has attracted so much attention that Disney World sends cast, mostly the various "Princesses" and the Dragon*Con Parade Sunday morning has become a feature of Atlanta's Labor Day Weekend.

However, as the sun goes down, the con's tone slowly changes to become more Mardi Gras and less Disney. This is, in fact, specifically recognized with the event that has slowly been gaining notoriety, the Dragon*Con After Dark Costume Contest of which the author has had the privilege of being the co-master of ceremonies several times. For persons interested in being contestants, I will remind you that "no costume means no costume." And Dragon*Con After Dark complies with relevant Atlanta and Georgia laws regarding nudity.

Barely.

(On a further note, my good friends Rogue and Jessica DuPont of Cruxshadows are usually among the judges.)

This has been my only attempt to describe Dragon*Con and I really could not do it justice. It is one of those things in life that truly has to be experienced to be believed.

However, it was not until I was doing research for "fiddly bits" of this story that I realized (or even in fact noted) the amazing architecture especially of the Hyatt Regency Hotel. I'm not an architecture fan. It's the sort of thing you throw into a book to lend authenticity. So when this novel was in its final draft I desperately asked my lovely and talented (and much more architecturally oriented) fiancé Miriam to look up the architectural details and explain them to me. In small words.

Although Miriam had been involved with the design of the new walking bridge between the Hyatt and the Marriott (one detail that was left out since the Dragon*Con of Janea's spiritual journey was from an earlier period) she had, surprisingly, never really paid much attention to the architecture of the Hyatt itself.

Prepare to be enlightened.

Built in 1967, the Hyatt Regency Atlanta is generally described as "the first contemporary hotel." Designed by "visionary" (and I agree) architect John Portman, it incorporated several novel design features that remain subjects of study and use to this day. The "bubble" (glass open) elevators that Janea so casually dismissed were in fact the first of their kind in the world. All subsequent glass elevators simply drew on the Hyatt design. The "modern art sculpture" in the middle is anything but. The Flora Paris is, in fact, one of the most brilliant examples, ever, of a critical structural necessity being turned into pure art. The gold and silver plated steel tubes run in parallel from the foundation up to the lobby level then spread out into hundreds of separate tubes, twenty-two stories high, in the architect's own words, "arms in praise of the sky and the sun."

However, their purpose is purely structural. The top of the Hyatt is a (now closed) rotating restaurant. The basic structure of the building could not support its weight. The Flora Paris is what supports the *entire weight* of that massive and essentially separate building. It floats on beauty.

Brilliant.

There was no place to include those details in the story but the author thought that some people (including long-time attendees of Dragon*Con such as the author) might be interested.

See you in Atlanta at Labor Day.

John Ringo
Chattanooga, TN
March 2012